Praise for Finding Grace and Grit

"To read Khristeena Lute's *Finding Grace and Grit* is to be swept into a gently twirling caduceus—to experience two women, two worlds, two times simultaneously through interlocking narratives. A young nineteenth century writer, 'Grace King of the New Orleans Kings,' climbs from her family's post-bellum fall from socioeconomic grace to become an independent woman in elite literary circles while twenty-first century budding scholar, wife, and mother Meredith Mandin builds her social chops to rise from a struggling, dysfunctional Appalachian family to establish her own family and career. In discovering Grace King as a fiction writer and breathing woman who transcended her time and place, Meredith discovers her own path toward personal purpose, gender equality, and stability. These women confront societal constraints, bigotries, sexual oppression, misunderstandings, violence, and betrayals, growing in strength with every step. After we encounter such luminaries as Harriet Beecher Stowe, Samuel Clemens, and George Sand through Grace's eyes and a pair of abusive and predatory parents, naysayers, and the controversial King herself through Meredith's eyes, a shared vision emerges. The healing caduceus begins its liminal work. With humor, grace, and grit, Lute tells a complex tale of redemption with such lucidity that the reader can virtually see her winking behind the page."
—KATHLEEN McCOY, author of *Green and Burning* and *Ringing the Changes*

"In this debut novel, Khristeena Lute creates a compelling tale about two southern women separated in time by more than a century. Each struggles to find her own voice despite domestic and cultural obstacles; each longs for adequate reward to ease the financial burden for herself and family. Told in tandem as alternate chapters, the two dramas become more entwined as the story's protagonist, graduate student Meredith Mandin, digs deeper into the subject of her dissertation: a real-life nineteenth-century writer, Grace King.

At first glance, King's experience seems a distant shore, almost quaint, as her family escapes from New Orleans during civil war. However, as the fictional character Meredith deepens her own search for an emotional and professional haven, the two women's lives become more parallel, their determination more profound, their yearning to feel safe more universal. Margins of time slip away as Grace and her beloved city inhabit the grad student's head and heart. Like her subject, and over the course of academic and personal milestones, Meredith reaches epiphanies, girds her courage, and discovers the redemptive power of trust.

The aptly titled *Finding Grace and Grit* will convince readers that Khristeena Lute is a sensitive storyteller. Part of the pleasure of the book is its unadorned everydayness. She tells it simply but considers weighty themes. In addition, readers who know Grace King from her letters, journals, and memoir will find this factional version delicious. Lute captures an essence of the too-little-known writer and pioneering historian. She might well send readers in further search of King's life and works which, of course, is what Meredith Mandin would want her dissertation to do."

—MIKI PFEFFER, PhD., Author of *A New Orleans Author in Mark Twain's Court: Letters from Grace King's New England Sojourns* (LSU Press, 2019) and *Southern Ladies and Suffragists: Julia Ward Howe and Women's Rights at the 1884 New Orleans World's Fair* (University Press of Mississippi, 2014).

ꕥ

"Through the thesis of Meredith Mandin, a fictional graduate student, Khristeena Lute reveals the life and works of Grace King. King, a Civil War survivor, achieved some fame as a self-supporting writer whose works were admired by Mark Twain. In her debut novel, FINDING GRACE AND GRIT, Lute releases King from the 19th century and gives her as a compelling gift to readers in the 21st."

—BEVERLY FISHER, author of *Grace Among the Leavings* (2013), a Civil War novella told from a child's point of view.

ꕥ

"Khristeena Lute's *Finding Grace and Grit* touches upon the ways ambitious women throughout history must navigate their particular societal norms and challenges to reach their highest potential. Throughout the novel, with history in step with the present, both Grace and Meredith are each seeking their unique voice and defining their passion and purpose. The circumstances of their lives and their place in time may be different, but the core remains: women have to work harder and smarter. Both women are strong and both are survivors. *Finding Grace and Grit* bestows the reader with the parallel lives of two female characters who in the face of financial ruin, familial trials and heartbreak, professional triumphs and adversities, find their way to their best selves."

—MELISSA CORLISS DELORENZO, author of the novels, *Talking Underwater* (2015) and *The Mosquito Hours* (2014).

ꕥ

Finding Grace and Grit

Finding Grace and Grit

ℬℭ

Khristeena Lute

Thorncraft Publishing
Clarksville, Tennessee

First Edition, 2021

Published in the United States by Thorncraft Publishing.

This novel is a work of fiction, though it was inspired by historical characters, places, and events. The author does not claim this book to be historically accurate portrayals of factual events or relationships. Names, characters, incidences, and places are the products of the author's imagination or used fictitiously. Any resemblance to actual individual people, living or dead, places, or events may not be factually accurate, but are fictionalized by the author.

Cover Design by etcetera...

Cover Image: "A vista through iron lace, New Orleans" by Arthur Genthe. Genthe photograph collection, Library of Congress, Prints and Photographs Division
Back cover: "Spanish Moss, New Orleans" by Arthur Genthe.

ISBN-13: 978-0-9979687-7-4
ISBN-10: 0-9979687-7-X

Library of Congress Control Number: 2020948747

Thorncraft Publishing
Clarksville, TN 37043
https://www.thorncraftpublishing.com

10 9 8 7 6 5 4 3 2 1

To creative imposters searching for confirmation.

To nervous graduate students looking for a place.

To future-writers looking for a sign.

To empty journals waiting for ink.

ೱ೦೫

Contents

Finding Grace and Grit

ꕥ

Part I

"The past is our only real possession in life. It is the one piece of property of which time cannot deprive us; it is our own in a way that nothing else in life is. It never leaves our consciousness. In a word, we are our past; we do not cling to it, it clings to us."

—Grace King, Memories of a Southern Woman of Letters, 1932

Chapter 1

March
Dear Ms. Mandin,

On behalf of the graduate program here at Tennessee Valley State University, I want to congratulate you on your acceptance into the doctoral program in English. I would also like to extend an offer of a full graduate teaching assistantship, which will pay not only all of your tuition but also a small monthly stipend of $1200. Upon your formal acceptance of this offer, I recommend meeting the graduate advisor to select your courses and register for fall semester. Welcome, and congratulations.
Dr. Dougal

* * *

There are places in the world to which some souls are inexplicably drawn. The heart aches with a sense of homesickness to return to its soul place, perhaps to find peace, acceptance, or belonging. If a person is lucky, the wind will push them towards their soul place, where they can begin to put down roots and grow anew.

Meredith Mandin felt the tension already leaving her body as the airport escalator carried her to the arrivals taxi stand. Looming over her, a mural of Louis Armstrong and a brass band played silently in the background of the real band playing nearby. She walked outside, welcoming a blanket of humidity and a soft breeze after being inside various airports and planes all morning.

Minutes later, she handed her luggage to a cab driver.

"Thanks," she said, as the driver, a middle-aged man, placed her small, worn suitcase in the trunk. The edges and corners were frayed, and the black material had faded in places, leaving it an uneven, splotchy gray.

She paused for a moment before getting into the backseat of the beat-up taxi, an older, cream-colored Malibu that had seen better days. The breeze lifted her shoulder-length hair off the back of her neck, bringing some relief from the heavy summer heat. The wind here smelled sweet and salty, even by the airport. She inhaled deeply before sliding into the backseat.

"Where to?" The driver asked as he climbed into the driver's seat.

"Hotel Royal," she answered, feeling a little embarrassed saying it.

"Nice," the driver said, nodding appreciatively.

"Yeah, it's kind of a treat," she said, feeling the need to show that she doesn't usually get to stay at such fancy hotels, as if the state of her luggage could ever give that impression. Having grown up in a family that penny-pinched and considered the Red Roof Inn a splurge, Meredith felt almost embarrassed to be staying at the lovely boutique hotel in the French Quarter.

"Aha," the driver replied, as he navigated traffic. "What are you in town for?"

"Research," she said. "I specialize in New Orleans literature." It was a small lie, but one she hoped would one day be a truth.

"Wow, that's kind of cool," he said, his voice changing in tone from monotonous chit-chat to quasi-interest as he glanced in the rearview mirror. "You from here?"

"No, but it feels more like home than actual home does, if that makes any sense."

"That's the way it is with some people. Some places just fit," he said with a nod as he smiled in the rearview mirror.

They rode for a bit in silence, and she watched as Metairie Cemetery appeared on the right. Grace was buried there, and Meredith planned to visit her grave. A few minutes later, they pulled up to the hotel curb, and the driver retrieved her bag as she swiped her credit card through the machine and climbed out into the muggy afternoon.

"Thanks so much," she said, as he placed the bag on the sidewalk. Her mousy brown hair frizzed up around her face, and she squinted her blue eyes up at the hotel balconies. Flowers and vines draped over the wrought iron and dripped halfway to the sidewalk.

"My pleasure," he said. As he opened the driver's door, he paused and called out, "Oh! And welcome home!"

She smiled and waved goodbye. *Home*. What would it feel like to be *home*? Was this it? Relief?

She entered the small lobby of the boutique hotel she'd booked as a June special. There's a reason New Orleans hotels are cheaper in June, and the sheen of sweat forming on her forehead from the extreme humidity was part of it.

"I'm sorry, miss, check-in isn't for a few hours, and the room isn't ready yet," the young hotel clerk told her over the counter without looking up. The phone rang, and several other employees rushed in and out, assisting other clients. From the look on the receptionist's face, he braced himself for a fight, pursing his lips and trying to avoid eye contact.

"That's okay. Any chance you could lock up my bag for the afternoon?"

He looked up and finally made eye contact. "Absolutely!" He said, relieved, as he waved for her to follow him down the small brick hallway to a closet.

Just then, her phone buzzed. "Excuse me," she mumbled, fumbling the phone out of her pocket. Recognizing the number, she answered. "Hi! Is everything okay?"

"Yes," her husband, Liam, replied. "Just wanted to check on you."

"I'm checking my bags into the hotel right now, then I'm heading out for some research. Are the girls doing okay? It feels so weird not to have you three with me."

She mouthed, "I'm sorry" to the waiting receptionist and handed him her bag.

"I know, but you need this. And we're fine." A crash sounded in the background, and she could hear their older daughter crying. Liam sighed. "Well, Lila's tower just collapsed. Gotta go. Meredith... you'll be careful?"

"Of course."

"Okay, call me later. I love you!"

"Love you, too!" She smiled at the receptionist as she put her phone back in her pocket. "Sorry about that. My husband's outnumbered by our kids. I needed to make sure he was okay," she said with a nervous laugh. Lila could be a handful, especially after Liam's last year-long deployment to Afghanistan. Meredith worried that he had more than he could handle between Lila and her six-month-old sister, Emmy.

The receptionist tucked the small bag into the closet, locked the door, and handed her a retrieval ticket. He smiled and said, "Not a problem! What brings you to New Orleans?"

"Celebrating both finishing my masters and starting a doctoral program this fall."

"Wow! Congrats! Well, you give us a few hours, and we'll have that room ready for you."

"Sounds great. Thank you so much!" She started to walk away. "Oh, um, could you remind me? The Canal Street streetcar goes all the way to Metairie Cemetery, right? I need to pay a visit."

"Sure does. But be careful—it's a hot one out there!"

"Thanks again!"

She stepped back out into the heavy June afternoon. Nearby, street musicians played on Royal Street, behind the cathedral. She walked a few streets over to a local florist and purchased a small bouquet of irises and lilies before heading to the streetcar on Canal Street. Time to find Grace's grave.

* * *

Two hours later, her feet were blistered and sore from a style-over-function shoe choice, and she was completely lost in Metairie Cemetery. How did all those gorgeous women walk around town in heeled sandals? Even her low wedges had been a disaster. She frowned at the angry blisters her cute leather sandals had left. For added fun, the sky now darkened with storm clouds, and of course, she'd left her umbrella back home in Tennessee. She stumbled into a frigid, air conditioned office in a funeral home at one end of the cemetery—blistered, frizzed, and flustered.

"Excuse me?" she asked an elderly lady in a blue cable-knit cardigan at a desk. "I'm trying to locate a grave in the cemetery and failing miserably. Is there any chance you have a directory handy and could point me in the right direction?" She shifted the wilting flowers in her hand.

The woman seemed confused by the question. "No. But there might be someone back here who does. One minute, please."

A few minutes later, an elderly woman in a matching mauve pencil skirt and blouse appeared in a cloud of drugstore perfume. "Yes, sweetie? You're looking for a grave?"

"Um, yes. Grace Elizabeth King," Meredith said, her eyes tearing up from the perfume.

"Aw, is that your granny, sweetheart?" the woman asked, as she opened a dusty ledger and skimmed the pages.

"Um, no," Meredith said, coughing on the perfume in her throat. "She's a writer."

"Oh, I see." The warm tone disappeared. "King. Yes, here." She showed her a map of the cemetery, with all of its lanes and such and pointed to a spot just a few rows in from the entrance. Meredith had walked right past it multiple times.

"I see. Okay, thank you very much!" Meredith said, bracing herself and her burning feet to keep going.

She limped back across the bulk of the huge cemetery as more dark clouds rolled in. Her anxiety shifted between panic over the storm and panic over being mugged in the fast darkening cemetery.

Scanning the graves, Meredith turned her ankle on a rock on the walkway and stumbled, as thunder growled in the gray skies and the wind plucked sharply at the trees. Almost three hours had passed since she'd first arrived, but this visit to the cemetery she'd imagined for months seemed to be for naught.

Just as Meredith was about to give up and head toward the streetcar stop, she saw it: King.

The family headstone rested above the raised plot, and Grace's plaque lay flat. Meredith sat on the stone edging and pulled at the weeds that grew around the edges.

Why *Grace King*? Why did *her* writing pull Meredith to it? She'd never even heard of the writer until she started researching lesser-known women writers of the south on a hunch for a graduate class a year ago. But there were so many...so, why *Grace*?

Grace had spent most of her entire life right here in New Orleans, occasionally traveling for awhile but always returning home. She knew her place. In her time, Grace King's fiction had brought a great deal of attention to the city, inviting writers and artists there, ready to experience and be inspired by the exotic city. It had been Grace's great love, the city of New Orleans, and it had loved her in return.

What would that be like? Meredith wondered. *To feel so connected to a place—a deep sense of belonging. Of purpose.* Grace knew her purpose in her early thirties—to write. Meredith was of a similar age now, but she felt untethered, as though she might float away without the roots of place or family to hold her steady. Meredith's own family hailed from the Appalachian foothills of northeastern Kentucky, but the military had moved her and Liam around a few times. The thought of "going home" to Kentucky with her own children wasn't a happy one. She saw her childhood home as a place of loneliness, failed adulthood, drug use, run-down buildings, and near empty towns. Where could she go to find the same sense of place and belonging Grace had experienced? Meredith wanted an anchor, and she wasn't sure where to look.

Liam had separated from the Army to avoid more year-long deployments and separation from her and the children. Meredith would become the breadwinner now, giving Liam time to reconnect with the children and find his own path again. In the meantime, they would survive on her graduate stipend and his VA disability benefits, something they knew was not sustainable in the long term. A family of four's fate, ultimately resting on her.

Meredith felt the weight of the air grow even heavier on her skin before finally standing up when fat rain drops began to plop on her arms. She left the flowers on the grave and began limping her way back to the streetcar stop nearby.

By the time she reached the Quarter again, she felt a bit rested, but the heat still flushed her face and dampened her clothes. She walked slowly from the streetcar stop toward the hotel, the heat weighing more heavily with each block she passed. She paused on a side street behind the cathedral as a wave of dizziness wafted over her. She looked around for a place to sit, get a drink, or even find some air conditioning—anything—to help her rest. To her right was a closed wooden door to a used book shop.

She opened the heavy door and was met by the sweet cool kiss of air conditioning and the musty scent of old books. She tiptoed around the waist-high stacks of books on the floor and made her way to the back of the shop. She wiped her forehead and tried to not drip sweat on the books.

"Hello there!" called a chipper voice from somewhere in the stacks. A kind-faced, middle age man walked by, carrying an armful of heavy texts.

"Um, hello," she said, embarrassed to the core to be so sweaty and still dizzy to boot.

"Can I help you find anything?" He wiggled his nose to push his wire-rimmed glasses back up into position without having to touch them.

"Um, not really. Just poking around."

"No problem! Boy, it's a hot one out there today, isn't it?" He set the books down on a nearby table.

She smiled nervously. "Yes, it sure is." She looked around at the stacks and stacks of old, leather-bound books. Some looked like collectors' items, but many of them seemed simply old and dusty. Affordable. She ran her eyes up and down the stacks and shelves and tried to discern any sense of order. Was there a chance she might find an affordable edition of one of King's books? "Actually, um, is there any chance you might have any books by Grace King?"

He stared blankly for a minute.

"She's a writer from—"

"Here. She's a New Orleans writer. Nobody ever asks me about her! But," he said as he walked quickly over to a stack on the floor beside the counter. "I have a whole stack!"

"Seriously?" She walked over to join him and knelt on the floor to peer through the books.

"Oh, *Pleasant Ways*—you'll have read that one, right?" he asked.

"Yes! My master's thesis was on it," she explained, quickly forgetting her red-flushed face and sweat-soaked shirt.

He stared again. "Fantastic," he said sincerely. "And what about *Balcony Stories*?"

"One of my favorites!"

"Oh, too wonderful! Well, here's one you'll find interesting! Here is a collection of King's journals. It really shows the personal side of King—you know, the stuff she doesn't include in her fiction." He handed over a thick, hardback book.

"Wow," she said. "I didn't know about this. Thank you!"

She placed the book on the counter to purchase it. She covertly tried to spot a price on the cover and braced herself for what could be an expensive text.

"I'm Roger, by the way. The owner. Now, I also have a lecture that I gave in Canada on King a few years ago. Any chance you'd like a copy?"

"I would love that!"

He grinned and opened a file drawer to the left of the paper-strewn counter. He flipped through a few folders and removed two stapled packets.

"I assume you read French, so here's the original," he said. "Would you even want a copy in English?"

"Oh, um," she said. "I read French, but how about the English copy, too, just in case?" She glanced up nervously to see if her white lie had worked and silently begged the universe to not let this man speak to her in French.

"Wonderful! Well," he pulled over a calculator and tallied up the cost of the book. "So, you did your thesis on King?

Remarkable! I always knew she had to come back into academia!"

"Yes, and I'm hoping to do my doctoral dissertation on her, as well."

He looked up and blinked for a moment. "Remarkable," he said again with a sigh. He pulled out a card and placed it inside the cover of the book. "And here's my card. Contact me anytime you're in search of something."

She flinched inwardly at the cost of the book but decided it would be her "big purchase" on this trip.

"Thank you so much," she said, picking up the book.

She stepped out of the bookstore and back into the wall of heat outside and limped back to the hotel—sore but happy—and retrieved her bag from the little closet. The same receptionist showed her the staircase and gave her directions to the room.

"Now, you just...Oh, you know what? I'll just go with you," he said. "It can be a little confusing. This way!"

He picked up her bag, and she followed him up the stairs. They turned a corner to the left, and he opened the door.

"Now, we had an upgrade available, so..."

She stepped into the biggest hotel room she'd ever seen. A king size, four poster bed was layered with a crisp white duvet and matching pillows. Gray, hardwood floors ran the length of the double room. A small kitchenette was stocked with pralines and coffee.

"And here," he said walking over to the drapes, "is your private balcony." He swept the white curtains back to reveal a wrought-iron balcony covered in vines and flower pots.

"Wow," she whispered, stunned. "This is amazing. Thank you so very much!"

He smiled and set her bag down on the luggage rack.

Suddenly, she panicked. She didn't have any cash on hand. Her face clearly revealed her momentary panic, because he laughed and waved his hands.

"No, no, don't worry about a tip! Congratulations! And enjoy your reward," he said as he let himself out of the room.

She turned to her bag and set out the books she'd brought with her: *Delta Wedding* by Eudora Welty and *The Collected Stories of Katherine Anne Porter*. Pre-reading for her upcoming fall semester. Underneath the books, she found an empty journal for the writing she kept telling herself she would start doing. She was starting a doctoral program at age thirty with two small children at home and a husband who was trying to readjust to civilian life after recently separating from the United States Army. She could see herself, past and present—a poor girl from Appalachia, half a step out of the trailer park—in her favorite city, in the most beautiful hotel room she had ever seen.

For a moment, she thought about calling her stepfather, Gene, to tell him about her day, and she even picked up her phone to dial. They'd often chatted on the phone during Liam's deployments. Gene once spent an entire afternoon talking Meredith through how to fix a lawn mower, patient as could be through the whole process—Meredith in Tennessee, and Gene in eastern Kentucky. They had spent a lot of time talking about his wanting to move to Tennessee to work on a ranch with his uncle, which Meredith had supported and encouraged. Gene, as far as either of them were concerned, was her dad.

But last summer, Gene had died suddenly of a severe heart attack. She sighed and tossed the phone back onto the bed.

She walked into the bathroom to begin assessing the blistered damage to her feet and the chaffed burning of her inner thighs. She found a chilled bottle of champagne on the dresser and a marble bath so large she could barely see over the top once she sank blissfully into the cool water.

Outside, horses clip-clopped down the street, and tour guides projected their voices as they told ghost and vampire stories.

Home.

Chapter 2

New Orleans
1862

"Sissy?"

Grace heard her little sister whisper in the dark. She felt May press closer against her in the bed they shared.

"What's that red light in the window? What is all that noise outside?"

"It's probably nothing, May. Go back to sleep." Nine-year-old Grace stared at the window, too. Orange light filled the sky, and the smell of smoke wafted inside. Finally, she sighed, stood up, and crept over to the windowsill.

The King family lived in a large house: three stories with wide porches, called galleries, in the front. They had a small garden and simple backyard, a brick cellar, and servants' quarters. Pictures hung in gilt frames throughout the house. The main floor had a parlor that opened up into the dining room, where a giant, wooden sideboard sat opposite a heavy bookcase packed with volumes. Bedrooms were on the second floor, including Mimi and Papa's—as the children called their mother and father—whose rooms took up the front of the house and opened onto its own balcony. The Creole governess, Coralie, also slept on this floor.

The children gravitated to the third floor of the house where theirs and Grandmamma's rooms were located. Grandmamma's room was bright and airy and always welcome to children. The nursery was here. The boys had their own room, but the girls slept in Grandmamma's, in a trundle bed alongside her own grand, mahogany bed. The walls hosted pictures of Grandmamma's Georgia family, including her father and ancestors. Every day, Grandmamma watched over the children's dressing and prayers in her great, bright room.

On that particular night, Grace noticed that Grandmamma was not in her bed, so she crept to the window and crouched below to gather her courage to peak outside. The children spent hours looking through this window at night, while Grandmamma taught them the constellations. Grace edged her eyes up to see the city of New Orleans on fire. The smoke seemed to come from the river. Just yesterday, boats there were loaded with supplies, according to Papa. Grandmamma usually described the stars and constellations as God's gifts; but tonight, God's gifts were blocked by fire and smoke. It seemed as if someone had set fire to the Great Mother River herself.

May and Nan, Grace's younger sisters, crept up to see, as well. No one spoke.

Something clanged in the hallway, and they looked at each other with wide eyes. They all started to hop back into their trundle bed, expecting Grandmamma. The door opened, and their younger brother, Will, bounded inside.

"Can you see it from here?" he asked, enthusiastically. Grace rolled her eyes at first but then gave a little nod. They all gathered back around the window.

"Where are Fred and Branch?" Grace asked Will. Their older brothers would probably have more information from listening in on the adults.

"Dunno. Probably downstairs, eavesdropping."

"Think tomorrow they'll tell us what they hear?"

"Probably not. They think they're grownups, now, too. Big brothers are a pain," Will said.

Five-year-old Nan's eyes were widest of all. "What's going to happen to us?" she whispered.

Grace looked from Nan's tiny face out to the fires.

"Those Yanks will enslave us. Or kill us," Will answered in complete confidence.

"Will! How could you say that?" Grace hissed, gesturing at the younger girls' faces, filled with fear.

"Well, that's what happens in Grandmamma's Bible," Will pouted. "Papa was right; the South never should have seceded."

"You don't know what you're saying," Grace said, as she looked over the fires.

Nan stared thoughtfully, too. “What if the fire reaches our house? What if we have to run away from home? Where would we go? What would we take? I’m taking my dolly.” Nan squeezed the rag doll to her chest.

“I’m taking the cat,” said May, still staring through the window.

Will’s eyes lit up. “I’m taking my rifle.”

“That thing won’t help anyone,” Grace said haughtily. “It’s just a toy.”

May turned and tugged on Grace’s sleeve. “What are you taking, Sissy?”

Grace sighed. “I guess I’m taking all of you. And books. As many as I can.”

“Sis?” asked May, as they filed back into their bed. “Will you tell us a story?”

Grace smiled into the dark. “Has *Maman* told you about her school when she was little?”

“Yes, but I like it when you tell it,” said May, putting her head on Grace’s shoulder. Nan curled up on Grace’s other side and snuggled into her.

“Mimi had been a sickly child with blonde hair and red sties always bothering her eyes but never her mood. She was raised a Protestant but attended a Catholic boarding school in the day. That means she went home at night,” Grace explained to Nan, who nodded. “She picked up French from her Creole classmates and became as like them as she could. As the girls were being prepared for their first communion, she finally admitted to the priest that she was Protestant. ‘What a pity! You made such a lovely Catholic girl,’ the priest had said. She continued at the school but did not attend his religious classes anymore after that day,” Grace finished.

May and Nan giggled.

“*Maman*’s stories are always fun,” May said, yawning. “She’s a good story teller, but Sissy, I like your stories even better.”

“Everyone loves Mimi’s stories, even the adults. If I’m half the storyteller Mimi is, I’ll be happy,” said Grace. She watched May and Nan close their eyes, but Grace stared at the window anxiously for hours, with Will's words about what would happen if the Yanks took New Orleans hanging in the air.

* * *

Life for the children did not change much overnight after the Union occupation of New Orleans began. Dinners were a bit simpler, but everything else seemed normal. Grandmamma and Mimi still made them attend lessons with Mademoiselle Coralie, and Papa still went to work daily at his law firm.

Until the knock at the door. Jerry, one of the house servants, answered it. Jerry came to the door of the parlor, where the children sat around Mimi in her chair while she read to them in French.

"Mistress? My apologies, but..." Jerry's voice trailed off, and he gestured behind him. Jerry's face was taut and his eyes wide. Two soldiers in blue uniforms approached on either side of him. Grace glared at the men. *How dare they come into our home!* she thought.

"We're here to search the house, ma'am," said one soldier. "We have reason to suspect hidden Rebel weapons and supplies here." One of the Yanks wiped his boots on the fancy rug in the hallway, spreading dark mud and muck.

Mimi straightened her back and sat tall and proud. "You will find nothing of the sort here." But she gestured with her hand for them to proceed, as though it were she giving them the order to search her home. It was like a script she'd practiced or a scene in a play. As soon as the men walked away from the parlor, she leaned over to Fred and Branch.

"Go," she hissed.

They jumped up quietly and fled to the back of the house.

Will scowled. "Why can't I go?" he demanded a bit too loudly.

"Because," Mimi answered. "We need you here. To protect the girls."

Will beamed. "Yes, ma'am!" Will sat taller on the floor and looked smugly at Grace, somehow victorious over the girls. Grace pursed her lips and drew May and Nannie closer to her on the rug. Mimi picked up Nina, the baby of the brood, and settled her on her lap.

The soldiers searched through the family's things. They ripped open mattresses, threw clothes in piles on the floor, and emptied the wardrobes and dressers. They bumped into shelves and knocked the good porcelain to the floor, shattering it. They walked over the broken glass, crushing it under their boots. But they didn't find any weapons and eventually left. They informed Mrs. King that her husband was a wanted man, and he needed to report to the Union officers immediately.

Fred and Branch had arrived at Papa's office in time to warn him not to come home. Instead, he fled to the countryside, leaving Mrs. King and their seven children behind in an occupied city.

* * *

A few days later, Grace sat in her mother's room and watched as she dressed in her finest emerald green silk gown.

Grandmamma watched from the doorway. "What will you do?" Grandmamma asked.

"I will go right in and get my family the passports we need," replied Mimi, her head held high. "We have to leave the city, and we have to do it now."

"How? How will you do this?"

Mimi sighed. "I will think of that when I get there."

"Why do we have to leave?" asked Grace, her face betraying anxiety.

"Because the Yanks are making life here too hard. Papa cannot return, and it could get worse before it gets better," Mimi explained.

"But where will we go?" asked Grace.

"L'Embarrass Plantation," answered Mimi.

"But where is that? We've never been there, have we?" Grace asked, confused.

"No," Mimi said with a sigh, looking at Grace through their reflections in the mirror. "But we will find it together.

Papa says it is lovely." She turned around to face Grace and smiled. "Not to worry, Sis. I'll be home soon."

Grace nodded. "I'll help Grandmamma with the children while you're away."

"I would expect nothing less," Mimi said, reaching out her gentle hand to pat Grace's head. Mimi stood, took a deep breath, picked up her nicest lace parasol, and left the room.

Grace looked at Grandmamma. "Now what do we do?" Her voice trembled a bit.

"We pray, Sis. We pray."

* * *

Hours later, Grace read to May and Will in the parlor, while Grandmamma carried baby Nina. Hearing the front door, Grace shot to her feet, her excitement and anxiety too much to hide. "Mimi?" She called.

"Yes," came a tired reply. Mimi stepped into the parlor, her face pale, but a smile affixed nonetheless.

Grace looked at Grandmamma, and Grandmamma looked at Mimi. "Well?" Grandmamma prompted.

Mimi smiled coyly. "How about tea? And I will tell everyone a story!"

Grace grinned and ran to the kitchen in the back of the house.

"Aunt Mathilda! Mimi is home! She wants tea!" Grace said, almost hopping up and down.

Aunt Mathilda, Jerry's wife, smiled patiently. "Of course she does, Sis. But you better calm down, Miss Gracie, or you're going to get one of your fevers!" Aunt Mathilda reached out to gently pat Grace's hand. "You take that tray over there, and I'll get this one." Grace picked up a tray of small sandwiches and tea cakes and licked her lips. Some of the cakes had sweet sugar icing.

She and Mathilda carried the trays into the parlor and found the children gathered on the floor around Mimi's chair. She had removed her flowered hat and shawl and was settling in. Grace joined them as Mathilda poured tea for Mimi and Grandmamma.

Mimi took a dramatic breath and began. "I needed passports signed by the Beast himself: General Butler!" The children, Grace included, gasped and looked at one another excitedly.

Mimi continued, knowing full well the dramatic air she created. "Papa had escaped the city and sent word that the rest of his family was to meet him on the faraway plantation for their safety. I was the leader now, but could I sway the most heartless man in New Orleans?"

Grace and her sisters and brothers exchanged wide-eyed looks.

"I dressed in my finest silk gown and hat and carried my most expensive lace parasol, trying to be the perfect Southern Lady to show my respect."

Will burst out, "But those damn Yanks don't deserve respect! I should've gone, and I would have shot that old Beast with my gun!"

Grandmamma scowled and reached out to box his ears. "Language, young man!"

Mimi smiled gently, always Will's defender. "Leave him, Grandmamma. His energy is to be admired!"

Will grinned at Mimi, but Grace noticed that he scooted a little further away from the reach of Grandmamma and her cane. Grace knew that Grandmamma's strictness with Will was just an act; she regularly saw that Grandmamma slipped him cookies before dinner.

"I spoke directly with the Beast. I explained our situation, that all I wished was to leave the city for the safety of my seven children. But the Beast was indeed as heartless as they said, and he refused to sign the passports." Mimi's face saddened, and the children's faces all fell. Grace felt tears welling behind her eyes and a lump forming in her throat. *How would they live here, without Papa? What if Will was right about what happens to the children when a war is lost?*

"But then..." Mimi said, and every face in the room lifted in hope. "Another high-ranking officer overheard my gentle pleas and took pity on me. As I left the office, this officer took me aside and signed the passports. And," she paused for even more dramatic effect and removed a paper from her pocket. She held it up for all to see. "Here it is: *October 1, 1862, to Mrs. William King, seven children, servants, and personal baggage to go to the Parish of Iberville. By order of Major Gen. Butler.*"

Grace grinned and grabbed May into a hug, while Will, Fred, and Branch jumped up and shouted their excitement.

"So, we're going?" asked Fred, his face flushed.

Mimi nodded gently. "Yes. We will venture through the countryside to find Papa and be together for a few months until the city returns to normal."

* * *

A few days later, the family finished packing what little they could take and loaded their things onto a wagon.

"Don't worry, children," Mimi called through the house as she walked from room to room, gathering items. "We'll return in a few months, maybe a year at most. Our home and things will be waiting for us!"

Grace stared at the books in the family library. Mimi walked past the doorway and paused.

"Sissy?" her mother asked gently.

"What about the books?" Grace asked, tearfully.

Mimi sighed. "They'll be here later. They're too heavy to pack."

Grace looked back up at the shelves sadly, her lower lip trembling.

Mimi walked over and placed a hand on her shoulder. "Select a few. But make them good for the whole family!"

Grace smiled sadly and nodded. She removed a few history texts from the shelves. History, to make the adults happy; stories and adventure to make the children happy.

As night fell, they piled into a wagon and headed for a steamboat. Grace began to feel cold and tired as they hurried—and frightened. In the night, there were crowds of people everywhere. Grace looked at the yelling mobs of people and felt panic rising in her chest. Her heart began beating rapidly, and her eyes filled with tears suddenly. As she looked away from the other children to hide her distress, a man grabbed the side of the wagon.

"Where you going, little girl?" he leered. His dark blue jacket was unbuttoned, and his breath smelled sickly sweet and stale. Someone else in the crowd knocked him to the ground, where people began treading on top of his body.

Grace's hands began to shake. As a wave of the crowd pressed forward, someone pushed something into her hands: an ugly rag doll. The fabric was worn thin, and her hair was stringy. Grace had outgrown dolls, but right then, the doll was a small comfort. She clung to it and kept her eyes pinned to the floor of wagon. Grace edged to the center of the seat, where Grandmamma put an arm around her to protect her. May and Nannie were on the floor, where Grandmamma kept them covered, hidings their faces from the frightening scenes around them.

Fred and Branch rode on the back of the wagon with Will, who watched the crowd, wide-eyed. Grace couldn't tell if he was excited or frightened. Mimi and Jerry sat up front, Mimi holding a screaming Nina against her shoulder. Soon, they walked onto the steamboat and took refuge in a cramped room, all together. The girls hid under the blankets until morning.

The family traveled on the boat for a week, enjoying the peace and the boat ride. Grace began to grow tired and cold much of the time. Grandmamma let her sleep during the day, even while she made the others go on deck and play after the daily Bible study. Coralie, the governess, had a brother to care for in New Orleans, so Mimi and Grandmamma took over the children's lessons, and they were set on keeping the daily schedule, even while traveling up the great river.

When the boat docked, the crew began removing their things from the ship. Grandmamma told Grace to go rest in the waiting wagon.

Nearby, Mimi spoke quietly with the steamboat captain. She gestured with a frown at some barrels the captain set alongside the family's things. The captain looked at his sheet and nodded again, assuring her the barrels were part of the delivery. Mimi frowned again but gave in. Grace dozed and felt the wagon creak and bump as they began the next part of their journey.

She continued to cling to the rag doll, even though her stringy hair and yarn-grin scared her a little. The yarn holding the doll's head on began to unravel a bit, and soon, the head lolled to one side. Grace weakly held the doll out to Grandmamma, as though she were a much younger child.

"Oh, we can fix her soon enough," she assured Grace. She examined the doll and paused. Holding it at an angle, she reached her fingers inside the cotton body and removed a small lump, tied in string.

"Wow, what's that?" Will cried, jumping closer and knocking Grace to the side.

"Now, watch out for Sissy," Grandmamma gently scolded. She unwrapped the small bundle. A piece of paper was tied around a lump of Confederate money. "The note says, 'Please give this money to Private Nathaniel Jones in the ninth regimen.' Whoever gave this to Sissy needed help and knew where to look."

"Can't we keep the money?" asked Will.

"Absolutely not," chimed in Mimi, who sat on the front of the wagon, beside Jerry, who drove. "Someone trusted us to do the right thing, and we will." She reached back and took the small bundle before Will could squirrel it away. Grace leaned her head against Grandmamma's skirts, too tired to care anymore about the doll. Mimi looked over her shoulder and frowned. She reached back and placed her cool, slender hand on Grace's forehead. Grace closed her eyes and felt Grandmamma tuck her shawl around Grace's shoulders.

May whispered nearby, "I don't want Sissy to be sick. I want her to read to us and tell us stories."

"Me, too," said Grandmamma.

Mimi and Jerry spoke quietly, and the wagon sped up a bit.

"Is she getting the fever again?" Grace heard May ask.

"Shush now. She just needs rest," Grandmamma replied softly.

Grace lay her head down on Grandmamma's skirts and half dozed and half watched the scene around her through a feverish haze.

When she opened her eyes again, she saw they were unloading at a beautiful plantation.

"Grandmamma?" she said sleepily. "Are we there? Is this it?"

Grandmamma smiled and put her hand on Grace's forehead. "No, child. But your fever is a bit better, so that is good. We are stopping for the night. A nice Creole man has offered us shelter, and they are unloading everyone right now. Come now!"

That night, the family slept in several beautiful rooms. The next morning, the owner of the plantation urged them to stay and rest for awhile, but Mimi was adamant: they must continue on their way.

They borrowed a carriage and cane cart from a nearby farm and moved on.

The road went alongside the river, and the older children were allowed to walk along the top of the levee. The children gathered pecans and piled them into Mimi's lap, laughing.

Several days into their journey, they stopped in front of large home to take refuge for the night, but no one came to the door. Grace sat in the wagon, feeling tired and woozy again. She didn't notice Mimi's eyes constantly glancing in her direction.

"Hello?" called a woman from behind them. She had a red tignon wrapped over her hair and a yellow calico dress. "Can we help you? The family left a week ago."

Grace watched as Mimi walked to her, but her walk seemed different somehow. She seemed tired. "Yes. We're seeking refuge for the night. My children are weary, and my daughter is coming down with chills," she said as she gestured to Grace.

"Mistress, I can't let you in there. The family left because a child died of scarlet fever in the home. We're supposed to let it sit for awhile. It's not been long enough," she said, almost pleading, glancing at the children with concern.

Mimi sighed. She looked at the wagon, loaded with seven children, her elderly mother, and five servants. Everyone was tired and hungry. Then her eyes rested on Grace, curled up on the wagon floor. "We'll stay in the front rooms only."

"Mistress, please," said the woman. "We're not supposed to...."

"Say we forced you. Because we are. My girl needs rest, or her fevers will return."

The woman stared at Mimi and then at Grace. Mimi raised her eyebrows as she waited for the woman to respond, then nodded to Jerry.

"You're sure?" he asked.

She nodded again, her head held high. Jerry opened the door, and Mimi entered first, as gracefully as though she were attending a ball and was the expected guest of honor. She swept through the bottom rooms, surveying.

After a few minutes, she returned to the doorway. "This will do just fine. Children, unload, wash yourselves outside, and come in. Could we bother your cook for tonight?" She asked the woman.

She sighed. "We can send up some hominy and grits."

Mimi nodded. "Thank you." The woman nodded and walked away, clearly happy to get away from Mimi. Jerry walked over to the wagon and scooped Grace up in his arms.

"Come with me, little miss," he said softly. He brought her inside to a soft sofa in the front room. She stretched out her legs, sighed, and fell asleep.

The next morning, the woman from the night before brought up hot milk and biscuits for breakfast, and after eating, the family began loading back into the wagons. Jerry carried Grace out to the first wagon and sat her beside Grandmamma. May and Nan piled in with them, and the boys hopped in the second wagon with Mathilda and the other servants. Jerry and Mimi approached the wagon.

"Mistress, the extra barrels. What should be done with them? We've been carrying them along, but the load is slowing us down quite a bit," Jerry said, pointing to the barrels the steamboat captain had loaded into the wagons.

"Yes," Mimi said. "Let's open one quickly and see what we find."

Jerry climbed into the wagon and pried the lid off of one. "Flour, mistress. No, wait. There's something else in here." Jerry reached through the flour and pulled out a parcel, wrapped in cloth and twine.

He handed it down to Mimi, while he searched the barrel for more parcels. Mimi balanced it on the wagon wheel as she carefully opened it.

"Medicine," she said. "Quinine, calomel, morphine, blue mass, chloroform. We have to get this to the nearest army camp. They are in desperate need."

Before long, they started on their bumpy journey again to a farm they'd never seen and hoped to find Papa.

* * *

Eventually, the family reached a wide river and searched for the ferry crossing. Mimi located the ferryman near the roadside, but he shook his head at her request for assistance in crossing the river.

"I'm sorry, ma'am, but the Union troops burned the boat just last week." He gestured to its remains nearby. One end was submerged, and the boards were blackened halfway to the other end, which floated above the water at a precarious angle.

"I have to cross that river," Mimi said, as though this need outweighed the reality that there was no longer a boat. From the wagon, Grace watched Mimi haggle with the man, who grew frustrated with her continued harassment.

"Ma'am, I really can't believe I'm saying this, but we'll try it. But if we capsize, the burden is on you," the man said. "I won't have it said that I put women and children at risk."

They loaded some of the family's things on the undamaged end of the boat, and a few of the children and servants went in each trip across. Mimi, however, made each trip herself to see to everyone's well-being, standing tall overlooking her precious cargo.

They crossed successfully both times.

That night, tales of the brave and devoted woman from New Orleans swept the town on both sides of the river. The family was invited to spend the night at the largest plantation in the south, Nottoway Plantation. The main house was large and white, with black wrought-iron trim, soaring ceilings and porticos, and grande, double stairs to the front entrance.

The next morning, Mimi contacted a lawyer connection to help them hire two barges to make their way through the next step: the bayous. Grandmamma rode in the stern with the girls, and Mimi stood at the bow, where she could command her crew for the final leg of their journey, through waters rumored to be filled with Yankee troops.

* * *

Just as in the wagons, the girls cuddled up with Grandmamma and tried to sleep. Sometime in the late afternoon, they heard a small steamboat in the distance. The servants pulled up their poles and looked to Mimi. She stood at the front of the boat, simultaneously their little vessel's captain and figurehead. She stared forward and pursed her lips, carefully avoiding the children's frightened eyes.

The steamboat came across the bayou towards the family.

"We have passports," said Mimi calmly, though her voice shook slightly. "They cannot detain us."

May's eyes were wide with fear. "What if it's Yanks, and they won't let us go to Papa?" she asked Grace. "What if Will was right all along?"

Grace reached out for her trembling hand and squeezed. No one spoke as the air grew thick and heavy the closer the boat came to them.

As the boat neared, they could finally see men in uniforms: gray uniforms.

Grace and May breathed a collective sigh of relief.

"Halloo!" called one of the men.

"Hello," Mimi returned, relaxing a bit but still cautious.

"Have you any news?" asked a soldier, as their small steamer came alongside the barges. Huge trees shaded the water, casting dark shadows over the water.

"What about supplies? Do you have any supplies?" asked another, more intensely.

"Excuse us, ma'am," said a young man leaning over the side of the boat. "My name is Jonathan Smithfield, from Pass Christian. Our small unit here has been separated from our larger contingency, and there are Yanks patrolling these waters."

"Please get these men the medicines we were given," Mimi said to Jerry. "It was clearly meant for them. In the meantime, Mr. Smithfield," she said, turning to the young soldier, "Perhaps you can help us. I am traveling to a farm to find my husband. Have you passed any farms on these banks in the last day or even few hours? We should be very near it, but the waters here change often, I understand. We've travelled from New Orleans, and the children are quite tired."

"You mean, ma'am, you've been traveling with this large bunch all the way from New Orleans?"

"I do, sir," replied Mimi, lifting her head high.

They began exchanging stories and pleasantries, as though they were at a dinner party, rather than in the middle of a bayou. Jerry brought forward the parcels from the barrels, and Mimi handed them over to Mr. Smithfield. She also reached down into a bag of her own and retrieved the bundle from the rag doll. "Might we ask another favor of you?" asked Mimi, as she explained the contents, and Smithfield accepted the challenge of trying to find the intended recipient of the money and note.

Before long, they parted ways, and the family followed the edge of the bayou as the sun slid down on their left. The soldiers had seen several nearby farms in one direction, and so the family headed that way, hoping to find the plantation—and their father.

* * *

The swamp air was cold as night fell, and fog dampened their clothes, making the children shiver. Grandmamma wrapped them up with her shawl, and May, Nan, and Grace huddled around her skirts. The sun slid behind the trees, leaving the bayous even darker. Every so often, Grace saw a log on the surface of the water, moving smoothly along—or at least, she hoped they were logs.

Mimi sat in the front of the boat, gazing at the banks, straining for any glimpse of a white farmhouse through the trees, but there was just darkness.

Suddenly, the boat ground against something and pitched frighteningly to one side. Grace squealed and clung to May, who squeezed just as tightly back. Grace shut her eyes and pretended, for just a moment, that they were home, safe in their bedroom.

Nannie began to whimper. "I want to go home," she said in a tiny voice.

Even Will was by now tired of this adventure. "Well, we can't, now can we?" he said angrily.

This made Nannie cry in earnest. "Why'd you do that?" quipped May, who reached over to comfort Nan, while Grandmamma tried to hush all of the children. They were finally silent and listened to the swamps around them. Chirps and croaks were all they could hear. Mimi walked to the front of the boat and faced the darkness alone.

"Halloo!" She called. No answer. She shook her head, and the servants began to poke their long poles into the dark water, trying to find out what was wrong.

Jerry grunted as he leaned over the side of the boat. "It's no use, Mistress, we're stuck on a sand bar." As Jerry, Fred, and Branch tried to dislodge the boat, Mimi sighed. She glanced over at the children, huddled on the floor around Grandmamma. Grace watched fear cloud Mimi's eyes and began to panic herself, feeling her heart start hammering in her small chest. If Mimi was afraid, then there was truly something to be afraid of.

Mimi's eyes met Grace's, and Grace saw Mimi's back stiffen and her shoulders roll back in resolve. She gave Grace the tiniest of smiles to reassure her, and Grace nodded in return. Mimi would save them.

She held her head high and called out into the darkness again, her bravery restored. "Halloo! Is anyone out there?"

Grace could hear a tiny waiver in her mother's voice, but Mimi kept calling out. Soon, her shouts for help became part of the swamp sounds—just another noise in the background. The fog grew heavier, and Grace was frightened and cold, but somehow, she slept anyway. Every time she awoke, the scene was the same: Mimi standing alone at the front of the boat and calling for help, surrounded by fog and the croaks of swamp frogs.

Mimi held vigil over the boat until her voice was cracked and hoarse. Every now and then, Grace thought she heard a sob of panic in Mimi's voice.

Gators moved through the water, occasionally knocking the side of the barge. The cypress trees were tall and frightening, casting looming darkness even against the starry sky.

In the second boat, Grace heard Branch ask Fred, "You think someone'll find us in the morning?"

"If we make it 'til morning," Fred answered quietly.

Mimi either hadn't heard or decided to ignore them.

Finally, at the darkest hour before dawn, they heard it: an answer. Grace couldn't make out what it was, but it was there, very far in the distance. Someone was out there. She began to stir excitedly. She looked over to realize that Will had snuggled up with her sometime in the night, looking more like the little boy he was rather than the young man he'd been pretending to be. He opened his eyes groggily and looked up.

"What if it's Yanks?" he whispered. "What if they take us prisoner?"

No one answered him.

"Is someone out there?" Mimi called, her voice raspy.

"Yes, ma'am! We're here to help!" Out of the darkness and cover of the trees, a boat with lanterns and several men came into view. "Our master sent us to help. Is everyone okay?"

"Yes, but we're stuck on a sand bar. Can you help?" Mimi answered, relief evident in her tone.

"Yes, ma'am," said the man in the front of the boat. "Let's spread out that heavy load between all the boats, and then see if we can free you."

The servants and Mimi began moving items carefully from one boat to another while Grace snuggled down against Grandmamma's skirts. The boat rocked under them and finally slid free from the sand bar. Grandmamma crossed herself and thanked the heavens repeatedly. They set out once again, but this time with an escort.

Grace watched the banks slide by in the dim light of the lantern and drifted in and out of sleep until she felt May shaking her arm.

"Sissy," she hissed. "We're going to stop. We're almost to the men's farm."

Grace reached out in the semi-darkness and took May's hand. They both squeezed.

"Halloo!" called someone from a nearby bank.

"Halloo!" responded the men in the boat. As they pulled up to the bank and began to disembark, Grace wandered what this next leg of their journey would be. Wagons? More boats? Walking? How long until they reached this farm?

Jerry stood between the boat and the bank to help Mimi step over first, always their scout and emissary. As she did, she walked up the little slope to speak to the tall stranger standing in the shadows.

Mimi cried out loud enough for the children to hear from the barges. "William!" She wrapped her arms around him in a warm hug.

"Papa?" May squealed, her eyes wide and excitement filling her voice. Fred and Branch jumped right out of the boat and sloshed through the water to the bank, with Will fast on their heels. May, Nan, and Grace rushed Jerry all together, and he scooped them up all three at once and dropped them onto the bank. They all ran full tilt at their father as he stood, laughing. He opened his arms up as the children all piled into them, knocking him to the ground.

"Welcome home!" he shouted. "Welcome to L'Embarrass Plantation!"

"But," Mimi stammered. "How did you know we needed help?"

From the ground, Papa hugged and kissed the children's heads repeatedly. "I went into town and overheard a group of our soldiers telling stories about a brave woman in the bayou with boats full of children and luggage. They said she told the most amazing stories, and then gave them much needed supplies and news from the city. From their descriptions, I knew it had to be you, but you didn't arrive earlier as I thought you would. So, I sent Julius and the men out to search for you."

"Thank goodness you did!" Mimi said, wiping at her wet cheeks. Through the whole trip, this was the first time Grace had seen Mimi cry.

"Hey, now," Papa said, climbing to his feet. He put an arm around Mimi's shoulders. "You made it. A more daring feat has never been attempted by anyone in New Orleans! And now. Let's go to the main house and get you all something warm to eat and warm beds for sleep." The children began walking around Mimi's skirts and Papa's legs, but he never took his arm from around Mimi's waist.

They stopped in front of a medium sized, grayish-white farmhouse in bad need of repair. The peeling paint was evident even in the dark. No galleries. No flower gardens or brick pathways. Just dirt, sand, and bayou.

"Welcome home!" said Papa proudly again, waving at the simple farmhouse as though it were the most glamorous house in the Garden District.

Chapter 3

Barely a month later after returning home to Tennessee, Meredith's short trip to New Orleans to gather research and notes was almost a distant memory.

She sat in the car, enjoying a blast of air conditioning and taking a last sip of her latte. She looked at the back of the four story library. Somewhere in there was the University Writing Center, where she would work for the first year of her doctoral program. The rest of campus seemed empty, except for this parking lot, which steadily filled for the first few rows. She sighed and turned off the car. As soon as she opened the creaky door, a wall of heat blasted her face. She grabbed her brown leather shoulder bag, a gift from Liam, and set across the parking lot to the library entrance. Butterflies thundered through her body, leaving her hands almost shaking. She expected the worst case scenario: to be in the wrong place at the wrong time. To look out-of-place. To find there was a mistake, and she didn't have the position after all. To find she had the position but had missed a deadline and had now lost her place.

The two sets of glass doors slid open as she neared them, and a blast of icy cold air conditioning wrapped around her. The short walk from the car to the door was enough for her to start sweating, but she had a feeling she would need the light sweater tucked in her bag. Air conditioning in the South is either too much or too little. She stood in a black and white tile, atrium-style entrance and looked up at the towering spiral staircase that went up four flours. The atrium echoed from even the slightest sounds, let alone her kitten heels on the marble floor. Heavy wooden circulation desks stood to the left, the security and information desk held vigil right beside the door, and the reference desks were behind a glass wall to the right. She walked to the large staircase and began climbing to the third floor. Others trudged slowly beside her or took one of the four elevators that were just behind the staircase. She continued climbing, trying to walk slowly so she wouldn't be out of breath by the time she reached her floor.

The third floor housed book stacks in the middle and special sections on the wings that wrapped around the atrium. On one side, the wall read, "Education Curriculum," and on the other, "UWC," the University Writing Center. She walked cautiously toward the UWC, determined to find her social niche as soon as possible. She turned the corner down a short hallway lined with the UWC's glass wall and saw twenty or so people moving around inside, carrying small plates of breakfast food. She almost turned around and left, right there, but she paused, steadied herself, and walked inside.

"Hi, there! Welcome to the University Writing Center!" a chipper blonde around Meredith's own age said as she hesitated near the door. "I'm Jen Cooke, the Assistant Director. Let's get you a name tag!"

In two minutes flat, she had a name tag, a packet, a goodie bag, and a styrofoam cup of bitter coffee with bland creamer. She found an empty table in the back and set up shop. Normally, she was right in the front of a class, ready to go. But here, she wanted to see her new colleagues. How would she stack up compared with this group of academics?

"Is this seat taken?" asked a young woman in her early twenties—a good ten years younger than Meredith. Her thick dark brown hair was pulled into a messy bun at the nape of her neck, and she wore comfortable jeans and a soft tee shirt. Meredith glanced down at her own striped pencil skirt and blouse.

"No, not at all," Meredith answered, adjusting her things on the table to make more room. "How do these things work? Have you done this before?"

"Well, here at the UWC, no, I haven't," she said as she plopped down in the teal chairs. The table was small and round. "But, orientations usually open with a terrible ice breaker, then move on the business stuff." She had a pleasant voice—relaxed and sincere.

"Aha," she replied. "I'm Meredith, by the way."

"Reagan," she answered. "I just spent a year abroad, exploring and learning a few new languages."

"Wow," Meredith said. She'd spent the year nursing a newborn baby. She double checked her skirt to be sure no baby food stains had tagged along. Just a little one, and she tried to deftly brush it away.

Soon, Jen and the other administrators began the orientation. Reagan was right; they opened with a terrible ice breaker before getting down to writing center business. Meredith tried to remember people's names as they introduced themselves and their areas of interest, but it was difficult in a group this large. She wasn't the only mother with young children in the room; she wasn't the oldest in the room, either. She wasn't the only American Southern Literature student, and she wasn't the only married student. She blended right in. Nothing unique about her.

* * *

Each day, orientation began exactly like the first. Bitter coffee, small talk, and that ever awkward moment of finding a seat in a crowded room of strangers. The exact same feeling, maybe a little less intense, as a high school cafeteria.

By the end of the week, Meredith still didn't know with whom she fit, but she damned sure knew a few with whom she didn't. Where were the folks who could take their studies seriously but still keep a sense of humor?

Finally, it was Friday, the last of five days of intense orientation sessions. It was two o'clock, and they'd been doing Q&A for forty-five minutes. A very large and soft spoken man with a lisp raised his hand—again. His hands are quite tiny for such a large person, Meredith noted. She couldn't remember his name, and so began mentally calling him Tiny Hands. His hands reminded her of the opening of Sherwood Anderson's *Winesburg, Ohio*, grotesque in the way that Wing Biddlebaum's hands were.

"Yes?" Jen asked cautiously, clearly trying not to sigh openly. She failed. The week had exhausted her as well.

"What do we do if someone opens fire in the writing center? Like, if they're angry about a tutoring session..."

Run, bitch. Meredith coughed and choked on her afternoon coffee, gone cold.

"Excuse me? Like, with a gun?"

"Yes. Or maybe a knife."

Meredith flicked her eyes from face to face around the room, looking for anyone else who looked shocked by the question, but not one person looked up or seemed to even notice the conversation happening around them. Meredith sighed and sank back into her seat.

* * *

The following week, classes started. Meredith's nerves roared as she walked into an old, musty conference room: Bush Hall, Room 301.

Other students walked easily into the room, it seemed, but she stood outside it. The room seemed to whisper, *You don't belong here.*

She swallowed the lump in her throat and walked in, selecting a chair closest to the door. The room was claustrophobic. A large wooden table took up most of it, with chairs placed all the way around. They barely had room to pull the chairs out before hitting the overfilled bookcases holding old literary texts and past dissertations and theses. A few crooked pictures hung above the shelves, and a white board ran along the left side of the room. A computer cart and an old, scratched wooden podium were shoved into the corner—in front of the room's only window.

A petite woman with soft, shoulder length silver hair walked to the far side of the room to the head of the table, carrying a small stack of books. She sat carefully, arranged her materials, and set her mug of tea to one side: Dr. Bradford. Other students joked with one another, smiling and chatting easily across the table, while Meredith sat quietly, checking and rechecking her materials. Eudora Welty's *Delta Wedding,* notebook, folder for handouts and syllabi, and three pens, in case two of them ran out of ink. She triple-checked that her cell phone was on silent. A text from Liam read, *Have a great first day! I want to hear all about it later tonight!* She smiled and texted back a quick, *I love you.*

Finally, she sat, listening as others chatted.

Dr. Bradford opened the class with the basics: attendance, syllabus review, and project overview. Her voice was measured, soft, and low, and Meredith struggled at times to hear her. Then, they began discussion of Welty's novel on this very first day. The conversation continued naturally for about thirty minutes.

"Yes, indeed," replied Dr. Bradford to another student's comment. "I can certainly see where you would develop that perspective." A slightly awkward pause followed, the kind that happens in a class when the professor wants someone to say something profound, but no one wants to brave that kind of pressure. So, everyone sits in silence for that long, heavy moment— waiting for the professor to pick up and continue.

"Meredith," said Dr. Bradford. "You have a look that says you have something to say. Would you share your thought?"

"Um, well," Meredith ventured, her heart pounding in her chest. Speaking in a classroom shouldn't be this terrifying.

"Go ahead, there are no incorrect responses."

Meredith exhaled slowly. "Okay. So, here's my question. The main character, Laura, has no mother. The other characters also lack motherly guidance at times. In other books we're covering this semester, there are no mothers, or there are just really terrible ones. Why are there no mothers? What does this say about our society, that we must remove the mothers—just erase them as though they don't matter? Clearly they do. Look at all the dumb shit that happens when they're gone. I mean..."

Meredith stopped talking abruptly as she scanned the room and realized that every student in the room was staring at her, some of them with open mouths. "Um," she stammered. "Maybe I'm misunderstanding or have overlooked something..." She began scanning her eyes over the pages of the book, as though any second now, the answer would jump out and grab her, saving her from the social awkwardness that threatened to drown her.

Dr. Bradford smiled gently. "No, you didn't miss anything. I think that is a very good question indeed, and you might consider exploring it this semester for the main project."

"Oh, okay. Thank you."

After class, Meredith slowly packed away her things as others filed quickly out of the room.

"You have studied southern literature before, I wager," said Dr. Bradford to Meredith.

"Well, I did my master's thesis on Kate Chopin and Grace King, and I want to focus solely on King for my dissertation," Meredith explained.

Dr. Bradford watched her, emanating stillness. She didn't shuffle papers or fidget with materials. She stood perfectly still—calm and graceful. "King," she repeated. "King is a good choice. Not much has been done. Remind me about King. She was from New Orleans, I believe?"

"Yes. She lived there her whole life, traveled to Europe from time to time, and then devoted her whole career to writing about women in the south," Meredith explained. She paused and thought about the obstacles in King's path: family circumstances, poverty after the Civil War, and society's outlook on women writers as dabblers rather than true artists. "I just think there's more there to study."

"And how did you find King? Not many graduate students stumble down a path that untraveled," Dr. Bradford said with a soft smile.

"I took a New Historicist class at Claxton State, and we studied Chopin. I enjoyed that a great deal, but I wanted to study someone...a little less studied, less noticed, I guess, but still connected to New Orleans."

"Well, I studied at Claxton State myself, many years ago. Do you by chance know Professor Matthews?"

"Actually, yes," Meredith said. "I took my southern literature course with him, and he was the second reader on my thesis."

"Oh, how wonderful! I took that class with him several decades ago," she said, with a smile.

"Well, it was probably the same set of notes for both classes, since that notepad he carried looked pretty faded," Meredith blurted.

Dr. Bradford looked surprised but then laughed quietly. "It's quite possible," she murmured.

"I'm still not sure what angle to study with King, but I figure it will become clearer as I go," Meredith said, almost apologetically.

"Much has come from less. Follow that road, and we'll see where it goes."

* * *

"Okay, you see that off-ramp on the right? Take that, but stay to the left as you exit it. Go left on Fort Campbell Boulevard," Meredith explained to her mother over the phone, sitting on the front porch on a chilly November night.

Liam opened the glass door behind her. At six feet tall with broad shoulders and dark hair, he completely filled the doorway. "Is Gayle doing okay? If she needs it, I can go meet her and drive the truck in for her."

"I'll tell her. She's almost here, though," Meredith answered, as she stepped forward with a smile and removed a small, sequined bow from his hair. He nodded, took the bow with a straight face, and closed the door. Meredith repeated his offer on the phone.

"I'm almost there. I just want to get there and be done. Oh my God," Gayle said over the phone. "I'm so tired! This truck is huge! Wait till you see it!" She half laughed and half cried.

"Okay, do you see a big church on the right yet? At a traffic light?"

"Um...yes! I see it!"

"Good. Turn right there. We're just a few blocks from there. Do you remember how to get here from there?"

"Yes, I'll see you in a few minutes!" She hung up.

Meredith sat on the porch in the quiet, dark night. Thanksgiving was in a week, and Gayle had decided to move from Kentucky to Tennessee. Meredith had been offering to help her mother move since her stepfather's death, but Gayle had married a man suddenly this past summer before finding out he was an addict. They'd known each other for six months.

After that, she and Meredith had finally put the plan into motion: Gayle would rent a nearby apartment and help Meredith and Liam by watching the girls while they worked and went to class. In return, they would help with her bills and expenses. They had originally offered to turn the garage into a fully finished apartment for her, but she had declined, preferring to be on her own, so instead, Liam and Meredith paid the apartment deposits to help her get set up. Meredith and Liam's home was a simple brick ranch with three bedrooms and a large, detached garage. The backyard was flat, so they had set up a large wooden swing set for the kids and spent most days either on the deck or on the screened-in porch along the garage. Liam had finished the interior of the garage with heat and A/C, and they often used it as an extra family room or study space. The house was simple, but they were happy and willing to share whatever they had.

Meredith glanced inside. Liam was feeding Emmy while watching Lila dance in the middle of the room. She couldn't be happier that her grandma was going to live just down the street. Meredith thought about her leather bag resting beside the dining room table, overflowing with books and articles to review. Finals were coming up, and she still had so much to do. She sighed. It would be a late night tonight, or, more likely, an obscenely early morning tomorrow.

A large moving truck turned the corner. The truck must have been the largest they made, and it pulled Meredith's stepdad's old, rusted Ford pickup on a trailer behind it. Gayle parked on the side of the road as Meredith walked across the lawn to open the passenger door.

"You made it!" she said as Gayle's elderly dog, Vienna, wagged her tale and tried to waddle over the passenger seat. Gayle's other dog, a little dachshund named Peanut, wiggled on her lap. She swore up and down that Vienna was a "standard size dachshund—you know, like a standard size poodle." In reality, Vienna was some kind of labrador-corgi mix with a high pitched bark that could break glass, but Gayle insisted that her dog was a purebred—just a breed that no one had ever heard of.

"Yeah, well, no thanks to your terrible directions! Nothing was where you said it was!" she said, her voice revealing her exhaustion. She brushed her long blonde hair over her shoulder. Gayle had been dying her hair the exact same shade of blonde since the mid-80s, but at least she'd finally lost the Aqua-net along the way.

Meredith sighed. "Well, I'm sorry about that. I listed every step along the way. I thought it was clear." She decided to change the subject. "How did the animals fare? And how did you drive with Peanut on your lap?" He wagged his thin tail and growled at Meredith simultaneously.

"Yeah, it was easier than him barking the whole way. But the little shit peed on me," she said, wrinkling her nose. "What do we do about the truck?"

"We leave it here for tonight," Meredith said as she carefully lifted Vienna out of the truck and placed her on the grass. "You take a shower and change clothes. We'll order a pizza. In the morning, Liam and I will drive the truck over to the new apartment and unload it for you. Do you need help to get out of the truck?" Meredith asked, as her mother groaned, trying to move her legs to the side. She had surgeries on her legs in the past, but she almost always refused physical help. Gayle had been physically disabled with degenerative bone and joint disease since Meredith was in junior high.

"No, I'll get it just fine," she said as she climbed down from the cab. She set Peanut on the ground, and he ran off to pee on every tree in the front yard.

Meredith walked over to give her mother a hug. "You're here now," she told her. "Everything's going to be okay."

Gayle wiped a few tears off her cheeks. "I didn't think I was ever going to get here. I didn't plan on ever leaving northern Kentucky, you know."

"I know. But Liam and I are here, and we'll help with whatever you need."

Later that night, after settling Lila and Emmy in for the night, Meredith saw her mom go outside for a cigarette and walked out to check on her. She sat on a chair, slowly inhaling, the embers glowing red in the dark. "Hey, you doing okay?" Meredith asked softly.

She sighed. "How expensive is a divorce in Tennessee, do you think?"

Meredith stared at her, speechless.

"He was stealing my pills. I didn't want to tell you that, but he was. I had to keep them locked up. But Dave's coming to see me next week, and he's nothing like that."

Meredith choked back the "I told you so."

"We'll figure it out this week. Maybe we can chip in, to help move the process along. And we'll find you a local doctor, too, so you'll have someone here. I have a few names and places, already," Meredith said. Her grad student stipend and Liam's VA benefits didn't go far, but surely they could find a way to stretch them further.

"Thank you. Oh, and please don't tell Dave nothing about the divorce. I don't want him to know I was married again." Dave was the new guy. Before Dave was the Pill Head. Before the Pill Head was some random man she met on the internet ("He's a wealthy man from Italy! He says he wants to take care of me and marry me!").

"Okay," Meredith said and sighed as she walked back inside. If she hurried, she could get a few hours of sleep before getting up to read several articles on Grace King and start a paper on Jesmyn Ward's *Salvage the Bone*—all before unloading her mother's massive moving truck into a two-story townhouse apartment.

* * *

The next evening, Meredith sat on the sofa, exhausted. She sipped a glass of wine to relax after a hard day of unpacking boxes. Her laptop and stack of books rested on the dining room table, waiting impatiently.

Gayle poured herself a glass of sweet tea and came into the living room. She stepped over several toys and brushed the couch cushion with her hand before sitting down.

"Don't you ever clean?" she asked.

Meredith sighed. "With what time? I already get up at four thirty, at the latest."

"Well," she said, lowering her voice. "That husband of yours should be doing more."

"Mom, he's caring for the kids," Meredith said, feeling attacked. "And doing as much housework as he can, while taking online classes of his own."

Liam had recently separated from the Army after several year-long deployments, and they were slowly readjusting to their new roles with Meredith working and Liam becoming the primary parent while working on his Bachelor's degree. He took online courses so he could stay home with Lila and Emmy. Crowds and classes still set his nerves on edge, and the kids made it difficult to complete online classes, but he was making steady progress.

"I know that, but look at this place. Toys everywhere."

"We're doing the best we can," she sighed. "I've just got a few weeks left in the semester, and then I can catch up here."

"I'm proud of you for doing what you're doing, but don't forget: Those girls come first."

"I know that. I'm doing what I'm doing so I can provide more for them," Meredith said, bristling.

"Whatever," Gayle replied, setting her glass on a large volume of Shakespeare and looking at Meredith while she did it. "I'm just saying that once you have kids, your life isn't yours anymore."

"Mom, please. That book's expensive," Meredith said, reaching over and lifting the glass. It had already left a wet ring on the cover.

"Maybe you should clean up in here, and I'd have somewhere to sit my glass."

Embarrassed and exhausted, Meredith began picking up toys and books.

"You think you're doing something positive for them with all this studying and working, but it's not your turn anymore. It's theirs," she said. "It's time for you to take a backseat. Stop spending all your time with books. Those girls need their mother."

Guilt began swelling up in Meredith's throat and chest. She said softly, "This is my path to teaching in a college or a university."

"You're doing this for yourself. You could teach anywhere. Any grade, any school. Besides, I raised you just fine, didn't I? And on a part time job, too," Gayle said stiffly. "Money isn't everything."

Meredith struggled to find a response. She remembered back in junior high when she had filled out her mother's tax forms after one of Gayle's hand surgeries. Her mother's income had been eleven thousand dollars that year. Meredith thought about how she had never invited friends to her house as a child and teen from embarrassment that their house was small and on a busy road, far from the nicer brick homes on tree-lined streets where her classmates lived. She knew her mother had done her best under rough circumstances, but Meredith wanted more for Lila and Emmy. What was wrong with that?

And then she remembered something else she needed to tell Gayle. "So, um, I wanted to let you know that Dad's coming in to see the kids next week."

Gayle rolled her eyes. "What's that asshole want?"

"I told you. He drives in every few months, we go to dinner, hang out in a park with the kids, then he usually heads out the very next day. I just didn't want you to be surprised," Meredith explained. Her parents had a very messy divorce when Meredith was young, and they couldn't be in the same room with one another. For legal reasons.

"You know he's just doing this to be near me," Gayle said, sipping her tea. "He just can't leave well enough alone. That's the only reason he fought for custody of you when you were a kid. He didn't love you. He just couldn't let go of me. Twenty-seven times we went to court over custody! And not one of them were actually for you, you know. He just could *not* let me go!" Gayle shook her head at the memory, while Meredith sat quietly.

She remembered many of those custody scenes. The big, empty courthouse corridors, marble and echoing. She remembered being frightened of the judges and attorneys. While in a room alone with just the attorney and the judge, her father's attorney had said that Meredith had asked him if she could live with only her father, but this wasn't true. Meredith remembered trying to speak, to say he was lying, but instead, he'd turned to her and claimed she was lying right then to the judge. "Is that true, young lady? Are you telling tales?" the judge had asked in a stern voice, leaning over his desk to look down at her. She was maybe seven or so at the time.

He'd sounded like the Child Protective Services agent who had visited her father's house numerous times. Meredith never knew who had called CPS, but the man who showed up every time was intimidating and mean. He, too, had finally said to Meredith that she was lying to someone. "Do I have to keep coming out here and wasting my time?" he had asked her, his angry eyes and voice terrifying Meredith.

She had been about ten years old by then.

Meredith didn't reply to Gayle. She had been estranged from her father for most of her life after those custody battles had finally ended when she was around twelve, but when she'd had Lila, her father had reached out, asking to be part of their lives again. Meredith had acquiesced, though the relationship was strained and sometimes forced. Lila liked spending time with her Papaw, though.

"You know, I'm not feeling well," her mother said suddenly, standing up. "I don't think I can watch the girls this weekend."

Meredith sighed. She had just purchased tickets to an IMAX movie for a date with Liam. Their first real date in months.

"Oh, would you happen to have a few bucks? I'm out of smokes."

Chapter 4

L'Embarrass Plantation
1862

Grace tapped at the doorway to Papa and Mimi's room. Mimi looked up from her bedside post. "Thank you, Grace." She nodded to the dresser, where a large fan rested. Grace picked it up and took Mimi's seat as Mimi stood and stretched her back.

"I'll be back soon," Mimi said quietly as she left the room, hesitating in the doorway.

Grace turned to the bed and began fanning her sick Papa slowly, to keep away the mosquitoes and give him a bit of air. One by one, most of the family had come down with malaria, as did the slaves. Mimi alone seemed unaffected. A few of the field hands died from fever, with Mimi by their side. She had wrapped their bodies in linens for burial. She spent more and more time down in the field hands' cabins, washing the sick or caring for those on the mend only to return to the house and provide care for the children or Papa.

Papa, in all his strength, had been in bed, moaning and half weeping for days, while the children took turns fanning him.

In the hallway, Grace heard Mimi lower her voice to Jerry as they watched Papa from the doorway.

"Are there no doctors anywhere?" she said, pleading.

"I'm afraid not," Jerry replied. "We've sent for anyone for miles. No replies."

Mimi sighed deeply. "What will we do, Jerry? We can't lose him."

Mimi returned to Papa's side and took up her cold cloth routine yet again, gently patting Papa's forehead, face, and neck. Grace heard Jerry's steps fade away down the hallway.

"Sissy?" asked May, appearing in the doorway. "Can you help me find linens? Aunt Mathilda needs them."

Grace set down her fan and walked to the trunk in the corner of the room. She pulled out a set of fine linens from the trunk.

"No," said Mimi from across the room. "Not those. We might need those..." she swallowed hard "...later."

"Why? Are they for something special?" May asked innocently. Grace held her breath and waited for Mimi's response.

Mimi hesitated in answering. "Yes." She never elaborated, but her face was white and her eyes troubled. She glanced at Papa's face and looked away quickly. Grace put the linens back in the trunk but hesitated to return to Papa's bedside just as Aunt Mathilda appeared.

"Mistress?" she asked softly. Mimi didn't respond or give any signs that she'd heard Mathilda's voice. Aunt Mathilda swallowed and glanced at Grace and May. "Miss May, would you go on down to the kitchen and help Patsy with the biscuits?" May nodded and left as Aunt Mathilda wiped her hands on her apron and approached Mimi's side and reached out a hand to her elbow. In a voice so soft Grace could barely hear, Mathilda said, "Sarah."

Mimi started and looked up into Mathilda's dark eyes.

"You need to rest," said Mathilda gently.

"Oh, I will later," murmured Mimi, turning back to Papa.

"No, ma'am," said Mathilda. "You need rest now, not later. Everyone here needs you, and they need you healthy." Just a few weeks ago, it had been Mathilda's bedside Mimi had occupied, with Papa reminding her to rest.

Mimi sat up a bit and suddenly remembered Grace was in the room. "Sissy, could you..."

"Of course, *Maman*," replied Grace as she scurried to pick up the fan and return to the bedside. "I'll stay right here until you return."

Mimi nodded grimly as she stood and patted Grace's shoulder. She turned to Mathilda, who nodded at Grace and took Mimi's hand, leading her to the door and down the hallway.

Grace sighed and looked back at Papa's ashen face. She waved the fan slowly over him as her thoughts floated over the events from the last few weeks.

Every day had been much the same on the farm. On Sundays, the family read to each other most of the afternoon, while Grandmamma took her bible down to the slave cabins and read to the men and women there. Other days, the children awoke and had bible study with Grandmamma in her small cabin, where she lived with the boys. They took breakfast after that and studied French and handwriting with Mimi. This was Grace's favorite. She loved the sound of the French words and how they rolled and curled off her tongue. When she held the pen and dipped the tip into the inkwell to practice the loops and swirls of cursive, her mind usually froze from the importance of whatever she was about to write. Whatever touched that paper had to be important, so she had to choose her words and ideas carefully.

After morning lessons, they joined Papa for walks around the farm or nearby forests and bayous.

"How do you know so much about farming?" Grace had asked Papa one afternoon. As far as she knew, Papa had always worked in an office.

"A little here and there from when I was a boy and a young man in Alabama, but I mostly read a lot of books," Papa explained conspiratorially, lowering his voice and winking at Grace.

"Papa, when is Uncle Edmund visiting?" Branch had asked, as they walked alongside the fence line. The rains had been heavy of late, but this afternoon, they'd had a short break. "I want to hear his stories about helping the soldiers!"

"He'll be visiting soon," Papa said. "His last letter sent his gratitude for you all helping to run the farm while he is away." Grace thought sadly about their comfortable home back in New Orleans and all the books and toys they had to leave behind. She missed her books and lessons, her friends, and their daily lives. She thought about Coralie, the governess, still in New Orleans.

"Why couldn't Coralie come with us?" she'd asked. "I miss her."

"She has a brother that needs her care," said Papa. "So she stayed. But I'm sure she'll fare somehow, and we'll see her upon our return. Once the city is safe for us again, that is."

"But if it isn't safe for us, how can it be safe for Coralie?" she'd asked. "Those Yanks are terrible people. They burned our city. How can they be good and right if they burned our city and made us leave?"

Papa had sighed. "It's a lot more complicated than that, Sissy. Much more so than I can explain to a little girl."

"I *hate* the Yankees," Grace had said bitterly. "They made us leave everything behind. Our home, our books, our friends! What if they come here, too? Where will we go if they come here and take this home, too?" With each question, Grace's voice grew shakier and her face whiter. In her mind, she saw the white farm house on fire, just as the city had been.

"Whoa, there," said Papa, reaching out a hand to her forehead. "They can't hurt us, Sissy, so don't you worry or fret yourself into a fever. Mimi won't let you come out with me if I return you with a burning forehead."

Grace had nodded, but all she could think about were the red fires burning in the city as they had fled.

That evening, Papa had been teaching the older children math and grammar. May and Grace were always included, as Papa wanted educated girls. Grace was proud of this, that her Papa wanted his daughters as educated as his sons. Many evenings, Papa made them practice oratory, too, but Grace hated these lessons. Everyone stared at her, while Grace tried to remember all of the words and project her voice across the room.

"Louder, Sissy," Papa had coaxed. "You have to project your voice, so people in the back of a room can hear you. You're so tiny, it's hard to make your voice heard, so you'll have to work extra hard at it. Branch, show her again."

Before Branch could speak, however, they heard a splashing near the front door. Fred jumped up and ran to the doorway. "There's water coming in! It's everywhere!"

The rest of the children and Papa ran to see for themselves, and sure enough, dark muddy water was running in tiny rivulets under the front door and over the floor boards. "Don't play in it," scolded Mimi, as Will sloshed gleefully through it. "It's not regular river water. When floods rise up, the waters bring all sorts of disease with them. Children, everyone upstairs for tonight," said Mimi. "Open the windows for a breeze."

May, Nan, and Grace opened every window, and a sticky breeze trickled through the house, carrying the heavy smell of silt and sand. The boys were instructed to bring the furniture upstairs, where they stacked chairs and small tables in chaotic messes.

In the middle of the chaos, someone was pounding on the front door and forced it open.

"William!" thundered a deep voice from downstairs: Uncle Edmund. "William! You fool! You left the cows out! They're in a flooded pasture, water up to their bellies! Get up! All the damned books you read about farming, and you still left the damned cows out! Get up!"

Everyone stumbled to the hallway to face a fuming Uncle Edmund. Moments later, Papa and Edmund went out into the flood waters.

Grace looked at May. She nodded, and they both ran to a window to watch through the darkness as the men sloshed through the water toward the cow field.

"I hate Uncle Edmund," Grace said quietly to May.

"He's just mad about the cows."

"Maybe, but he called Papa a fool." She fumed as they watched through the darkness, trying to see what was happening below.

Mimi stepped into their room. "Girls, time to sleep," she had chided.

"We just wanted to watch," Grace had said. "Why does Uncle Edmund have to be so mean?"

Mimi sighed her tired sigh. "He was rough, but he was right. We depend on those cows, for milk and meat. If they sicken or die, we could be in danger."

"Oh," Grace said, still not ready to forgive.

"There they are!" said May. They watched as Papa and Uncle Edmund led the cows toward the barn, but it, too, was flooded. The men argued about something, waving their arms in the air, but the girls couldn't hear what. Then, Uncle Edmund led his cow by the halter, making the others follow. He took them slightly uphill to the sugarhouse and led the cows inside. Papa followed, leading another cow and small herd.

The children settled in for the night, sweating from the humidity and yet chilly from the breeze, the sheets sticking to Grace's legs as she tossed and turned.

Over the next few days, the waters had slowly receded, and Uncle Edmund returned to his work as a scout. The cows were able to leave their shed, and the family began the slow work of cleaning up the farm. The field hands did the heavy work, but the children were assigned this area or that to pitch in, though Grace's share, admittedly, was always a bit less than everyone else's. She'd been picking up debris near the house when she felt a wave of dizziness pass over her. As she swayed on her feet, she heard Mimi call out from a great distance, but Grace had already lost consciousness before she hit the ground.

Now, as Grace moved the fan over Papa's face, she felt a lump rise in her throat. She'd rested in her own bed for days, restless from her fever. She'd dreamt they were still safe in their New Orleans home, only to wake and find the ramshackle farmhouse was the reality. By the time she'd been able to swallow a little broth and follow conversations again, she'd learned that first Mathilda and then Papa had contracted the same illness. Guilt ached in her stomach, tightening her throat and burning her eyes.

If they lost Papa, what would happen to them? They would be completely dependent on Uncle Edmund or perhaps Mimi's brother, Uncle Tom.

Grace sighed and continued fanning Papa's face. "I'm sorry if I made you sick, Papa," she whispered, her lower lip trembling. "And I know you're tired, but we need you to wake up, Papa. We need you. Mimi needs you."

Tears slipped down Grace's cheeks and landed on the bed linens with a plop. She leaned back in the chair and rested her head on the arm, just for a moment. The next thing Grace remembered was Jerry lifting her up and carrying her to her own bed. "But I'm fanning Papa..." she protested weakly.

"Your Papa is looking better, thanks to you," Jerry told her. "But it's time for you to rest, Miss Grace."

The next morning, Grace awoke and tip-toed into Papa's room to see him sitting up drinking tea.

"And there is my angel!" Papa called weakly as Grace stood by the doorway. "There I was, floating in the ether when I heard a tiny voice say I was needed, so I'd better wake up." Papa set the tea cup down and held out his arms for Grace.

"Easy now," Mimi called, as Grace flung herself into the bed with Papa. Mimi's face was white with exhaustion and worry, but she topped off Papa's tea cup and went about fluffing pillows and tidying linens. "Why don't we let Papa get some rest?" she asked, gently herding everyone out of the room.

Grace picked up a book and ran downstairs to join May and Nan in the front yard, where they were settled on an old blanket. Grace sat with them and began reading aloud from her book when the girls heard movement in the bayou nearby. Grace paused in her reading to listen.

"You think it's another gator?" asked Nan. "Jerry said to let him know if there was another one. He wants it for shoes and meat."

The shrubs rustled nearby, and Grace's heart nearly froze in her chest: soldiers in dark blue uniforms approached the house. They were finally here, and Grace was frozen in fear.

Nervously, she glanced around and saw no one in the yard but May and Nan, both younger than herself. It was up to her, then.

Her breath caught in her throat, but she swallowed it with a gulp and reached down and picked up a heavy stone. She curled her fingers around it until they ached.

"Where is the master of this farm?" demanded one man, leading several others behind him. His stained uniform was missing buttons, and the elbows were worn thin.

Grace stood, speechless, squeezing the rock behind her back.

Mimi appeared behind her in the doorway. "I am the mistress of this farm," she said stiffly. "The master is unwell."

"His health is not our concern," said the man, clearly an officer. "He is to come with us."

"But he is un—"

Suddenly, Papa stood beside her, looking disheveled and pale. Mimi stopped speaking and looked panic-stricken at Papa.

"I am the master of this farm," he said calmly.

"Then, you, sir, are under arrest. Please come with us."

Papa looked down at Grace, his eye falling on the rock in her hand. "Go on inside, Sis. Take May and Nan. I'll be back shortly."

Then, he walked, faltering occasionally, down the steps to stand in front of the Union soldiers. The soldiers were much younger than Papa, but they towered over him. His frame was frail and weak in comparison.

They filed in front of and behind him and led him toward the bayou. Grace ushered Nan and May inside and turned for one more look at Papa. Out of the corner of her eye, she saw something moving quickly across the field between the house and the bayou. She gasped.

Fred ran toward the troops with his recently acquired shotgun. They turned and saw him, but he hid behind a tree. Leaning out, he shot his weapon toward them.

"Fred! No!" Papa shouted weakly. Fred's shots bounced off the ground well away from his targets. "He's only a boy! Please don't hurt him!"

"Return fire!" ordered the officer.

"Please!" Papa shouted again.

Mimi held her hand to her chest, her face so white, Grace thought she might faint. Mimi opened her mouth to say something, but no sound came out.

"But, sir, he's just a boy defending his pa," said a young soldier. "Look—his shots ain't even coming close!"

The other soldiers looked at each other. Another spoke up.

"Captain, we don't shoot children."

"The boy is no longer a boy if he can take up arms! Return fire!"

"But the gun is barely more than a toy! He might as well be throwing rocks!" shouted the first soldier.

"You will do as you are commanded, private, or you will be punished! Heavily!"

The soldiers hesitated as they raised their guns to their shoulders, continually looking at each other for reassurance of what to do. Grace panted, her breath unable to fill her tightening lungs.

As she gasped for air, a pair of arms reached out from behind her, and Aunt Mathilda pulled Grace into her chest to hide her eyes as the soldiers shot their guns.

Mimi screamed and fell to her knees in the yard as Grace peeked under Mathilda's arms to see if Fred had been hit. The soldiers continued to fire, but Grace couldn't see where the shots were landing. She saw Fred run, jump a fence, and disappear in the nearby woods, all under the gun fire.

Grace finally drew her eyes back to the soldiers. Were they really just terrible shots? Fred had been right there in clear range...

When she saw the soldiers, tears spilled down her cheeks. Their guns were pointed straight up. They were missing Fred on purpose, as their captain yelled and fumed at them, his words unheard by Grace over the gunshots and the ringing they left in her ears. The soldiers continued on their march with Papa, away from the house.

Mathilda pulled Grace inside as Jerry helped Mimi. The family sat in heavy silence as they waited.

Eventually, Fred circled around to the back of the house; his cheeks tear-stained and boots muddied.

Later that night, Papa, too, returned to the main house unscathed. He said the Yanks went on and on about what a brave thing Fred had done. Foolish, but brave. Papa said that until his last breath, he would be grateful for those soldiers' kindness toward Fred.

* * *

1865

Papa had been away from the farm for some time, having escorted a large group of men to Texas and headed to New Orleans himself. Now that the war was officially over, the King family hoped to return home as soon as possible. In the mean time, Mimi and Jerry were tasked with managing the farm and readying the children.

Several nights after Papa's departure, the children sat on the front porch, being bored together. Lessons were done for the day, and they heard a rumble in the distance. And then something sharper. A thin trail of smoke wafted above the horizon.

"What's going on over there?" asked Fred, his eyes brightening a bit.

Ever cautious, Jerry walked down to the barns and began closing up the heavy doors. A few of the field hands came up to check in with him while the children watched from their post on the porch. The rumbling in the distance grew louder, and the smoke turned darker above the trees.

Mathilda came onto the porch. "Alright now, everyone inside. *Maman*'s orders."

"But, Aunt Mathilda!" said Fred, panting in excitement. "They're coming! The battle's coming, and I'm going to..."

"You're going to follow your *Maman*'s orders, young man," scolded Aunt Mathilda. "Everyone in!"

After starting up the stairs, Grace realized she'd left a book on the porch. She went quietly back down and opened the door.

"What'll we do if it gets here?" she overheard one of the men, Joseph, say to Jerry.

"Hunker down, keep quiet. Maybe they'll pass us on by," Jerry said, examining the sky again.

"Why? Why not leave and join them?" asked the man. "Why should we stay here? Why do you stay here?"

Jerry frowned. "Cause that's my family."

"That ain't your family," Joseph said, angrily. "Mathilda's your family. Not the others."

"They're all my family," Jerry said stubbornly. "Mathilda, the mistress, you. Everyone."

"You think they're going to protect you? Or support you after this is all over?"

Jerry hesitated. "I hope so. Because I've been with them longer than I've ever been anywhere. She's good to me and mine, and she needs me here. Those children in there," he gestured to the main house. "And down there," he pointed to the cabins. "They all need a man here to protect them. And for right now, I'm that man."

"You're a fool, then," replied Joseph, as he turned and walked away.

Mimi sighed deeply from behind Grace, making Grace turn around. Her face flushed red and her eyes teared over. "I love Uncle Jerry, *Maman*. I do," she said to Mimi. "I don't want him to leave. Or Mathilda, either."

Mimi sighed and put her arms around Grace. "It's all a big mess," she said quietly.

"I thought...I thought..." Grace said, hiccupping so hard her voice caught in her throat. "I thought they were my friends. All this time. The servants' children. Joseph's children. Everyone. I thought...everyone was happy. I knew we were poor now, but I thought we were all happy. But they're not, are they? Why don't they love us? We do our best to take care of everyone..."

"Grace, they are slaves. Like in Grandmamma's bible. Just as Will feared would happen to us," Mimi explained softly. "They don't get a choice. As women, neither do we. We're all stuck in a situation we didn't create, but we will do our best to make each day better for those around us. What more could we possibly do?" Mimi nodded her head toward the book outside, and Grace went out to fetch it.

When she went upstairs, Grace found that Mimi and Mathilda had arranged everyone's beds around Mimi's own.

"What's going on?" Grace asked.

"Battle's coming closer," Fred said, excitedly. He and Will stared out of the window longingly. Mathilda came in with a plate of corn bread and cold ham.

"Take some down to the others, too," said Mimi from the doorway.

Soon, the sky darkened, but they could hear the cannons thundering even louder. The air smelled of burning fires, and the tree line seemed to glow red in the distance. Branch, the best reader of all the children, read aloud stories from *The Scottish Chiefs* to keep them distracted. Stories about brave men and war.

The next morning, the smell of burning had lingered in the air, but no one came to the farm. The adults had seemed relieved, but the children were oddly disappointed. Fred and Will moped for days, setting aside even their play battle practice. It turned out no one needed the battle-ready skills of children with their small weapons.

Barely a week later, Grace, Fred, and Branch sat at the top of the stairs eavesdropping on Jerry and Mimi discussing the sudden return of the men Papa had sent to Texas. They'd come home in the middle of the night, unexpectedly.

Jerry explained, "They say they weren't treated right. Worked without regular meals for more hours than they usually do with no breaks through the day. That's not fair treatment and was not the arrangement I know Mr. King made."

Mimi remained quiet.

"They abandoned the ranch in Texas and walked all that way back here to rejoin their families. But," Jerry hesitated. "Some took sick and died on the way here. Mistress," Jerry said, with some hesitation in his voice. "They know. They know the war is over. They know they are supposed to be free," he said gently.

"What do I do, Jerry?" Mimi had whispered, just barely loud enough for the children to hear her. "I can't just tell them to leave here. William has not instructed me to send them away, and if they leave the farm...I'm not sure what will happen to them out there. I can't in good faith keep them here, but I can't in good faith let them go with no shelter or food." Mimi's voice cracked, and Grace could tell she was crying. Grace looked at Fred and Branch, her eyes wide and filling with her own tears. Fred signaled that they should go back up. They paused by Grace's bedroom, where the other girls slept soundly.

Branch and Fred walked to the rear stairs and quietly descended, so they could slip unheard out the back door and return to the cabin. Grace slipped back into bed with May.

The next morning, they ate breakfast in silence. As Mathilda began gathering dishes, they heard men shouting outside.

"Stay here," Mimi instructed them, as she went to the kitchen door to face a small gathering of men, the children crowding behind her to see.

"Mistress, we're placing a complaint. We don't belong to you anymore!" one man shouted. Grace recognized Henry, one of the strongest of the field servants. Will often fished and played with Henry's son, Jimmy. The others behind him nodded.

"I understand you are upset," Mimi said.

"Upset? No, ma'am. We are angry. How dare your husband send us to that place!" Henry's voice rose up and rattled the very shingles on the porch roof. "We deserve better! Your husband made a bad decision! That fool—"

Something in Grace snapped. In her eyes, Papa was everything good in the world. Everything strong, secure, and comforting. Papa meant safety.

"How dare you insult my father!" Grace screamed. She jumped forward and darted around Mimi.

"Sissy!" Mimi said, failing to catch Grace in her arms.

"He is a good man!" Grace screamed, as tears began rolling down her cheeks.

"No, little miss! He isn't!" yelled Henry. "And it's best you learn it now! Men lie and cheat and take all they want, no matter how it hurts everyone else!"

She ran at him, raking her fingers like a cat's claws at his shirt. Henry waited, looking around for someone to take the thin little girl railing at him, but he didn't lift a hand to peel her off himself. Jerry appeared suddenly and scooped her up, like the spitting cat she was. He practically scuffed her by the back of the neck and carried her inside the house.

The yelling outside continued, but Grace was shaking, crying, and hiccupping beside Jerry on the sofa in the parlor. Mathilda appeared and took his place beside her, as Jerry left to rejoin Mimi.

Eventually, Mimi came in and took over from Mathilda. She did not hold or comfort Grace as Mathilda had.

"Grace Elizabeth King," she said quietly and slowly. "What in heaven's name did you think you were doing?" She didn't yell. It was much worse. Her voice dropped to a gravely deep tone, and her eyes seared into Grace's own.

Grace opened her mouth, but no sound came out.

"You could have been hurt. They could have reacted to you and hurt the other children. You *must* control your temper! You are not a child any longer."

Grace felt her face heat up. "They can't say those things about Papa!" Angry tears began rolling again.

"They can say whatever they want," Mimi said. "They are free men, now. And they outnumber us. We are in danger here. Don't you see? And they are in danger out there!" She gestured to the trees. "I cannot send them away for what may happen to them. And now we cannot stay here for what may happen to us. Children," she called, finally taking a deep breath and including the others, who had gathered silently in the doorway. "Pack a bag. We must leave here now."

"Where will we go?" asked Will. "Jim and I are supposed to go fishing..."

"The Tally's farm."

Before long, they were seated in an old wagon and making their way toward the neighbor's home some miles away. Jerry and Mathilda stayed behind in the main house. Grace overhead Mimi and Jerry whisper about being afraid the house would be burnt to the ground.

By night, the children were settled in pallets on the floors of their neighbor's home, much like their own: simple and rustic but functional. Mimi penned a letter to Papa in New Orleans, but they could not tell how long it would take to reach him. A few mornings after their hasty departure, some of the servants arrived on foot at the neighbor's house, asking for Mimi. Again, the children crowded behind her to listen, but this time, Branch kept a hand firmly on Grace's upper arm.

"We've come to ask you and the children home," Henry said, looking nervously at the others. He wrung his hat in his hands in front of him. Several women came with them, as well. "I was angry and spoke out of turn."

Mimi stood tall and firm. "And what is the situation at the farm right now?"

Henry took a slow, shaky breath. "Nothing's damaged, if that's what you mean, or...or...burnt. And we...we didn't mean to run you and the children off. We're all confused. We don't know what to do or where to go," he said, staring at the dirt.

Mimi sighed. "I don't either," she admitted.

"Please, ma'am," said one of the women, Maria, from the back of the group. She was round and clearly pregnant. "Please don't call the authorities. No harm will come to anyone, not from us." She looked and sounded near tears.

"You're close to your time, now, aren't you?" Mimi asked.

"Yes, ma'am, but I'm worried. I don't know what's coming. I don't know..." Maria's voice trailed off as her hand cradled her belly and unborn baby.

Mimi swallowed hard and looked at the dirt in the distance, thinking. "I will come with you and see to a few things, before the children return."

"But," Will started. Fred punched Will's arm before he could say anything else. "Ow," he grumbled, flexing his shoulder.

"Jerry and Mathilda are still in the main house?" Mimi asked.

"Yes, ma'am," Maria said, gaining a little confidence in her voice. "Please, let us help bring your family home."

The neighbor had the old wagon brought around. Mimi sat up and took the reins to the old farm horse. She held them up to Henry. "Henry, drive us home, please. Maria will sit with us up front," she said. "Everyone else, climb in the back. Let's go home. Children," she said. "I will return in a few days, once things are settled and safe for you. Fred?"

Fred stepped forward and pushed his shoulders back. "You are in charge of your siblings. Take care of them. I'm counting on you. I'm counting on all of you."

Three days later, the children came home to the farm and settled back into the routine.

* * *

A month later, Mimi received a letter from Papa, and the children grew excited about what could possibly be in it. Were they finally going home? Fred brought it inside for Mimi, and Branch and Will danced around him, trying to catch it. Grace stood on the stairs, watching, with May, Nan, and Nina on the steps behind her. Nina held Nan's hand.

"Boys," said Mimi as she swept into the room. Fred stopped hopping and stood still beside Branch, who frowned at Will.

"You're going to open it now, right?" asked Fred.

Mimi looked at them, all standing and waiting. "Oh," she said. "Should I? Or perhaps we should finish our tasks and chores to give the letter the attention it deserves?"

The children looked in horror from one to another. How could she make them wait that long?

"Out you go, all of you," said Mimi. "Grandmamma needs a few things repaired at the cabin, Fred and Branch. Will, go along with Jerry to check the pasture fence. May and Grace, you're to help Mathilda with the mending and sewing. We need to finish up those clothes for everyone. Nan, Nina, Grandmamma and Aunt Mary are waiting for you outside."

Her missives complete, Mimi waved her hands, dismissing her unit.

Grace headed to the front room, where Mathilda had set out their current sewing pile. Half-finished dresses and shirts littered the tables and sofa arms.

"Here you go, Grace," Mathilda said, handing her a light blue dress. "You do such nice work. Could you do the hems? May and I can work on piecing the larger sections together."

Grace and May nodded and settled into a quiet rhythm with Mathilda, the only sound the pull of the thread through the cloth. Grace's mind began to float. She wondered again what would happen to everyone now. The war was over, and this meant large changes for them. She cast small glances at Mathilda and wished she could ask her questions. What would happen now? Will she come with them back to the city?

She thought about asking Mathilda if she loved them, if Jerry loved them, but she bit her tongue. She was too afraid of the answer.

Grace rested the skirt she'd been hemming on her lap and sighed just as Mimi came in to join them. Mimi smiled gently, and Grace noticed the lines deepening around her eyes now. A few gray streaks now ran through Mimi's hair. When did that happen? Grandmamma's hair, too, had lightened, but Grace had expected that.

"Gather round, everyone," she said, as she led the procession into the parlor and took a seat in her favorite chair. The boys were behind her, jumping in place with excitement. Mimi opened the envelope carefully.

"When do we leave? Should we pack tonight?" asked May, setting her sewing aside.

Mimi's eyes scanned the note as the children tried in vain to read her expression.

"Out loud! Read it out loud!" Will said.

Mimi held her breath for a moment but then began reading out loud. Papa had returned to find their home had been confiscated, with all of their beautiful furniture, clothing, and books. It no longer belonged to them. Papa's law firm had been ransacked, as well; his books and legal documents gone.

Papa said the city was full of confusion and chaos. He would have to find them a new home to rent, and they would have to start completely anew with whatever they could bring from the farm.

"But my toys..." began Will, confused.

"My dresses..." said May.

Grandmamma mouthed a prayer and clutched her bible to her chest.

The only thing Grace could think of was Papa's books. The family library was gone. She would never hold those leather volumes or practice the languages in them. Three generations of beautifully bound books were gone. Their home, their previous lives, and hopeful futures...all gone. They would be returning to the city just as penniless as they'd been living in the country—worse, even, for Jerry, Mathilda, and the others would not be returning with them. Grace felt like her family was splitting. There would be no grande return to their lives. Nan had started crying, and Nina followed suit, while Will sulked, his lower lip protruding angrily.

In tears, May ran to the bedroom she shared with Grace, and Fred and Branch hid their cussing from Mimi until they were outside.

Grace felt her heart drop to the floor and walked toward a nearby field, leaving the house behind. She had thought—they had all thought—their hardships were temporary, dutiful even. Who was she, if not the first-born daughter of a wealthy family? What would she do once they returned to the city?

She circled along the edge of the bayou as the sun slid further across the sky. A golden tint soon made the trees magical, the shadows darker, and the green more subdued. Not scary at all, like on their arrival three years before. It turned out, there were scarier things in the world than shadows.

She sat near a group of cypress trees and listened. Birds chirped in the distance, chattering and singing. Somewhere nearby, some small critter rustled in the bushes. A squirrel, maybe. Her heart felt a stirring, and some small energy filled her, from her tingling toes to her buzzing scalp. Her fingers itched. The buzzing feeling swam through her head, and she stood up to clear her thoughts. She stumbled a bit, her legs wobbly underneath, and suddenly, the forest sounds were silent. No birds. No chirping squirrels. No rustling leaves. Silence. Her sadness hardened a bit, and she felt that she could carry it easier that way.

She looked up to the golden sky to see silent clouds rushing by. In her imagination, she saw ladies in balls, brave men and women in boats in bayous, and New Orleans' cobbled streets filled with colorful dresses and head scarves. She could smell chicory coffee and sugared pastries and see endless stories rolling out in front of her...characters, plots, and settings.

She felt a deep desire to begin writing. Not just a desire...a *calling*. A commanding. She would write. She was supposed to write stories and letters and tales and ideas. She felt it in her very bones: She would be a writer.

Chapter 5

Hey Meredith,

It was good to see you and the girls last weekend! Kay and I were wondering if you four might be able to join us at the beach house we're renting this summer in Panama City, Florida. The beach is the most beautiful I've ever seen, and I'd love to spend more than a few hours with you all. Let me know!

Love,

Dad

P.S. What's Lila's favorite color? I'll buy her some beach gear.

Writing centers are places on college campuses where the students can receive extra support on their writing projects and goals. Many students think of it as a place for "bad" writers, but the reality is that everyone needs support to grow as writers. The tutors in the writing center at Tennessee Valley State were all students in the doctoral or masters' programs or advanced undergrads. It was clear, however, from their conversations during slow shifts that an underlying sense of competition existed no matter what their kind words or social media invitations suggested.

Tiny Hands spent much of his time either digging up what he thought was dirt on other grad students or finding ways to belittle them. "How long was your thesis? Mine was so long, the director told me I could have a full book out of it."

One young woman attached herself to virtually every female grad student in the room. "Oh! I'm so glad to see you!" Lyn said one day and ran forward to hug Meredith, holding onto her elbow afterward.

"Oh, were you looking for me?"

"No, silly, I'm just so happy we met! Was your weekend lovely? I spent time with friends, and we passed the loveliest evening! Such wonderful tidings! I even took a walk with a man I met in my church," she whispered excitedly, blushing and looking down at her feet.

She spoke and acted as though she were living in a Jane Austen novel. *This girl needs to get laid,* Meredith thought. *Bet Jane Austen never thought of that as a remedy for most of these characters' problems.*

"That's nice, Lyn," Meredith replied warily. "How are your classes going?"

"Oh," she said, her face falling. "I'm struggling. My professor critiqued my writing, and it was very disheartening." She looked near tears. Meredith stared for a moment, too distracted by Lyn's fast turn of emotions to respond.

"Oh, um, that's okay," she finally stammered. "Take note of her recommendations and move forward."

Tiny Hands piped up suddenly and said, "Lyn, you said something the other day that really bothered me."

"Oh, if I did, I'm truly very sorry, indeed," she began. "May I ask what it was?"

"You said that homosexuality was a sin. And you should know, I'm gay."

Lyn stared, speechless. "Well..."

The receptionist, an undergraduate tutor with more professionalism than most of the grad students, chimed in, as though she had no idea what the conversation was that she interrupted—though Meredith could tell she knew exactly what was going on behind her. "Your appointment is here," she said to Tiny Hands. She gave Meredith a look that said, "Well, we side-stepped this for now..."

Tiny Hands joined his student at a small table nearby. Lyn wiped a tear and excused herself to the restroom. Meredith sighed, relieved to have dodged the issue for now.

* * *

That spring, Meredith met Preema, who came into the center for help with her writing.

"Oh, my sentences are bad, Meredith," Preema said, shaking her head. She stared at the papers in front of her sadly. "I been in this country for thirty years, but I learned English to speak, not write proper, you know?"

"Well, looking at your writing style, I'd say you learned English in a British colonized country. See here? The letters are flipped in places, and the punctuation is a tiny bit different. Not wrong. Just different. But we can work on these and other little things, too. The ideas are here, and they're wonderful. We'll just focus on little things to show them off a bit more."

"You can tell that from my writing? You are very good!" she said with the certainty of a grandmother bestowing compliments on a beloved grandchild. "I moved here from Nigeria. I married a man. An arranged marriage, so we didn't know each other at all, and he took a pastor job here in the church, and we moved thirty years ago." Her accent beautifully shaped her words.

Meredith sat, stunned. "Preema, you mean you just moved to a whole new country with a new language? You must've been very scared."

"Oh, I was, but I wanted to raise my children in a safe place. I was very lonely for a time, but the church helps, you see. That's my community. It's important to have a community, to belong."

"I'm glad you had that community to help you, Preema," Meredith said, truly meaning it.

"But this—this is hard," Preema said, pointing at the paper in front of her.

"What led you to come back to school?"

"My children are all grown up now, having their own babies. I do work for the church, but I want to do more. So, I study to be a social worker. I want to help the children. They need help the most, so alone with no one to fight for many of them. I will do that. But this English is hard." Her brown eyes were deep but bright with unshed tears. Sincere.

Meredith smiled, feeling tears behind her own eyes that, like Preema, she refused to let fall. Forging ahead when the odds felt overwhelmingly against you was something Meredith understood on a deep level. She thought for just a moment about the Grace King story collection, *Balcony Stories*, sitting on top of her books in the corner of the center and the first few paragraphs in it: *Women's stories, as only women know how to tell them.*

"Well, let's get started then, Preema. We'll go slowly, and you tell me anytime something doesn't make sense. We'll figure it out together."

Preema reached out a hand to touch Meredith's, and for once, Meredith didn't flinch. She let Preema hold her hand through many sessions after that day, without any hesitation whatsoever.

Later that afternoon, Meredith stopped by the Library Circulation Desk to check out her most recent stack of materials.

Lyn turned around and smiled from behind the desk. "Oh, hi, Meredith!"

"Oh, Lyn," Meredith said. "Hi. Are you working here, too?"

"Yes, a little moonlighting to help pay the bills," Lyn explained, scanning Meredith's student I.D. and handing it back. She began scanning each text and glancing at Meredith in between. "So, I noticed in your account the other day that you have some interesting titles checked out."

"I'm sorry?" Meredith asked, confused.

"In your account. For the library. You have some interesting titles checked out. Some about women writers, some theory, and a few collections of journals and such. Find something interesting for your research?"

"You, um, went through my account?"

Lyn smiled a sugary smile. "One of the perks of the job," she said, as she slid the stack of books toward Meredith. "So, what do you have cooking? Anything you can pass along for me?"

"Afraid not," Meredith said, seething inwardly. She felt breeched, but what could she do? If she reported it to anyone, she would be a snitch. If she didn't, she would have to put up with it continuing. As she put away her I.D., Meredith suddenly paused. She had it. She knew exactly how to stop Lyn's prying without bringing anyone else into the situation.

"Just dabbling in this and that. And I just realized there are a few texts I forgot to pick up."

She swept her stack of books from the counter and headed back upstairs. Twenty minutes later, she set down a second set of texts on the counter for Lyn to scan.

"So, you asked about my research. I'm happy to discuss this project, if you'd like?"

Lyn glanced at the titles and blanched as she waved the scanner over the spines. *The Body in Ecstasy: Reading Pornography; The Pornography Industry: What Everyone Needs to Know;* and *The Ultimate Guide to Kink.* "Um, I'm actually heading out for the day after this," she said so quietly Meredith could barely hear her.

"Oh, okay. Some other time then!" Meredith said with a bright smile. "Have a great day! I know I will!" she said as she left the counter with a wink.

* * *

"Okay, so the kids are safely delivered to Gayle's for the night, and we have a whole night to ourselves for the first time in months. What do you want to do?" Liam asked excitedly.

Just then, Meredith's cell phone rang. She answered, seeing her mom's number on the preview screen. "Hey, what's up?"

"The baby won't stop crying. She just keeps crying and crying," Gayle said. "I've been trying to get her to sleep since you left."

"Mom, it's six o'clock. She usually eats when we do, around seven, then bath and bed by eight or eight-thirty."

"Well, she's inconsolable. You have to come and get her."

Meredith sighed. "Okay. Can you give her a few minutes to try?"

"Fine. But if she's still crying in a bit, you need to come and get her."

Meredith hung up.

"Let me guess. Come and get them?"

"Yes. Emmy won't stop crying. I guess I'll get dressed."

"No. Sit here and enjoy your glass of wine. She said she would watch them for one night. We're financially supporting her so we can have some help, remember? We need rest. You need rest. This running ourselves ragged physically and financially is not sustainable."

Meredith sighed, stuck. They'd been struggling for weeks to get some time to themselves and did manage to go out for a few hours on New Year's Eve. Gayle had not been feeling well since her arrival in November and refused to see a local doctor. Liam had registered for a few on-campus classes this semester, so he and Meredith were working double-time, often handing off the kids in university parking lots. This was the kids' very first full night at Grandma's apartment.

Another phone call. Emmy was still fussy.

More phone calls. One last try. As they sat on the couch, Meredith burst into tears. Liam wrapped his arms around her shoulders. Finally, he said, "You know what. I have a crazy idea."

The phone rang, interrupting. Emmy was finally asleep. Gayle would watch them until tomorrow morning, but next time, Meredith would need to make sure Emmy was asleep before she left. Meredith agreed and hung up.

"Okay, tell me about this crazy idea. And it better not be to sell everything and move onto a sail boat."

"It's not, but that idea is always a valid option. We'll need to make a few phone calls tonight..."

* * *

The next morning, they woke early and went to Gayle's apartment. The kids were eating ice cream for breakfast. Meredith had just called her before they left the house, and Gayle knew they were on their way over to pick up the girls.

"Oh, you're here. Well, if you want to pull them away from their treat..."

Meredith sighed and shook her head a tiny bit when Liam raised his eyebrows, dumbstruck by Gayle's actions. They sat on the sofa and brought up Liam's idea.

They could see Gayle was unhappy. His mom, Maggie, would come down from Kentucky for an extended visit for spring semester. Liam had already called and discussed it with her, and she was thrilled to come and stay and help with the children. Gayle could leave.

"Thank you," Gayle said, as tears filled her eyes. "I'll leave everything here. Maggie can use the apartment as hers for the spring semester, and I'll just come back in a few months to pack my things when the lease is up."

"That's fine," Meredith said.

"I'll call Dave today! The divorce papers came a few days ago, but I'm done with all that marriage stuff. No more! But he's been wanting me to come down to Arkansas with him."

Meredith and Liam made the drive to pick up Maggie. She couldn't drive that far alone, so Meredith followed behind as Liam drove his mom's car with his mom back to Tennessee.

When Meredith called to check on her, Gayle cooed about the girls and how easy they were, but only because she was leaving. As soon as they arrived with Maggie, she warned that they were a handful again. Dave arrived a few days later, and Gayle took her dogs and went to live in Arkansas.

A few days later, the electricity in the apartment was cut off and was quickly followed by the water. The bills had gone unpaid, even though Meredith and Liam had been giving Gayle money to pay them. When Meredith called Gayle, the phone went unanswered.

Maggie paid the bills, and Meredith burned with embarrassment.

The girls began spending one night every week with their Nana. Meredith would call or nudge Liam to call every few hours to make sure they were fine. Gayle had said repeatedly that they were a handful, and Maggie was twenty years older than her.

"They're fine," Maggie said gently, every single time. "Don't you worry about them. Lila is making some arts and crafts, and Emmy cried for a bit at bedtime, but I held her until she slept, and she's doing just fine now. By the way, I was going to make eggs for them for breakfast. I know you want them to eat healthy, and some people aren't okay with eggs nowadays. Is that okay?"

Meredith had teared up with relief. "Yes. Eggs are just fine."

* * *

One Tuesday morning in mid-April, Meredith made her way to the foreign language building. She had a ten o'clock appointment to take her French reading fluency exam. Last week, she had sat through a four-hour qualifying exam. Faced with several questions in each section and the sections arranged to cover all of British and American literature, Meredith had written on everything from *Beowulf* to *Beloved*. She had spent the rest of the day and the next one in a fog, playing in the backyard with the children. She had given everything she could on the exam and felt oddly at peace now with her performance on it, even if her nerves had been fired up before it. Now, it was done. There was naught to be done about it.

This morning, however, Meredith felt anxious, even if less so than for her qualifying exam. Her French exam she could retake next semester...or even the one after that...or the one after that. If the exam proved too difficult, she could opt to take the full class in translation, but it would add a considerable weight to her already heavy semester workload. But if she passed the exam, this would be one more step closer—one more box checked.

She made her way inside the newly renovated building. New sitting areas with modern sofas and heavy wooden tables were nestled in every nook and cranny, and wide hallways were well-lit by the skylights above. She glanced inside a few of the open offices, curious. New cherry wood wide desks were inside each one with towering floor-to-ceiling bookcases. Most of the offices had large windows and skylights above. Meredith thought about her English professors' offices back in Bush Hall: Cinder-block, airless cubes with no windows or natural light whatsoever. Most had rickety metal bookcases, old desks from decades prior, and were barely larger than a broom closet.

Meredith found the French professor's office and frowned when she saw the heavy wooden door was firmly closed: the signal that the office was empty. Meredith glanced at her phone, 9:53 a.m. Seven minutes early for her exam. She shrugged and began to slowly read every bulletin board in the hallway as she meandered up and down, waiting. Twice, she knocked hesitatingly at the door, just in case. No answer.

At 10:15 a.m., she pulled up the confirmation email from the professor to reassure herself that she had not mistaken the date or time. Nope.

By 10:30 a.m., Meredith had memorized most the flyers on the walls. She had started walking slowly down the hall, turned right, and followed the hall in a complete circle, reading each professor's door, posters, and flyers. She wanted to reschedule, but the exams were only offered in a two-week window each semester—and today was the last day.

She scrolled through pictures of Panama City on her phone, looking forward to the four days she and the girls would spend there in July. Liam had finals that week, so she and the kids would venture out alone. She was nervous to be without him for the few days, but she looked forward to playing on the beach with them. *How did I do those year-long deployments without him?* she wondered.

At 11:00, a frazzled young man carrying a half-open backpack rushed past her, slammed to a halt, and turned back to face her.

"Professor Banks' office?" he asked, panting.

"Third door, other side of the loop," Meredith answered flatly, now familiar with every door on the floor.

At 11:15, she was torn: Should she walk away? What if the professor showed up just minutes after Meredith left? What if she'd just had a crazy morning—a flat tire or something? Didn't things like this happen all the time?

She set a deadline for herself: If the professor still wasn't there by 11:30, Meredith would leave. At 11:30, Meredith sighed and looked at the professor's door one last time. She turned to walk away just as a woman in maybe her early forties approached at a slow pace. She wore a patchwork light jacket and had a faraway look on her face.

"Professor Perkins, by chance?" Meredith asked. The woman paused and looked at Meredith in surprise, as though she had not noticed the only other person in the entire hallway though they stood less than five feet from one another.

"Yes?"

"Hi, um, I'm Meredith. I was supposed to take a French translation exam this morning?"

Professor Perkins furrowed her brow and frowned. "I don't think so. I don't recall anything on my schedule."

"Oh, um," Meredith said as she pulled up the confirmation Professor Perkins herself had sent. She awkwardly showed it to the professor.

Professor Perkins rolled her eyes, pulled her glasses out of her pocket, and squinted at the phone to read the email. "Hm," she said, frowning even more. "That's my email account, but I certainly do not recall scheduling anything for today." She stared at Meredith suspiciously, as though Meredith had somehow arranged this entire episode on her own. Professor Perkins pursed her lips as she handed the phone back to Meredith and fumbled with her keys to open the office door. Once she entered and tossed her things into a pile on the floor, she waved Meredith.

"You might as well come inside," she said with a sigh. "Students use that desk over there." She pointed to the corner of a table overrun with stacks of papers and books. Meredith sat down and started to move a stack of the papers to make a small amount of room in which to work.

"Oh, don't move those. They're in a certain order. Just work on top of them."

"Yes, ma'am," Meredith said, feeling increasingly irritated.

"I have to leave, but just leave the finished exam on my keyboard and shut my office door behind you. Oh, and you'll have to finish in forty-five minutes instead of the usual ninety minutes. I have students in my *own* department to work with. And remind me: Which department?"

"English."

Meredith took a breath to steady her nerves and anxiety. She glanced at the clock on the wall. Students were given a full-length article in French from their fields of research—in her case, literature—that they were to translate into English. If the translation was deemed acceptable by the overseeing language professor, the student passed. Other grad students had warned Meredith that the article would be on Dickens—and had been for several semesters.

Professor Perkins handed her a manila envelope with a thick article inside and walked to the door. "Good luck," she said as she walked out.

Meredith took a steadying breath and opened the envelope. She skimmed the title of the article and frowned.

"Professor Perkins," she called quickly. She hopped up and looked down the hallway, but it was already empty.

Meredith plopped back down on the hard plastic chair. She looked up at the clock and considered her options, her eyes tearing up. Should she walk out? Try to reschedule for fall semester? It would still be the same overseeing professor then as now. And the class? Taught by the same professor. But if she passed the exam today...

She made her decision, picked up her pencil, and began translating the twenty-page article on nineteenth-century Canadian anthropological theory.

In what felt like minutes, Meredith finished the translation—just as several of Professor Perkins students came into the office. She left the packet on the professor's keyboard and headed back outside. As she walked by a small sitting area tucked back between some shrubs, she recognized Jennifer, another graduate student in the program. Jennifer's face was tear-streaked and splotchy. Meredith froze. She didn't know Jennifer very well at all. Should she say something or give her some privacy?

Jennifer looked up and caught Meredith's eye. "Oh, Meredith. Hi," she said with a sniffle.

Meredith walked closer. "Hey, Jennifer. You okay?"

Jennifer tried to gather a shaky breath. "I, um, didn't pass the qualifying exam."

"Oh," Meredith said, sitting down next to Jennifer. "I'm so sorry to hear that."

Jennifer gave her a tight smile in response. "The thing is, that's my second fail. I'm done. I'm out of the program."

"Oh, Jesus, I'm so very sorry," Meredith repeated. She inwardly reproached herself for being terrible at consoling a friend.

Jennifer shrugged. "Just not my path, I guess. But I have no idea what to do now."

Meredith sat quietly with her for a few minutes before speaking. "What was your favorite part of the program?" she finally asked.

Jennifer thought for a moment. "Working in the writing center. I was really looking forward to teaching my first class next year."

"You like kids?"

"Love 'em."

"Why not teach in an elementary school? Junior high? High school?"

Jennifer took a deep breath. "You think I could?"

"I don't see why not. You have a master's in English, right?" Jennifer nodded. "Charter schools and private schools could hire you straight away, pending background checks and stuff. And a public school could, too, if you took a little time and switched to an education program to get the state certs. In the meantime, you could always substitute teach different grades until you find your fit."

"Huh. I didn't think of any of that," Jennifer said, with a bitter chuckle. "I was dreading having to switch my facebook from Graduate Student to Barista."

"Well, you still could," Meredith said in a positive tone, leaning back against the bench. "Probably make more money as a barista."

Jennifer snorted. They sat together on the bench for a few minutes, emailing the education program director and advisors and laughing about a few of their classes over the last year. Meredith realized with regret that she was finally making a friend, but a friend who was leaving the program.

By the time Meredith left Jennifer, her phone buzzed with a new email. Her own exam notification. Her heart pounded as she waited impatiently for the message to download and show up on the phone. The little wheel turned and turned, trying to process the weight of the message as Meredith fought her impulse to throw the phone on the ground in frustration. Finally, the text popped in: *"Hello Meredith, I'd like to congratulate you on passing..."*

She almost fainted with relief.

Chapter 6

L'Embarrass Plantation 1865

On the morning of their departure from the farm, Grace and Mimi stood beside the wagon as her brothers finished loading supplies and their belongings into the back.

"Oh, Jerry," said Mimi softly. Jerry stood in front of her, holding his hat in his hand. "Must you stay?"

Jerry and Mathilda would be joining a group of the former slaves from the plantation in starting their own camp and settlement.

"I'm afraid so," he replied kindly. "My family wants to go their own way now, and they need me, mistress."

"But we're your family, too," Grace said, but from behind Jerry, Papa caught her eye and shook his head. She sighed and looked away. Jerry had kept them safe on the farm. It had been bad enough when Mathilda left them a few weeks back to go ahead of Jerry to their new home, but now she would lose Jerry, too.

"Jerry," said Papa. "I think we're all set here. The boys will bring supplies for everyone at the camp each month for as long as we can."

Jerry nodded. "Thank you."

Tears misted over Grace's eyes.

"Oh, now, miss," Jerry said. "It's not all that bad, now."

Grace sniffled. "Everything's changing," Grace said, leaning her head on Mimi's shoulder. "Everyone is leaving. I want to go home to the city, but I want things to be like they were. Our big house, and our big family."

"Things change, and people grow. I'm afraid that's just how it is, Sis," Mimi said, leading Grace to the wagons.

The family left the farm and traveled back to the city. The return trip was much less daunting than their arrival had been. The family rode on a large steamboat, which the children were happy to see after spending several years in the countryside. It was filled with golden lights that reflected upon the great mother river that carried them back home.

Even though Papa had said Will's dog was the only pet that could come with them, Nan hid a kitten in her basket. All the children helped her mask the small meowing that occasionally drew Papa's attention, as they slowly made the way to their new home, which Papa described as grand and luxurious in this *new* New Orleans.

As they rode through the city, things looked vastly different from the city Grace had known three years prior. Or maybe Grace was different. She was thirteen now, and she was beginning to see the world through her new, writer's eyes. People darted this way and that, but their clothes looked more worn. Not as bright or cheerful as she recalled. The city she remembered had been festive and happy, filled with music and color. This one seemed...less so. The people more beaten down, and the clothing more threadbare and drab.

They switched wagons and carts a few times, and each transfer led to a neighborhood more derelict than the last. Grace exchanged looks with May and Branch. Mimi sat up front with Papa, sharing a quiet conversation. She frowned and pursed her lips frequently, scanning her eyes back and forth across the neighborhood buildings, but Papa didn't seem to notice.

Grandmamma rode in the wagon behind them, fanning herself with her worn, lace fan, occasionally reprimanding Will for horse-playing in the seat beside her, though it was clear to Grace that she didn't truly mind.

Grace began to feel dizzy and deeply fatigued from all of the travel and sighed deeply. May squeezed her hand and held it as they turned yet another corner. They were now in a part of the city Grace had never seen or even knew existed. The brick buildings were worn smooth, and the corners were often crumbling. The sidewalks here were made of wooden planks—not red bricks in nice patterns. There were no shade trees that Grace could see in any direction, something she thought they would sorely miss come June. With no tree roots to hold the dirt in place, mud squished from underneath the wooden planks, where men shouted, and people crammed the narrow, wooden sidewalks. The houses and buildings now looked dreary and ugly, with no green plants, flowers, or beauty to be seen.

Her eyes swam with sudden tears. She suddenly missed their farm. May squeezed her hand again and leaned forward and gently tapped Mimi's elbow. Mimi glanced back at the girls, frowned, and started to turn forward again. She looked back a second time, this time looking into Grace's eyes. She leaned back and placed her cool, now work-worn hand on Grace's forehead. Mimi sighed deeply, shared a concerned look with May, and turned forward again.

"How much farther?" she asked Papa, seated beside her.

"Not much, and the crowds will thin out a bit," he assured her. "This house was the nicest we could afford. And I spent nearly three times the amount of money on furniture we would have donated to charity as would have cost new before the War. Basic supplies, like wood or bolts of fabric, are still lacking, but that will change. I'll return to my practice, and we'll watch the city grow around us!"

By the time they reached their new home, Grace's developing fever made her overwhelmingly tired. The new landlady, a large woman with a kerchief around her head, waved from the front door of the small house. She took one look at Grace and stepped forward to help her inside into a narrow bed. The other children unloaded from the wagons and began to look around their new neighborhood.

"Cribiche!" the landlady called to a young boy playing outside. "Run to the churchyard garden, and bring me some of the herbs in the corner patch!" The boy hopped up and ran from the room. "He's a good boy," the woman explained in her thick, Creole accent to Mimi, who sat beside Grace. "He's the neighborhood orphan. Everyone takes turns feeding the boy in their kitchens, and he run errands and messages, like a good boy."

Grace fell asleep after that, but she saw Cribiche a number of times in the few years that they lived in that small house on the corner of Delery and Chartres Streets.

* * *

Mimi took charge of the new home and quickly put things to order. Her first order of business, after stocking the kitchen and unpacking the crates, was arranging for the children's education. Mademoiselle Coralie, their beloved governess, was nowhere to be found upon their return.

Instead, Mimi and Papa had selected two small schools, one for the girls and one for the boys. Before the first day at their new school, the children traveled with Mimi to Canal Street to shop for new clothes.

As they walked down the busy sidewalks, Mimi pointed out all the stores and sights that she had described during the stay in the country, like the famous hat shop where silk flowers were imported from Paris. Many rainy days on the plantation had been spent begging Mimi to take her beautiful pink hat out of the box for the girls to see. Now, she pointed to the shop where the hat had been purchased.

As Mimi looked inside the store, she paused.

"What is it, Mimi?" May asked.

"Children, wait here for a moment," Mimi said quietly, leaving them together on the sidewalk.

Grace and May glanced at each other and watched as Mimi approached a young woman who walked inside the store on the arm of a Union soldier. The woman felt familiar though Grace couldn't place her exactly.

When Mimi returned a few minutes later, she shook her head. "I could have sworn that young lady was Coralie, but she looked so different. She said I was mistaken, so now I feel foolish," Mimi said with a sigh. She kept glancing back at the young woman inside, though, and Grace followed her gaze. She could see it a little now; the woman's eyes were darker and her face had new lines, but she could see some resemblance to their former governess. And there was something about the dress that the woman wore that struck Grace, as well.

"Her dress looks like one you used to wear, Mimi," Grace said, realizing now why the color struck her. She had seen Mimi wear just such a dress many times for afternoon visits and tea in their previous life in the city. She had left the dress behind in their exodus, deeming it too frivolous for the countryside.

Mimi smiled sadly and steered her flock away to continue their errands, but Grace still noticed the sideways look Mimi cast at the woman as they walked away.

"Mrs. King?" said an elderly woman walking by them.

Mimi looked away from the young woman and greeted the elderly one kindly. "Madame Girard, how wonderful to see you!" The women embraced, and Mimi turned to Grace, May, and Nan. "You remember the girls."

"*Oui, mais* they have grown," Madame Girard said in her blend of French and English, as was typical among the Creole community. "You have enrolled them at the Institut St. Louis, I hear?"

"Yes, we have," Mimi answered.

"Ah, it is a good institute, girls," Madame Girard said, raising her eyebrows. "I fully expect you to study with Mademoiselle Cenas after that, and return to me for polishing your French and history, *oui*?"

"*Absolument, Madame*," said Grace with a curtsy.

"*Bien*," Madame replied. "*Bonne chance* with your studies, girls," she said as she walked into a nearby store for her own shopping.

Mimi then led Grace, May, and Nan into several shops and selected new items, but it was the shoe clerk that brought Grace into harsh reality.

As they sat on the cushioned stools, a middle-aged man bent over Grace's feet. He delicately tilted her foot from one side then to the other. Grace gazed at the shoes displayed behind his counter, imported and Parisian. *Expensive*.

"Madame?" he asked Mimi. He had a thick French accent. "Who made these...rough...looking shoes?"

Another patron in the store waited patiently to the side of the counter with her daughter in tow. The daughter appeared to be of a similar age as Grace, but the girl's snort of laughter cut through Grace's momentary excitement at the purchase of new shoes.

Mimi's face flushed red from embarrassment, and Grace's did, as well. "Well, I did, I'm afraid," she admitted. "With the hide of some gators we caught."

The girl in the shop snorted again and muffled a giggle as her mother elbowed her gently. Grace looked over to glare at them both, but they expertly avoided eye contact.

Grace had been quite proud of her shoes, because Mimi and Jerry had cobbled them for her on the porch while she watched. Mimi had guided the shape as best she could. But now as she looked at them, all she saw was a hideous pair of worn shoes that looked like they belonged to an old woman living in a swamp. Certainly, these were not the shoes of a young lady living in New Orleans and part of genteel society.

The clerk, too, wrinkled his nose. "These will not do." He removed the shoes and set them aside as though they disgusted him. Grace felt her face burn red from embarrassment—and anger.

"Here. Proper shoes for a young lady." He slid black leather shoes onto her feet and buckled the single strap across the top. There was the tiniest of heel heights to this shoe—shoes fit for a young lady and not a child's flat shoe as she had always worn. *Maybe he wasn't such a terrible person, after all,* thought Grace. She saw herself suddenly dancing at balls on the arms of gallant young men, whispering behind silk fans dressed with feathers. Just as quickly as the image had arisen, it faded.

"How much?" asked Mimi. The simple question brought Grace back into their present circumstances. There would be no balls. No fancy dresses, no gallant young men. They were barely scraping by now. What would happen in a few short years when four young women all entered the social scene in a very short span of time? How would they ever afford dresses like the one the girl in the shop was wearing?

"Madame, *women* ask the price of shoes. *Ladies* instruct where to deliver them," the clerk said, without even bothering to make eye contact.

Grace looked at her mother and thought Mimi was going to faint from embarrassment right then and there. For a second, Mimi's eyes filled with tears, but then her countenance changed dramatically. She straightened her back, pushed her shoulders down, and changed her voice to an entire octave higher when she giggled sillily. "Oh, my! In my silliness, I've let these little things go by the side, clearly!"

The clerk nodded and now smiled kindly at the silly wife who knew nothing about financial things and never needed to worry her pretty little head over them. Grace frowned. Of course Mimi understood money. She'd run the farm—and by herself a great deal of the time. But when she giggled and acted like a young girl, the clerk treated her with greater respect. This infuriated Grace.

Mimi didn't ask for prices on anything else for the rest of the shopping trip. The shoes and stockings were delivered that evening, but Grace noticed that they didn't return to Canal Street for quite some time after that.

New Orleans
1867

Grace fluffed the slightly faded silk flowers on her hat one final time and frowned as they remained as faded and wilted as they were before she fluffed them. She thought briefly about the hats she'd seen other young women wearing now with fresh, bright colors and new silk flowers.

She had recently graduated from the Institut, and the graduation ceremony had been filled with girls in expensive dresses—alongside Grace in her slightly faded one.

Some of her classmates were from families like the Kings; that is, families that were rebuilding their legacies. Most of her classmates, however, were from wealthier Creole families, and though Grace loved spending evenings at their beautiful homes, admiring the inner courtyards lit with dozens of candles, part of her grew frustrated that they simply did not understand the challenges families like hers faced.

Just yesterday, one such classmate had asked when Grace's brothers would leave for college in Paris, and how excited Grace must be to be able to go and visit them there. And the beaux! Of course, Grace and May must be purchasing all new wardrobes and having new dresses made for them, since they were to attend so many social functions in the coming year to meet the beaux!

Grace had almost scoffed out loud, and even now she rolled her eyes at such vapid stupidity. *Those girls didn't understand how the real world worked,* Grace decided firmly. She might be a little faded, but at least she had her wits and intelligence and came from an honorable family. She tilted her chin up at her reflection and left the bedroom to join Mimi and May waiting by the door. She'd secreted her history books into their luggage and hoped no one commented on the extra weight.

"Ah, here's Sissy. All set, then?" said Mimi, smiling up at her.

"Mimi," Grace said firmly. "You know I'd rather you not call me Sissy anymore. I'm sixteen now."

Mimi smiled gently. "*Oui, ma chere, je sais.*" Grace was by this time fluent in French and had been practicing her reading of Spanish and German.

Mimi walked them outside to the wagon. May and Grace were traveling by train with a friend of Papa's, the Judge Charles Gayarré, and the girls were quite nervous to be leaving home to spend a holiday with complete strangers. And yet, Judge Gayarré was a famous man— a politician and scholar— so Grace was excited for this journey as well as anxious. He often worked with Papa on cases. The Gayarrés were childless, having married later in life, but they adored children and had invited Grace and May to spend some time with them at their country home.

May and Grace exchanged wide-eyed looks as they sat side-by-side in the wagon. Judge Gayarré was to meet them at the station, where Papa was to introduce them. May reached out a hand to squeeze Grace's own as the wagon bounced down the lane.

Mimi sat up front, but she reached her hand back to clasp hands with both girls. "Now, girls. Do be lovely guests for the Gayarrés. Their offer for your visit is a great one, and the opportunity for you will be invaluable. But, they are an elderly, childless couple, so don't expect to be entertained every moment of every day. And remember your manners. Don't giggle too much, May, and Sissy—"

Grace blew out the breath she'd been holding and stared at Mimi pointedly.

Mimi smiled. "Grace. Don't let that temper flare up in conversation—or anywhere else."

"Mimi," Grace said. "May and I know how to behave."

Mimi smiled a thin smile in return as they arrived at the station. As servants lifted their bags from the hired carriage, Papa walked over to help the girls and Mimi down.

"There you are!" he said in his deep voice. "Judge Gayarré is waiting on the platform."

Papa led them to where a stately man in his sixties sat waiting patiently. He wore an expensive black suit with silk hat and had a close-cropped beard. His eyes were dark but kind.

"Ah, *bonjour, mademoiselles!*" he called as he stood up and removed his hat.

"*Bonjour, monsieur,*" Grace replied with a deep curtsy. He smiled as he took her gloved hand in his in greeting.

"Ah, Miss Grace, I have heard wonderful things about you! Congratulations on your recent graduation from the Institut St. Louis! A fine school, indeed! And Miss May, your own studies progress quite successfully, as well, I hear!"

May and Grace exchanged quick glances. Judge Gayarré's first comments were about their studies...not their curls or looks or prospects for marriage, as most adults commented on. Grace began to relax a bit as they were led to their seats on the train. They traveled with him to Roncal, his plantation in Mississippi, and along the way, he asked about their studies in detail: which histories did Grace best enjoy, what poems were

May's favorites, which writers did Grace respect and why. All too soon, they loaded into a small carriage, this one a tad nicer than the rented one in New Orleans. May and Grace watched the winding road, lined on both sides with overhanging trees. Grace had missed the country since their return to New Orleans.

As they pulled up to a small, yellow cottage, she felt a bit disappointed. She'd expected a grand Creole mansion with sweeping, wrought iron staircases leading up to second story galleries—not this tiny house.

"*Bienvenue à* Roncal!" said Judge Gayarré. A matronly woman walked out to meet them with a warm smile on her face.

"Welcome, welcome!" she called, opening her arms to embrace them each in turn. "You must be Grace," she said, kissing Grace's cheeks as though they were old, dear friends or long lost relatives. "And you, May." She kissed May's cheeks. She linked her arms through the girls' own and led them inside. "Let me show you to your room, and you can get settled."

As they stepped into the cottage, Grace gasped. The room was filled to the brim with ornate, carved furniture, clearly imported from Europe. The walls held paintings on every available space, from the floor to the ceiling. Books were displayed in beautiful glass cases throughout the first floor. The walls were a sunny yellow and were contrasted with an overabundance of green potted plants. This cottage was more like an Italian or Spanish villa, with the sunlight glowing through the windows.

Grace suddenly realized that Madame Gayarré was waiting patiently for her to continue walking, a soft smile on her face. "Your home is the most beautiful home I've ever seen," Grace said. As she spoke, her eyes fell more completely on the bookshelves. Leather volumes, multiple matching sets, itching to be opened.

Madame Gayarré laughed kindly. "She is certainly an academic, ready for fine study and discussion, dear husband!"

She called to Monsieur Gayarré, who approached to stand beside them.

"Aha, dear Grace. Consider these your open library, my dear. Any text you wish to borrow, do not hesitate to do so."

"Oh, thank you, Judge," Grace said, gratefully. They continued to their bedroom, which was just as beautifully decorated as the rest of the house. The stay was restful and invigorating, simultaneously. They spent the mornings reading or walking around the forest near the villa, their afternoons having tea on the gallery, and their evenings chatting about all topics, great and small, over dinner.

Judge Gayarré treated Grace as an intellectual equal, which was a new occurrence for her. For any guests that he welcomed to Ronal, he introduced Grace and May as dear friends, not as children of a dear friend, and seated them at the table as equals. He asked Grace's thoughts and opinions about various histories or philosophies and offered his own but never in a pedantic manner.

For the first time in Grace's life, she felt she was an academic, and she relished it. *This* was the life she wanted, but how could such a life ever be obtained? She was expected to marry well and spend her life in service to her husband's career and aspirations. But what about her own?

Chapter 7

Dear Ms. Mandin,

I'd like to congratulate you on successful completion of the French Translation Exam. This requirement of your doctoral program has now been officially completed.

Sincerely,
Dr. Perkins

Hi Meredith,

I'm glad you and the kids will be here in July! And I'm glad your mom made the move to Tennessee. It's good to have family nearby. Try to be patient with her new guy. She never really could be alone.

Love ya,
Dad

"Mom?" Meredith said into the phone as she paced the back deck. She'd been calling Gayle's phone for hours. Rain drizzled, but Meredith stayed dry under the roof. It was now late-April, and the back yard was filled with blooming irises.

"Hey! What's going on?" Gayle said nonchalantly, as though it hadn't been two months since Meredith had stopped calling, trying to find out why none of the bills had been paid or where the money had gone.

"Mom, we have a situation. A close friend of Maggie's has passed away. We need to get her back to Kentucky for the service, but we're a little stuck right now. I know we talked about you coming back in three weeks to pack when the lease is up, but is there any way you could come now?" Meredith felt guilty asking for help once again, but she had another few weeks left in the semester, and she and Liam were struggling to keep up—academically, financially, and emotionally. Luckily, they were a team and worked together to help each other, but it didn't change the circumstances: they were both needed in more places than they could physically be.

"Of course, honey. But I'll need you to come and get me. Dave needs my truck for a few more days. I'll send you directions."

"Thank you," Meredith said, relieved. She dreaded the next few days, knowing she would get little to no sleep or rest, but it's what was needed.

"I'm in Arkansas, near the Texas border. Should be only, what? Seven or eight hours' drive from you?"

Meredith drove the eight hours southwest to Arkansas, then the eight hours back to Tennessee to drop Gayle off to stay with the children, followed by another six hours farther northeast to follow Liam and Maggie who drove in Maggie's car to get her and her car home, and finally another six hours back southwest with Liam to come home. *Thank you, Red Bull.*

After all the driving, she arrived home to find an email from a classmate she had never spoken to outside of class: *Hey Meredith, just wondering if you could share your notes for class this past Thursday? I couldn't make it. Headed out to Cannery Row Wednesday, and partied a little too hard! But if I could get your notes, that would be great! Thanks!*

* * *

A week later, Liam, Meredith, and the kids sat in their favorite restaurant in Clarksville, the Blackhorse, for a much-needed break. A plate of beer cheese and tortilla chips sat on the table in front of them, and Gayle and her newly-arrived-to-Tennessee boyfriend, Dave, sat opposite. Liam skillfully juggled a now eighteen-month-old Emmy on his lap while he ate, handing her little tidbits to try throughout the meal.

"Dave, my daughter reads about New Orleans a lot. She just loves it! Tell her what you told me about New Orleans," Gayle said, turning back to Meredith. "The stories he has! You know, he's been there a bunch of times. To Mardi Gras, even!"

"That's nice. It's a beautiful city," Meredith started to say.

"You been to Mardi Gras?" Dave asked. He was tall and skinny, almost all knees and elbows. He was closer to Meredith's age than Gayle's and seemed more like an overgrown child than an adult.

Meredith replied, "Not to Mardi Gras, but to New Orleans, yes, quite a bit. I specialize in New Orleans lit—"

"Well, you must not specialize in it much, if you ain't even been to Mardi Gras!" he joked loudly.

"Someday. That trip would be too expensive right now, for us," Meredith said. She thought for a moment about the deposit money they'd recently lost on a vacation rental in New Orleans, after Gayle had stuck them with her unpaid bills.

"Hell, Mardi Gras don't cost nothing," he explained as if Meredith were a child. "You believe that?" he said to Gayle. "She thought it cost something for Mardi Gras!"

Gayle laughed heartily and rolled her eyes at Meredith. "How you been studying that city so long and didn't even know that?"

"That's not what I meant..." Meredith started to explain, but she stopped herself. There was no point.

When the check came, Liam paid for dinner quietly.

"Oh, you got that already?" Dave said, feigning surprise when the server returned the bank card. "I was going to get that. Well, let me get the tip at least."

"Sure thing," said Liam, focusing on packing up Emmy's things. Meredith held Lila's hand and started to follow Dave and her mom away from the table, but she glanced down to be sure. Two dollars. Four adults, two children, and a two dollar tip. Liam tucked another tip under his plate, catching Meredith's eye and giving a tiny nod.

As the semester began to wrap up, Gayle began to pack up her apartment, and they scheduled the move-out inspection. Dave returned to Arkansas in Gayle's old truck—presumably to return in a few weeks to pick her up. Unfortunately, the apartment management informed her that the apartment had bed bugs.

Her mother cried herself into hysterics on Meredith's deck.

"Mom, did you get a second opinion?"

"What? Why? Management says it'll cost over two thousand dollars to treat it! I don't have that! They want it paid up front! I'm going to lose everything! All my furniture! All my things! My home is ruined and gone! You have to do something!"

Meredith tried to keep an even voice as she asked, "Shouldn't we get a second opinion from another company? Something doesn't sound right about this."

"I can't help how it *sounds*! I've lost everything!" she wailed.

"Mom, we'll help," Meredith started.

"I don't want your help! Your help caused all of this!"

Meredith sighed and walked away, completely lost about what to do.

* * *

The next morning began calmly enough.

"I'm sorry about everything," Meredith said over tea and coffee in the living room.

"I know. I'm just overwhelmed. So overwhelmed," Gayle said sadly.

Meredith nodded. "I can understand that. Look, I'll call off work for today and stay home..."

"No, you can't do that. You need to get to work," she said. Inwardly, Meredith agreed; she needed to keep work stable. If work was stable, then funds were stable. Funds must remain stable—for the whole family. Gayle continued, "I'm okay. I'll just hang out here with the baby, then start dealing with everything tomorrow morning."

"Okay. Take the day. Rest. If you'll just give me the day, I'll wrap up some things on campus, and we'll tackle this together."

Gayle nodded and sipped her tea. "That'll be good. Thank you, Meredith."

Meredith nodded and gave her a hug. "Hey, until we figure this out, will you stay here at our house today? I'm not sure what's going on, so it may be best to keep Emmy here. We're still trying to figure out what triggers that poor kid's eczema." Emmy had battled the skin rash for months, and they were finally starting to get it cleared up, but every now and then, something caused a flare up, and Emmy would need a series of baths every day and an ointment routine. The poor kid could be rashy and itchy within hours after exposure to a trigger.

"Fine. I can't deal with that mess today, anyway." Gayle opened a prescription bottle and took one of the tablets inside.

"Thanks," Meredith sighed. She felt guilty even asking, as though it implied the apartment was dirty or tainted. It wasn't, but she was hesitant to expose Emmy to anything. Her skin was extremely sensitive.

Liam had class on campus that day, as well, so they planned to reconvene that night to figure out what to do. Meredith headed out.

Late that afternoon, her cell phone rang as she walked across campus. Gayle.

"Hey. I need the keys to the truck. I can't find them."

"Oh, is everything okay?"

"No. The baby's out of diapers."

"Oh, there's another box in the garage. By the door," Meredith said, relieved.

"Fine. I'll check there. Bye." Click.

Five minutes later, the phone rang again. "I still need those truck keys. Where are they?" Gayle demanded.

"Were the diapers not there?"

"No, they were. But I need the keys."

"I'm not sure. They should've been on the key hook, but what's going on? Are you okay? Is Emmy okay?"

"Yes, she's fine. But I need to get out of here. I need a cigarette."

"Okay. I thought you had a full pack on the end table when I left..."

"Well, I didn't. Stop grilling me. Where are the damn keys? Did that asshole husband of yours hide them?"

"What? Why would he do that?" Meredith said, knowing full well that he probably did, but for good reason. "I'll call him and see. Call you right back." She clicked the off button and called Liam.

"Hey, did you hide the truck keys when you left this morning?"

"Well, yeah. She was acting weird, but she said she was fine. I had a feeling she would take Emmy to the apartment, and her skin is finally starting to get to better. What's going on?"

Meredith explained the situation as she made another lap walking around the library. "I think I need to cut class tonight and come home."

"No, I'm closer. I'll cut my class, if needed. Call her one last time and see if we can get through another hour, so I can get through class. I had to cut it week before last for the Arkansas-Tennessee-Kentucky road trip, so I'm afraid of pissing the professor off."

"Okay. One minute."

Meredith called back and asked if her mom could wait for another hour, so Liam could attend class.

"What? Are you kidding me? I'm here, and I say I need to leave, and you won't tell me where the keys are? Fine! I'll walk!"

"Mom, you can't walk with a baby in a stroller down that road! It's too dangerous! Please! People get hit there and die all the time!"

"Well, you won't help me, so what else am I going to do?"

"Give me a minute. Just don't walk with her out the door! Please!" Meredith said. Panic was rising in the back of her throat. Gayle was going to get Emmy killed for a fucking cigarette.

She called Liam.

"Liam? She's wigging out. I don't know what do," Meredith said, feeling her own panic rising. "I'll leave here, but I'll be too late! It's an hour and a half drive. She's going to walk down that dangerous road with Emmy!"

"No, she isn't," he said dejectedly. "I'm already on my way there. I'll be there in under five minutes. Call and tell her. I want to know what happens. But then, you're going to class.

God knows what will happen next week, and you're already on campus."

She fought the little wave of nausea that threatened and reached up to rub the tension from her eyes.

"Okay." Meredith switched calls again.

"Liam'll be there in five minutes." Meredith heard Gayle pull a breath on a cigarette.

"Okay," she said, her voice suddenly light and cheery. "Thanks."

"Wait. You said you were out of cigarettes," Meredith said. "I can hear you smoking right now."

"Well, I called my friend, Gloria, who lives by my apartment. She brought me some."

"Oh," Meredith said, knowing that no one named Gloria lived near her mother's apartment. "I see. Well, Liam'll be there. And you won't have to watch the kids anymore. He and I will figure it out."

"Oh, well, that's fine," she said, as though shocked about why they would do such a thing. "I can handle them, you know. I can."

"Yes, I know. Our schedules are just changing, that's all," Meredith lied. "I'll be home late tonight. I have class until nine, then that long drive home."

"Whatever. Bye."

Twenty minutes later, Liam called her. "Everyone's perfectly fine," he said, reassuring Meredith. "There's no crisis. Lila is home from school, and the kids are playing happily. Go to class. She's won part of this, but she's not winning you. We need you to be in class."

By the time Meredith made it home, it was nearly 10:30, and the kids were safely in bed. Liam was angry but calm, and Gayle sulked on the back deck. Meredith collapsed on the bed and fell asleep, fully clothed.

* * *

The next morning, her alarm went off at 4:30 a.m. Time to study and head to campus. She started fixing coffee when Gayle came down the hallway, fully dressed and shoes on.

"What's going on?" Meredith asked, her voice hoarse from fatigue.

"You need to take me to the hospital," Gayle said in a shaky voice. "I'm having a heart attack." She opened her prescription bottle and took a tablet.

"What? Are you sure? Are you in pain?" Meredith asked, shocked. "Is there pain down your left arm? And what are those? The pills you're taking?"

"I'm throwing up, and I have chest pain. And this is just my pain pills. I take them all the time."

"Why didn't you wake me up?"

"I didn't want to be a bother."

"Should you be taking that pain pill right now?"

"I'm having a heart attack, and you want me to skip taking my pain pills?"

Meredith sighed and left the room.

She dressed quickly and explained to a very sleepy Liam what was happening before returning to her mom in the kitchen.

"I'll email my boss and cancel today..." Meredith told her as she grabbed her bag to take it to the hospital.

"No," she said. "I don't want you to stay with me."

"What? But..."

"No," Gayle said, raising her shaking voice. "Just drop me off and leave me alone."

Meredith nodded to placate her, and they climbed into Meredith and Liam's old Honda.

"God, it smells terrible in here. It's disgusting," her mother said as Meredith started the old car. It was musty, but it was an old car Maggie had given to them when they badly needed a second one. It ran just fine and was easy on gas, so they were glad to have it. "Can't you keep anything clean, ever?"

Meredith sighed and tried to ignore her. Gayle repeated her complaints as they drove to the hospital. The sun wasn't up yet, so she couldn't see the hurt on Meredith's face at every insult.

As they neared the hospital, her mother screamed, "Stop the car! I have to vomit! It's too disgusting in here!"

Meredith barely had time to stop before her mother opened the door and vomited on the side of the road.

When she was ready, they continued their trek, with the windows down in the cold morning air. As Meredith walked her mother into the emergency room, the attendant brought a wheelchair and immediately took her to the room adjacent to the check in. Meredith sat in the lobby, texting Liam an update.

The nurse waved her over. "Okay, so we don't think she's having a heart attack, but we're going to keep her for the morning so we can run some tests," she explained. "You won't be allowed back with her right now."

Meredith looked behind the nurse to see her mother sitting on a hospital bed, cracking jokes with another nurse.

"Mom?" she asked. "What do you want me to do? I can't come back with you, but I can work from the lobby for the morning and be here..."

"No, I told you," Gayle said coldly. "Go to work. I'll call Liam when I'm ready to leave," she said, barely making eye contact with Meredith. "Just go."

Fighting back hurt and tears, Meredith went. Liam texted three hours later with Gayle's diagnosis: panic attack. He had picked her up around lunchtime, and everything was fine.

By the end of the day, Meredith had been barraged with concerned calls from Kentucky; her mother had told family members on social media that she'd had a heart attack—from a broken heart, Gayle had said the doctor had told her.

* * *

Two days after Gayle's hospital visit, Meredith waited patiently by a conference room door at Claxton State University, where she'd completed her master's degree and where Liam had been working on his Bachelor's. Claxton State is in Clarksville, so the short drive was a relief. She was presenting at the Robert Penn Warren Annual Meeting, and she was shaking from nerves. She sipped a too-hot Earl Grey tea, wincing at the burn on her tongue, and waited for the society members to arrive for the first presentation of the day: her panel.

She'd presented at a few graduate conferences in the last year, but this presentation was technically a national one. She hoped to see even one familiar face, but she found herself in a room of complete strangers. She sat at the table with three other panelists, facing about thirty audience members. The other panelists were in their fifties and sixties and treated Meredith as the child on the panel, but at least they were kind. She read her paper on Warren's novel *All the King's Men* and the film noir.

Afterwards, several members invited her to lunch, but she politely declined. They needed to save money, so she planned to grab lunch at home, and then drive out to a cemetery in nearby Russellville, Kentucky for a poetry reading with the society members. She was very excited by this: reading poetry in a cemetery with academics—*how much cooler could this academic thing get?* And she relished the idea of just one drama-free afternoon.

As she drove through the lunchtime traffic at a major intersection in town, she decided to call and check on Gayle. She said she would be at her apartment for the day and late into the night, cleaning and trying to save what she could. Meredith and Liam had been putting everything they could in the dryer and treating their own house for bed bugs, too, just in case, and, to their relief, it worked.

"Hi," Meredith said when her mom answered.

"I'm leaving in a couple of days," she said in reply.

"What? What about the apartment? I thought we were getting organized, getting a second opinion, and trying to sort everything out?"

"I'm not going to do that. There's no point," she said, an edge to her voice.

"Where are you going to go? Back to Arkansas with Dave?"

"Not yet. I'm going to go back to Kentucky. Dave will join me in a few months, when his construction job brings him back to that area."

"Um, okay," Meredith said, trying to think.

"And you need to tell that mother-in-law of yours that I expect her to pay for everything."

"Wait, what?"

"Liam's mom brought those damn bed bugs in here, and now I've lost everything. I expect her to pay the damages."

Meredith was stunned into silence. She and Liam had canceled their first real vacation in years because they had given the money to Gayle for bills. And when those bills apparently went unpaid, Maggie had paid hundreds of dollars to catch up the accounts—without an angry word to Meredith about it.

Feeling a wave of perfectly calm anger, Meredith's voice dropped an octave, and she said, "There's absolutely no way that's going to happen."

"Well, why the hell not? I never had bed bugs before her! I'm not dirty! I'm not a dirty person!"

Meredith sighed. "Mom, bed bugs just happen. It doesn't mean someone is dirty. And Maggie's never had them, either..."

"Well, the pest control guy said neither of the apartments on either side of mine have them, so it's just me! And it's not fair! I don't deserve this!"

"You're right. You don't. But neither does Maggie. I'm not going to ask her to pay for anything, because that's just not right."

"Why not? She has the money!"

"Mom, the woman already paid your overdue bills and even gave me and Liam a car to help us get back and forth to school. She's been a saint. I'm not asking her for a damn dime!"

"Then *you* pay for it!"

"You know I don't have two thousand dollars. I already gave you everything I had for the bills, your divorce, and the rent that we found out later that you didn't even pay,"

Meredith said, her voice climbing up. She never yelled at her mother—or anyone else for that matter.

"I did what I had to do!" Gayle screamed. "And you need to tell that husband of yours to get off his ass! He just sits there on his computer all day!"

"He runs a website and is a student, like me! We work from home, so yes, we spend time on our computers!" Meredith yelled.

"Well, I don't give a shit anymore. I'm leaving. Dave's going to meet me in Kentucky, and then we're going back to Arkansas together."

"Are you serious? You're just leaving everything? To run off with some dude you met at a pizza place and have known for a few months?"

"Dave and I are meant to be together! We're *soul mates*! I told you that! *He* loves me, and *he* takes care of me!"

"In a used camper parked in his mom's front yard? Are you fucking kidding me? Stop acting like a fifteen-year-old whore, and start acting like my mother!" Meredith screamed into the phone.

The line went dead. Meredith tried to call her back, but there was no answer.

When she arrived home, she told Liam what happened as she sobbed angry tears on his shoulder, in between pacing the house, cleaning as she went. She didn't make it to the cemetery poetry reading.

That night, Meredith made dinner for her family, but Lila wouldn't eat much. Gayle didn't come by and wouldn't answer her phone. Lila seemed incredibly sad, but they'd been careful to keep the drama with Gayle away from her as much as possible. They took her to her soccer team's practice, but she didn't want to participate, so they brought her home and put her to bed early, in case she was coming down with something.

"What do you think's wrong?" Liam asked.

Meredith watched Lila's sleeping form from the doorway when her thoughts clicked.

"My mom's leaving tonight," Meredith said, the intuition tingling in the back of her mind. "She's probably already gone.

She's told Lila goodbye and not to tell us anything, so Lila is struggling to deal with keeping a secret from us."

"Do you really think so? Why would she ask a six-year-old to keep that kind of secret? How do you know?"

"Because she asked me to do things like that when I was six."

Meredith recalled Gayle telling her not to tell her Grandpa about her friend, Rob, or about her other friend, Scott. Meredith remembered being in the third grade and coming home to find her mother had remarried while she was at school. She was divorced by the end of the month, and she had asked Meredith to never tell anyone about it.

She patted Liam's hand. "Let's give Lila time and just love her. When we can, we'll talk to her."

The next day was Lila's annual checkup. Her elderly pediatrician seemed to take on the role of every child's grandfather, and he was good at it. Both girls loved him. Coincidentally, as Lila sat on the exam table, he talked to her about keeping secrets from Mom and Dad.

"I always tell my patients," he explained. "That they should never keep secrets from Mom and Dad. If a grownup ever tells you not to tell Mom and Dad about something, that grownup is not making a good decision. That grownup is being dishonest. You tell Mom and Dad, right away," he explained.

Damn, thought Meredith. *He's good.*

She and Lila made it to the parking lot, Lila sucking on her grape sucker. Meredith buckled her in and settled herself into the driver seat.

"Mommy?" said a voice from the backseat, tinier than her usual bombastic self. Meredith expected her to ask to stop by the Cupcakery, the usual doctor-trip bribe.

"What's up, sweetie?"

Lila started crying immediately.

"Grandma asked you to keep a secret, huh?"

Lila nodded in the rearview mirror, too upset to make eye contact.

"Grandma's having a hard time right now making good decisions," Meredith said, as much to herself as to Lila. She consoled her by telling her she did the right thing by telling her mommy. They bought giant cupcakes on the way home.

More than a few times, Liam and Meredith traded off the kids in various university parking lots to make sure they could each attend everything they needed to. Meredith passed more than one afternoon riding in the fancy glass elevators in the student center with the kids—kids love glass elevators. She finished the semester, tutoring in the writing center and sitting in classes with her classmates and professors, as though nothing had happened, and the most stressful thing in the world was simply final exams. Year one was finally over.

* * *

At the beginning of the summer term, Meredith sat in Dr. Bradford's office in Bush Hall, planning their summer reading list. Dr. Bradford had agreed to do an independent study course, which would allow Meredith to meet the needs of her assistantship while letting her stay home with the kids over the summer. Liam was taking a heavy load of courses, since Meredith could be home more. Or as Meredith called it, Shift Change.

"So, I don't know much about King personally, but let's pair her with Edith Wharton and George Eliot. This transatlantic angle will be an interesting first foray into possible dissertation topics for you," Dr. Bradford said, looking over their proposed reading list. "What works by King would you recommend for me?"

"*Balcony Stories* and *The Pleasant Ways of St. Médard*," Meredith said. "These are the two I tend to use more than the others. There are some additional works, like her 1932 memoirs and a collection of her journals, but that's an awful lot for you."

"Yes, but if I have them on my radar, I can look up things if needed. Are these in our library here?"

"Most yes, but not the journals. They're on Google Books, though, most of them. And I can scan my book and email you a pdf, if something is missing in the Google book. I really do appreciate you doing this course for me. I'll stay on the schedule we proposed. Would you like weekly updates by email? You mentioned you'd be traveling a lot, so I don't want to be in the way."

"Not at all. Weekly updates work just fine. Mostly, just tell me what your thoughts are. We can have a discussion about the texts and work out some ideas for the papers as we go. Oh, that reminds me. I have something for you." She shuffled around on her desk and pulled out a flyer. "This came across a listserv that I follow. It looks like the idea of transatlantic literature is a growing subfield. Take a look."

The flyer was a call for proposals for a conference on transatlantic literature—in Wittenberg, Germany. "Wow. This looks amazing."

"You should draw up a proposal for this, if you can. If nothing else, it would be good practice for you."

"Okay, I'll think about it. Thank you so much for thinking of me. So, I'll email you in about a week?"

"Sounds good. Have a great weekend!"

* * *

The next week, Meredith stared at the blinking cursor on her Word document.

"What are you working on?" Liam asked as he came in and set up Emmy's play rug on the living room floor.

"Dr. Bradford thinks I should send a proposal for this conference in Germany."

"Holy shit. Germany? That's amazing! Do it!"

"You think? It'd be expensive."

"Can you get some funding?"

"Maybe a little."

"Do it anyway. We'll figure it out."

"It probably won't get accepted."

"Not if you don't send the proposal. Just do it. If it works, great! If not, no big deal."

"Okay." Meredith sighed and started typing. Liam walked over and kissed the top of her head lightly.

By mid-July, the summer heat had settled over Tennessee, and each day was heavier and muggier than the one before it. But kids are kids, so they still spent most of their days in the backyard, playing in sand...while Meredith read. Playing with bubbles...while Meredith read. Playing with Barbies...while Meredith read, struggling to balance her thick copy of Grace King's book, *Memories of a Southern Woman of Letters,* in one hand.

"Mommy, let's do the swings!" Lila sprinted across the yard to her yellow swing and plopped in.

"Mommy, push Emmy red swing?" Emmy asked, looking up with her bright blue eyes.

"Well, of course. Off we go," Meredith said, scooping up Emmy and heading to her red toddler swing. She settled her in and took turns pushing each girl in her swing. At the same time, she skimmed the pages of the book in her hand.

"Mommy, what's your book about?" asked Lila.

"Ladies in the south after the Civil War," Meredith told her. "About how brave they had to be and their adventures. This one girl, Grace, she and her mommy had to run away from their home through the swamps to find her daddy far, far away."

"She must have been scared," Lila said, squinting at some birds in the distance.

"I think so, too," Meredith said.

"But she had her mommy, right?"

"Yes, she did."

"What did her mommy do?"

"Her mommy led the whole family. She found wagons and boats and food and led them on a very big trip to a place she'd never been. She even called for help for hours when they were stuck in the swamp."

"That's neat. Can we read *Harry Potter* later?" Lila's interest had shifted, and Meredith had lost her audience.

"Of course," Meredith said, giving in. "Want to make chocolate frogs, too?"

"YES!"

Chapter 8

New Orleans
1874

Early one morning, Grace, now twenty-two years old, sat down at the breakfast table and picked up the copy of the *Picayune*, one of the local newspapers. The King family had moved again to Erato Street in their slow attempt to climb back up the social ladder, but the house itself was little better than its predecessor.

As she absentmindedly spooned sugar into her morning coffee, her eyes scanned the columns for anything of interest. The society columns held only disappointment for her now; her name was hardly ever listed there, but maybe this wasn't such a terrible thing. Upstairs, she could hear the family members readying for their own days.

Papa had hoped to climb back into his position as a prominent lawyer, but this was proving much more difficult than he had expected. He spent most of his time in his office, trying to procure cases that were yanked away from him at the last minute.

Grace sighed and continued to scan the social columns. She and her sisters had recently returned from Pass Christian, Mississippi, a town on the Mississippi coast. It was a frequent retreat for the family thanks to her Uncle Tom's generosity, but she had hoped to see some familiar names from a recent gathering that she had missed.

Many of these trips to Pass Christian were to meet eligible beaux from good families, and Grace half-smiled, thinking about her first meeting with Garry.

On most of their stays, May and Grace would walk for hours, arm-in-arm around town and to the beaches. They would stop for picnic lunches and reading, enjoying the breezes and fresh air. In the evenings, they attended garden parties and were introduced to eligible young men.

At one such gathering, Grace had found a moment to escape the idle chatter common among this type of gathering. She had hidden herself away in a corner of the garden and pulled out a small volume of history. She lost herself to the reading and didn't hear someone approaching on the gravel walkway. When a young man turned the corner, he tripped over her skirts. Grace had gasped and dropped her book in surprise.

"Oh, I'm sorry!" said a young man. "I didn't mean to startle you. Are you quite all right?"

Grace had tried to catch her breath. She opened her mouth to speak, but no sound came out. She glanced down and frowned. "My book. You have my book," she had said, rather crossly.

He had stood up, dusted himself off, and smiled down at her. He was tall, in his twenties, and had dark hair and eyes to match.

"I'm Garrett Walker, of the Pass Christian Walkers. And you are...?" He held out her book.

"Grace. Grace King, of the New Orleans Kings," she said, taking the book.

"Might I join you here for a bit?" he had asked.

"Of course," Grace had said, but almost immediately her situation dawned on her: she was in a hidden corner of a garden alone with a young man. "Actually, on second thought, I should rejoin the party."

"Of course," he had said. "Might I walk with you, then?" He held out his hand to help her from the bench but he didn't let go of her fingers after she stood. Instead, he casually placed her hand in the crook of his arm. "And, if you would, please tell me why this book is of such importance to you?"

Grace had hesitated. Usually, boys wanted to chat about parties and kissing or horse races or boxing or sports—all things that bored her. "Well, I..."

"And do you prefer reading histories? Most young women do not, you know, so you see, you pose something of a challenge for me."

Grace's face had tilted up, slightly offended. "A challenge? How so?"

Garrett had laughed kindly. "Most young women fawn over parties or balls, not volumes of history. I am intrigued by this."

"Oh. Well, it seems you know only foolish girls, then, and not intellectual women," Grace had said, with a bit of a coquettish tilt of her head. As they walked, she explained about Judge Gayarré and her love of history, and, thus, the importance of the book. He had listened and occasionally asked questions. They had reached the rest of the party and chatted for the rest of the evening. A few days later, a special box had arrived, with Grace's name on it. A beautiful volume on French history, with a simple note: For Miss Grace King from Mr. Garrett Walker.

Since then, they had exchanged frequent letters and visited whenever she was in town. Garry had even spoken to Mimi and Papa about future marriage, once his position and career improved. Grace was in no rush, though, as the idea of marriage and the duties it brought seemed too heavy to carry. Garry was nice, though, so if it had to happen, it might as well be with him.

Grace turned the newspaper page, moving on to a different section.

As she focused on one column in particular, her hand stopped stirring the sugar.

"Something interesting?" asked Papa, entering the room and joining her at the table.

"Actually, yes. This newspaper column says that on July 4th, several Black Leagues are to march on New Orleans," she said, furrowing her brow and looking over at Papa. "Have you heard word of this?"

Papa frowned. "Keep reading, please, Sis."

"It says negroes want access to all public spaces and saloons, and on that date, will attempt entrance to spaces all around the city."

Will walked in to join them, picking up a hunk of bread and tearing into it, leaving crumbs on the table. "Well, so what? We played together as children. I don't see why we can't live together peacefully now."

"Oh my," Grace said, pausing her reading. She swallowed hard. "Listen to this. The article says that if resisted, they plan to attack and take any women they like."

Grace stopped reading and stared over at Papa.

Papa shook his head sadly. "What is the world coming to. I wonder what it will be when you reach my own age, dear Grace."

"But, Papa, we should do something! They can't just...just *take women...*" said Grace, setting down the paper so forcefully she rattled her coffee cup. Her mind flashed back to her childhood, seeing New Orleans on fire.

"You mean, like people do to Black women?" Will asked innocently, without making eye contact.

Grace took a breath to argue, feeling her face turning red. She opened her mouth for a retort when she remembered that she'd recently seen Will on a streetcar when he should have been in class. She stopped herself, paused, and smirked. "How are your classes going, Will?" She thought about all the lectures and school lessons Will had skipped, always preferring to run around with his friends, instead. By the time *she'd* been fifteen, she was graduating with honors, visiting the Judge, and being prepared for marriage. Will, however, was allowed to continue just being a boy. It simply wasn't fair.

Will stopped chewing, sighed, and stood up. He dusted his hands on his pants and walked to the doorway before he turned to face her. "About as well as your engagement. When is the wedding, again?" he said, turning the corner before she could form her next insult.

Grace glared at the doorway and contemplated throwing something at him, but nothing substantial was in reach, and Papa still sat beside her.

"Not to worry, dear Grace," Papa said, hardly looking up from the paper or seemingly noticing the heated exchange between Grace and Will. "I almost guarantee, this event won't happen, and things will blow over. And stop baiting your brother."

Grace sighed, and finally took her first sip of her now overly sweetened chicory coffee. She wrinkled her nose and rose to empty the cup and start a new one.

"Oh, Papa, I saw Louise Marie Drouet the other day," Grace said. Grace had followed the Drouet family scandal and case of the previous years, fascinated by the fate of the mixed-race woman who had been raised as a lady and expected an inheritance, only to have her beloved deceased father's family retaliate and refuse her even a pittance, casting her aside to a life of poverty and hardship.

"Mm," Papa mumbled.

"She was riding the streetcar. She looked well enough, considering," Grace said with a frown. Louise Marie had been raised to be a lady, just as Grace herself had been. She had been beloved by her father, raised in a convent, and was rumored to be a perfect embodiment of the Southern Lady. Her father, however, had not left a will or considered her welfare after his passing, and so his extended family had cut her off, leaving her destitute. "Do you think she might be able to appeal? It seems wrong for a lady to suddenly be expected to work when she's not had that lifestyle or upbringing."

Papa nodded. "I agree, Sis. It's wrong. I don't support what happened to Miss Drouet. But the law is the law, and I do not think Miss Drouet will be able to fight this."

"But if women had more power, a voice even..." Grace started.

Papa lightly scoffed but then broke into a coughing fit. After he regained his breath, he said, "Women do not need power, Sis. They should have gentle lives that best fits their natures. And power does not fit their natures."

"But what about Miss Drouet's nature? Without her father or a man to speak for her, she was—" Grace started, but Papa cut her off.

"For now, I must head to the office," Papa said, standing. "I suggest you worry less about Miss Drouet and more about minding Mimi." He left the room without another word.

Grace sighed and sat back in her chair. If she and Louise Marie had had similar upbringings—education, emphasis on their roles in society as ladies—then what kept Grace from facing the same fate as Louise Marie? Being thrown out of the family, penniless?

Later that afternoon, Grace sat in the parlor, reading a French novel, when Mimi walked through, half singing to herself.

"You are in an exceptional mood today," Grace said, without looking up from her book.

"Yes, I am," Mimi replied. "Will is finally doing well, don't you think?"

Grace looked up. "Yes, Mimi, but he does act the child much of the time. Did you know he's been skipping classes and lessons?"

"Oh, I know, but I want to support him, and he's finally smiling more and happy. He's had such a tough time," she said, arranging the flowers in a vase on a side table. Grace opened her mouth to respond, but Mimi spoke before she could say anything. "Oh, I am arranging for you and May to visit some family friends over the summer down on Grand Isle."

"Grand Isle? That's fairly new." The small peninsula was south of New Orleans and was oft-visited by wealthier patrons.

"Yes, well, I think you're more likely to meet beaux there."

"Technically, I am engaged, Mimi, remember?"

Mimi looked at Grace pointedly and tilted her head to the side in a half shrug. "Are you? His career has been moving slowly, has it not? Do you see him focused on improving his situation? Has he purchased a home or prepared for you in any way?"

Grace could say nothing to Garrett's defense. She hated to admit it, but perhaps Mimi was right about the situation. Garrett hadn't done any of those things.

"Remember how hard life has been for us, Sissy. And then imagine navigating it with children and servants depending on you. For everything," she said sadly.

Grace looked up at that and saw the deep sadness in Mimi's eyes. Her hair was thinner than it used to be. She was afraid for Grace. For all of her children. Mimi broke their stare and left the parlor just as Nan brought in the mail tray.

"Here, Sissy," she said kindly. "From Garrett."

Grace opened the small envelope and saw his now-familiar scrawl. This time, though, it looked as though he had dashed off the letter rather quickly.

My dearest, Grace,

It has come to my attention that your mother has informed several acquaintances that our engagement should now be considered an informal arrangement to which you are not bound.

It's like you are two people, Grace. The public version of you is the one everyone sees—I think, perhaps, even your family sees only this version. This Grace is fiercely proud of her family and heritage. But the other Grace, that one is sweet and shy. That private Grace is religious and kind, loves flowers and reading quietly for hours. This Grace is my favorite, because very few truly know her.

Although I am hurt by your mother's actions, I hold no ill will toward you. I know you must abide by your family's guidance, and I love you all the more for that loyalty.

Yours—
G.

Heat flushed her face. She tried to reread the letter with eyes that simply would not focus. Her fist clenched the paper as she stormed from the parlor in search of Mimi.

Grace found her in the kitchen, surveying a basket of produce.

"What have you done?" Grace demanded.

"Whatever do you mean?" she said without looking up from the basket.

"Garrett says you wrote to someone. Informed them that our engagement was not binding."

"Oh, Sis," Mimi sighed. "I've done what a good mother is supposed is to do. Guide her daughter through the process. Marriage is not a simple thing! You must consider all of the possibilities before selecting one option. It's business, Sissy, not love." Mimi sighed. "For you and your sisters, I will compromise and give a little to love, but ultimately, the arrangement must be a sound one. Garrett will still be there, plugging away at the railroad company, if a more promising match isn't found. What's the harm? If you continue to exhibit this temper, however, I dare say no man will have you," she said, muttering the last sentence.

"Then maybe that's the answer," Grace said. "If I can't marry whom I choose, I will not marry at all."

"Very mature and ladylike, Grace," Mimi said.

"You don't understand, do you?" Grace said, exasperated. "There aren't beaux anymore! They're all dead! The very idea of a beau is extinct! I will not wed someone I find stupid or immoral, and, whether you choose to see it or not, pretty much all of the young men are one, the other, or both! The gallant ones died from being gallant. I would much rather be independent than tie myself to a dead weight that will sink my life into the gutter!"

Mimi stood straight up, and her shoulders tucked back. "Now," she said, lifting an eyebrow.

"What?" Grace said, confused and angry.

"Now," Mimi repeated. "Now, you get it. Do not tie yourself to someone who will take you down with him and sink you under a burden of financial debt or children." Grace and Mimi stared at each other for a long, hard minute before Mimi finally said softly, "No ordinary man will do for you, Grace." And with that, Mimi turned and left the room.

Grace stood for a moment, trying to wrap her head around the exchange and what that meant for her—was she back to looking for beaux? Was she free to accept her spinsterhood? Before she could come to any conclusions, she heard several people in the entryway. She looked over to see Fred, Branch, and another friend of theirs pulling on their vests and readying to leave.

"Fred? Branch? Can I ask you about something before you leave?" Grace asked.

Fred sighed. "Fine, but make it quick. *We* have plans."

Grace pursed her lips at the not-so-subtle slight against her evening at home. She looked at the other young man standing in the entryway and hesitated.

"Oh," said Fred, glancing up. "Grace, this is George Préot, a colleague from school. George, this is my sister, Grace." Fred had been studying to become an attorney, like Papa.

George nodded politely and offered a shy smile, which Grace gently returned.

"There are rumors that something is about to happen. In the city. With the League. Are they true?"

Fred and Branch exchanged a look. Branch sighed and turned to Grace. "Possibly. Just stay away from the court house section of town this week."

Fred and Branch were constantly going on about the beautiful women they favored that month; beautiful women who flirted openly with men and danced too close for Grace's comfort. How could they get away with behavior like that? It wasn't fair. The men only liked them for the women's forwardness, but Grace didn't want to be so forward and inappropriate. And so, her dance card began to have a few more empty lines.

"Oh, Sis," Fred said as he rolled his eyes. "Just do as Branch said."

As they turned to leave, Grace saw Branch tuck a woman's handkerchief into his pocket. She pressed her lips firmly together, because she recognized that just last week, the handkerchief Branch carried had contained different initials embroidered on the corner.

"It was nice to meet you," George said with a polite nod, as he followed in Fred and Branch's wake through the front door. If he noticed the peeling paint or worn furnishings, he said nothing. Grace had noticed, however, that his own trousers were a bit worn on the bottom hem.

The next day, Grace walked through the family garden, occasionally pulling a weed. This was mostly Grandmamma's domain, the garden, and Grace had no desire to dig her own hands into the dirt to work, but she did enjoy the space and helping Grandmamma from time to time. She couldn't settle into anything or focus on any of her books, anyway. She sighed repeatedly and watched the street in front of the house. She listened for any sounds in the distance to reveal what was happening in the rest of the city. Anticipation and frustration raged a battle in her head, and she grew irritable.

Will came down and stepped onto the side gallery. "Has Fred or Branch been by?"

"No," answered Grace. "Have you heard anything? What's happening?"

"I don't know," Will replied. "Fred wouldn't tell me anything. Said to stay out of it. Said I was too young."

"Will, maybe you should just listen to someone, for once," Grace said, looking away.

"Why? No one knows what I go through. It's not like any of you ever listen," Will said.

Grace sighed. "Will, we all struggle. But you—you can do anything you wish. You are intelligent, but you won't study. You are able-bodied, young, and not terrible to look at. How is your life so terrible?"

"Oh, you think it's all that simple, do you?" Will said, scoffing. "Well, try being surrounded by idiots whose families will buy them their positions after finishing school, so my intelligence doesn't matter. Fred and Branch are off doing their own things, leaving me out, like always. Fred says it's men's work. So what does that make me? A boy? And besides, what they're fighting is ridiculous. Everyone is out there waging a fight against...what? Integration? It didn't seem to bother anyone that we grew up playing with the exact same people they're trying to exclude. Why were they good enough to be our playmates, but not good enough to sit in the same saloon? Why are they fighting over who sits in the streetcar together when just a few years ago, we hid in the same rooms together, shared the same food?"

"That's not the point," Grace said stubbornly.

"Then, Sis, what *is* the point? Because I'll be damned if I can figure it out," Will said with a sigh. She paused for a moment, considering Will's words. On the farm, he *had* spent much of his time playing with the slaves' children, fishing and exploring the countryside. Since their return, Fred and Branch had paired off, as had Grace and May and Nan and Nina—leaving Will on his own much of the time.

"The point is that if the North truly just wanted to reconcile the north and the south back into one country, then they wouldn't have destroyed everything. They wouldn't have burnt our cities, salted our fields, or...hurt...our women," Grace said. "This is less to do with integration and more to do with not standing for the oppression we've faced." She held her head high and pushed her shoulders back.

"But if that were the *real* point of this, why on earth would folks be taking it out on Black people, making things even tougher than they already are?" Will asked.

"Well," Grace said, trying to formulate her reasons. "Why don't you suggest a better way, then? It's not like anyone will listen to women, anyway," she muttered. "What are you going to do to make the world better?"

Will shrugged. "I want to join the navy, but when I brought it up, Mimi refused to even discuss it."

"Oh," said Grace, surprised. She had never taken her younger brother for a military man. "Why did she object?"

"She said being in the military isn't a viable career choice, that I'll just get hurt," Will said, with a defiant look that hovered between a childish pout and a man's resolve. "There are limits, you see, to what I am allowed to do, too," he said coldly.

"What limits?" Grace asked, exasperated all over again.

"Look around you, Sis. You are a limit. May and Nan and Nina and aging parents and grandparents, you are *all* limits. Fred, Branch, and I alone have to carry the financial burden of everyone, and if I join the navy, then Fred and Branch will bear it all. I can't move forward if everything and everybody is holding me back!"

Grace grew impatient with Will's attitude. At least he could work! He could go to college and be anything he wanted. He could dedicate his life to something worthwhile, instead of domestic drudgery or social calls. He could study law, like Fred, or business, like Branch. If only she could be in Will's shoes, she thought with a cold scoff. "Maybe you should have been the one to enter the marriage market, then. Maybe you could land a spouse with some finances? I mean, those were my instructions, so maybe we should switch roles," Grace said, her anger at Will quickly turning into merriment at his expense.

Will rolled his eyes. "Maybe we should. Then I could stay at home and sit around and do nothing."

As he went back inside, he let the gallery door slam shut behind him. *Clearly he doesn't understand the irony in our situations,* she thought.

She continued pacing the garden until sunset, when Papa joined her. They paced together, without saying much, until Mimi joined them, as well. She sat on the gallery, watching them both. She would pick up a book, pretend to read, and put it down. Pick up her embroidery, stitch a few stitches, and then put it down and go back to the book.

In the distance, gunshots suddenly fired. Grace looked in panic to Papa. Everyone froze.

"Inside," Papa ordered, taking Grace's elbow.

"But—"

"Now."

Grace hurried, picking up Mimi's sewing basket as she went. They filed into the parlor, and Mimi began closing the curtains. Grace could hear Papa outside, quickly closing the wooden shutters, as though preparing for a hurricane.

"Grace, get your sisters. Tell them to close the shutters and curtains upstairs," Mimi ordered.

When the house had been secured, they all gathered in the parlor together. Papa's shotgun leaned against the entryway. Most of the lights in the house had been extinguished, save for the small hurricane lamp in the parlor.

"Can't we at least have a little more light to read by?" asked Nan, squinting at the book in her hand.

"No," replied Mimi. "We want the house to look empty. We want to be overlooked by anyone outside."

They waited. Nan read aloud from her book, leaning over to catch as much light from the lamp as she could. Nina dozed on the sofa, covered by a thin coverlet Mimi had placed over her. Grandmamma prayed continuously through the night.

"Papa, maybe we should..." Mimi said.

As they turned to Papa for guidance, Grace heard someone on the side gallery.

They all listened, collectively holding their breath. Papa reached for his gun.

The gallery floorboards creaked under the intruders' steps as they rattled the door, stopped, rattled it again, stopped, and rattled it a third time. Then, they knocked out a rhythm on the door.

Papa sighed and set down his gun. "It's Fred," he said, going to the door. Papa unlocked the door and opened it to find Fred and another man waiting.

"It's about time. Get inside, quickly," instructed Papa.

Fred leaned on the other man as they made their way inside. They were both covered in dirt and smelled of sweat, blood, and gunpowder. The man helped Fred to the wooden chair Papa had set down for him.

"Now, don't get blood on Mimi's nice chairs," Papa said. He leaned over Fred's leg. "What are we dealing with, here? And any word from Branch?"

"Nothing much," Fred said. "A little graze is all. And word is Branch was arrested, but we can get him in the morning."

Papa nodded and frowned as he gently examined Fred's leg. He leaned back. "Grace, take your sisters and get these fine boys something to eat. We'll clean Fred's leg and hear all about their adventures."

Thirty minutes later, Grace and the rest of the family, even a sulking Will, who had, in fact, been left out of the evening's adventures, sat in the dining room, sharing a feast of cold ham sandwiches and potatoes. Grandmamma had gone to bed, exhausted.

"This is a good friend of ours, Rene," Fred said, gesturing to the Creole man at the table.

"Thank you for opening your door to me," Rene said to Papa, the words lilting with his French accent.

"Any comrade of Fred's is welcome here," said Papa. "So, tell us. What's happened?"

The young men paused their eating to look at each other in solemnity before they all grinned like boys. The rest of the family looked from one to another in confusion until Fred finally said, "We won. We took control of the courthouse!"

Grace put her hand over her mouth. "But, what does this mean?" she asked.

Fred looked at Grace, his grin still plastered on his face. "It means, dear sweet sister, that those carpetbagging, thieving sons of bitches got a little taste of a southern ass-whooping!" He whooped loudly before tearing a ferocious bite out of his sandwich.

Grace laughed heartily as Papa scolded Fred. "Now, now, boys. Ladies are present," but Grace saw Papa's own smile even as he said it. He tilted away from the table as he fought a small coughing fit and Mimi frowned at him. Will, Grace noticed, had rolled his eyes and leaned back in his chair.

"What happens now?" asked Mimi. Grace turned and realized that, like Will, Mimi was not cheering. Her face still looked drained and pale, as though she were still worried.

"*Maman*, the plan currently is to hold the house until those interlopers understand that we here in the South can take care of our own. We don't need all those northerners coming here making a mess of everything," said Fred. Grace inhaled sharply through her nose and held her breath.

"How many died?" asked Mimi quietly.

"Don't know. Not too many, I don't think. A few negroes, I heard, maybe one or two from our side," Fred said, patting Mimi's arm across the table. The news didn't relieve her of her concerned look.

"Mimi, we won this," Fred assured her, furrowing his brow.

"Anytime there is violence," Mimi said slowly. "No one wins. How many mothers on both sides tonight are grieving for their lost sons?" She stood, pushed her chair in, and sighed. "If you'll excuse me, I'm feeling quite exhausted." Mimi turned and left the room.

Grace sat quietly thinking about the newspaper column and how it had frightened her and again how Fred's words had energized her. The article had carried fear to its readers. Its words held such strength that people had reacted strongly, even committing violence in its wake. But Mimi's words had silenced the room and brought everyone in it back into the present. People *had* died. Those people had other people grieving for them tonight. What if it had been Fred? Or Branch? Mimi's words had been few, but they had been enough to shift the air in the room completely.

If words could incite people to violence or halt the flow of energy as they had, what else could they do?

Chapter 9

Dear Ms. Mandin,

We would like to invite you to participate in the Transatlantic Currents conference this December in Wittenberg, Germany. Your proposal on Grace King will fit in nicely with our other panelists. We look forward to seeing you in Wittenberg.

Sincerely,

J. Fitzgerald

* * *

While sitting in the quiet living room one early morning, Meredith tried to let it sink in: She would be going to Germany for an international conference.

Her.

She didn't speak any German.

Liam wouldn't be able to go, so she'd have to travel alone.

Completely alone.

Just then, her phone buzzed with a text from her mother, *Let me talk to Lila. Ur keeping me from my granddaughter.*

She responded, *Not now. You told her to lie to us. She had stomachaches for days.*

Let me talk to her!

Meredith turned off the phone. The whole thing reminded her of her own childhood, suffering stomachaches almost every day through elementary school. Meredith had spent more time in the nurse's office than anywhere else, until one day the nurse had said she wasn't welcome there anymore. Either she had a real problem, or she needed to leave. Meredith didn't go back; instead, she hid the stomachaches better.

A few hours later, Meredith turned the phone on, too curious not to. She read, *You are a terrible mother and you owe me money.*

That one got her. *For what?* She asked.

Remember when you needed to finish your degree?

Meredith did remember. It was the one time they thought Gayle would be able to help with Meredith's college tuition.

Yes.

I took out a parent loan for you—$3000.

Meredith shook her head. Her mother had taken out a loan, but she'd never had to make a single payment. *But you didn't have to pay for the loan. Your disability waived repayment, remember?*

Yeah, well, I had to go to the doctor to get that paperwork, and co-pays add up!

Meredith sighed. *So, you want me to pay for a co-pay from almost ten years ago?*

The response was immediate: *Yes. Oh, and stop calling the family. Everyone tells me all about it.*

Meredith had emailed her aunts to see if Gayle had arrived safely back in Kentucky.

So, I'm not allowed any contact with the family, then? I'm out? Just like that?

Deedee and Candace show me the messages. We laugh about you. They tell me everything. And they said to stop bothering them. They know ur a liar, and they don't want anything to do with you, either.

Meredith sighed and turned the phone off. She opened another bag from a recent trip to Florida that she had taken with the girls and dumped the sand out on the floor.

* * *

Hours later, when her excitement for Germany had been fully replaced with anxiety, the children and Liam joined her in the living room. She showed Liam the texts from her mother, and he gently suggested they change her number. After weeks of relentless and cruel messages, Meredith agreed to it, cutting all ties with her mother and that side of her family completely.

In mid-November, Meredith found herself doubled over the commode vomiting at three in the morning. She crawled back into bed, trying not to wake Liam.

"What's going on? Are you okay?" he mumbled.

"Don't know. Just sick," she said, trying not to cry. Every muscle ached, and she felt like she couldn't catch her breath.

"Hey," he said, more alert. "What can I do?"

Meredith shook her head in the dark, the lump in her throat preventing anything more. He brought a cold cloth and iced water for her to sip, lay back down, and gently rubbed her back. Even nauseated as she was, Meredith felt guilty. She knew Liam must have just fallen asleep; he was up late most nights with insomnia. The transition from the military was taking some time.

Before long, they were both asleep again.

Meredith lost over ten pounds in less than two weeks. A stomach bug shouldn't last this long, so she finally went to the nurse at the university health center.

"You're too worked up," the nurse practitioner said. "Physically, you're fine. But your anxiety is upsetting your stomach."

"I'm traveling to Germany in a few days for a conference. Am I going to make it?"

"Aha. Well, that'll do it. Here," she said as she wrote a prescription for an antacid. "Start taking these when needed, and try to calm down. Good luck."

* * *

A few weeks later, Meredith stood gazing at rows of tudor-style buildings and winding streets. Wittenberg. She'd traveled through Miami and considered staying there on the beach for a few days, rather than finishing the trek. But she'd managed to get herself on the plane to Berlin and then on the train for Wittenberg. She dragged her old suitcase over cobblestone sidewalks, the bag clack-clacking behind her. The streets were narrow and empty, and Meredith glanced at the printed copy of the map to guide her. The bitter cold stung her eyes, making them ache.

She turned through a small archway that opened onto a stone parking area. A three-winged building sat to her left, and she entered the main door in the middle section. A young woman smiled when she entered.

"Welcome," she said. "You are here for the conference?"

"Yes," Meredith replied.

Within minutes, she was handed a packet and a key to her room. She would be staying there, in a former monastery. Her room was tiny but clean—and so quiet, she was almost uncomfortable. She lay down for a short rest before the evening reception began.

* * *

A few days later, Meredith nervously sipped cold water from the glass in front of her. She sat at a table with three other presenters, facing an audience of about twenty-five people from all over the world. The presenter ahead of her finished, the audience clapped, and the moderator began introducing her. She stood, carried her essay over to the podium in shaking hands, and looked at the room staring back. She'd been in this audience for days listening to other presenters, but from here...

She took a deep breath to steady her nerves. "Wow, y'all are a little scarier from up here," she joked nervously. The southern accent she'd been trying to hide all week rolled out unhindered. Light laughter circled the room, and Susan, the moderator and a highly-esteemed professor and scholar, smiled warmly. She mouthed, "You've got this" from the front row.

Meredith began reading, her voice evening out as she went. She heard her tone drop into a softer, well-paced rhythm. She explained how a thirty-three year-old Grace King had read an essay of hers nervously to a crowd in New Orleans in 1885, when she tried to describe what she felt did not yet exist at that time: A truly American Heroine. She explained that this essay was the start of a long writing career for King, even if few modern scholars were familiar with her work.

Twenty minutes later, Meredith finished and returned to her seat as the audience applauded. She nervously sipped her water as audience members asked other panelists about their topics, both relieved and disappointed that no one had questions for her.

One young woman raised her hand. "I have a question for Meredith. In the 1870s in New Orleans, a lot of families were involved with the Battle of Liberty Place, which was racially motivated. Was the King family involved, as well?"

"Yes, they were," Meredith said. "There aren't many references to it in Grace's works or her journals, but I think there are a few veiled mentions of it. It looks like her brother, Branch, was arrested and released the next day, and I think her oldest brother, Fred, would have been involved, as well. This is the same battle," she added, for other audience members. "That involved Oscar Chopin, Kate Chopin's husband. Shortly after the battle, the White League returned control of the courthouse back over to the proper chain of command. The battle restored some pride for the men, especially those who had been too young to have fought in the Civil War—like Fred and Branch King. But, ultimately, it was intended to reinstate white control and supremacy. In 1891, a monument to the battle and the White League was erected, and in 1932, an inscription was added stating that white supremacy reigned in the South. Because the monument was a symbol of racism, finally in 2017, it was removed under police protection due to threats of violence from people upset by its removal. Today, it sits in storage, rightfully so."

The young woman nodded. "Do we know if the youngest brother was also involved?"

"I'm afraid it's unclear. Will would have been very young—maybe fifteen or so?—at the time of the incident. And beyond the sadder aspects of his tough life, little is known about his own political or social leanings," Meredith explained. "Grace, herself, is difficult to decipher, at times. What she writes in letters differs from what we see in her fiction."

At the end of the final presentation, the group decided to combine efforts and put together a book of articles on transatlantic women's literature—Meredith's first real publication. That night, they ate dinner together, laughing over episodes of television shows across the language barrier. Many times, one person translated for another. "Oh! Betty Draper! I hate this Betty Draper!" Shared laughter. Academics from around the world, bonding over a shared hatred of Betty Draper.

That night, Meredith sipped hot, spiced *glutvien* and walked around the Christmas Market, marveling at the lights, wooden toys, and delicious smells coming from every direction. Church bells played in the distance while she purchased a few items for Liam and the girls.

The next morning, she made her way to Berlin, where she made her flight but landed in New York's JFK in a blizzard. Flights were being canceled, people were yelling, and lines were atrociously long. Meredith was exhausted, but there was nothing to do about it. She trudged along through the airport crowd, trying to see the front of a monstrous line to make sure it was the right line to join. She couldn't see the front signs, so she asked nearby TSA agents.

One glared in response. "There's one line, sweetheart, and it's back there." He pointed down the line.

"I'm sorry," Meredith stammered. "I was just making sure it was the right one. Thank you." Her voice wavered from exhaustion, and she began walking back to the end of the line. A Middle Eastern man walked, carrying several bags in his arms while a little boy, maybe four-years-old, followed, trying to get into the giant line. The boy's stuffed bear fell out of his backpack without him noticing. Meredith picked it up and held it out to him, smiling. He hid behind his father's legs, so she gave the bear to the man, who smiled in thanks. She waved her hand for them to join the line ahead of her. The man smiled and nodded thanks again.

"Ma'am," said the grouchy TSA agent behind her. The same man who had snapped at her just moments ago. "I need to see your papers."

Fuck. "Yes, sir," Meredith said. She handed over her passport and boarding passes.

"Come with me, ma'am."

Inwardly, Meredith panicked. This was it. She was about to be strip-searched.

"Where are you coming from?" he asked, as they walked alongside the line.

"Germany."

"Why were you in Germany?" He unclipped a security tape and gestured for Meredith to come through.

"A literary conference. I'm a grad student."

"And where you heading?" His Brooklyn accent was spot on with all the Hollywood versions she'd heard of it. She'd never heard it in person before.

"Home, I mean, Nashville. But I don't think I'm going to make the flight home."

"Southern girl, huh?"

"Yes, sir." They reached a security table. "Um, I've never been searched like this before, so be patient with me, please. I'm nervous and exhausted."

He stared and suddenly smiled. "Nah. I'm not going to search you. You're adorable. You go on through, sweetheart, and try to catch the flight home. It might be the last one out tonight, with the storm."

"Are you serious? Oh my god! Thank you so much!" He opened a gate for her to pass through.

"Bye now!" he called as Meredith waved over her shoulder.

She ran through the airport, dragging her bag behind her, and arrived at the gate, where boarding was stalled due to the ice storm. People shouted over the check-in counter, crying about getting onto this flight or that one. One man had to be removed by security after he tried to punch a flight attendant.

When she finally boarded the plane, Meredith settled into the single seat row with a sigh of extreme relief. It was ten p.m., and she'd been awake and traveling for almost twenty-four hours at that point.

"Ladies and gentlemen, this flight is overbooked. We will be removing the last three passengers who purchased their tickets."

Other passengers moaned, rolled their eyes, and began cursing—some under their breath, others openly. They called out names. Meredith wasn't one of them, but a young blonde was. She carried a guitar and began to wail. "This is my big break! I need to be in Nashville tomorrow night! It's my big break! PLEASE!" She screamed at the other passengers. No one volunteered to trade her places, and the attendant escorted her off the plane.

For a moment, Meredith felt guilty, but it was a very short moment. *Sorry, Dolly*, she thought, *you should've booked an earlier flight*.

After all the excitement, the pilot announced, "Ladies and gentlemen, due to the extended time on the runway, we need to de-ice the plane again. This should take about thirty minutes, and then we'll be on our way." Collective moans from the other passengers. Meredith turned to lean her head on the wall and closed her eyes.

Hours later, she arrived at the Nashville airport, found the little Honda in the dark parking lot, and drove an hour north to Clarksville. She made it home around three in the morning and crawled into bed with Liam. Three hours later, she woke to a sleepy little girl hugging her, waiting for presents. They spent some time together that morning, and Meredith walked Lila to the school bus stop. Shortly after, she drove to the university, where she gave a final presentation in her Teaching Composition course and drove two hours back to Clarksville, where she curled up against Liam for the rest of the evening and night. She was home, she was done for now, and all was well.

* * *

Two days later, Meredith's cell phone rang in the early morning.

"Hello?" she asked. She sat on the edge of their unmade bed, listening to the sounds of Lila getting ready for school down the hallway.

"Meredith?" her stepmother, Kay, responded in a strained voice.

"Kay? What's wrong?" she asked. If Kay was calling, it was because her father could not. *Heart attack*, Meredith thought. Down the hall, she could hear Liam calmly explaining to Lila that she could not wear a princess dress to school.

"Something's happened."

"Okay. What's going on?" Meredith asked, forcing patience to keep her stepmother calm. She braced herself for dire health news. Hospitals. ICUs. IVs.

"It's your dad."

Clearly, just get to it...

"He was arrested."

"What? Why?" *Tax evasion*, Meredith thought immediately. It has to be tax evasion. Why else would a middle age, overweight man be arrested?

"Sexual assault," Kay said, sniffling.

"What the fuck?" Meredith demanded.

Kay began openly crying. "When Ginny was twelve or thirteen, he touched her. There's video proof. The police came last night. They came into the house—into *our* house—and they took him. He did awful things—made her do awful things..."

Meredith sat in stunned silence, trying to piece all of the information together. "He raped Ginny?" she asked softly, thinking of her younger stepsister. She had always thought of her as the perfect girl: Happy, blonde, blue-eyed cheerleader. She hadn't spoken to her stepsister since they were in their early teens, before Meredith went to live with her mother and stepfather full time. Twenty years. Even at the beach last summer, Ginny and her family were not there. In the years since her father had wanted to start rebuilding their relationship, Meredith had noticed that Ginny and her children had never been around.

"Yes," Kay said. "I didn't know about it. Ginny told her husband not too long ago, and they went to the police. Your dad was arrested last night. I know he'd really like to see you."

Meredith sat, silent. Rape. He'd raped Ginny. She felt the anger starting in her legs, inching its way up. Her chest felt tight, and her neck and face began to feel hot.

"Your dad, I mean. I know he wants to see you," Kay said again, to fill in the awkwardly long pause.

"How is Ginny?" Meredith asked, her voice dropping to a quiet, controlled tone.

"Oh, I don't know. I haven't spoken with her this morning," Kay said.

Meredith barely stopped herself from asking, *Why the fuck not?* "And you? Are you okay?" She heard herself ask.

"I can't stop crying," Kay squeaked into the phone. "But I'm going to church this morning to pray."

"Kay, did they freeze the bank accounts? Are you okay financially?"

"Oh, I have access to everything," she said.

"So," Meredith asked carefully. "You're okay, physically?"

"Yes," Kay replied. "They've taken him to the jail in the courthouse downtown. He's meeting with the attorneys soon, and they'll set bail or whatever. Will you come up?"

Meredith paused.

"I'll try," she lied. "Kay? Tell Ginny I said thank you. What she did was very brave and must have been terrifying. But if she hadn't, he might've hurt someone else." *My girls*, she thought. *He might have hurt my girls.*

"I'll tell her," Kay promised.

They hung up. Meredith told Liam, and they shared a moment of shock. Meredith put Lila on the school bus and drove again to the university for her final writing center shift that semester. She didn't say a word about it to anyone.

Chapter 10

New Orleans
December, 1884

Grace and May walked through the gates of Metairie Cemetery carrying small bouquets. They walked in silence out of a hushed respect for the departed and scanned the headstones as they passed.

Grace slowed her walk, and May, glancing at her older sister, followed suit. *This trip needs to take as long as possible,* thought Grace, doing her best to halt time in its place. She stole glances at May as they walked, noting her pale, drained look and sunken eyes. May had been ill again last night, and they'd sat up together for most of it. This afternoon, both sisters had their dark hair pulled back in a simple braid and bun and wore blue dresses with little adornment. They'd bought the fabric and sewed the dresses together, and this trip was special, so they wore their matching dresses.

As they approached their first stop on this visit, Grace watched for the dome shape of the tomb with the name carved over the top arch: Miller.

The King family had moved again to a nicer house on Terpsichore Street, but soon after this move, Grandmamma had taken to her bed, ill. Grace had been sent to find the doctor and bring him to examine her.

As the sisters had looked from one to another while pretending to work on their embroidery, May had finally broken the silence. "What do you think is happening up there?" she had asked in a soft voice.

Grace had looked over to the stairs. "Whatever it is, I'm sure it isn't good. Grandmamma has been through so much." They waited, trying to glean Grandmamma's health by the faces of the uncles, aunts, and servants as they left the bedroom.

"Let's gather flowers," Nan had suggested. "Grandmamma would like that, don't you think?"

"Excellent idea, Nan. Grandmamma is the best gardener in the city! Everyone in the neighborhood says so. She would appreciate being surrounded by her garden in her illness," Grace had said, glad to feel like they were doing *something,* even if only gathering flowers for Grandmamma's room.

The sisters gathered large bouquets from the garden and took their time arranging the blooms in as many vases and jars as they could find. Finally, they heard footsteps coming down the stairs.

Grace had led her sisters to the foyer, where Papa and the doctor stood quietly talking.

"What's happening?" Grace had said.

The doctor turned to Grace, with a quick side look at Papa. "She is very unwell. Your Grandmamma has endured much physical pain but said nothing of it. She is the epitome of a southern lady, I tell you. But her health now is fading, I'm afraid."

Grace had felt May and Nina reach for her hands, and the sisters held back tears.

The doctor's kind eyes had looked at each of the tearful faces surrounding him. "I think you'd best spend as much time with your Grandmamma as possible over the next few days. And please, no visitors, outside of family and the closest friends."

Grace had nodded and choked out, "Thank you, doctor." She had walked past Papa and led the way to Grandmamma's room, where Mimi started to send them away.

"No," Grace had said simply. "We're staying right here." She pulled another chair to Grandmamma's side. "May, will you and Nan start bringing the flowers in and arranging them? And Nina, would you find Grandmamma's bible? I will read to her."

Nina brought over Grandmamma's thick bible, the pages worn thin from her use. Grandmamma's glasses were tied with a ribbon and balanced on the cover, and Grace had carefully placed them on the night stand. Grandmamma had only needed them in her seventies, unlike most of the other elderly ladies Grace had known.

Uncle Tom and Henry had arrived, and the family took turns reading bible passages and telling stories to each other and Grandmamma, though she was beyond responding to the conversation.

"Remember the boats, Grandmamma?" Grace had asked. "In the swamp? You wrapped us up in your shawls and skirts and kept us warm and safe. We felt safe because you assured us God would not abandon us."

"Remember the cabin, Grandmamma?" Fred had asked. "You managed to keep three boys in line, almost every day," he had said and laughed. "And made sure we studied our bible and washed properly. Keeping three boys clean in the country—I don't know how you did it."

"Remember when Will tried to sneak in his dog, after Grandmamma told him not to?" Branch asked.

Fred laughed and then explained to the sisters. "Will tried to hide the dog under his bed, but the dog smelled so bad, Grandmamma made Will take three baths, thinking the smell was him! He finally gave up and admitted the dog was inside, just to stop taking baths!"

Grace had laughed heartily hearing some of their stories about which she hadn't known. *Why didn't we share more, like this?* She thought.

A few short hours later, Grandmamma died, and the family wept in grief.

Back in the cemetery, Grace reached for May's hand as they stood in front of the Miller tomb.

"I will always associate Grandmamma with flowers," May said in a quiet voice.

"Me, too," answered Grace. "She'd be proud of you, you know."

May smiled shyly. "I don't know about that."

"She would," Grace repeated. She stepped forward to place her small bouquet on the ground in front of the tomb and paused. Another bouquet was there, and Grace assumed it was from Mimi or another family member, but scrawled on the ribbon was the name Aza.

"May, look," said Grace, pointing. "Do you think it's possible? Could Grandmamma's Aza have left these?"

May stepped forward, her brow furrowed, and knelt to get a better look. She reached out her small hand to turn the ribbon over and trace a flower petal. "They're pretty," she said quietly. "Mimi said that Grandmamma and Aza grew up together in Georgia, but I don't see why Aza couldn't have made her way to New Orleans."

"Why didn't Aza come with Grandmamma to New Orleans in the first place?" Grace wondered. Before the War, it was normal for a woman to bring her closest servant with her into a new marriage.

"I'm sure there were reasons," May said. "But they both seem to have loved and missed each other."

Grace looked back at Grandmamma's tomb and realized that so many of Grandmamma's stories had died with her, untold. "I wonder whatever happened to Aza. She must be nearby, to have left these."

May shrugged. "I don't know how we'd ever be able to find her. It would be nice, though, for her to know that Grandmamma had loved her, too."

Grace sighed sadly. "Are you ready for our next stop?"

May took a deep breath, held it, and slowly released it. She nodded but said nothing.

They turned away from Grandmamma's tomb and walked hesitatingly. Oddly enough, Grace enjoyed their visits to the cemetery, even if they were often filled with painful memories. There was something about the ritual of remembrance that appealed to Grace. The Kings were Protestant, but Grace envied her Catholic friends' sense of and adherence to ritual. It made sense to her in a world where not much else did.

She and May approached the rectangular plot etched on the front with "King." May reached for Grace's hand as they stood in front of it, squeezing as though this would keep their tears from falling. Grace sighed as she looked over the etched words: William W. King. *Papa.*

Grace glanced again at May's pale face and felt a small lump tighten in her throat. May resembled him, with her dark features, but her countenance was much more subdued. Quiet. Papa had been a leader—always stepping forward to reassure them they would be fine. He was the one who made everything okay—even if they were struggling, wearing threadbare clothing, or eating the same soup for days at a time. Papa had said those struggles would only make them stronger, and Grace had to admit in hindsight that he was right. They'd survived. But he had not.

Papa had suffered from bronchitis and had become even more frail and thin from working endless hours since their return to the city. Grace had sat by his side all day and night after he had become bedridden, holding his hand. She mostly read to him, but he could not speak or communicate in any way near the end.

He had used himself up trying to rebuild a life for the family after the War, Grace was sure, and had been too weak to fight anymore. He'd already built them up twice in his lifetime: once before the War, and again after. If he could do that, why couldn't Fred, Branch, or Will? Why must they complain about every tiny thing they did for the family, when Papa had given his very life without complaint?

Grace stepped forward and placed her small bouquet on the grass at the foot of the headstone.

"Do you think Papa would approve of me?" May asked shyly.

Grace nodded slowly. "I think he would." She noticed that May gently worried a ribbon between her fingers.

May sighed suddenly. "I think I'm ready, Grace," she said so quietly Grace almost didn't hear her.

The lump in Grace's throat tightened once more, choking any words she might have said. She simply nodded and walked silently beside May, reaching out a hand to squeeze hers as though she could hold on to her. Keep her there with Grace in the present.

When they returned home, May's trunks were lined up beside the front door, and Mimi stood waiting, holding May's nicest hat.

"I can't believe it's happening," she said. She smiled and whisked away a tear as she tied the ribbon for May, who did her best to avoid eye contact.

Nan and Nina stood in a line to give May farewell hugs.

Grace waited until everyone else had said their goodbyes and walked with May to the waiting carriage.

"He'd better treat you well, May," Grace said, holding her head high and her chin tilted up.

May nodded. "I'm certain he will, Sis."

They stood beside the carriage, not ready to say their goodbyes. Finally, Grace sighed. "This is silly. I'll see you in a few months. Why is this so hard?" Tears trickled down her cheeks. "What am I going to without my sister-partner?"

"Stop that, Grace Elizabeth King," May said firmly. "Because if you cry, of all people, I will break. And you will do exactly what you've been doing: visit the opera with Uncle Tom. Travel with the Morris family. Aren't they returning to New York soon? You enjoyed Saratoga, remember? But this time, you will be able to stay with me on your way up and back."

Grace laughed and took a deep breath, willing the air to help her hold the tears inside. "Northerners. So well-dressed and polite—and so stiff you could break a board with them. Why do you have to marry someone so far away again? What kind of life will be possible in Charlotte, when you have had all of New Orleans?"

May reached out and pulled Grace into a tight embrace. "I love you, Sis. And you will come visit me, and together, we will make Charlotte a bit more colorful. Write me. Soon. I'll expect letters from you as soon as I reach North Carolina."

Grace nodded and smiled. "I mailed one a few days ago, just so you'll have it waiting for you. And, May," Grace said, glancing over her shoulder to be sure no one listened. "Tell me everything about marriage. *Everything*," she added pointedly. Grace's last beau, Atwood, had succumbed to a roving eye—

and she had lost both beau and a dear friend in the drama. She had decided marriage—and beaux—were simply not for her.

May laughed. "Sis, I cannot say goodbye to you, so I will say, I will see you soon."

And with that, May turned to the carriage door, where the driver stood to hand her up. He shut the door, gave a small bow to Grace, and walked to the driver's seat.

Grace stood on the sidewalk and watched the carriage until long after it had disappeared.

* * *

The next night, Grace woke up alone in the room she had always shared with May, thinking she was hearing Grandmamma's coughing. "Grandmamma?" she called, without thinking. Goosebumps prickled up and down her arms.

When no answer came, Grace remembered why and leaned back on her pillow. She picked up Grandmamma's old book, *The Lady of the Lake*, and read until she could sleep again.

The next day, she walked around the city and felt it again: that stirring in her heart.

An energy tingled from her chest to her fingertips, and she wanted to sing at the top of her lungs, to run across an empty field, to rejoice in warm sunshine on her face, and to weep—all at once. She wanted to expand her very self and feel her heart pound and her lungs burn. She remembered this feeling from the bayou, just before the family returned to the city. It happened most in times of deep change. It was time for her to write and create, but Grace was still at a loss for how to start.

For days after May's departure, Grace moped about the house, folding the same linens repeatedly and overwatering all of the plants and flowers. Nina and Nan were arguing one day over something trivial, when Grace simply could not bear another minute. She sighed and stood.

"I'm going for a walk. Alone," Grace said, glaring at them across the room.

They didn't notice, and Mimi was completely absorbed in their fight.

Grace rushed outside and walked the narrow sidewalks, making her way toward a row of shops. Grace and May usually did this walk together as they discussed what colors or types of fabric to purchase, or what style of blouse they might like to make. Now, Grace walked it alone, carrying the basket that used to hang on May's elbow.

As the afternoon passed, her sadness eased into melancholy. There was the small garden where they had talked about May's engagement for the first time. She had been excited but frightened. Grace had been, too.

Grace passed the shop where they had sat for hours, debating which lace May should wear on her wedding day. Grace entered it, alone, and set the basket on a stool by the counter. She spent time looking over fabrics and finally settled on a soft blue. She would make May a new blouse.

When she returned home, her melancholy eased again into a peaceful productivity when Mimi came into the parlor.

"Oh good, you're home. This came for you," she said, handing out a small envelope and settling into her own seat. It was addressed to Miss Grace King, in May's neat script.

Dearest, Grace,

Oh, how I miss you! I am settling in here, though I miss New Orleans terribly. The wedding was lovely, but in all honesty, I feel disappointed in the wedding night. Perhaps he had been a bit too heavy into his cups. The night was far from the gentle introduction to marriage that I had daydreamed about for so long. I had hoped for the knight from fairytales and am saddened to find a... rougher... beginning to my marriage. I am healing well, with only a little discomfort and pain left. But it is over, and now I am a wife.

I am lonely now, but soon, I will take on the role as Lady of this home in Charlotte, a very different place from Louisiana. The cuisine is blander, and the colors dulled somewhat. The flowers, though, are still vibrant and lovely, even if they are not as exotic as those draping our

windowsills back home. You must visit me often and soon, and bring a little bit of the sunshine with you.
Much love,
May

Grace read and reread the letter, her previous sense of peace completely gone.

"How could he?" she said aloud.

Mimi lifted her eyebrows. "I take it Brevard has stumbled in his first days as a husband?"

Grace half growled. "How hard is it to be kind?"

"Men are different, dear," Mimi replied, turning back to her embroidery basket as though that explained everything.

"That is no excuse," Grace muttered. She tucked the letter into her pocket and left to sit at the writing table in her bedroom.

Grace's hands shook as she lifted the pen to start a response to May. She started, blotted the paper, and stopped multiple times.

January, 1884
My dearest, May,

I am astounded and furious at Brevard's boorishness! You simply must be straight forward with him and demand his respect! It amazes me what married women must do for free, while working women at least are paid!

It is a terrible lot for all women—to be martyrs at all stages and formulations of our lives so men can do as they please!

But do not regret or miss your past self, my dear May. That May King has blossomed. The transition may have been painful, but it was not a worthless one. You are stronger for having survived it. Women gain strength from pain, more so, I believe, than men do.

But remember this, too: Look out for your own comfort. Do it boldly. And do not accept any more discomfort or pain out of a sense of delicacy or comport. Men do not accept such fates, and neither should we.

Much love,
Sis

Chapter 11

Hello Dr. Donnell,

I was hoping to submit a paper to be considered for the upcoming writing awards. I have heavily revised the final paper I completed in your class last fall, and I was wondering if you might consider signing off on it.

Thank you so much for your consideration,

Meredith

"Lila, we need to talk," Meredith said, as she sat on the floor beside Lila and her doll house. She had dreaded this talk for days but knew she needed to speak to Lila about what had happened. Inwardly, all she could hear was *what if...*

"About what?" Lila said, dressing her Barbie.

"About Papaw. Do you remember when the doctor talked to you about grownups asking kids to keep secrets?"

Lila looked up and nodded.

"Did Papaw ever ask you to keep a secret?"

"No."

"Are you sure?"

"Yes. Why?"

"Papaw..." How did she explain something of this magnitude to a child? "Papaw did some very bad things to another girl, a long time ago, and we just found out."

"What did he do?"

Meredith took a breath to stall and fought back tears. What if Lila told her he'd touched her? She mustn't cry. No matter what. Lila would think she'd done something wrong, so Meredith braced herself for whatever may come at her.

She looked up to the doorway where Liam stood, listening. He'd offered to speak with Lila himself, but they had decided if something had happened, Lila would be more likely to tell Meredith. After the deployments, they shared a special bond.

Meredith inhaled deeply. "Well, he touched her in private places where he shouldn't have. You know it's never okay for someone to touch you without your permission, right? And it's especially not okay ever for a grownup to touch a child like that."

"I know, Mommy, the doctor said so, too, 'member?"

"I know, honey, but I wanted to talk to you about it. It's never ever okay for someone to touch you without your consent. Consent means permission. You know, if he did touch you, you can tell me. You wouldn't be in trouble."

"I know. Why would I be in trouble?"

"Some kids think that kind of thing is their fault."

"That's dumb. I know you wouldn't be mad at me, and he didn't touch me like that, ever. I promise. Can we play Barbies now? Look, Helicopter Joe can spin his legs."

Lila held up an old G.I. Joe doll that had seen better days and flicked his legs, sending them into a fast spin.

* * *

Spring semester started smoothly but with occasional phone calls to the detectives assigned to her father's case. Meredith had to assure them that he had never laid a hand on her, which was true.

She'd spent hours ruminating over the past, turning over every stone she could find and kept mentally searching. She remembered wrestling with Steven at a young age. He would lay on the living room floor with his knees drawn up. Meredith remembered sitting on his feet and how he would reach down, grab her hands, and flip her upside down over his head. He had never been quick to hug and for the most part was never even physically affectionate, beyond that one type of horseplay. Even that, as she thought about it, stopped after Steven had met Kay. Meredith had been in the third grade, and at first, she'd been excited about having new members of the family—sisters, even! That had quickly been replaced with passive aggressive rivalries between Meredith and her stepsisters. In junior high, Ginny's older sister, Tonya, had moved a candle during a family gathering for Thanksgiving, placing it directly beneath Meredith's waist-length hair. In one swoosh, Meredith's hair was aflame, but it went out as fast as it went up, leaving her hair singed but ultimately unharmed. Right after that was when Kay had bagged up Meredith's things for her to move to her mother's home.

After moving out, she'd lost her closest friend, Ginny, and though they'd attended the same high school, their paths never crossed. It was like Meredith had been exiled, but she had never understood why.

Meredith wanted to support Ginny now as an adult, but she had no testimony to give, beyond simple family drama. She told the detectives she was sorry, but her father never physically abused her.

One rainy afternoon, the lead detective, Toni, called. Meredith nudged the basket of clean-but-unfolded laundry out of her path and answered her cell phone.

"Hello?"

"Hey, it's Toni. I'm sorry to bother you with more of the same, but...there's another young girl in another video we've located. Light-skinned, African American, probably around fourteen. Any chance you might know who she could be?"

Meredith began walking aimlessly through the house while talking.

"Um...that might be my cousin," Meredith said, as she reached the back door. In her head, Ashley was still five years old, though Meredith knew she was all grown up and had her own kids by now. Ginny and Meredith took Ashley hiking once near Meredith's grandparents' house in the winter, when the bugs and weeds were gone. Ashley didn't have gloves, so Meredith took hers off to give to the little girl, but Ginny had suggested they each give her one, so Ginny and Meredith would each have one glove, too, evening out the discomfort between the two of them.

Meredith turned and made her way slowly back to the kitchen.

"Or, if it's a more recent video or file," she said. "It could be my older stepsister, Tonya's daughter, but I've never met her. What about Tonya, by the way? Ginny's older sister? Did he ever hurt her?"

"Well, she says he used to watch her shower in her teens, but that's it," Toni responded.

"'That's it,'" repeated Meredith, as though that wasn't enough. "Is she going to testify?"

"No. She refuses."

"Why?" Meredith demanded.

Toni sighed, exhausted. "It's like that more times than I'd like to admit. Sometimes, people just don't help when they could. And, I'm sorry for asking this again," she said, hesitantly. "But you're sure he didn't touch you?"

"I know this is going to sound weird, but I'm sorry. He didn't. It's such a weird thing to say...to apologize that I wasn't raped or molested. But I wasn't. My mother was awarded full custody when I was around twelve, and my stepmother had my things bagged up when I visited after that. It was pretty clear: I didn't live there anymore."

"Have you had any contact with Ginny over the years?"

"No, I'm afraid I haven't," Meredith explained. "We were treated as rivals, growing up, so I kept my distance. In all honesty, I thought she hated me for some reason."

"Well, thank you for your help. We may call on you to testify, though, so be prepared for that," Toni said with a deep sigh. "If I hear anything else, I'll let you know."

"Thanks."

* * *

A few days later, Meredith sat in a slightly darkened section of the fourth floor of the library. She often drove to campus to be there as soon as the library opened at seven, which meant leaving the house by five thirty. This early, the library was mostly empty, especially this far from the main entrance and computer labs, and she relished the quiet stillness.

She opened the collection of Grace's journals in front of her and reread a few paragraphs, making the occasional note in the margin or underlining a passage.

Grace had been the eldest daughter in her own family, just as Meredith was before her stepsisters came along. Tonya was two years older than her, and Ginny one year younger. As they grew up, Grace's three sisters had looked to her to help guide the family when it was in strife, but then they rebelled and challenged her need for control, too, especially Nina, the youngest. Meredith knew the King family had been challenged and their relationships strained, and yet, they remained a family.

Meredith shook her head in wonder at it all. It was hard enough making ends meet in twenty-first century Tennessee, let alone Reconstruction Era New Orleans. She and Liam had changed roles as the bread winner several times in their marriage, and it usually worked out just fine.

This time, however, Meredith found herself struggling more than usual; her anxiety lurked in the shadows and tightened her chest when she least expected it. She had her small family of four depending on her for financial security, but what if she failed? What if the chaos of everything swallowed her whole?

Meredith flipped to the middle of the book to look at the pictures there. Various black-and-white images of Grace King looked back. A young Grace, looking hopeful and elegant. A middle-aged Grace, looking confident and sure of herself. An elderly Grace, looking regal and poised.

Would Meredith ever feel these things?

* * *

Later that week, the weather hit full "Spring in the South," and the sun beat down on the hot pavement on campus. Meredith walked to the writing center to start a shift and set her things down, sweating slightly from the walk across campus and the heat of the room.

"Good Lord, it's hot in here," she said, setting her books on the table.

"That's because you're here now," said Scott, grinning up at her. Scott was in his late forties and was infamous for disagreeing with professors.

Meredith stared at him and frowned. "Excuse me?" She didn't work with Scott often, and she made a point of not sitting near him in classes. Something about him made her uncomfortable, but she couldn't put her finger on exactly what.

"Sorry," he mumbled, looking down and turning away as his face and neck turned red.

Meredith walked away and began reviewing the session schedules and questions waiting with the receptionist. She had taken on a little more leadership in the writing center and wanted to make sure their young receptionist had no questions or issues needing resolution.

"Meredith? Can I talk to you?" asked an undergrad tutor, Anna, quietly by the desk.

"Of course," Meredith said, immediately concerned. She and Anna were friends, but this was clearly of a larger nature. "Let's go for a walk. Sky, we're going to step out for a minute," Meredith said under her breath to the receptionist. He nodded and gave a tight smile as he hung up the phone only for it to ring again immediately.

Meredith and Anna walked down the wide hallway away from the center and sat in comfortable armchairs near the stairs. "What's going on?" Meredith asked.

"Someone...has been saying... things that bother me," she said haltingly.

"Can you tell me more?" Meredith asked, concerned. Inwardly, she braced herself. Anna was a very conservative young woman, and arts and humanities grad students were typically very open about their lifestyles and opinions about—well, everything.

"Scott's been making weird comments about my chest," she blurted.

"Holy shit," Meredith stumbled. "Are you serious?" Anna was barely nineteen.

Her eyes teared up, and her face flushed red. Meredith thought at first from embarrassment but quickly realized it was anger. "He said a blouse I was wearing wasn't appropriate for work, but Summer said it was fine." Summer was another Ph.D. student, and she, too, was religiously conservative, but Meredith had noticed that she had been open and accepting of other grad students, regardless of their differences. Meredith was glad that Summer and Anna had connected. Summer would be a good mentor. She was the very definition of a "good Southern Christian," including her strong Alabama accent and impeccable fashion sense.

"Anna, if he made you feel uncomfortable in any way, I'm sorry you had to deal with that," Meredith said. "Would it be okay if I quietly pursued this? Has he been saying things to others, as well?"

"I think so, yes." She listed a few other names, and Meredith made a mental list.

"Okay, I'll talk to these ladies. Would it be okay if I chronicled our talk today? I won't list your name, if you'd prefer," she added.

"Okay. Thank you. I don't want to get someone in trouble..."

"But if someone is making work difficult for others, that person has caused their own trouble," Meredith said.

Anna nodded.

Later that day, Meredith began an important email to her stepsister, Ginny. They hadn't spoken since junior high. Kay had stopped calling with updates, and Meredith had a feeling that her gratitude had not been passed along to Ginny. She found her email address at the elementary school where she taught first grade.

Ginny—

First, my apologies for using your work email; I didn't know how else to get in touch with you directly. I want to thank you for your bravery and actions. You may have saved my own daughters from similar events from him. I'm so sorry that I am not able to help as much as I'd like to, but I assure you that I support you one hundred percent. I'm working with Toni and giving any information that I can.

You don't need to respond to this email if you're not ready or simply have no desire to do so; I would understand completely if you didn't. If you need time and want to respond in the future, that's okay, too. I'm here, ready whenever you are.
Meredith

* * *

Late that night, Meredith awoke in a panic.

"Liam?" she whimpered into the dark.

"Hm?" He mumbled.

"Sick again," she said, hating how tiny and weak she sounded. She sniffled, trying not to vomit, but she couldn't catch her breath. Her skin felt hot, but she was shivering and covered in cold sweat.

"Hey, it's okay," he said. He slipped out of bed and returned with a cold washcloth and water for her to sip on. Her muscles began cramping up, and her legs ached, drawing up involuntarily. "Can I touch you?" Sometimes, she could handle being touched during an episode, and sometimes, it made the nausea worse.

"Don't know," she choked out, half sobbing, half gasping.

"Okay. I'm going to rub your back, but stop me if you feel worse," he said softly.

She nodded in the dark, resting on her side facing away from him, in case she had to vomit onto the floor. His hand very lightly touched her upper back, and at first her stomach did a flip. She half dry-heaved. He moved his hands up to her shoulders to the base of her neck and squeezed gently, not moving his hand. The tension in her legs lifted a bit. She let out a breath she didn't know she was holding.

"I really wish you would see a therapist. A counselor. It's been helping me," Liam said gently.

Meredith shook her head. “Yours is part of your VA benefits. We can’t afford one for me right now," she said through gritted teeth.

He simply held his hand there, squeezing between her neck and shoulder, as she began to breathe again.

“There now,” he said, sleepily. “I’m here. And everything’s going to be okay. I’m not going anywhere.”

Silent tears slid down her cheeks and wet the pillow. Eventually, she slept.

* * *

The following week, Meredith sat at a beige, formica conference table in the Teaching Assistant Office in Bush Hall. The room was claustrophobic from too many desks and shelves having been shoved into the space in an attempt to fit in more grad students. Nicknamed the Beige Palace, every surface in it was a generic shade of beige. Every table, every cinder block in the wall, every partition, every cubby. Even the tiled floor: beige. The only windows were too high for anyone to reach without standing on a table. Summer sat across from her, frowning and tapping her foot under the table.

“Yes, what Anna says actually happened, and she’s not misreading it. I overheard the whole thing,” said Summer.

“Did he ever say anything inappropriate to you? Or make you feel uncomfortable in the writing center?” Meredith asked.

Summer looked away. “Um....”

“So that’s a yes, but you don’t want to get him in trouble. Is that it?” Meredith asked.

“I told him to back off, and he did, to me,” Summer said. “But I notice he still says weird stuff to the others, especially the younger girls.”

“Okay,” Meredith said as she jotted down the information. “I won’t include any names on anything without your express permission. Does that help?”

Summer let out the breath she'd been holding. “Yes.” She paused and stared at Meredith for a moment before continuing. “Okay, he’s been saying we should set up the writing center like a strip club, so the tutors could take students into the 'back room.' Then, he asked me if I was afraid of men staring at my hot ass. Not really sexual harassment, but it was still weird."

Meredith sighed. "Got it. Okay, I'm heading over to meet with Jen later today, but like I said, I won't hand over any names whatsoever without express permission from each person, in writing," she assured her.

She gathered up her things and left the TA office. She had arranged to meet with Suzy, another peer mentor for the writing center, so she headed over to the campus Starbucks and settled in to study while she waited.

She set out her laptop and notebook and leaned back, sighing deeply, trying to shift her attention back to her own studies—even if just for a few minutes.

Meredith had begun drafting a new conference proposal on Grace King. A scholar she'd met in Wittenberg had sent the conference information: An entire conference on just King. Meredith had been tweaking her proposal for weeks—adjusting a few words here or there, moving one line forward and back again. She stared at the Word document—one single-spaced page—for a full half-hour.

She finally gathered up the courage to hit the "Send" button just as Suzy walked in.

"Hey," she said, as Suzy set her heavy bag on the floor.

"Whew, these bags just get heavier," she said with a laugh. "So, what's up?" She tossed her smooth blonde ponytail over her shoulder and looked at Meredith with bright blue eyes. She reminded her of Ginny.

"Well, I've been meeting with several writing center ladies about Scott," Meredith said.

"Oh, that whole mess," she said, rolling her eyes.

So...she is aware of this? "I was wondering," Meredith ventured carefully. "Scott and most of the women coming forward are actually in your peer group, not mine. I just happened to be the mentor one shift the other day when a tutor approached me. I was wondering if you might represent their interests, instead of me. Several of the instances happened during the group meetings, and as a peer mentor, this might be better fitting for you to take it over, as the leader of that group." Meredith wanted to shout that being surrounded by asshole men and the women they've violated wasn't helping her mental state. A break would be nice.

"Oh, well, I was never offended by Scott. He never said anything to me, so I would feel uncomfortable doing that," she explained. "I'm not going to get someone in trouble."

"I see," Meredith replied, shocked and dismayed.

"So, is that all?" she asked.

"Um, yeah. I guess so. Thanks," Meredith said. Suzy shrugged and heaved her bag up on her shoulder.

"Okay! See ya!"

Meredith sighed and slowly walked over to the library for her meeting with the director and administrators. She'd spoken with them candidly and provided a document listing each woman's story of harassment.

Meredith took her time crossing campus, trying to catch her breath and appreciate the warmth of the day just a tiny bit, but her thoughts continued to spin. It seemed everyone else got to shirk responsibilities when they were stressed, so why didn't she get to do the same?

Meredith sighed deeply. No running from this. No hiding. When she arrived at the writing center, Jen was already in her office waiting, along with Dr. Jones, the writing center and graduate teaching assistant director. Dr. Jones was the southern grandmother everyone wanted: kind, intelligent, humorous—and could bake the best Mississippi Mud in the state. The offices here had windows for walls, but today, the blinds were closed—giving their meeting even more mystery for those hanging out in the center.

Dr. Jones spoke first. "So, I want to thank you for stepping forward to handle this." Meredith had mentioned to her a tiny bit about her father's arrest, in case she was subpoenaed and had to miss work suddenly. "I know this can't be easy for you right now."

Meredith nodded her thanks. "Well, the women needed someone to do it, so I'm here. I'm not trying to get anyone in trouble, but they've had enough, and they deserve to be able to come to work and not be harassed," she explained.

"Of course," she said. "No one likes these kinds of things, but they have to be addressed."

They reviewed each account by each woman, whose names Meredith had carefully replaced with numbers to keep the accounts separate but anonymous. Jen sighed a number of times, running her fingers through her hair and mumbling, "I just can't believe this guy..." while shaking her head.

After they were done, Dr. Jones looked at her. "Meredith, I'd like to check in with the ladies. Do you think you could tell us who they are?" she asked carefully.

Meredith paused. She knew Dr. Jones meant well, but she'd told the women she would not reveal them until they each gave permission to do so. She sighed. "I can't. I'm so sorry, but I told them I wouldn't, until they gave me permission. I know that if this goes to judicial affairs, we'll need their names, and I'll cross that bridge when I get there. For now, though, I have to keep my promise to them."

Dr. Jones nodded and smiled. "I understand that, and I respect it. Greatly. They chose the right person to represent them, I'll tell you that. So, Leigh over in Judicial Affairs will take over the case from here on out. We'll need to give her your notes, without the names, and she'll arrange for you to meet with her in a few days. If you can, try to get the women to add their names soon, since that will clarify the case and allow greater transparency."

Meredith nodded again. "I'll try."

Jen offered her a thin smile as she stood to leave the room, but Meredith noticed that her face was looking drawn and stressed.

* * *

Meredith,

If I had found your paper of value for the writing awards, I would have said so in my comments on it last semester.

Best of luck,
Dr. Donnell

* * *

Meredith,

I want you to know that it meant so much to me to read this message. I have so much respect and admiration for you, because despite the circumstances, he is still your father. You are right. My Mom did not tell me anything you said at all.

It is too difficult to accurately describe the feelings I have experienced the past several weeks. I have been so angry at him, of course, but also so many people in my family for not having the courage or decency to protect me when the abuse was going on. I think that is a big part of why I couldn't tell anyone else until now. Maybe I realized that my Mom and sister should have known and when they lived their lives normally, I thought there was no one at all who would help me. Still, I loved them, and Steven knew this. He said if I ever did tell anyone that he would kill me or my Mom.

Despite this, I still have felt so guilty for not telling sooner. I actually did tell Mom as soon as I moved out (so she for sure knew then) because I was worried he would abuse my niece, but Mom stayed with him. That was nine years ago. He tried to pretend to her like he was sorry and that he got "saved" by the church, but that's no excuse to me. That gave him years to destroy or relocate many of the pictures and videos he made of me.

Thank you, Meredith, for your email and support—it means a lot. I'll be in touch as the trial progresses.
Ginny

Chapter 12

New Orleans

By late 1884, the World's Fair had settled into New Orleans, bringing with it a host of wonderful influences, but at the same time, the crowds of people were often overwhelming. Grace had been frequenting many of the lectures in the Women's Department and even became a member of the Pan Gnostics, an intellectual group that met each week.

Fred, Branch, and Will provided for the King family, but Grace found it increasingly challenging to run a household of seven people on fifty dollars a month, especially when the family loved to entertain guests. Will made more money now and was very generous with it, when he had it. The family held high hopes for him, but still, they struggled to support so many of them on relatively little funding.

One day, Fred arrived home from a business trip as Nan and Grace were sewing a new curtain in the parlor.

"Sissy, Nannie," he said, as he sat on the chair nearest them. "I've invited a new acquaintance to dine with us tonight. A young man I met on the riverboat on my return trip this morning. Joaquin Miller. He's a poet, and I found him most eccentric and interesting!"

"Oh, how lovely," Grace said and immediately began planning simple menu changes and seating arrangements in her head. "Mimi can make her famous bouillabaisse."

That evening, they were charmed by the simple pleasure of Mr. Miller's conversation. A conversation is more than simple "talk," though many do not understand the nuance of the difference. A conversation is an intellectual pursuit that allows the participants to learn from one another. Talk is the simple family exchanges and local gossip.

Mr. Miller brought conversation to the family table in the same way that Judge Gayarré did, and Grace relished this.

As she walked with Mr. Miller to the porch after a lovely evening discussing Romantic poets, he paused.

"Miss King, I wonder that you yourself do not write," he said, raising an eyebrow at her.

"Oh," Grace replied, blushing. She lowered her voice. "In all honesty, I've tried. I've composed a few sketches here and there, at the Judge's encouragement. I sent them up north to the publishers, but they were all declined."

"Miss King, I wonder," he said with a slight hesitation. "I wonder if you would mind assisting me tomorrow afternoon with my writing."

"Why, of course, Mr. Miller, I'd be delighted, but how can I be of assistance to a poet such as yourself?" Grace's mind raced. Had he been interested in her bright ideas over dinner about poetry? Had she expressed linguistic talents? Was this the support she needed?

"I prefer to dictate my poetry, and I need a secretary."

Grace sighed but smiled, anyway. "Of course, Mr. Miller, I'd be happy to oblige." She patted his arm, and they continued on to the gallery.

* * *

By December, Julia Ward Howe, the famous speaker and activist, arrived to the city, along with her beautiful daughter, Maud. After meeting the women at a dinner party, the Kings suggested a tour of the countryside and local bayous.

As the day arrived, their rented open carriage pulled up to the Howe's temporary home. Julius, the driver, dismounted from his seat, adjusted the reins, and patted the old horse comfortingly on the neck.

Mimi smiled at him fondly as he walked to the Howe's door. In a lowered voice, she said, "I'm so glad Julius is our driver today. He reminds me so much of Jerry, and how I miss Jerry!"

Grace nodded in agreement.

Julius returned to the carriage door and waited to help the Howes.

"Hello, Miss King, Mrs. King," said Mrs. Howe as she approached the carriage. She looked hesitantly at the steep step and handle, took Julius's hand, and climbed into the carriage with a grunt.

Julius handed Maud in, as well, before returning to driver's seat and picking up the reins. He clucked to the horse who started a gentle plod.

"Good morning," Grace replied. "We should have a lovely day ahead of us! And I am excited to show you the beauty of our bayous and countryside here in Louisiana."

"Oh, I am so excited!" chirped Maud, smiling at each person in turn. As the carriage bumped along the country road, Maud continually put her hand to her hair, as though remedying what was a perfectly coiffed style.

Grace pointed out the various types of trees, towering oaks, and draping Spanish moss. The water in the bayous and channels was a bit high from the recent heavy rains, and they approached a small bridge to cross the dark water.

"I'm sorry, missus," said Julius, stopping the carriage. "The bridge is washed out. We'll need to go on down to the shallow section and wade across."

"Of course, Julius. Whatever you think," said Mimi.

"Is that safe?" asked Mrs. Howe, lowering her voice. "Just wading across?"

"Oh, Julius would never take us across if he felt it unsafe," Grace said, reassuring the older woman.

As the carriage approached the shallow water, Grace realized they had crossed here before. Julius paused the carriage and stared at the still water, scanning his eyes to the left and right. No current, and so they could cross safely.

He nodded to himself and clucked the horse forward again. The carriage slowly eased down the shallow bank and into the water.

"Oh, my," said Mrs. Howe, alarmed. She grabbed onto the side of the carriage as it rocked gently through the water. They proceeded to the middle of the stream, which at its deepest came almost to the bottom of the carriage. The horse trudged along steadily, but the Howes began to panic.

"Oh, no!" Mrs. Howe squealed as the carriage bumped a bit.

Mimi and Grace exchanged looks. The carriage wheel nicked a rock, and a slosh of water came up, splashing Maud's elbow.

"Oh, dear lord!" she screamed, grabbing her mother. "We'll drown, surely!"

"It's truly quite safe, I assure you," Grace said, trying to calm the screaming women.

Mrs. Howe began fanning herself as though she might faint. "We're going to die in this bayou!" she said, as she tried to pull her feet up into the seat of the carriage.

Grace pursed her lips. These squealing, screaming women were supposed to lead all women into the future? They couldn't even cross a creek without nearly fainting.

They finally finished the crossing, returned to town, and dropped off the Howes.

* * *

Dear Miss King,

We at the Pan Gnostics invite you to present a lecture at our meeting in the second week of April. Your thoughts on the current state of literature have been most interesting at our meetings of late, and we invite you to expand on this topic. We hope you accept this invitation, and we look forward to your response.

Sincerely,
M—

A few weeks after the carriage ride with the Howes, Grace surveyed the parlor one last time, having spent her morning cleaning and tidying the house. She kept the Pan Gnostics' invitation in her pocket and occasionally paused to reread the invitation.

"Grace?" called a weak voice from upstairs.

Grace sighed. "Yes, Nina?" she called, her patience wearing thin. Nina had gone back to bed that morning, claiming to be ill, but only after she'd realized it was cleaning day.

"Do you need help with the housework, still?"

"Actually, I could use some help..." Grace said, calling what she knew was Nina's bluff.

"Of course." She heard Nina's bed creak. "Oh, my. I'm so sorry, Sissy. I thought I could, but I'm just too weak."

Grace gritted her teeth in frustration. "Not to worry, Nina. I'll be fine."

Grace turned down the hall to head to the kitchen when Mimi swept in.

"Oh, Sis," she said happily. "We've been invited to the Howe's next reception!"

"That's nice," Grace said flatly.

"Oh, now, Sis, buck up," Mimi said. "I've ordered new hats for everyone, and we can make new dresses! Won't that be nice?"

"But," Grace said, panic starting in her chest. "But, Mimi, we can't afford that. We already owe more than we have coming in!"

"Yes, but we'll manage. We always do!" Mimi said, setting her things down on the hallway bench. "Where are your sisters?"

"Upstairs. Both have taken ill. On cleaning day," Grace added sourly.

"Oh no, poor things! I'll cheer them up with my news!" Mimi headed upstairs.

Grace sighed and went to the kitchen to clean. She swept and ran figures in her head. How were they to pay for these hats? They owed money to the grocer for last month's stocks, and she still needed to find a way to pay the pharmacist for his recent care for Will.

Branch came into the kitchen with heavy boots, leaving mud on the floor with every step.

"Sis, here's the money for the rent," he said, placing an envelope on the table.

She walked over, opened the envelope, and stopped. "Branch, this is only half."

"Yes, well, that's what I have."

"But...we need to pay the last two months' rent or we're going to be in trouble," Grace said.

"Then maybe you should get a job," Branch grumbled. "Or find some way to be useful here, without constantly nagging."

"Why, then who would clean the house? Manage the bills? Order the groceries? Air the laundry? Sew the clothes? And perhaps most importantly, who would make excuses to all the people to whom we owe money!" With each sentence, Grace's voice rose a notch in volume.

Mimi clattered down the stairs. "Grace Elizabeth King! What are you going on about?" she hissed.

"She's demanding more money," Branch said, glaring at Grace.

Grace opened her mouth to speak. "That's not—but I—"

"I can't believe you, Grace," Mimi said. "I thought I'd raised children who knew that money wasn't everything. Your brothers work hard to put food on the table and a roof over our heads!"

"But Mimi—" Grace began.

"No. You're wrong to berate Branch, and I won't stand for it in this house."

"Fine," Grace said, throwing her hands in the air. She walked down the hallway towards the front door. "Then maybe I shouldn't live in this house anymore."

"Sis!" called Nina from the stairs. "Did Mimi tell you? We're going to a reception at the Howe's, and we're to have new hats!" She practically jumped up and down on the stairs, smiling and giggling.

Grace turned away and slammed the door behind her. She spent the entire afternoon walking around New Orleans, alone.

* * *

Dearest, May—

Such a busy season we are having here, and I wish that you were here to share it with me. The other day, I had such a row with Branch. To make matters worse, Mimi took his side and rebuked me! I cook, clean, conduct social expectations—I even sew dresses and linens for the whole family! Nan is no help & goes almost catatonic for long periods of time while embroidering at a tediously slow rate—when she has not taken to bed during her monthlies, that is. Nina takes to her own bed for long spells then rises full of energy for half the day—noticeably after I've completed the day's chores. She now completely embodies the bossy youngest sister—she wants all of the privileges of adulthood but none of the responsibilities!

Mimi & her societies are never ending—she proposes new hats for everyone—but with what money? I was exhausted by it all when Branch came in & started on me. Without thinking, I responded sharply, & Mimi heard. After our row, I walked for hours, trying to find a resolution. I think I will have to ask Uncle Tom if I might come live with him—I don't know that I can survive in the house any longer.

However, in the darkness comes hope! I have been asked by the Pan Gnostics to speak at an upcoming meeting! I am terrified but ready! I have started the speech already—dabbling a little here and there. I will devote myself to it completely, but I will need to practice my speaking with a steady voice.

This could be my greatest accomplishment to date—or my most audacious failure.

Your ever affectionate sister-partner,
Sis

* * *

The Howes hosted many receptions at their temporary home in the city, and Grace frequently attended them. In introducing Grace to others, Maud continually referenced their water-crossing. She regaled her numerous male admirers with her tale of near-death-by-drowning as the young men gushed about her bravery.

One evening, they were gathered in the Howe's home for another reception. As Grace hesitated by the door of the parlor, Nan hurried up to her, her face white.

"Sissy," she hissed, pulling Grace to the side and half-clawing at her arm.

"Nannie," Grace said, scowling and taking Nan's hand off of her arm. "What's gotten into you?"

"Atwood is here," Nan said.

"Oh."

"And he's not alone."

Grace sighed, dejected at first. "Well," she said slowly, pulling her thoughts together. "That's fine. What am I going to do? Stay at home and sulk?" Grace stopped suddenly, realizing her error. Nan had been sulking for weeks after her own beau, a Yankee soldier, had suddenly been re-located to Montana just when their relationship began to become serious. Grace had wondered if Mimi had had anything to do with the sudden orders.

Nan opened her mouth to speak but shut it, as her eyes teared up.

"Oh, Nannie," Grace said. "I didn't mean anything by it!" Nan turned and walked briskly away.

Grace sighed deeply. She would talk to Nan later. For now, she needed to navigate the room as carefully as she could. Would it be possible to avoid Maud, her numerous suitors, and Atwood, too? But she had also heard that a powerful editor from the North was to attend the party, as well, and she had hoped to meet him. She hesitated in the doorway to the candle lit parlor, hearing Maud's higher-pitched voice telling her narrative again.

She stood to the side of Maud's adoring crowd and grew increasingly annoyed at the stupidity of it all, as with each retelling, the water rose higher, the carriage tipped more, and the horse grew older.

As she stepped back to attempt to slip away unnoticed, she bumped into someone behind her.

"Oh, I am sorry," she said, turning to see Fred's colleague, George Préot, right behind her.

"Quite all right," George said, reaching out a hand to steady Grace's elbow. "It was my fault completely. I was trying to..." George's words trailed off as his eyes glanced across the room. Grace followed his gaze and smiled. Amelie De Buys stood near a small table, chatting with another young woman. Amelie had always been kind to Grace, who had spent many an evening with the De Buys family at Amelie's invitations.

George cleared his throat and did his best to avoid eye contact with Grace. She liked George, and he had spent several dinners with the King family. Grace knew George sometimes missed his family in Virginia. She also knew that, like the King children, he was working to climb the social ladder.

"Mr. Préot," she said kindly. "Would you like me to introduce you to her? She's a friend of mine, you see. An old schoolmate."

George's face flushed, and he opened his mouth to speak, but no sound came out. He finally nodded.

Grace took George's arm and walked over to Amelie. "Amelie, my friend, it's been too long! You look absolutely lovely!" Amelie smiled and stepped forward to exchange kisses on the cheek with Grace. Amelie's other companion excused herself politely and joined another small group chatting nearby.

"And you! I hear you've been attending so many lectures lately! You always were so intellectual, my dear Grace," Amelie said, turning her eyes to George.

"Amelie, I'd like to introduce my dear friend, Mr. George Préot," Grace said, turning to George. "Mr. Préot studied law with Fred and has begun a wonderful career here in New Orleans. And Mr. Préot, this is my wonderful friend, Amelie De Buys, of the well-known De Buys family."

"It's wonderful to meet you, Mr. Préot," Amelie said, dropping into a curtsy that Grace noticed was just a bit lower than was necessary.

"And you, Miss De Buys," George said softly.

Seeing that George and Amelie kept their eyes on one another, Grace smiled mischievously. "Oh, I think I just saw my sister. Would you both excuse me?" And with that white lie, Grace slipped away, leaving them to chat.

No one noticed as Grace slipped through the doorway to escape to the side garden. She sat on the red brick edge of the flower beds and looked around her. People gathered in every corner inside, and the piano music drifted through the open windows and french doors. She could try to flirt with some of the beaux, which was what Mimi had encouraged her to do. But as she looked around, they were entranced with younger, more beautiful women than her. Their dresses showed them to be women of wealth and financial means—things Grace grudgingly lacked. And besides, she found most of their conversation bored her to tears.

She watched through the glass as two attractive men in their thirties spoke to a group of three young women. The ladies were in their late teens, and they listened, completely enraptured of whatever the men were saying. One woman put her hand over her mouth in shock, and her eyes opened wide. Another blushed fiercely, but she patted the arm of the man closest to her. The men tilted their heads this way and that, clearly on stage and enjoying the attention of the women. They reminded Grace of peacocks, all dolled up and tilting their heads at funny angles. *How would they react if one of the women challenged the young men's ideas? Or spoke at all?* Grace thought. It was all an act. Those girls. Their perfectly styled curls and hats and dresses—all a facade. But the men were too foolish to notice. Or perhaps they did notice but didn't care. It was a theatre put on just for them, wasn't it?

Many young women had been attending the sessions put on the Women's Department for the World's Fair. Grace had attended many of the lectures and intellectual gatherings, but what was the point in claiming the gatherings were intellectual exchanges, only to have all the women dressed to the nines to flirt? It had been such a farce, as far as she was concerned.

Grace sighed and looked around the small courtyard. It was getting late, and though she'd met a few interesting people, the night overall had been a bust. She sat her champagne glass on the nearest table and gathered her skirts to stand.

"Oh, I do hope you're not leaving just yet," said a middle aged man from the doorway. "I was just coming out to join you." He walked over and held out his hand. "I am Charles

Dudley Warner. And you, I am to understand, are Miss Grace King. Is that correct?"

"Yes, yes, I am," Grace said, as excitement fluttered quickly through her heart, her throat, and her head—all at once. Mr. Warner was the literary reviewer, critic, and editor from the north. This was not a man she needed to flirt with, but one she did need to court, in a sense.

"And I hear that you'll be speaking soon at the Pan Gnostic gathering. Care to share a preview with me?" he said, as he settled himself on a chair by the small table where Grace had set her glass. A sudden burst of squealing laughter erupted from the group she'd been watching earlier.

Mr. Warner glanced over at them. "Ah. Another flippant group with not much to say, I wager."

Grace huffed a small laugh of agreement.

"So, your talk. What will you discuss?"

"Literature," she replied. "Specifically, the role of the American heroine, and what makes her distinctly American."

"Well, well," Mr. Warner replied. "That sounds most interesting, my dear. I will try to be in attendance. Am I to understand that you have studied these last few years with Charles Gayarré, the historian?"

"Yes, sir, I have. Judge Gayarré has been like a second father to me for quite some time, actually."

"Might I call on you to introduce me? I would very much like to meet Mr. Gayarré," he said.

Grace laughed. "I would love to, but you must address him as Monsieur or Judge, rather than Mister."

"Truly? But this is an American city, is it not?" he said warmly.

"Indeed, but barely. And Judge Gayarré is of old honorable, Creole heritage, and so, he is Monsieur, not Mister," Grace explained. She softened her voice. "He would be deeply offended if addressed as Mister."

"Aha. You Southerners are an odd lot, but I do confess, I find your city beautiful and filled with inspiration. I can't wait for my wife to join me soon."

"She will be most welcome! Please do introduce us, so I can show her around," Grace offered, slightly disappointed at the word *wife*.

"Yes, I hear you give the most interesting tours of the countryside," he laughed.

"Well, yes, I do," she replied, slightly ruffled. "And maybe by then, the poor horse will have calmed down from all the Yankees screaming the other day and scaring it near half to death."

"Oh," Mr. Warner said, clearly amused. "You southern ladies with your fire! Absolutely wonderful. Might I call on you later this week?"

"Of course, Mr. Warner, I'm looking forward to it."

* * *

A few days later, Grace paced the length of the side gallery. She read and reread her speech, scratched things out, and rewrote the same sentences. The sun shone through the vines and flowers hanging down from the balcony and cast long shadows on the wooden planks of the house. She sat on a wicker chair only to rise and begin the whole process again.

"Hello, Miss King," called a voice from around the garden path. She glanced up to see George Préot entering the garden from the side of the house and making his way back to her.

"Why, hello, Mr. Préot. I wasn't expecting you today," she said. Grace nervously shuffled her papers and set them carefully under a book, so the breeze wouldn't send them flying.

As he stepped up onto the porch, George smiled and said, "I wanted to check on your progress for the lecture. But also," he paused, his face flushing a tiny bit. "To thank you."

"Ah," Grace said with a small smile. "You are most certainly welcome. I hope you and Amelie get on quite well."

He glanced at her stack of papers as she tried to hide the ink spots on her hands. "I hope you aren't fretting too much?"

"Well," Grace said hesitantly.

“My dear Miss King,” he said kindly, taking a seat at small table. “What assistance might I offer?”

“Might I read a few passages to you? I’m worried about the content. There will be so many more educated members than I...”

George smiled kindly. “Yes and no. I think you’ll find your own education quite extensive compared to most women. But, I am more than happy to serve as your practice audience.”

“Thank you, Mr. Préot. Why don’t I fetch some tea?”

* * *

A few weeks later, Grace stood in the front parlor at the weekly Pan Gnostics meeting, wringing her hands nervously and trying not to blot her papers. Members poured in and filled the rows of seats, chatting warmly with each other. Grace anxiously adjusted her skirts, a dark navy to set the tone of serious intellect that she wanted to convey.

“Miss King?” asked Mrs. Howe, gently taking her elbow. “How are you, my dear? You needn’t be nervous, I promise,” she added in a whisper.

Grace smiled as confidently as she could manage and started to speak. Mrs. Howe, however, took her elbow more firmly and steered them both into a quiet corner.

“I remember my first time speaking to an audience,” she said. “I was terrified,” she admitted, smiling. Suddenly, Grace liked her a bit more than before. “I was so nervous, my hands crushed my papers, and I had to give half of my speech from memory! And yet,” she paused dramatically. “I absolutely loved it. It was such a thrill,” she said, laughing quietly. “I knew right then and there that I was supposed to be a speaker, a person to represent others and help get their voices heard, too. And that’s why I’m here, remember. To get women’s voices heard. Your voice deserves to be heard, Grace. You are an uncommonly intelligent woman, and your ideas are well-founded and interesting. Now, go up there, read your words, and share that part of you with this audience.”

Grace smiled and nodded, momentarily speechless at Mrs. Howe's kindness. She suddenly felt a tiny bit guilty for her snark and bite towards the Howes and the Women's Department in general.

"Now, let me introduce you, my dear," Mrs. Howe said, walking to the narrow wooden podium at one end of the parlor.

"Welcome, all!" Mrs. Howe's voice suddenly boomed across the room. People scurried into seats, and the women waved small fans, which created a gentle fluttering around the room. "Today's speaker is the lovely Miss Grace King, who will speak about the most interesting topic of the American heroine!"

The audience clapped politely as Mrs. Howe and Grace traded positions. She arranged her papers on the podium and licked her lips. Her heart pounded in her chest and threatened to drown out her small voice. She felt weak and tiny and shifted her weight from foot-to-foot.

"Forgive me," she said with an embarrassed smile. A gentle wave of smiles swept across the room, and Grace slowly drew in an even breath, casting her eyes down at her paper. The words swam in blurry black marks, and she stared at them, willing the room to disappear into the walls around her. She remembered suddenly her father's voice: *Speak up, Sissy. Make yourself heard in the back of the room*. Mrs. Howe's words also came to her: *I'm here to make women like you heard. Speak up.*

Suddenly, a quiet sense of confidence settled into her chest, and she began to read.

Twenty minutes later, she was startled to hear applause. She had focused so heartily on reading her speech that she hadn't heard her own voice. Grace couldn't remember a thing, but the audience smiled, nodded, and clapped. She breathed a sigh of relief and walked away from the podium. A crowd of well-wishers gathered to congratulate her on the essay, and she felt such a wonderful buzzing in her heart. Pride? Happiness? Whatever it was, it was new—and she recognized that a weaker Grace had stepped up to the podium, but a new, stronger Grace had stepped down from it.

Chapter 13

Dear Ms. Mandin,

We have reviewed your proposal for the upcoming conference on Grace King, the very first devoted solely to King. We welcome your participation in this conference and happily invite you to present this November in Metz, France. We look forward to hearing your work this fall.
Sincerely,
B. Xaio

* * *

Dear Mr. Mandin,

Congratulations! Your application to Tennessee Valley State University's Master's in International Studies has been accepted. The university would like to offer you a full assistantship working for the department. Again, we congratulate you and look forward to working with you.
Sincerely,
A. Smirnov

* * *

Dear Ms. Mandin,

We would like to invite you to speak at Le Salon des Amis this November at our first salon meeting of the 90th year of the Salon. As you know, Grace King was our first president in 1924, and we would love to know more about her. Our previous president spoke quite highly of your research. We will hold a tea and reception following your presentation. As a polite reminder, our Salon is extremely private in order to respect the privacy of our esteemed members; as such, we ask that no photos or videos be taken while at the Salon nor any members' names shared. We look forward to meeting you this November in New Orleans.

Sincerely,
L.—

* * *

In early May, the magnolias sweated and swayed lazily on their dark, glossy leaves all around the campus. Meredith walked into the writing center, brushing away the thin layer of sweat on her forehead. She set her things on the shelf in the corner and walked to the reception desk to check the schedule as usual, but it boasted mostly empty appointment slots. Meredith sat at the communal table and took out a laptop to work on her own projects.

David, another grad student, came in and joined her.

"Slow day today, huh?" he said, propping his feet on another chair.

"Looks like it," Meredith replied. Mallory walked in to join them, as well, setting down her own bag.

"Good morning," Mallory said, grinning. Mallory had returned to grad school in her fifties and was a bit ahead of Meredith in the program.

"So, I'm taking over editing the school journal, and I noticed we don't have any submissions from you, Meredith," David said.

"Yeah, I don't really have anything ready," she said. The other grad students had become increasingly competitive, and the idea of competing for inclusion in the journal made Meredith's stomach lurch.

"She thinks she's too good for our journal, don't you, Meredith?" Mallory said with a teasing smile.

"No, not at all," Meredith replied, returning back to her laptop screen. She had begun drafting the presentation for the France conference scheduled for this coming fall.

Dr. Jones swept into the center, her arms loaded with tote bags and books. "Good morning, everyone!" She called, as she unlocked her office in the corner. "Meredith? Could I ask you to run the reports? If anyone hasn't completed theirs, kindly let them know, so they can do so. I'd like to have the reports done before everyone leaves for the summer!"

"Sure thing, Dr. Jones," Meredith said, grateful for an excuse to leave the table and work on something else—away from chatting. With her father's trial pending, Meredith had begun isolating herself even more—trying to keep the personal away from the professional. Each thing in its tidy little box.

Meredith sat a computer on the other side of a partition from the tutoring table and began running reports on the tutoring sessions for the whole semester.

As she printed out the list of entries that were missing for each tutor, she overheard Mallory.

"Someone's getting a little too important for us little people."

"You think?" David responded, confused.

"Pff, yeah," Mallory retorted. "You ever notice that whatever position Meredith wants, Meredith gets? The admin just gives her whatever, while the rest of us plow away in the fields."

Meredith's face grew warm. That's what the other grad students really thought? She cleared her voice as she walked around the corner shuffling the papers back into order.

"Here are your incomplete reports, guys," Meredith said, making a point of avoiding Mallory's eyes and smiling through gritted teeth.

"Not me. I didn't miss a single report this semester," said Mallory, sitting back in her chair and crossing her arms over her chest.

Meredith handed a sheet to David and set another down for Mallory. "Looks like just one or two. Not a big deal at all, but it would help the writing center if you would take a look and jot a note or two, in case it's needed later," Meredith said. "I've got one to take care of, too. Thanks!" She turned and sat back down at the computer on the other side of the partition.

She heard Mallory scoff, just as Reagan walked in. Meredith smiled. "Morning, Reagan! I hear you passed all of your exams! Congrats!"

"Thanks," Reagan said, sitting down beside Meredith. "I need to talk to Dr. Jones, but she looks like she's busy."

Meredith glanced over just as Mallory entered Dr. Jones's office and closed the door.

"I'm sure she'll be free in a minute," Meredith said, trying to ignore what she knew had to be a complaint about her. "You doing okay?"

Reagan sat down beside Meredith. "Not really."

"What's going on? That is, if you want to talk. If not, that's okay, too," Meredith said.

"I'm not too thrilled about coming back to the writing center," Reagan said quietly. "I hate the chaotic schedule. Sets my bipolarness on edge, since I can't ever tell if I'm going to be working with people or not. Predictable routine is a major thing for me."

"I see," Meredith said. "So, lack of predictability causes additional stress?"

"Yeah. I've finally got my meds straightened out, for the most part, and I'm afraid of what might throw that off."

"Got it." Meredith thought for a minute. The admins viewed grad students tutoring as an introductory stage to teaching, giving them time to adjust to the program and rigor of their own classes or to focus on their own studies without the added pressure of teaching a full class. Tutoring was also an option when teaching became too heavy a workload. But the grad students often saw tutoring as childish—as though the assignment was a punishment for remedial teaching abilities. Meredith noticed that no amount of explanation seemed to ease this stigma, and grad students often fought against being assigned to the writing center. "What if there were a middle ground?" she asked.

"What do you mean?"

"Well, the writing center sometimes does those studio classes, remember? Where we pair a tutor with a small group to review mechanics and grammar? So, like a mini-class. They're scheduled, so they'd be predictable for your needs, but it would still meet the admin's needs for tutors, too."

"That's actually a really good idea," said Reagan slowly. "I hadn't thought of that. Thank you!"

"Let's talk to Dr. Jones, and see what she thinks," Meredith suggested, just as Dr. Jones's door opened, and Mallory returned to the table with David.

"Dr. Jones," Meredith said from the doorway. "I think we may have found a nice solution for those studios for next semester." She nodded to Reagan, who stood beside her.

"Oh, good. Reagan, come on in," Dr. Jones said.

Meredith closed the door softly and returned to her computer. She kept an eye on the clock, since today was a Mother's Day party for Lila's class. Lila had been giving them some trouble lately, fighting with Emmy and slamming doors. Meredith was afraid that the events with Gayle had upset her.

Minutes later, Reagan left Dr. Jones's office, gave Meredith a thumbs up, and headed out of the center.

"Meredith?" Dr. Jones called. "Could I see you a minute?"

Meredith stood and entered Dr. Jones's office, closing the door softly behind her. "Everything okay?"

Dr. Jones smiled. "Well, Mallory has a problem with another grad student being in a position of management over another, so I think I will relieve you of running the reports."

"But," Meredith said, confused. "Last semester, an MA student ran the reports, and that was fine. An undergrad ran them, too, just a few weeks ago. I'm confused."

"Look, she's clearly just got a thing against you. And I don't want you to have to deal with her..." Dr. Jones said kindly.

Meredith opened her mouth to speak, then shut it. *Mallory is going to think she won this.* Swallowing her words, Meredith smiled. "Whatever you think. No problem."

"Thanks, Meredith."

When she left the office, Mallory smiled overly sweetly from her corner of the center, like a cat licking cream from its whiskers. Meredith spent the rest of her shift working on her own projects and avoiding Mallory, who wore a pasted-on smirk.

After her shift was over, Meredith headed up to her corner on the fourth floor to do a little bit of work before she headed to Lila's school. She opened her laptop and notes to begin organizing for the Salon speech.

She had read that in the late 1800s and early 1900s, the ladies of New Orleans often replicated the old French fashion of a "reception day". Salon days are quite similar, but they were by invitation only. Salons were intellectual clubs where members could exchange projects of interest, invite speakers, or chat about whatever topic interests them. Le Salon des Amis, in New Orleans, had no webpage or web presence beyond a few articles written by historians catalogued in obscure pdf files. No pictures were allowed to be taken of the interior, and the members respected each other's privacy to the utmost level. Men were not allowed to attend the weekly meetings.

Meredith felt goosebumps on her arms at the idea of just being in the same space—the very rooms!—where Grace had once spent time. She wondered if Grace had felt nervous when she first stood up to speak, like she did. Grace's own career didn't begin until her thirties, giving Meredith some reassurance that there was still time for her. To do what, though? To teach? To write?

She pursed her lips. How could she even be wasting time thinking about writing? Her children needed her, and her husband needed her.

She sighed. She wouldn't even know what to write *about,* anyway. Meredith turned back to her laptop and began typing. Academics were safer. Controlled. It stayed in its nice, neat box, no matter what chaos swirled around it.

* * *

Two hours later, Meredith sat in her car in the elementary school parking lot, enjoying the quiet and stillness before heading in to a chaotic classroom.

Sighing, Meredith turned off the car and went inside. She picked up her name tag at the school office, where a gaggle of other mothers stood. Meredith had never felt she fit in with the other mothers. They always seemed to have this parenting-thing down; whereas she felt she was flying by the seat of her pants almost every day. Each mother received a pink carnation. Meredith smiled gently—and awkwardly. She walked to Lila's classroom, looking at the hand drawn pictures and projects posted to the walls.

Inside the classroom, she waved to Lila, who was arranging something at a table in the back of the classroom. Lila smiled but didn't come over to say hello.

Meredith stood uneasily, unsure of where she should be and what she should be doing, so she walked slowly around the classroom, looking at the artwork on the walls.

Lila's teacher, Mrs. Neill, clapped her hands. "Okay, boys and girls, let's get these wonderful mothers a treat and sit down at our desks!"

Meredith found Lila's desk and sat down. Lila joined her with a small plate of cookies. "Hi, Mom," she said, sitting the plate on the desk. "I'll get us juice!" As Lila bounded off in a different direction, Meredith scanned the desks and noticed that every other child's desk had a packet of papers on it—but Lila's was empty. The other mothers smiled, laughed, and shared the booklets' contents with each other, while Meredith shifted uncomfortably in her seat. Did Lila lose her packet? Was she shy about sharing it?

Meredith glanced inside the desk and saw a jumble of wadded up papers and pencils sans erasers. She thought she spied a little piece of the ribbons that she saw bound the other books, but she left it inside.

Lila returned and sat the Dixie cups of red juice on the desk. "Hi, sweetheart," Meredith said. "How's your day?"

"Good," Lila said, sitting down on the other side of the desk, where an extra chair had been placed.

Mrs. Neill clapped her hands in a rhythm, and the children clapped their answer. "Very nice job, boys and girls. Now, let's start our Mothers' Day program! First, Sarah has a lovely poem about her stepmother. Sarah?"

Meredith smiled kindly and listened to most of the children recite lovely poems or stories about their mothers. Lila listened patiently while she needled the petals off of the carnation. The mother next to her, holding her own carefully decorated packet, glanced at Meredith's empty hands and torn up carnation and then up to meet Meredith's eyes.

Meredith smiled and shrugged. "Kids," she whispered, with a fake laugh.

The woman smiled sadly and turned away.

Don't cry. Don't cry.

The children's program continued for another twenty minutes before Meredith could politely escape to the solitude of the car. Lila had said barely two words to her during the entire event. Meredith had barely closed the door before a sob broke out. *Lila hates me*, she thought, as another sob thumped in her chest and tightened in her throat.

She breathed in slowly through her nose, trying to calm down. She put the car into drive and slowly left the parking lot, feeling silent tears slipping down her cheeks.

* * *

A few weeks later, Meredith walked through the empty rooms in their Clarksville home. Liam was tying down the last boxes in the moving truck, and the girls were outside playing in the driveway. Liam had finished his bachelor's degree and had accepted a position at Tennessee Valley State, so they had decided to move closer to the university. Renters would be moving into their home in a few weeks.

Meredith stepped into the kitchen, which she'd recently painted dark taupe with white cabinets. Liam had hand-laid new slate tile floor, which gleamed under the new stainless steel refrigerator and small dishwasher. She walked into the empty living room and looked over the taupe walls here, too. The room had a big picture window where their great dane used to sit on the couch and people watch. He had passed away awhile back from old age and cancer. She walked slowly down the hallway to Emmy's blue and white room. It had been

Meredith's office before Emmy was born. Meredith used to sit at the black desk, reading Chaucer at midnight while working on her master's degree while Liam was deployed to Afghanistan.

Across the hall from Emmy's room was the bathroom. It was white with teal tile from decades before and emitted memories of kids, bubbles, and bath time. Their dog always jumped out of the tub and ran down the hallway, slinging water over everything. At the end of the hallway, Lila's room had also been recently painted taupe to cover the purple paint. She glanced inside, thinking about the gauze canopy and soft quilts that had filled it just a few days before.

She smiled gently and turned to her and Liam's room. It had received the same paint, as had the tiny bathroom. She walked inside it, glancing at the tiny shower. Meredith thought she had miscarried there while pregnant with Emmy. She looked through the small window into the backyard. Their dane's ashes had been scattered around his favorite napping places in the backyard, where her irises were large and blooming a glorious purple.

This place was safe. She and Lila had felt safe there during Liam's deployments. They'd been safe through every tornado watch and even the great springtime floods. This simple brick ranch home was *her home.*

And she had to leave it all behind.

Meredith walked back through the house toward the driveway. Liam stood in the dining room, performing his own walk of memories. They looked at each and smiled sadly.

"It's a good thing," he said. "This house served us well, but it's time."

Meredith nodded. "I know. But it was comforting to be here for so long. It felt safe. And now we're leaving that safety behind."

He opened his arms for her, and she snuggled into his embrace. "I know. But I'm here. We're together. 'Home' is here," he added, squeezing gently.

"It's going to be a long night. A two hour drive, then unloading, and getting the kids settled in at some point. Oh, my God," she breathed, feeling the weight of the next day of activities pressing down on her.

"Nah, we've done it before. It'll be okay," he said, squeezing her shoulders. "You know, we could always..."

"We're not selling everything to go live on a sailboat!" she said, wiping a few tears from her cheek.

"Okay. Well, then, we better get going. You sure you got the girls okay for the drive?"

"Yeah, we'll be fine. You'll be okay in the moving truck?"

He nodded and tilted her chin up to meet his before planting a soft kiss on her lips. "Ready?" He hugged her one last time in their home. One more moment of stillness before the hours of chaos.

She nodded silently, and they walked together out of their home, loaded the girls into their seats, and set out for the drive.

Chapter 14

New Orleans

Grace was still flying on the success of her paper when she and Branch attended a Pickwick Club dinner a few days later, their brawls set aside for public events. Branch escorted her into the hall for the dinner. They had been trying to get on better for Mimi's sake. Grace's suggestion that she move out had deeply upset Mimi so much that she'd wept for days, finally taking to her bed. The idea had been abandoned. For now.

Branch glanced into the parlor, and Grace noticed that his eyes lingered for a moment on a woman talking to a group of young men by the piano.

"Ah, I see *you* have goals for this evening," Grace said.

Branch smiled slowly and nodded. "I might. Might you excuse me, my dear little sister?"

"Indeed," Grace said in a flat tone. She turned to begin a slow walk of the gallery, nodding her head at various acquaintances as she did so. Before long, they were seated at the dining table. Mr. Richard Watson Gilder, a well-known editor, sat to Grace's left. She had hoped meeting Gilder might lead to a publishing opportunity, since Gilder had first published George Washington Cable, another local writer. They exchanged pleasantries as the hors d'oeuvres and light dishes were served, with Grace carefully playing her role as warm and welcoming southern Lady.

When the main plates arrived, Mr. Gilder turned to Grace and said, "Well, Miss King, I do confess I have had a distaste for the South ever since the War."

"Oh, Mr. Gilder, I am sorry to hear that. I do hope that your experiences on this journey are quickly changing your mind," she answered with a smile that she hoped hid the unease she felt creeping into the conversation.

"I'm not sure it could, to be quite honest, Miss King," he said. "You see, my brother-in-law was a Union soldier killed during the Civil War. During his funeral procession here in New Orleans, a New Orleanian woman laughed as the coffin was walked past her balcony. I mean, can you imagine such a dreadful act? Laughing at a man's death? Anyway, the soldiers responded to her after the funeral, so I'm told, but still. Such a deplorable act," he said, turning to address the blackened shrimp on his plate.

Grace stared at him with her mouth rudely open for an instant. She clamped it shut. *Do not lose your head,* she tried to calm herself. She tensed and released her shoulders multiple times, trying to force her voice into gentle evenness before finally speaking.

"Mr. Gilder," Grace said, forcing honey to ooze from her words. "I do believe you have only heard one side of this story. You see, the lady in question and her tale are quite famous here in New Orleans. She did not, in truth, laugh at the funeral, but at a small child dancing on their gallery. She meant no disrespect to the deceased at all." Grace paused for a moment before finishing the tale. "The lady was arrested that night and sent to Ship Island for imprisonment, with no trial. No one has heard from her since. All because she laughed at the wrong moment."

Grace braced herself for his angry retort, but part of her didn't care anyway. How could a man be so blind and deaf as to listen to only one side of a story? She turned to her own shrimp and delicately sliced a prawn into smaller pieces before lifting a single, tiny piece on her gracefully held fork to her mouth.

Mr. Gilder stopped his fork halfway to his mouth and stared at his plate with his mouth hanging open in shock. He returned the fork to the plate and carefully cleared his throat. As they finished the main course and a sweet dessert, they managed to stay on more polite topics. Coffee was served to the women as the men took brandy and cigars in the adjoining study.

Before long, Grace stood outside on the cobblestone walkway, waiting for a small group of walkers to form. They were to walk from the club around the neighborhood, delivering each member to their home. Branch joined her.

"I've heard some mention of tension between you and Gilder," he said softly under his breath. "Do be careful, Sis."

She started to answer him when Mr. Gilder joined their small party. "I am staying nearby, as well, and thought to walk with you," he said to the group, before his eyes landed on Grace.

As the group departed and fell into pairs on the walk, Grace found herself side-by-side with Mr. Gilder, much to her dismay. She had hoped meeting Gilder would lead to publishing opportunities, but once again, her hopes were crumbling.

"So, tell me your thoughts on my favorite southern writer, George Washington Cable," he said, focusing on their shared interest of literature.

Grace thought for a moment. To play the part of gentle acquiescence? Or to speak her mind? She released the breath she'd been holding. "I'm afraid Mr. Cable has not studied the full range of his subject," she said as politely and simply as she could. She noticed that several of the walkers around them had stopped their conversation and were listening in on theirs.

Mr. Gilder's breath hitched and his shoulders tensed. "How so?" As he was Cable's editor, Grace knew she had struck another punch.

"I'm afraid Mr. Cable has conflated the definition of what it means to be Creole," she explained. "He seems to think that all Creoles are of mixed racial descent, but this is false and quite misrepresentative of some Creole families. He also seems to be under the false impression that all Black women are young, beautiful, and exist purely to be desired by white men."

"Amen," muttered Branch. Grace had not realized that her voice had carried so far.

"Why," Gilder said, turning away. "If Cable is so false to you, why don't some of you write better and tell your own stories?"

Grace was speechless. She walked a few steps as the old energy filled her again. Her fingers itched, and her heart pounded. This time, however, was different; the energy combined with her temper and spilled over.

"Mr. Gilder, I do believe we may finally have found something we agree upon."

* * *

Grace sipped her coffee the next morning at the breakfast table, thinking.

"Grace, you are very quiet this morning," Nan said over her own coffee. A plate of warm bread sat in between them, and Nan reached for the jam jar. "Are you feeling well?"

"Yes, I am. Just thoughtful this morning." That familiar buzzing energy warmed Grace's body, tingling in her fingers and arms. This morning, though, for the first time, the energy felt controlled–focused. Grace stood, picked up her cup, and left the room.

"Grace?" She heard Nan calling behind her.

Without answering, Grace walked upstairs to her room and stood for a moment. *No. Someone will come to bother me here*, she thought.

She walked to the hallway and to the attic door. There. It wouldn't be too hot there just yet, and an old desk stood vigil in one corner. She gathered paper, pen, and ink and climbed the narrow stairs. Grace swept the dust quickly from the desk, sneezing as she opened the small windows. They were more for ventilation than an actual breeze.

Finally, she settled in. She would create a story to show the love and familial bonds between White and Black women. But how to start? Her old school, the Institut St. Louis, would make a good locale, and then she could base the setting around something with which she was familiar.

A quadroon named Marcelite had been the hairdresser at the school, and Grace remembered her fondly. The girls who boarded at the school had loved her deeply. Perhaps she could be her first character. She remembered Marcelite's warm smile and yellow tignon.

Grace lifted the pen, dipped the tip in ink, and immediately blotted the corner of the page. Her hand shook with nervousness as she began writing,

It was near mid-day in June. A dazzling stream of vertical sun-rays fell into the quadrangular courtyard of the Institute St. Denis.

Marcelite could always manage her own affairs without the assistance of anyone...

She scribbled away for hours, until the light began to fade in her writer's nest. She looked up, surprised to see the setting sun through the window. Her first creative work lay on the desk: "Monsieur Motte."

* * *

For weeks, Grace spent her afternoons writing on the side gallery, where the shade and soft breezes were more tolerable than the attic. Though she had written the story, she would need to find a *nom de plume*, as she didn't wish to embarrass Mimi or become the family eccentric. *A woman writer!* As she scratched out a sentence and rewrote it below the scribbles, a *halloo* called from the garden gate.

"Yes?" she said without lifting her eyes from the paper.

"Hello," called a man's voice. Grace looked up to see George Préot approaching. "Miss King," he said. "I'm glad to find you at home."

"Mr. Préot, how lovely to see you again. I've heard you've been doing some writing for the local paper of late. How are you finding it?"

"Well, I've come to ask you about the essay you read at the Pan Gnostics meeting not too long ago. I think it was quite well done, and I wonder if you'd be interested in publishing it in the paper."

"Oh." Grace lost her words for a moment. *A publication!* But—"But I'm afraid publishing under my name might not be..."

Mr. Préot smiled gently. "We can use your initials, perhaps. Or maybe 'P.G.' for Pan Gnostics?"

Grace frowned in careful consideration. "Yes, that would be nice, I think. And you think it might be well-received? Really?"

"I do. And might I ask, are you working on another project?" His eyes looked to her scratched and ink-blotted pages.

Grace hesitated but then sighed. "Yes, but I'm afraid the writing here is stunted. I have a story, I believe, but what I need is better description, less sentimentality."

"May I?" He gestured a hand toward the discarded pages on the porch floor. Grace nodded. He picked a few pages and scanned his eyes over them. "Not bad, Miss King."

"Well, thank you, but those pages were terrible..."

"I might disagree. You see this passage?" He held the page at an angle. "This passage could easily be expanded to allow for more description of the setting, as is the current trend."

"Oh. I see what you're saying. And if I do that, I could introduce my character earlier," Grace mumbled, taking the sheet from his hand. "By the by," she added. "How are things with Amelie?" She cast a quick glance up and back at the page in her hand.

George cleared his throat. "Quite well. I can't thank you enough for introducing us. Miss King," he said, hesitating. "I see in you the beginning of a fine writer, and New Orleans needs to foster her writers. Might I offer my services as editor, critic, and friend? No strings attached. No fees, no obligations," he said. "You needn't publish with the *Times* if you choose not to. I only wish to help you begin publishing. The World's Fair has shown us that in other cities, the mentorship of burgeoning writers is more pronounced. But here, we have failed to do so. I'd like to change that, and I find in you and your voice a uniqueness that is distinctly New

Orleanian. And without your kindness...I might not have met Amelie. I'd like to return that kindness, if I may."

Grace sat back in her chair, surprised. She opened and closed her mouth several times before finding words. "Mr. Préot, I cannot thank you enough for such compliments. I'm not sure I have earned them, in earnest, but if you feel I might be able to strengthen myself as a writer, then I welcome your guidance."

Mr. Préot smiled warmly and sat on the gallery steps. "Wonderful! Well, then. Would you share with me the premise of the story?"

They spent the afternoon discussing "Monsieur Motte," how the devoted quadroon hair dresser, Marcelite, cares so deeply for her mistress's daughter, Marie Modeste, that even after the girl's mother dies, Marcelite finds a way to care for and raise the girl to be a proper lady in society. Mr. Préot congratulated Grace's plot and characters.

Months of revisions later, Grace stood outside Mr. Hawkins' small neighborhood grocery store. She held the carefully wrapped manuscript clutched to her chest, too afraid to release it. She had decided to send it through Mr. Hawkins' store to avoid any questions her family may ask about a sudden parcel of this size. She wasn't ready to face the world—or the Kings. If the story was a failure, it would be hers alone. She would not have to share her pain or show her dashed hopes. She had addressed it to Mr. Gilder, since his words were her impetus, and she thought she might have the best chance of publication through him.

Except he would probably hate it. He'd probably laugh it off as a meager little attempt from some simple southern girl before tossing it in the fireplace. This was silly. No one would ever *want to read* her writing, would they? *No*, she assured herself. This was a lovely distraction for a few months, but that's all it was.

Grace turned to leave the corner and head home, still clutching her manuscript. As she walked, she noticed a young woman out of the corner of her eye.

"Miss King?" she said shyly.

Grace paused and looked over. "Yes?"

"Hello, I'm Adele, a cousin of Amelie's," she said, her face turning a bit red. "I wanted...I wanted to tell you that I really loved the article in the paper, the one you wrote awhile back—"

"Oh, I didn't—" Grace started. She had followed George's advice and simply put "P.G." on the article, to protect her reputation.

"Oh, I know," Adele said, with a conspiratorial smile. "I loved it so much that Amelie confided that her friend had written it. She said I mustn't tell anyone else, though, and I won't! I promise! But I saw you, and I just had to tell you that I loved it, and so did my friends!"

"Thank you, Adele," Grace said. "That's very kind."

Adele smiled, gave a tiny wave, and shuffled off down the street, glancing back every now and then as though she wanted to say more but was too timid.

Grace stood still for a moment, tapping her finger along the edge of the parcel. Finally, she sighed and went inside the store to place the parcel in the outgoing mail basket.

* * *

That fall, Grace walked alongside the river on the levee, enjoying the breeze and the quiet. Birds and seagulls squawked overhead, but she had left all conversation in the house behind her. The story was returned to Mr. Hawkins, without a single comment on it or even a note to show it had been read. Unopened and rejected. Unexamined and still unwanted. *If there was ever a metaphor for an unmarried woman in the South, this is it,* she thought. Tears threatened to fall, but she brushed them hastily away. In the distance, other walkers enjoyed the levee, but here, at least, she could be alone in the crowd.

She walked slowly on, alternating looking over the sun reflecting off the wide river to her left and the rooftops and cityscape to her right. She approached a small gathering of people and quietly navigated around it.

"Miss King?" asked a man's voice.

She looked up to see George. "Do excuse me," he said to the men with whom he was chatting.

"Hello, Mr. Préot, it's nice to see you."

"And you, Miss King. Any word from Gilder?"

"I'm afraid so," she admitted.

"Aha. Read or unopened?"

"The latter."

He nodded thoughtfully. "Might I walk with you for a bit?"

Grace gave a single nod of her head. They fell into step, side-by-side, as the river breeze pushed against them.

"Miss King, would you consider sending the story to another reader?"

"I'm not sure it's worth all that," she said, dejected.

"But I am. Truly, Miss King. I think you have the makings of a fine writer. At least consider sending it to Charles Dudley Warner. He will be true and honest with you."

Grace pursed her lips in thought as a gust of wind swept over the river and pushed against her, almost knocking her from the path.

Mr. Préot took her elbow to steady her. "Look, even the Great Mother River wants you to do this," he said, laughing.

Grace regained her footing and smiled shakily. She sighed. "I will try one more time and send the story to Warner. But if he, too, returns it, I will know that I am not meant to be a writer."

"I will still disagree, but I will respect your decision," George answered.

"Thank you. And now, I should turn back and begin my trek home. Do come by for tea this afternoon. Branch will be there, and I know he'd enjoy your company." Grace turned and began to retrace her steps.

"I would be happy to," he said. "Enjoy your walk, Miss King!"

* * *

Grace stood by the front door, holding the manuscript in her hand. She tied and untied the twine from the package.

"Sissy?" Nan called from the top of the stairs. "What are you doing?"

Grace paused. "Preparing to mail a package. That's all. To May," she lied. She'd decided the little deception was easier than her previous plan.

"Oh, well the post should come any time, so you better hurry," Nan said as she descended and walked into the front parlor. "And Will should be home soon, too."

Grace sighed and set the manuscript back on the table with the other outgoing items. The front door opened and both her brother and the postman stood on the porch.

"Ah! Grace!" Will said, a bit too loudly. Grace could smell the sickly sweet scent of bourbon. Will walked into the parlor to join Nan, leaving Grace staring pink-faced at the postman.

"Um, I do...apologize," she began, her face burning.

"No apologies needed, Miss," he said kindly. "Here you go." He handed her a small stack of cards and parcels. "Anything to send?"

Grace set down the letters and handed over the outgoing packages—all but one. She held the manuscript in her hand, neatly wrapped and addressed. In the parlor, Will was telling one story after another, his voice too loud and his words slurred. Grace hoped this show was in celebration of a promotion Will had been expecting. Though Fred and Branch earned an income, it was difficult for so many people to live on such small sums. Will had started working, too, but his income had yet to stabilize.

"Miss?"

"Oh, sorry," she murmured. She handed him the parcel.

"Thank you." He nodded as he placed the package into his satchel. "Good day, Miss," he said as he waved from the porch and walked away.

Grace sighed and walked into the parlor to join the others. She sat in the chair closest to the door and farthest away from Will.

"Did you hear about the promotion yet?" she asked. Will turned to look at her and clamped his mouth shut. His forehead was damp and flushed. A silence settled over the room.

Mimi sat on the sofa beside Will. “Now, Grace, we don’t need to talk about that right now,” she said softly. She gave Grace a pointed look. Grace stared back at her mother. What had happened to the Mimi who had led them through the swamps? But Mimi had always acquiesced to the men in the family, even when they were wrong. Why else had they made so many bad financial decisions since the war?

“I turned it down,” Will said, staring at nothing.

“What?” Grace asked, leaning forward. A white rage washed over her. “Why?” She managed to croak.

“Because they weren’t going to pay me what I wanted.”

“Was it still a raise in pay? Was it still a promotion in rank?”

He paused and swallowed hard. “Yes. But I didn’t want to agree to their conditions...”

They all sat in silence for a moment. Mimi’s face was white, and Nan looked panicked.

“You mean to tell us,” Grace said, quiet anger boiling through her words. “That you had a promotion and pay raise offered to you, and you declined it? Because it wasn’t exactly what you wanted?”

“You don’t know!” Will lashed out angrily. “You don’t know how hard it is! Working every day and having no time to spend doing what you want! You get to read and go to your foolish group meetings, while I toil at a desk! Why? Because I am a man, so I am supposed to provide for everyone! But what about what I want!"

“Do you not see that your advancement is all of our advancement?” Grace growled at him. “Not everything in life is about you! You are allowed in the work force! We,” she gestured to Mimi, Nan, and Nina, “are not! And what if you marry? Or have children? How can three men possibly support so many families?” Mimi began crying and shook her head.

Will’s face turned a darker shade of red. “How dare you! You stupid old spinster! You had one job: To marry some rich bastard! And you couldn’t even do that. I have to support you because you couldn't find a husband to do it! And no wonder! Who would want to be married to such a—"

"Will, you are an adult. Start acting like it!" Grace screamed back. She stood up, her heart racing.

Will stood to face her. His face had turned a mottled color of red and white, and he took a step as if to reach for Grace across the coffee table. Instead, he staggered, tripped, and fell. Mimi jumped up and ran to him. He rolled over to his side and snored loudly. He had passed out.

Mimi looked up angrily at Grace.

"Grace, you can't—"

"Why not? Look at him. He's a drunkard. And an angry one at that. And do you know what came in the mail yesterday? Another bill. For the money *he* owes!"

"You cannot talk to your brother this way," she replied. "Men are—"

"Weak," Grace responded. "And catering to this, telling them failing is okay, is unrealistic! It's not okay. People's lives depend on them. They've decided that women should stay home and shouldn't work outside of it, and yet, they fail to provide for us to do so. We are trapped."

"But our men provide for us. Their prides are sensitive, and we must build them up gently," Mimi explained.

"They aren't children. Do they not live in the same harsh reality we do? Why is it okay for him to drink and curse and waste money and put us into debt, but not me? What if it were me sprawled drunk on the parlor floor in the middle of the afternoon? Would you caress my face and treat me like a child?"

Mimi glared back. "You know the answer to that."

"You're right. I do. Because I'm an adult."

Grace stormed out of the parlor and slammed the front door behind her. She walked the city and rode the streetcars for hours to clear her head, dreading opening the front door when she returned home.

* * *

Months went by with no word about her manuscript. In December, Grace decorated the parlor for Christmas, tying red ribbons in neat bows above the mantle. Nan walked in with a letter in her hand.

"Sissy, there's a letter in the post for you," she said.

Grace took the letter from Nan's hand, curious. She perched on the wingback chair nearest her and slowly, painstakingly opened the envelope. Inside was a note from a Mr. William Sloane:

Dear Miss King,

I have recently acquired your story "Monsieur Motte" from Mr. Charles Dudley Warner and wish to publish it in the first issue of the New Princeton Review. *Please accept this payment of one hundred and fifty dollars, as well as my request that you continue to write. We would very much welcome a continuation of this lovely narrative.*

Yours most sincerely,
Mr. William Sloane

"One hundred and fifty dollars," Grace whispered slowly. "Nan, they bought it! *For one hundred and fifty dollars!*"

"Bought what?" Nan asked.

"My story! I wrote a story, Nan! And an editor bought it!" Grace said, a grin spreading across her face.

Nan squealed and pulled Grace to her feet. She wrapped her in a hug and danced in a circle, laughing loudly. Nan ran to the stairs and shouted up. "Grace is published! She's a writer!"

Grace read and reread the letter, looking at the check still clutched in her hand. Everyone was shocked to hear of her success, and Grace felt all the more proud for her big reveal.

"What will you buy, Grace?" asked Nina. "A new dress? Books?"

Grace thought for a moment. She gazed around the room and over each of her sisters. "Fabric," she said simply. "We need fabric for dresses, and I'll do the sewing myself, for the most part. We also need a few other household supplies. The money will go to supporting us, as a family. We owe several months of bills to the grocer. And Mimi. I want to pay for Mimi to visit May. She's been wanting to for so very long!"

Nan said, "And they say that literature doesn't pay! Can I help select the fabric?"

Grace returned her smile. "Of course!"

Nina frowned for a moment. "But, Sis, you can't...did you use a *nom de plume*, at least?"

Grace sighed. "Yes. Though the letter I sent had my real name, the manuscript was left unsigned. They aren't to publish my real name."

Nina nodded. "Good, then. Some of us are still hoping to marry well," she muttered.

In the middle of their celebration, Will stumbled into the parlor.

"Well, here I thought I'd left the party behind at the club, but it turns out, it's right here," he said, his words slow and slightly slurred.

Grace stood back and stared at her younger brother. She pushed her shoulders back and glared at him with her intense gaze.

"Yes," said Nina excitedly. "Grace has sold a story! She's a writer now!"

Will stared back at her. "Is that so? Well, then, now you can support the whole family, since I've proved such a disappointment to you."

Grace sighed heavily. "Maybe I will," she returned. "Maybe that's what we need. Fred and Branch have found careers, but you...you just drink away everyone relying on you. Maybe I will become the breadwinner in this household."

"You are nothing but an old bookish spinster," Will laughed. "Men don't want to marry women like you."

No one corrected him. Grace pressed her lips firmly shut and walked from the room.

She clutched Mr. Sloane's letter in her tight fist, taking deep breaths to calm her nerves and stop the tears threatening her eyes.

No matter what Will said, or how Nina had reacted, Grace had finally become a writer.

Chapter 15

Meredith pulled her battered suitcase out from under the bed and set it on top. She opened the flap and looked over her small pile of clothes to be folded and packed. It was October, which meant warm days and slightly cool nights in Tennessee, but tomorrow afternoon, she would be on a flight to Europe for the conference on Grace King.

She set aside a comfortable sweater dress and leggings for the flight and turned back to the pile just as a squealing Lila and Emmy ran into the room and jumped on the pile.

"Girls!" Meredith started to scold them but stopped. "Well," she said. "Most of it is already wrinkled anyway."

"Mommy, don't go," said Lila, her lower lip pushing out. "I don't want you to go." Lila wouldn't look her in the eye, and her brow furrowed as she stared across the room.

"I know, sweet pea," Meredith said for what felt like the twentieth time that day. "But Mommy is going to a conference for work."

"Then, I don't like your work." Lila pouted.

"Lila, I love you very much, and I won't be gone long. Just a few sleeps."

"I don't care. I want you here."

Emmy picked up a scarf. "Pretty 'carf," she said, holding it up. She pulled it to her cheek. "Soft 'carf."

"Thank you, Emmy."

Lila climbed over to the pillows at the top of the bed, plopped down, and glowered at Meredith and Emmy at the foot.

"Lila, you're going to have fun with Daddy while I'm gone."

"If you have to go, then I'll go, too."

"Oh, really?" Meredith said, surprised.

"Yes."

"Well, I hate to tell you this," Meredith said, lowering her voice. "But they don't have chicken nuggets in France."

Lila's eyes widened.

"Or...kids' meals."

"Wait...what?"

"It's true," Meredith said, turning back to the packing.

"But what will you eat for four days?"

Meredith raised her eyebrows dramatically. "Snails, probably," she said with a shrug.

"WHAT? You're going to eat SNAILS? Ew!" Lila shouted, jumping down from the bed and running to the living room. "Daddy! Daddy! Mommy's going to eat SNAILS!"

Emmy looked up curiously and wrinkled her nose. "'Nails? Ew! Emmy no like 'nails. 'Nails yucky!"

"That's okay, Emmy," Meredith said, laughing. "Mommy does."

Emmy opened her mouth in an exaggerated gasp as Lila returned.

"Come here. Can I hug you?" Meredith asked.

Lila came over and wrapped her arms around Meredith's waist. Meredith leaned down and kissed her head. "You know I'll always come home, right?"

"I know. It still sucks. Will you at least bring presents?"

* * *

The next afternoon, she flew from Nashville to Charlotte, and Charlotte to Frankfurt over night. The following morning, she flew into Luxembourg and took a train to Metz, France.

She stepped out of the train station to find a small, perfectly French town. Cobblestone streets, flowers and plants everywhere, and people strolling, coffee in hand. She hesitated as she left the station. *Pshaw. You don't need to reference the directions to the hotel. You can find it.*

An hour later, she gave up. She searched for another twenty minutes for a cab before finding one on an almost deserted street.

"*Excusez-moi, monsieur? Parlez-vous un peu anglais?"*

"Un peu, oui," said a man leaning against a taxi.

"Are you occupied now? I'm trying to find my hotel, and I could use a ride," she said, gesturing to the cab. It was the first cab she'd seen the entire hour.

"One moment," he said with a smile and walked into a nearby door. A few minutes later, he returned.

"Oui, quelle hotel? My employer isn't ready yet, so I will take you and return," he explained, opening the door for her.

"Oh, thank you so much!" She breathed, relieved. He laughed and shut the door.

"This town is small," he explained, as he pulled away from the curb. "But confusing for visitors. You are here for business?"

"Yes, a literary conference," she said, watching the quaint buildings slide by as they twisted and turned their way across town.

"Aha. You are a scholar," he said, glancing in the mirror. "Very young for such an important job." He smiled kindly.

She smiled in return. "Thank you again for taking the time. I was getting worried I'd never find it!"

"Ah, no worries, no problem," he said, as he pointed to various parks and city highlights along the way.

A few minutes later, they pulled up to the curb. "Now, this street is pedestrian only, so we stop here. But the hotel is right there. You see the sign?"

"Yes, I do," she said, reaching for her wallet.

"No, no," he said. "My employer insists he pay. *Bienvenue à Metz*!"

"Oh, thank you so much! Please give my thanks to your employer!" She gushed, as she climbed out of the cab. She waved goodbye as she clacked down the street, dragging her suitcase behind her. Within minutes, she was climbing four flights of winding stairs to a small room, where she found a perfect view of the cathedral spires from her window.

She glanced at her watch. Two o'clock. Time to call Liam so she could chat with the girls before they started their day. With any luck, she'd be able to sleep after that and maybe find a quiet dinner alone near the hotel—after stopping at the toy store she saw on the way in. But before all of that—*rest*.

* * *

The next morning, she made her way across a beautiful bridge. The river underneath surrounded a chapel on a small island in the middle, and swans swam by. *This must be where they make post cards of small French villages,* she thought. She walked to the university campus and easily located the building listed in the program. *Where was this sense of direction yesterday, Magellan?* she thought with a laugh.

As she entered, a short woman with red spiky hair looked at her curiously. “You must be Meredith. Welcome!” She opened her arms for an embrace. “I am Janis. I hope your trip was smooth?”

“Wow, I haven’t even spoken my terrible French yet, and you already knew who I was!” Meredith joked nervously.

The woman laughed. “No, no, it’s that I was expecting you! And our keynote is here, too. I will find her! You are our only Americans and our only experts on King! We’re excited to have you both!” She spun off down a hallway. “Wait here! I’ll be right back!”

An expert? I am an expert? Do they know I’ve been winging all this academic stuff?

Janis returned with a dark haired, middle aged woman beside her. “Amanda, this is Meredith! She came all the way from the States, too!”

Meredith smiled at Amanda. “Dr. Header, it’s so nice to meet you. I’ve read your work on King several times over...”

Amanda smiled in return and reached out to shake her hand. “It’s nice to meet you, too, Meredith. I’ve been on your website. You’re doing great things, and you’re still just a grad student! We’ll find some time to chat while we’re here.”

A small group of other conference participants walked into the lobby together. Introductions had barely been made when Janis clapped her hands and ushered everyone into a large lecture room for Amanda to present on Grace King’s life and most famous short story, “The Little Convent Girl.” Meredith took notes and tried to capture everything she said, even though she remembered not only reading much of it in the introduction to Amanda’s book, but even the page number and section where it was in the chapter. After her presentation, the group discussed the short story before departing to the home of one of the scholars, whose family hosted a beautiful reception with homemade hors d'ouerves and champagne.

Meredith found herself sitting next to Amanda that evening, as they told jokes about the demands of grad student life. Amanda even shared some of her own horror stories. "I've never received such a mean-spirited letter from anyone, especially from an academic that I admired!" She said, telling a story about another scholar in the field while she was completing her own graduate studies. "I told myself right then that I would never treat someone like that, if ever a grad student were to contact me!"

"And it's much appreciated," Meredith said, with a laugh. The host's husband came by with a tray full of small meats on toothpicks. "Oh, thank you. It's beautiful!" Meredith said, as she took one. Amanda did the same. As Meredith popped it into her mouth, she chewed thoughtfully. She realized then that Amanda was watching her.

She leaned forward and lowered her voice. "Okay, so how is it? It looks spicy!"

Meredith laughed. "A tiny bit, but not jalapeño-spicy. More like, andouille-spicy. Salty, but wonderful!"

"Great! Thanks!" She took a bite. "You're right. I was just nervous," she laughed. "So, are you flying out of Paris?"

"Actually, no," Meredith answered, shaking her head. "Luxembourg. Last year, I flew through Berlin for a conference in Wittenberg, but I was too nervous to explore Berlin while I was there. I regretted not exploring a new city. So, this year, I decided to fly into a different city and schedule myself a day there to check it out."

"Wow. That's so adventurous!" she said.

"Thanks, but it's more a decision based on the idea that I might not come this way again, or at least not for a very long time. I have preliminary exams approaching, a dissertation to write, and a job market to enter. It's all pretty terrifying."

"Yes, and the market will be the roughest of all of those things," she warned. "It's rough out there. But with your CV looking the way it does already, I think you'll find something.

But remember: even if you don't, that's okay, too. Sometimes it takes awhile to find your spot."

"Thanks," Meredith replied.

"You keep me posted, so we can stay in touch."

* * *

That Friday afternoon, Meredith presented her paper on King. The internet connection failed, so she abandoned her carefully prepared slides, reading through her paper smoothly. Afterward, there were a few genuine questions and connections to her argument that King's writing served as a transitional state between traditional nineteenth-century plantation novels and twentieth century modern American literature. The group headed out for a walk around town that evening and had dinner in a beautifully lit restaurant. Meredith was too shy to speak for much of dinner, since the whole group sat at one very long table, so she spent most of the night smiling and nodding.

After dinner, the group walked by the gothic cathedral in the city center, the one whose spires Meredith could see from her window. The air was chilly and crisp, but inside the cathedral, Meredith could hear music—a heavy organ was playing, but the music was somehow still soft. She crossed the road to the entrance, where numerous candelabra had been placed, inviting visitors inside. She stepped inside the stone entryway to find the entire knave glowing from candles. No electrical lights interrupted the soft scene as visitors whispered or sat in meditation in the wooden pews, listening to the music. Each alcove was illuminated by candles, and Meredith walked through in silence. She was not religiously-inclined, and so she made sure to provide space and respect for those who knelt in prayer. She just needed stillness.

And for that moment, she had it. She was simply there; all she had to do was breathe and absorb the gothic arches, statues, paintings, and music. For that moment, her shoulders eased.

* * *

Two weeks later, Meredith flew to New Orleans for her presentation at the Salon, and she decided to take advantage of the trip and fit in some research while there.

On her first afternoon in the city for this visit, she traveled uptown to Tulane University to look over some of King's documents on file there. She held King's honorary doctorate in her hands and marveled over the neatly typed poems and manuscript drafts.

Afterward, she rode contentedly on the St. Charles Avenue streetcar, watching the grand homes on St. Charles Avenue slide by when her phone buzzed with a new email:

Dear Meredith,

You have been awarded the prestigious Bush Award from TVSU. This award is a high honor, and we, the faculty, congratulate you on this success. There will be a formal ceremony and reception on December 17.
Congratulations,
Dr. C. Barnes

Meredith smiled to herself. She texted Liam the good news, put her phone away, and spent the next hour shopping for gifts for him and the girls. She found several quirky toys and as many fun beads as she could fit in her bag for Lila and Emmy. For Liam, she deliberated over purchasing an expensive, leather portfolio in an Italian stationary shop in the French Quarter. He had been the only steady support she'd had throughout her grad studies, but they needed to keep expenses down. They were surviving on graduate stipends and trying to save for their next move. As Meredith started to put the portfolio back on its display, the clerk walked over to her.

"Ma'am? Have you decided?" asked the clerk.

Meredith smiled softly. "Yes. Do you gift wrap?"

The next morning was the day of the presentation, and Meredith sipped on her too-hot ginger tea as she walked around St. Louis Cathedral in a light, misty rain. She was too nervous to sit anywhere, so she walked. And sipped. The morning was gray and unseasonably cold. A light drizzle came down, the air heavy for November. She glanced at her phone obsessively. Finally, it was time to go to the Salon to give her lecture.

She made her way slowly back around the cathedral and up St. Peter. On the left rested the Salon, with its iconic spiral, wrought-iron staircase behind locked gates. A bottom floor door was open. She cautiously entered the dark, stone walkway and followed it to the courtyard entrance. In the courtyard, the rain came a little heavier, and a light fog misted the cobblestones. She looked around carefully, fully expecting someone to pop out and challenge her being there, but the place seemed empty and quiet. It was nice to poke around a bit without needing to be social at the same time. Parallel to the stone entryway, the rectangular presentation gallery sat across from the courtyard entrance. She stepped in and began looking around at the books in the barrister bookcases. Literature. Philosophy. History. Posters on the walls advertised this person's book release or that person's art opening. The wood floors creaked as she made her way down the center aisle up to the wooden podium. All computer hookups were tucked inside the podium, so the look of an antique wooden platform remained, but it had fully functioning technology. The projection screen was already pulled down.

"Good morning," called a friendly, warm voice from the doorway. The current president embodied the image of the southern Lady, with a capital "L." Mrs. Allen's mauve skirt suit was impeccable, and Meredith found herself double-checking her own black dress and boots. Her camel colored boots were a bit worn, and though comfortable, they were beginning to show some mileage. "We are just so glad you're here!" Mrs. Allen gushed, opening her arms for a light embrace. "Are you finding everything you need? You help yourself to all that tech, and if we need to get our guy in here to fix anything, we'll do that!"

Meredith smiled warmly. "I think I'll be just fine. Is it okay if I go ahead and set up?"

"Absolutely! Let me get you some water to keep up there, too," she said as she swept back out of the room just as she'd swept into it: with distinctly southern style. Southern women anchor their worlds, moving with their own gravitational forces everywhere they go, like an extended magnolia-scented aura. When someone is in a southern woman's world, they know it. They are that woman's closest confidante, and they share a deep and meaningful connection; when she leaves the room, she takes her world with her, and the room is somehow emptier for having lost her.

Meredith smiled gently after her and turned to setting up. She adjusted her laptop, plugged in various cables, and checked the projector. Everything seemed to be working just fine, so she stood near the podium as ladies began filing into the seats. She smiled shyly in return as they smiled their greetings while taking their seats. She had thought—and feared—that the cold weather would lower the crowd size, and so, she expected around twenty people, if she was lucky. But the room steadily filled. Each row was elbow-to-elbow—every seat filled. Meredith tried to count the rows and seats and figured that roughly sixty people had filled the Salon. She tried to swallow the thick lump in her throat.

The former president, Mrs. Winston, stood to introduce her. She listed Meredith's recent accomplishments, which sounded much too grand to her own ear. *These must belong to someone else,* she thought, as she stood and took her place at the podium.

"Thank you so very much for inviting me here, today," Meredith began. She explained that she was not originally from New Orleans, but that she'd always felt at home here. Several ladies smiled warmly and nodded their heads in agreement, their feathered hats tipping back and forth. Then, Meredith fired up her first slide. She'd arranged the lecture as a literary introduction to Grace King but for a general audience. As she began telling one of King's most harrowing stories—the family's escape from New Orleans during the

Yankee occupation—she watched the faces in her audience. They were not only listening...they were enthralled. She reached the part where the family was stuck, alone and lost, in the swamps, and how the children hugged around the grandmother's knees for comfort and warmth, but that King's mother, Sarah Miller, stood and shouted for help until her voice gave out. The air in the room was tense. When she described their rescue by a stranger and how they stepped out of the boat onto land to find King's father, William King, waiting anxiously for them, several of the ladies gasped and fanned themselves.

It was the most rewarding story-telling moment Meredith had ever had.

As she transitioned into the next section of her lecture, she saw an elderly man being escorted to a front seat. *If a man is being seated here, he's important,* she thought. *Maybe even a King relative?* She quickly decided to drop Grace's utter hatred of the drinking habits of her brothers, as this man had to be a relation of one of them, since none of Grace's sisters had had children.

She continued her lecture and noticed a striking woman halfway back and right in the middle of the left hand section. Other women sat with slightly curved backs, slumped ever so slightly into their chair backs. This woman sat with a rigid spine and her face tilted up. Her eyes were dark, and her light gray hair short and curly. Many of the ladies were dressed for style in their skirt suits with corsages; this woman was dressed for function in a simple button down shirt. She made direct eye contact the entire lecture, smiling warmly when Meredith looked directly back at her. Whether she released it or not, the woman greatly resembled King in her later years. As Meredith spoke, she realized she was presenting to this one woman. This avid listener.

When she finished, the audience clapped warmly, but her heart was still pounding in her ears, so Meredith barely heard it. The woman in the audience held her hands at chest height so Meredith could see: she clapped and gave a deep, singular nod and smile.

Immediately, Meredith was presented with a small group of ladies shaking her hand, congratulating her on the lecture, and offering her their business cards. She was ushered upstairs to the parlor for tea and a beautiful reception. The room was decorated with antique furniture under a beautiful crystal chandelier. A piano stood in one corner, and people collected in small pockets throughout the room. Meredith was socially exhausted, but she smiled and thanked each one as they came up to speak to her. She had hoped to meet the woman from the audience, but she seemed to have disappeared.

Before long, Mrs. Allen approached. “There’s someone I’d like to introduce to you.” She escorted Meredith to the piano, where the gentleman from earlier sat on the bench. “Meredith, this is Mr. King.” The elderly man stretched out his hand to take hers.

“Young lady, you did a wonderful job,” he said. “I’m Fred’s grandson, Grace’s great-nephew.”

“Oh, wow,” Meredith said. “It’s so very nice to meet you!”

“I was a very young boy when Grace was still alive,” he said, as Mrs. Allen walked away to give them a few minutes alone. “She and her sisters were still living in the big house, you know.”

Meredith smiled kindly and nodded. “The beautiful home up on Coliseum, by the park,” she said.

“That’s the one. I used to play under the table in the dining room. We would visit with the sisters every so often, not too much. I couldn’t have been but five or six years old.”

“Do you remember much about Grace?”

“Not much, I’m afraid.” She wanted to ask him all sorts of questions, but she also recognized that he probably wouldn’t be able to answer very many of them, since he’d been so young when Grace was alive.

“What kind of aunty was she?” she finally asked. “The kind that complained when you ran down the halls making too much noise, or the kind that snuck you cookies before dinner?”

He grinned and chuckled. “Little bit of both, I s’ppose,” he answered. “Depending on the occasion.”

His wife approached and introduced herself. “I’m afraid we really must be going, but your talk was wonderful!”

“Thank you. I’m so glad to have met you both,” Meredith said, smiling.

His wife helped Mr. King stand and continued to steady his arm as they made their way out of the room. The crowd was beginning to thin, and Meredith found she could relax just a bit. She wandered back into the front parlor, near the piano again. Across from it stood a beautiful painting of Grace King. She knew from research that this one was done from a live sitting.

“Well, Grace, I think I’m getting closer to something, but I still have no idea what I’m doing,” Meredith said so softly no one could hear. “Any grand wisdom or secrets to share?”

Grace stared back from the painting, silent.

ᘓ

Part II

"Experiences, reminiscences, episodes, picked up as only women know how to pick them up from other women's lives—or other women's destinities, as they prefer to call them,—told as only women know how to relate them."

—Grace King, Balcony Stories, 1892

Chapter 16

1885

Dear Mr. Warner,

I continue to work on expanding "Monsieur Motte."

I do wonder—again—at the prospect of my using a pen name. Though I wish for literary success, I am abhorrent at the idea of advertising. My friends and family will think the worst of me for doing such. There must be a way to reconcile my writing and identity so as to remain in proper etiquette. I, also, fear a portrait being used with the article as you suggested. I find myself drawing more and more internally as this process unfolds.

Your Thoughts Deeply Appreciated,
G. E. K.

* * *

My dearest, Grace,

You worry overmuch about this issue. Using your real name—Grace King—already sounds like a wonderful pen name. The upcoming journal publication will include a small portrait of you, though I know how much you must despise this. It is your sweet humility that makes you react this way—but I wouldn't have it any other way.

How I wish I could spin out of the north and return to you in exotic New Orleans, have you tell me stories about the south. Have I told you I was an abolitionist and hated rebels as much as you hate Yanks? Isn't it odd how we grow and change with time?

Your affectionate friend,
C.D.W.

* * *

Dearest Mr. Warner,

There is no need to flaunt your Yankeedom at me; if you can tolerate it, so can I. How is it possible for such a southern gentlemen to be from the North?
Your Affectionate
G.E.K.

1886
My Dearest, Grace,

Congratulations are in order for the upcoming publication of your story, "Bonne Maman," in Harper's Magazine. I will be in New Orleans soon—giving a series of lectures. Perhaps we can find the time to sit down and go over the proofs of your wonderful little story. I hear you have another tale, "Madrilene," also in preparation for publication in Harper's for later this year. I am proud of you, Grace. Your career is on an upward scale, and I couldn't be more excited for you. I miss seeing that beautiful city of yours with you on my arm, in your lovely blue silk gown with your curls escaping your pins and hat. It is quite possibly my favorite thing in all the world to do. I am most excited that you will be joining me here in Hartford next summer. When I see you next, I will tell you all about it. But what I look forward to the most about your visit is so much more time with you.
Your Affectionate,
C.D.W.

Grace blushed as she read Mr. Warner's note a third time. She walked into the sitting room where Nina sat on the sofa reading a novel. Nina raised her eyebrows and set the novel beside her.

"You know," she said in a flat tone to Grace. "It's clear as a bell who has written when your face looks like that."

Grace tried not to face her.

"And I don't approve," Nina added. "All those letters about your affection for one another. It's not right, Grace."

"Oh, Nina, it isn't like that," Grace said. "He's a married man. He's just my mentor and guide, that's all."

"The flirtation is doubly inappropriate since he's married."

"Nina, it's nothing."

"You're going up to Hartford next summer. Without a chaperone. To stay with him for months."

"In the same home as his *wife*, Nina. Do you think a man would invite a possible mistress to his home *with his wife*? Now, for goodness' sake, drop this nonsense," Grace said angrily as she stormed out of the room.

"All I'm saying is Garrett and Atwood never got that blushing response," Nina muttered under her breath as she returned to her book.

* * *

Hartford, Connecticut
1887

Mr. Warner met Grace at the train station, and they rode together in the carriage to his home. They chatted about her trip north, her current writing projects, and possible outings during her stay.

"I'm thinking of doing a bit of writing on some historical subjects," Grace explained. "The Judge has been so kind in mentoring me for so many years, and I find history filled with amazing stories just waiting to be told."

Mr. Warner smiled kindly. "The Judge is a fine and intelligent man. I do encourage you, however, to continue in your purely literary pursuits. They are lovely and beautiful, and the world needs and deserves that kind of beauty, do you not agree? Literature is much more attuned to femininity."

Grace took a breath to respond, but as the carriage turned, she saw the mansion they approached.

The circular drive led them to a grand, red brick home. Steep, gothic windows and wrought iron decorated the third story. Two grand brick chimneys rose from the middle of the slate gray roof. The bottom floor had porches and bay windows across the front and side, all of which were draped with green vines and surrounded by trees and woods. A small pond with a fountain rested in front of the mansion.

"It's beautiful," Grace whispered. "And so grand!"

Mr. Warner laughed. "Consider this your northern home, Grace," he said, gently squeezing her hand.

Grace smiled nervously and squeezed his hand in return. He smiled and let his eyes linger on hers. The carriage pulled up to the main entrance, and the driver helped Grace step down, where a well-dressed older woman stood waiting for them in the doorway.

"Oh, Grace, I'm so happy to welcome you to our home!" Mrs. Warner said, wrapping her arms around Grace's shoulders and guiding her inside.

Polished wood trim bordered the dark green walls, and a wide, ornate staircase led to the second floor. Each wall was covered in portraits, and each and every one was ornately presented in thick, gold and bronze-brushed frames.

Mr. Warner stood to Grace's side, handing her valise to a well-dressed butler. "Please see Miss King's belongings to her room," he said.

"My dear Grace, I hope your journey was smooth?" asked Mrs. Warner, taking Grace's arm.

"Yes, it was. Thank you. And thank you, both, for such a wonderful invitation to spend some time in your home," answered Grace. "It's such a beautiful place! I do hope you'll forgive my getting lost a few times!"

Mr. Warner laughed. "Not at all, my dear! Now, Jackson here will show you to your room. Rest up, dear Grace, we shall dine in a bit, and we are expecting guests first thing in the morning!"

"Thank you," said Grace, blushing at the warm welcome but feeling suddenly timid. "But I hope my stay will not put you out or disrupt things too much."

"Oh, we don't entertain southern ladies such as yourself very often," said Mrs. Warner. "Our neighbors wish to visit you, as do a few others. Now, if you'll excuse me, I have a few things to see to before dinner." Mrs. Warner walked out of the room with a glance at her husband over her shoulder. Mr.

Warner stared at Grace, not noticing—as Grace did—his wife pursing her lips as she left the room.

"I see," murmured Grace, her anxiety rising. The thought of meeting guests who were used to the level of luxury she saw in this room made her second guess herself. She feared that the dresses she'd borrowed from her sisters and the faded silk flowers on her hat would not compare to the finery she was finding in Hartford.

Mr. Warner smiled and reached a hand to Grace's elbow. "Not to worry, Grace," he said kindly. "You need not feel timid here or with our friends. You've done wonderful writing, and I am more than proud to be your mentor." He squeezed Grace's elbow, and she felt her face flush red and warm at his praise. Mr. Warner shifted his weight to be closer to Grace. His proximity made her nervous, and she suddenly felt short of breath. He leaned closer toward her when a door slammed somewhere in the house, making Grace jump. "Let me show you to your room, myself," he said quietly, gesturing for her to proceed before him up the stairs. As they reached the top and turned to walk down the hallway, a door opened, revealing a slender and attractive woman.

"Oh, I'm so sorry," she said. "I didn't mean to startle you." She looked pointedly at Grace. "You must be..."

Mr. Warner cleared his throat. "Isa, we were expecting Miss Grace King's arrival today, remember? Grace, this is Isa Carrington Cabell, who is also staying with us this summer."

"Oh, yes, now I recall," Isa said, turning her attention to adjusting her clothing. She wore a white blouse open at the neck and a gray skirt. She had a look of sophisticated polish that made Grace envious.

She smiled nervously at Isa. "It's nice to meet you, Mrs. Cabell. I've read a few of your articles in the papers."

"That's sweet," Isa replied, turning to Grace. "I'm sure we'll be fast friends. Now, Charley, I believe you were supposed to work with me this afternoon. Shall we?"

"My office," he said to Grace, in explanation. "Is on the third floor. There is a large work table and shelves all along the walls, so do help yourself and feel at home. Isa, after you..."

Mr. Warner stepped to Isa's side and placed his hand at the small of her back. Grace noticed their physical ease with one another.

As they walked up the stairs, Isa glanced back at Grace. She winked and smiled mischievously and closed the door soundly behind them.

Grace stared for a moment, shocked.

Jackson came up the stairs and waited patiently in the hall behind her, holding Grace's small suitcase. Grace turned to him and smiled awkwardly.

"Right this way, Miss Grace," he said, gesturing down the hallway.

Grace nodded. "Of course," she said. "Jackson, do I detect a slight southern accent?" asked Grace.

"Yes, Miss, you do," said Jackson with a kind smile. "I'm from Virginia, originally."

"And what are you doing all the way up here?"

"Making a nice salary to send to my wife and children," he said, leading her down the hallway to the guest rooms.

"Your wife? And children? Surely you must miss them," said Grace, trying to take in every aspect of the house as they made their way through it.

"Yes, Miss," he said, opening a door and gesturing for her to go in first. "But my wife wouldn't hear of raising our children up north," he said under his breath in a conspiratorial tone.

Grace chuckled. "Your wife is a smart woman," she responded. "But it is quite beautiful here!" she said, as she looked around the room. The same thick wood trim decorated this room, and a four poster bed rested against the interior wall. A cream colored quilt draped over the bed, and fine lace pillows topped it. Grace walked over to the wall of opened windows and relished the cool air drifting in.

"Jackson, I noticed that every single door and window we passed was wide open. Is this a northern custom?"

"Yes, Miss. I thought it was odd, too, at first, but it does bring in nice air," he said, laughing. "Anything I can bring you, Miss Grace?" He said, as he made his way to the door.

Grace smiled in return. “Thank you, Jackson, but I’m just fine,” she said.

“Dinner will be served at eight, and I’ll ring the dressing gong at six. The Warners usually take drinks at seven thirty.” Jackson tipped his head gallantly and gently closed the door.

Grace sighed and looked at the grandeur around her. How could she rest when there was so much to see and write home about?

* * *

The next morning, Grace descended the heavy stairs to find Mrs. Warner giving instructions to two servants. She looked up and smiled at Grace.

“You look lovely, dear! Such a lovely dress,” Mrs. Warner said. Grace glanced down at her blue skirt and simple matching blouse. This one she’d made herself.

“Thank you,” she said. “From my window, I thought I saw a lady arriving, so I thought I should come down to pay my respects, but I don’t see anyone now.”

“Really, dear? There’s no one here just yet, I’m afraid. But soon, the house will be abuzz with people. What was this mystery lady wearing?”

“A light dress. She seemed quite lively, chatting to herself. I assumed she was a guest,” Grace said, truly intrigued. “I saw her walk up to the house and enter the side door.”

“Chatting to herself, you say?” Mrs. Warner said as she continued adjusting vases of flowers, moving a rose here and there, tying and untying ribbons. Realization suddenly dawned on her face. “Oh, that must be Harriet!” She laughed and shook her head. “Jackson,” she called as the butler walked briskly down the hall. “Has Harriet paid us a visit?”

“Yes, ma’am,” said Jackson from the hallway. “But she’s left already.”

Mrs. Warner nodded. “Thank you, Jackson.” She turned back to Grace. “That was just Harriet. She lives very near here. Poor thing has gone remarkably mad over the last ten years, ever since her book sales started dropping, really.”

"Harriet?"

"Yes. Harriet Beecher Stowe. You'll meet her sister, Isabella, as well. She's a delight," Mrs. Warner said.

Grace's eyes grew large. "That poor woman was Harriet Beecher Stowe?"

"Yes. Surely you've read her book?"

Grace shook her head. "Actually, no. Her book was banned reading in our house. The way my father spoke of it, I assumed it was bound in dragon skin!"

Mrs. Warner stared at Grace for a moment but then laughed.

Grace looked over the drawing room, now covered in beautiful floral arrangements on every surface. All of the windows and doors were opened to let in fresh summer breezes.

"Would you mind if I take a short walk through the garden before breakfast?"

"Of course not, dear. Make yourself completely at home."

"Thank you, Mrs. Warner," Grace said, as she turned down the wide, dark hall and found her way to the side door and stepped outside. She braced herself for a wave of heat but found the northern summer air surprisingly refreshing as she stepped lightly down the pebbled pathway.

Grace walked slowly through the narrow paths and under the tall trees on the outskirts of the Warners' property. As she did, she could hear a small group of people chatting in the distance. As she neared the entrance to a path through the trees, she spotted the small group led by an elderly man with a cane swinging in his hand. His wife, with a jovial, round face, walked beside him, her arm tucked through his. She wore a red silk dress with white sleeves and collar; he wore white flannel and smoked a pipe.

The man stopped at the sight of Grace.

"I say there, Miss. Are you a guest of the Warners?" he called out.

"Yes, sir, I am," Grace answered as she approached them.

"Well, well, looks like the visit's already over. If the ladies are leaving, there's no point in going!" he said, laughing at his own joke. The woman on his arm smiled patiently and patted his arm in support. Clearly, she had heard enough of his jokes and humor to expect them and knew best how to placate him.

"Hello, dear, you must be Miss King, is that right? From New Orleans?" said the woman kindly.

"Why, yes, ma'am. I am," Grace answered, her southern accent lilting her words.

"Aha!" shouted the man. "You are just who we were coming to meet!" He stepped forward and offered his hand. "Samuel Clemens, at your service," he said, with a dramatic sweep of his arm and an exaggerated deep bow. "Might I present my dear wife, Olivia?"

"Oh, my. Mr. and Mrs. Clemens, it's so nice to meet you," Grace gushed.

"I'm sure it is, my dear, I'm sure it is," Mr. Clemens said, as he propped himself up against his cane while he climbed back to an upright position. "Whew. That's taking longer than it used to. Might have to start budgeting the gallantry a bit, eh, Livy?" He joked to his wife.

"Youth, I have been encouraging you to 'budget your gallantry' for years. Why on earth would you listen to me now?" she said, laughing anyway. They linked arms again and turned to face Grace.

"We were heading to the Warners ourselves, to breakfast with you," Mr. Clemens said.

"I'm honored," Grace said. "Might we walk together?" As they turned to the pathway, Grace fell in step beside Olivia. "You know, Mr. Clemens, your *Innocents Abroad* was the second book my late Papa purchased after the War to begin rebuilding our library—just after Shakespeare."

Mr. Clemens stopped and looked at Grace earnestly. "I am deeply, most sincerely honored by your late Papa," he said, his eyes filled with kindness. "You hear that, Livy?" he said with a gentle elbow to his wife's side.

"Yes, Youth, I did."

He nodded, and they continued their walk back to the Warners'.

* * *

Dear Nina,

I hope you are finding the selection of novels I left to be to your liking! I cannot wait to return to New Orleans so we can discuss your thoughts about Maupassant. How I wish you could hear the conversations here in Hartford about literature! To be here has been quite an education for me, I must admit.

On my first morning here, I met Mr. and Mrs. Samuel Clemens! Papa would be most impressed, don't you think? I have been spending some time with the Clemens family and have gotten to know them quite well. Believe it or not, he is not at all refined! He even wears bed slippers around instead of shoes!

Yesterday, I met Isabella Beecher Hooker, the radical woman involved in the women's movement! She is the sister of Harriet Beecher Stowe, but they are not at all like the dragon women Papa made them out to be. Isabella is a kind, middle-age woman who spoke to me about the women's vote. I must say, Nina, I find myself quite in agreement with her; why should the men make all of the decisions? Why, if women could vote, we would certainly fight fewer wars, at least! But, of course, keep my newfound interest quiet! I do not want to embarrass Mimi or have Fred or Branch write me scolding letters! I am by no means a bluestocking and have no intention of becoming one!

Next week, I will be attending a grand dinner at the Clemenses' home! Oh, Nina, you would adore their daughters Susy, Clara, and Jean and become friends with them instantly! Susy is a musical prodigy, and her talent brings goose pimples to my arms and tears to my eyes. She has become almost like another sister.

Do write soon—the North feels like another planet, and I do find myself homesick for New Orleans and news of it!
Sis

* * *

The Clemens family wished to honor Grace with a dinner reception one rainy Sunday in June. At the last minute, they realized that a scheduling conflict had arisen: a famous Union general and his wife were also scheduled to visit the Clemens during the same week. Livy feared that having two parties would split the attendance at each, and so Grace suggested that they simply combine the events.

On the night of the dinner, Grace, the Warners, and Isa walked together on the path through the woods that connected the two homes. Isa took Grace's arm every chance she could, and Grace feigned every reason she could think of to pull away; she had to stop walking to adjust her slipper, loosen or tighten her sleeve, or pick up her fan. When Isa wasn't clasping onto Grace, she was on Mr. Warner's arm, walking so close that their hips brushed.

Though Grace had become a regular visitor to the Clemens' home, she still stood for a moment in awe every time the grand house came into view. The home had been designed to resemble a steamboat, as Clemens often felt nostalgic for the Mississippi River and the boats upon which he had spent much of his youth. The wide veranda wrapped around the home, mimicking the deck, while an octagonal section arose from it, resembling the captain's perch. Grace almost expected the double chimneys to billow steam and to hear the whistle blow.

From the wooded path, they entered into the two rooms that Grace considered the most beautiful in the whole house: The conservatory, overflowing with green plants and flowers, and the wood paneled library, its walls lined in books. Overstuffed chairs and sofas sat in the middle of the room, centered around the ornate fireplace. As Grace and the Warners entered the library, she inhaled sharply. Old books, wood smoke, and pipe tobacco. The room reminded her of the library at Roncal, the former country home of the Gayarrés, who had eventually sold it to pay off debts. As she looked at the small gathering of people, she felt excited and anxious. This event was a grand one; the women were dressed in their finest gowns, while she wore her sister's borrowed silk dress. *Thank goodness for May,* she thought, glancing at the beautiful dresses around her.

Typically, the dinners she attended at the Clemens' home were informal and noisy, with easy laughter. Grace had even begun to feel so at home with the Clemenses that she often found herself bantering right along with Mr. Clemens, much to the delight of the Clemens' children.

"Tety!" called Susy. Fifteen-year-old Susy had decided she needed a unique, personal name by which to call Grace, as she and her younger sister, Clara, had become very attached to Grace. They had settled on Tweety, but Jean, the youngest, had struggled to pronounce it, and so, Grace had become Tety.

"Thank goodness you're here," Susy said quietly. "Everyone is *so* boring!" She whispered to Grace. "Surely the balls you attend in New Orleans aren't as boring as these dinner parties?" Clara drew together with them to hear more stories about New Orleans.

"Well," Grace said, tilting her head. "That depends on who is throwing the ball, I guess."

"Why can't Hartford have balls like the ones you describe?" Clara lamented, laying her head for a moment against Grace's shoulder.

Across the room stood the Union general and his wife. General Lucius Fairchild was a tall, handsome man, who had famously lost an arm in battle at Gettysburg.

The Clemenses' butler, George, entered the room and announced that dinner was served. General Fairchild took Mrs. Clemens' arm, and Mr. Clemens took Grace's. Grace noticed that Charles Warner offered his arm to Isa, who batted her eyelashes up at him.

"Shouldn't you be escorting Mrs. Fairchild?" Grace whispered to Mr. Clemens.

"And miss the chance to escort a southern lady in my own home? Never!" He whispered back, feigning shock and laughing so his mustache twitched.

After the guests were seated, Grace looked upon the most beautifully arranged table she had ever seen. The table was round and made of the clearest glass. A large glass bowl sat in the center, holding daisies, ferns, and grasses. The contrast of green and white was carried over the ladies' plates, where small nosegays of white roses had been placed. All over the room, silver candelabra glowed with yellow candles. Olives and salted almonds were in small, silver terrines, and servants walked about, pouring expensive wine.

As a maid served sherry flavored soup, Grace breathed in the rich scent deeply. The soup reminded her of the flavors in a deep *coq au vin*.

General Fairchild said, "Clemens, this is quite a feast!" The General shoveled his spoon into his mouth, dribbling the fine soup on the table. Grace caught herself staring and had to force her eyes to look away.

Mr. Clemens said, "Well, of course, General! You are much respected and admired in this home!" Mr. Clemens, too, began attacking his food, tearing into bread and setting it on the table. Grace felt her eyes might pop out of her head. It was one thing to simply eat at a family dinner, but this was *dining! Were men not taught dining etiquette?*

She looked down at her own soup, determined not to be rude at such a fine dinner. She delicately lowered her spoon to the broth, tilted it horizontally, letting the broth slide into the spoon. She lifted it, waited a moment for drips, and then smoothly tilted the spoon against her lips, tasting the soup without spilling a drop.

"Good, good," Fairchild said, responding to Clemens's praise. "Did you see the responses I've gotten after I gave my most recent speech?"

"Yes, we have, General Fairchild," replied Mrs. Clemens, with a hint of nervousness in her voice. "But, perhaps—"

"Yes, indeed," said the General, soaking his bread in the soup and tossing it into his mouth. Grace cringed every time he tossed another small piece, thinking he would eventually miss. "Rogers thought I went too far, but I don't regret it! By God, President Cleveland ought to be ashamed! Reconciling with southern traitors! I still can't believe he ordered the return of their dreadful flags!"

Grace paused and braced herself.

"Well, General Fairchild," said Mrs. Clemens. "Our other guest here tonight is native New Orleanian, Miss Grace King." Grace offered a taut smile and a tiny nod but managed to hold her tongue.

"Aha, so you'll know all about the flags!" General Fairchild said. "The South waged quite a battle, but the War is over and done with."

"Not for us," murmured Grace, taking a small sip of her wine.

"Excuse me?"

"Not for us," she said a bit louder. "The War still affects our lives every single day," Grace explained politely, the sadness showing in her brown eyes. "Women struggle to feed their families, and men can't find work, even well beneath their status. Negroes struggle for place and survival even more. People starve for want of food. Children go hungry. It is still societal chaos. The War is never over for the women and children who must rebuild their lives after the dust on the battlefield settles."

"Then southern men are weak and have failed their families, unlike our good Yanks. Now, *those* are some *real* men. Good men are strong providers and do not fail their women," said Mrs. Fairchild, tilting her nose upward as she took a spoon of soup.

Grace felt her face grow warm and her temper rise. "You'd be surprised what 'good men' do in New Orleans when their good wives are not with them," she said flatly. She stared across the table with hard eyes as a heavy silence fell over the table.

Suddenly, Mr. Clemens guffawed, startling half of the guests at the table.

Mrs. Clemens scowled at her husband. "Well, George, I am to understand the main dish is ready?" she said, trying to change the subject.

"Yes, Ma'am," said George, signaling to the maids to bring in the next dish.

* * *

By the end of her visit to Hartford, Grace spent more and more time with the Clemenses and less with the Warners.

One afternoon after a lunch with the Warners, Clemens, and Isa, she sat on the veranda at the Clemens', reading Tolstoy's *War and Peace*. Russian literature had become a deep interest of hers, and she relished pouring over the volumes for hours. The surrounding tall trees provided shade, and a soft breeze occasionally lifted an escaped curl or two from her usual braided bun.

Her time with the Clemenses had been one of the most positive, joyful events of her life. They made her think of what *could have been* with her own family. Would she, Nan, and Nina have been closer, had they not been so desperate for any of them to marry well? The pressure to find a husband—a *wealthy* husband—had resulted in constant comparison with one another and with other young women in the same situation. And that pressure, she felt, had cracked many of their relationships.

If the War had not been, would they have had dinner parties and receptions, like the Clemenses did? Would her family be discussing a European sojourn, as theirs was?

Grace thought of Clara and Susy. Normally, Grace didn't gravitate to children, but this was different. Befriending Clara, Susy, and even little Jean felt like befriending a different version of her own family. At their age, she was studying in school, but the family was living on scraps. Her childhood memories were of hardship, fear, and hunger. The Clemens' children would have *these* memories—parties, dinners, laughter, music, and conversation. What an environment in which to grow up! What advantages they would have that may alter the course of their entire lives.

And yet. Grace realized with a sigh that her childhood hardships had crafted who she was now. Without them, would she have ever started writing?

She tried to shift her gaze to her book just as Isa walked over to join her.

"Well, hello, Grace," Isa said, sitting in the opposite chair. A small table sat between them.

"Hello, Isa," Grace said simply, smiling politely. She disliked Isa greatly and had up until now avoided much conversation with her. Isa was also a writer, publishing various types of newspaper articles. Not a creative or literary mind, in Grace's opinion.

"Have you managed to make travel arrangements?" Isa asked innocently.

"Yes," Grace answered, putting her book down. "I'll be heading out soon for a little solo work time. A few weeks should really help my writing."

"Ah. I find this surrounding quite productive for my writing, but I'm sorry it doesn't suit you," Isa said, pointedly.

Grace sighed. "It suits me fine, Isa."

"Well, you've not done much writing here, is all I'm saying. And Charles had written me about what a clever mind you are. I had hopes that we might exchange more pleasantries on your visit."

"Mr. Warner wrote to you about me?"

"Oh, of course. He tells me *everything*," Isa said, raising an eyebrow at Grace. "He has written me, let's see, every other day for over five years now."

Grace sat back, surprised.

"Yes, and he was excited to introduce us," Isa added, looking down at her nails. "Frankly, I think he wanted us to work together on a project or two. How silly, though! Us, writing together!"

Grace gave a humor-less chuckle. "Yes, clearly preposterous. I mean, you write simple little articles, while I write literature. What would we find to collaborate on!"

Isa's smile vanished.

"And what about your own travel arrangements? Surely your family must be missing you," Grace added.

"Since my husband's passing a few years ago, I travel when and where I please. And it pleases me to be here, with Charles," Isa said in a clipped voice. "Pity you couldn't form such a relationship."

"Oh, please," Grace said, lowering her voice. "You've shamed yourself. And in another woman's house. With her own husband."

Isa smiled a cat-smile. "And wouldn't you like to know what it's like?" she said, so quietly Grace could barely hear her.

At that moment, Charles turned the corner. "Ah, Isa! There you are—" He froze when he saw Grace was also at the table. "And Grace. My two favorite writers—"

Isa turned to Charles, with tears suddenly overflowing from her eyes.

"Why, Isa, what is wrong, my dear?"

"You wouldn't believe the horrible things Grace was saying to me, just now!"

Grace's mouth fell open in shock. "What?"

"Grace," Charles said, scowling at her. "You've upset poor Isa!"

"Oh, I'll recover. It's not the first time," Isa said softly, her lower lip trembling. "Charles, are we still working on my article this afternoon?" She batted her tearful eyes up at Mr. Warner.

"Yes, of course, my dear," he said. He reached out to take her arm. "Grace, I do hope you'll reflect on your words to Isa and make this right. I'm very disappointed in you!"

Grace sat in utter shock as Charles led Isa away, patting her hand comfortingly. Isa turned to smile at Grace before shutting the door behind them both.

* * *

The next morning, Grace left the Warners' for a six week stay at the Elm Tree Inn in nearby Farmington. She walked into her rented room and looked around at the writing desk and neatly made bed. She would spend this time writing. She settled her things, hung her dresses, and set out her paper and pens. She looked out the window into the green trees beyond and paced back to the desk. How to start? After the rush of parties, shopping, and visiting, she welcomed the peace and quiet, but now she was slightly unaccustomed to it.

Grace finally sighed and sank into the desk chair. She picked up her pen and began writing a letter. Letter-writing always helped her clear the cobwebs and prepare to write, as though getting her everyday thoughts out of the way helped her see the path ahead.

Dear Nan,

I hope you've been enjoying the summer resort season this year. I expect to hear all about your conquests, interests, and intrigues when I return home!

For now, I will entertain you with one of my own—Isa Carrington Cabell has also been a guest in Hartford this summer—staying, like me, with the Warners. She is most intelligent and sophisticated, and perhaps better able to navigate the publishing world than I. She attempted to force a close, sisterly relationship with me, but as you know, I despise forced—and usually fake!—relationships.

I was also uncomfortable with her relationship with Mr. Warner. I fear it is exactly what Nina feared would be my fate, if I were not careful. She works with him for hours on end, alone in his study, but Mrs. Warner does not seem to mind at all!

I've come to realize that though Mr. Warner has been nothing but kind and respectful toward me, he would do so for any writer—so long as such writer is a she. I will have to be careful moving forward to keep in these men's good graces, or else I fear what little career I have could shrivel up.

Give my love to Mimi,

Sis

Chapter 17

"Dr. Bradford?" Meredith asked, as she tapped on the professor's office door.

"Come in," Dr. Bradford called, looking up from her paper-scattered desk. "Ah, Meredith. Good. Have a seat. How is your research coming along?"

Her office had cream cinder-block walls, which were all lined with overfilled bookshelves.

"Not great," Meredith said with a sigh, setting her bag on the floor and settling into a chair opposite Dr. Bradford's desk. Meredith ran her eyes along the bookshelves while Dr. Bradford shuffled through some paperwork. Similar texts were beginning to collect on her own shelves: Robert Penn Warren, Evelyn Scott, Allen Tate, Zora Neale Hurston. "I'm struggling with a few things concerning Grace."

"What kind of struggling?"

"In her writing, Grace can show empathy and kindness toward her Black characters. But in her person, I keep seeing references that she was a segregationist. I can find passages that make me cringe, but I can also find passages that seem almost progressive. I'm worried about it. Dr. Bradford, I'm afraid that I am trying to save the writing of a racist woman. And what's the value there? And what role do I have in it as a researcher?"

"Ah," she said. "There's the challenge of literary and academic study, isn't it? Do we save the writing of someone because of its merit or value in one capacity, or let it become buried because their notion of society doesn't align with our more progressive one? Can you describe an example of each? So I can see the situation more clearly," she said, furrowing her brows in thought.

Meredith nodded. "So in the journals, she writes, 'To qualify themselves for an entrance into a novel they must first undergo a shameful connection with white men. Would that a pen were put into the hands of every virtuous colored woman, and she be bidden to write her own account not of the political but moral injustice done her.' Which sounds so promising. I mean, a little slut-shamey, but okay. And in her short stories, she has women of color as protagonists right alongside white characters."

Meredith took a deep breath. "But then, not only does she *not* do what she says someone ought to do—'put a pen in the hand of every colored woman'—but then, she writes in *Pleasant Ways* from Jerry's perspective, and perpetuates the stereotype of the childlike slave," Meredith said, frustrated. "At which point, I'm silently pleading with her to stop being such a racist and making my work so damn hard."

Dr. Bradford laughed gently. "And they never listen, do they?" She joked. "Well, does she use the n-word in her writing? As in, not in a character's voice?"

"No."

"Does she reflect the people of her time period?"

"Some, I think. Maybe not others. And the critics and scholars I read seem just as torn. Some of them state flat out she's a racist writer, and others say it's a lot more complicated than that."

"I had the same internal conversation when I wrote about Robert Penn Warren. I'm afraid they're creatures of their own generations. At least with Warren, as you know, he changed. Early in his career, he wrote of racist tendencies, but much later, he revisited these ideas, and his ideas evolved. But that's looking at a southerner from 1930 to 1950 or so. King is earlier than that, and for her to be any different than most white, patrician ladies of the time period would be truly exceptional. Frankly, the vast majority of white writers reflected complicated views on race. It's difficult, but I'm afraid you'll have to take her as-is."

"At the start of her career, she wrote a story about a former slave who loves her former owner's daughter so much, she raises the child even after the girl's mother died. Marcelite is an African American woman protagonist who is celebrated by the rest of the characters for her intelligence and strength...*but* she simultaneously perpetuates racial stereotypes," Meredith said, all in a rush. "This is why I keep going back and forth—because Grace does, too. She does this with other issues, too, like suffrage. In her personal letters, she is conservative and aligns with old causes and such. But in her writing, this is very different. And eventually, she comes out in support of women and the vote."

Dr. Bradford nodded thoughtfully. "Frankly, I'm glad that you're thinking so reflexively about your own scholarship. Most people don't. You're not going to find one answer that fits, I'm afraid. King may have done some things that were excellent and some things that weren't. Male writers are no different. Think about Mark Twain and Huck Finn. Some things are progressive or advanced for the time period, but then, some things are not. When we study the people behind their works, sometimes we don't always like who we find, and yet, historical figures, like King, are products of their time, just as we are products of ours. Your job is study the literature and its merits, not necessarily declare the writer a good or bad person."

Meredith nodded slowly. "The work she does representing women is amazing, and that's what she devoted her literary career to: Writing about women—*all* women. Writing across class and color lines, showing the lives of impoverished women and celebrating their strengths, after most of them were abandoned by the men in their lives. Most of the women in her works survive by loving one another and working together to survive, and yes, that's often across the color line. It's amazing."

Dr. Bradford smiled. "And how about the job search. How's it going so far?"

Meredith sighed. "I've been applying to a few generalist positions, but nothing has turned up yet."

"That's normal. Just keep an eye out, and there's also the option of you taking another year with a fellowship. Let's plan your dissertation with both outcomes in mind: One in which you wrap up quickly. In other words, write the dissertation you have to write to finish in a hurry. And place markers as you go to expand that version, in case you end up taking a fellowship for the extra year, in which case you can write the dissertation you want to write."

Meredith thought about her words for a minute. "If at all possible, I need to find a placement. Our girls need stability. They've moved too often." She needed stability. She needed roots—fast—or she feared she would spin out of control at any moment.

"That's understandable. The things we push ourselves to do for our children," she said kindly. "I did the same thing, with my own doctorate. I was a single parent, and I pushed to finish my diss, as well. I took a tenure-track job while I finished, but once I completed the Ph.D., the university refused to pay me the agreed upon salary, since it took me another few months to officially finish. I eventually left, because they treated me as hired help, rather than a full member of the faculty. I don't want that for you." Dr. Bradford paused and looked kindly at Meredith. "You are basing your diss on the notion that we must embrace ambiguity and be okay with simply not knowing," she said, reaching out a hand to squeeze Meredith's. "I'm afraid that means you have to, as well. For both the struggles with King and the ambiguity of the job search."

Meredith sat in silence, reflecting over the words. The professor she most admired had struggled, too. On the one hand, that was heartening. On the other, if someone with Dr. Bradford's skills had struggled, what would that mean for Meredith?

* * *

Later that afternoon, Meredith waited on the third floor of Bush Hall. She shifted her weight on the wooden bench and glanced nervously around her. Today, she was interviewing for a new graduate assistant position: Program Assistant. This position was considered the highest grad position, as it involved administrative duties related to the other grad students. She would be expected to work alongside faculty in maintaining the program.

Finally, the door across from her opened, and Jen smiled.

"Meredith, we're ready for you," Jen said.

Meredith sat in the only empty seat at the table, facing Jen and Dr. Helen Jones, head of the graduate program.

"Tell us," started Jen. "Why you want the position of Program Assistant."

Meredith took a breath to speak and sighed instead. "I don't." She let the words sit there for a moment. "I don't want the job. And yet, I'm the most qualified, and the least attached to any particular group or cohort. I operate independently from the others, ensuring I'll be more fair and equitable."

"And would you feel comfortable observing your grad student colleagues teaching and offering feedback on that?"

"I really enjoy teaching and pedagogy, and I'd love to help folks as they enter the classroom," Meredith said. "My own background before my MA in English was in teaching and pedagogy."

"And what about meeting the needs and representing your fellow graduate students?" asked Helen.

"I feel I am equipped to do so," Meredith answered. "For example, when Reagan was struggling to settle into the unpredictability of the writing center schedule, we chatted, and I suggested she try to be a small group tutor so she would have a more controlled schedule. She had a need, and the writing center had a need. It was just a matter to balancing those needs to benefit as many as possible."

"We've noted your handling of the sexual harassment issue. Well done on that. That was quite a challenge. It's unfortunate that Scott made the decisions he did, but now at least, he won't be teaching any incoming freshmen girls," said Jen. They continued chatting for over an hour.

As Meredith stood to leave, Jen followed her. "I'll walk out with you. I've got to stretch my legs."

Jen walked beside Meredith for a moment before gently touching her elbow. "Hey, you know you can reach out to people when you need it, right?"

Meredith smiled tightly. "Sure."

"No, really, Meredith. Academia is hard enough as it is. You don't need to isolate yourself on top of it."

Meredith paused, unsure of how to respond.

"I mean, this job is tough. Find your team." As she spoke, another adjunct faculty member passed them, giving Jen a tiny nod. Meredith saw the same gaunt face she had noticed in Jen lately, and she looked quizzically at her.

Jen sighed. "All the adjuncts and junior faculty have to re-apply for our jobs next fall. Every one of us. Rumor is they're going to cut seventy percent of us, and none of us are protected. Even those who've been here ten years or more."

"Holy shit," Meredith muttered. "Jen, I'm so sorry."

Jen shrugged. "Find your team, Meredith. You'll need it." Jen looked kindly at Meredith as she headed back to the graduate office. Meredith let out the breath she didn't know she was holding and walked down the hall.

When she rounded the corner, she saw Reagan.

"Hi, Reagan," Meredith said as she neared. Reagan raised her eyebrows ever so slightly to show the snub was intentional and kept walking to the office Meredith had just left. *She must be interviewing, too?* she thought. Meredith stopped in the middle of the hallway, surprised at the change in Reagan's treatment of her.

She doesn't understand yet that nothing about our applying for the same job is personal, Meredith thought. She started to shake her head, and then realized that Reagan's face was paler than usual, and there were darker circles under her eyes. *If she thinks this semester is stressful, she doesn't know what's coming in her third year: Preliminary exams*—and Meredith's were only a week away.

* * *

The next day, Meredith gazed over the living room floor. She had dropped Emmy off at day care and Lila off at school, and now it was time to settle in to work. She kicked out her half-destroyed yoga mat (thanks, kids!) and placed a footstool at one end. She scooped up armfuls of texts from the dining room table and placed them around the mat and set down a freshly filled cup of coffee on the footstool. Highlighters, pens, pencils, and index cards were scattered all around her.

She sighed and cued up yet another online Yale lecture video on literature. After five hours of mixed studying and light stretching, she sighed and gave up for the day. She piled the texts back onto the table and pulled on her workout clothes and walking shoes.

This was Meredith's normal routine several days a week for the entire year: study until she was mentally exhausted, then go for a three-to-five mile walk, or a hike if trails were nearby, to let off steam. Hiking had become something she enjoyed—something she found that gave her strength.

She slipped her earbuds in and set out towards a nearby park that included a paved trail that led to a small river. Once there, she took out the earbuds and watched the water glide by over the large rocks for a minute or two before replacing them to drown out the world and turn back toward home.

* * *

Liam gently shook Meredith awake on the morning of her exams. "Hey, you okay? Sounds like you're having a bad dream."

"I was," Meredith said, rubbing her eyes.

Liam looked worried in the early morning light. "Wanna talk?"

"Wasn't that kind of dream," Meredith said, rolling to face him. "I dreamed I had to take all of my exams in the Notes app on my phone. The app wouldn't save properly. It was awful," she whispered.

Liam snorted. "You know that's not going to happen, right?"

Meredith climbed out of bed to start getting ready: today was the day. She cast a quick sideways look at Liam and headed into the bathroom.

"Right?" Liam repeated from the bed.

* * *

Later that afternoon, Dr. Avery, the director of the grad program, stood in the front of the classroom, holding various manila envelopes—two for each doctoral student in the room. Computers lined three of the four walls, and the blinds barely shaded the hot afternoon sun. Doctoral students spaced themselves out at the computers, opened their various candies and waited nervously. Dr. Avery wavered between wanting to be the serious, no-nonsense director and the friendly coach.

"Now, remember: once your time is up, it's up. There's nothing I can do. But," he added. "I mean, finish your sentence or whatever, but that's it."

He kept checking his watch to start at the exact time. "Here are the envelopes, but don't open them yet."

The students scurried to the stack, sorted, and passed the envelopes out to each other. The air felt thick in Meredith's throat, and she could barely swallow.

"In a moment, you will start your primary area written exam," Dr. Avery said. "You will have exactly four hours to complete the packet. This exam will conclude at 5:00 p.m., but you must return tomorrow morning at 9:00 a.m. for your secondary area written exam. You will have the results of both in approximately one week. If you pass the exams, you will then schedule 90 minute oral exams with each set of your examiners. That means, you will complete one written and one oral exam for each of your two areas of specialization. Any questions?"

Everyone shook their heads no. This was common knowledge and had fueled their fears and nightmares for years.

"Then, you may begin."

Meredith opened her envelope. Two simple typed pages. Three questions.

Somehow, four hours seemed to pass in a matter of minutes, and the students were excused from the testing room at 5:00 p.m. sharp. Meredith had used her full four hours and cranked out fifteen pages of essay responses. She knew most of her colleagues were heading home to study up for tomorrow's exams, but she had two little girls needing her attention.

The next morning, she was up and out before any of them woke up. She walked around an empty campus, feeling exhausted and anxious—and oddly, peaceful. There was nothing else to do this morning besides do her best on the exam. No amount of last-minute reading would help.

She headed into Bush Hall and took her seat at the same computer as yesterday. The testers around her laughed or smiled nervously. Dr. Avery repeated his instructions from the previous session, and Meredith picked up her envelope for round two.

* * *

Meredith,

Your examiners have responded with your test results: American Literature 1910 to Present: Pass. Film Studies: Pass.

You will now schedule 90 minute oral exams for each testing area.

Congratulations,
Dr. Avery

* * *

Her oral exams were scheduled about two weeks after her written exams.

"I'm sorry, could you repeat that?" Meredith said loudly across the round table in the cafeteria. Two of her graduate professors, Drs. Barnes and Becall, shouted their questions over the lunch-hour cacophony, and Meredith shouted her answers in response. Most oral exams were done in a quiet classroom space, but Meredith's examiners had chosen the cafeteria, perhaps not realizing how busy the lunch hour truly was.

Meredith's nerves were failing, and she felt completely depleted.

One professor leaned forward to repeat her question, pointing to the paper in front of them, but all Meredith could hear was the buzzing in her ears and the loud lunchroom. People laughing too loudly. Other people shouting to be heard over their tables. Wrappers. Trays slamming.

Meredith pursed her lips and forced herself to stare at the paper for a moment. A class. They were asking her to plan a class in the middle of this chaos. But on what?

Meredith looked again at the paper: *Special Topics.*

The lunchroom noise slowly shifted to the background as Meredith stared at the paper. Suddenly, she could hear her own thoughts again. She picked up the pen.

"War," she said loudly. "I'd focus on war. Our country has been fighting in the Middle East for decades, and there's a ton of literature and writing that could be brought into a class like that. I'd use literature and film connected to the Vietnam War, as I think there are a great deal of similarities between Vietnam and the wars in the Middle East. A class like this could even be bridged to the Veterans Affairs office on campus for special speakers or presentations, and the students in it would have a stronger connection to the material—many of them being either vets themselves or related to veterans. Now, I'd start with Tim O'Brien's *The Things They Carried*, of course, and then, I might pair that, actually, with Sebastian Junger's documentary, to start those connections right off the bat."

Meredith rattled off half a dozen book and film titles, writing them on the paper as she went. "Now, for assignment sequences, I'd include the traditional research paper, but I might also include some sort of interview with a veteran or VA agent, a report on a veterans' issue, or even a creative writing piece or presentation. Oh, a nice addition of immigrants serving in the military, or women warriors, would be great, too!"

When Meredith looked up, the two professors were smiling and nodding. "I would take that class," Dr. Becall said loudly. They exchanged a look and asked Meredith to leave the table for a few minutes.

Meredith sat on a nearby bench, trying not to look like her academic fate wasn't riding on the conversation happening at that table. With no phone or notebooks, she watched the crowds in line for sandwiches and pizza, and after what seemed like an eternity, the professors waved for her to return.

"Congratulations!" they said, as soon as Meredith walked to them. They each shook her hand, and before she knew it, Meredith was outside on the hot sidewalk.

She left the chaos of the lunch room behind and took up residence in a hidden corner to rest and prepare for her next oral exam in three hours. She texted Liam her results, but she purposely hid out from the rest of the world for the afternoon.

When she entered the second oral exam, the professors sat in a half-dimmed, quiet classroom. The three of them chatted easily about film for the same ninety minutes, but this time, it passed quickly.

"I noticed," said her first examiner, Dr. Benner. "That you used comedies a great deal more than most students do. Most rely on dramas because of the more intense stories. Why such a choice?"

"I like them more," Meredith replied honestly. "Life is already filled with a lot of drama. I love the art behind a good drama, but I like the wit and humor in a well-done comedy just as much. A really well-done comedy should do both: Tell a riveting story but make me laugh, too. Honestly, comedy and laughter are what enable us to get through all the tough stuff. So, why leave out comedy in the serious dramas?"

He nodded thoughtfully. Soon enough, it was time for the same procedure.

Meredith left the room and returned a few minutes later.

Pass. Congratulations. Well-done. Thank you.

She left the room and walked slowly to the car. She sank into the hot driver's seat and rested with her eyes closed for a moment.

Professors and grad students alike said at this point, she would feel a huge wave of relief, having those exams completed. The weight would decrease, and the burden would lighten.

But Meredith felt nothing. No release. No lightened load to carry. She didn't feel proud of her accomplishment; she just felt complete and utter indifference. Her internal thoughts began a loop: They gave it to her. She was kind and didn't make waves. She was a decent teacher. So, why stop her during the exams? They gave this to her. They felt bad for her. She was a fraud—an exhausted fraud—and she felt it down to her very bones.

* * *

A few weeks later, Meredith logged into an online court case database. She logged on every single day, without mentioning it to anyone, even Liam.

Finally, after doing this for months on end, there was a change. Steven had taken a plea bargain: twenty years in prison. She also saw that her stepmother had filed for divorce.

She texted Ginny: *Twenty years.*

She answered almost immediately: *Yes. He tried to say my mom was involved, too, but she wasn't. He said she gave him permission to hurt me. She denied it. Then, she filed for divorce. I'm still not talking to her. She knew about his actions for years and took his side. Hope you're doing okay.*

Meredith responded just as quickly: *I'm doing fine, but what about you? I know family isn't much right now, but whenever, if ever, you're ready for one, I'm here.*

No reply from Ginny, but her phone buzzed with a call from Liam.

"Hey," he said, his tone off. "Um...so something happened."

"What? Are you okay?"

"Well, yeah, but I seem to have gone into a fugue state of some sort and missed my exit."

"What do you mean?"

"Well," he said, taking deep breaths. "I was just thinking, and then I looked up, and it had been an hour. I was almost in Chattanooga."

"What?" Meredith demanded. "You're not driving now, are you? I'll come get you...wait, I'll get the kids, then I'll come get you...but then, how will we get the truck back..."

"Meredith, stop," he said calmly. "I'm okay. I'm almost back now. I'm okay."

Meredith took a few deep breaths. "Are you sure?"

"Yes, I'm okay. And I'll call my doctor as soon as I get home."

* * *

A few days later, Meredith woke up in a cold sweat in the middle night. She felt hot and claustrophobic. She leaned over the edge of the bed, in case she threw up. *Oh, God. Don't throw up.* She'd been with this man for how many years and never thrown up in front of him? *Don't do it, don't do it, don't do it.*

"You okay?" Liam asked. He sounded alert, awake. He must have been sitting up, reading.

"You're still awake? Isn't it, like, four in the morning?" Meredith whispered.

"Yeah. Nightmares. But I'm okay," he said softly. "What do you need?"

"Nothing yet," she said. She felt dizzy with panic but rolled her legs out of the bed and half stumbled into the bathroom. She sat on the toilet and ran a wash cloth under the faucet. *Ahhhh, cold.* She dabbed the cold cloth on the back of her neck, her wrists, her eyes. Anything. Anything to keep from throwing up. *Please.* Her lower lip trembled, and her eyes filled with tears. *Please, no dry-heaving. It hurts. Please.*

After what felt like an eternity, nothing happened. She began to breathe a tiny bit and left the bathroom. She stepped gently across the floor, as though even a single incorrect placement of her foot could cause a complete reversal and send her into a full, vomiting mess. She sat on the edge of the bed, ever so lightly. *No sudden moves. Must be still. Be very still.*

She eased back on the cool pillow, still clutching her cold compress like it was her lifeline to sanity. *Cold. Good.*

The world seemed to spin around her, and the bed seemed to tilt dangerously under her, like a raft in a muddy, raging river.

Liam leaned, moving the bed. Her stomach flopped.

"I'll get you some cold ginger ale. Do you have your cold cloth?"

"Mm-hmm."

"Be right back."

Within minutes, an icy glass of ginger ale sat on the bedside table, sweating onto the wood. Meredith still clutched her washcloth to her face, childlike.

Liam lay back down, shaking the bed the tiniest bit. *Oh, God. This is it.* She was going to throw up.

She flashed back to when she was a very little girl. Her father took her to Florida for vacation. This was one of the times he had disappeared with her. Hid her from her mother. They stayed at a little motel with a small swimming pool. Meredith kept feeling sick to her stomach and telling him so. He'd ignored her. Later that night, she woke to him being sick in the bathroom. The next morning, he'd looked her in the eye over their breakfast cereal. "I'm sorry. I should have believed you," he'd said. She'd felt heard and grown-up when he'd apologized. How could she reconcile this person with the one who had hurt Ginny?

Meredith clutched the rag tighter and whimpered, her chest tight with unspilled tears.

"Everything's okay," Liam whispered. "I'm here. I'll do anything you need me to. Let's breathe together, like the therapist taught me the other day."

He took a deep breath, and Meredith tried to follow along.

Fear still ripped through her stomach, and her lower lip wouldn't stop trembling. Her leg muscles contracted, pulling up and locking in place. She lay still and quiet for what felt like hours with Liam's hand on her shoulder, until finally she slept, her pillow wet from the cloth and tears she didn't realize had spilled over. When she woke hours later, Liam was exactly where he'd said he would be, right beside her, snoring softly.

Chapter 18

November 1892
My dearest May,

Nan and I sailed out of New York a few weeks ago. Our first stop was England, and I was so excited—just to think about the adventure made me shake with anxiety.

Once we reached London, I received the page proofs for Tales of a Time and Place. *I could barely contain my excitement as Nan and I walked to our room. Imagine—your sister—a writer and a world traveler! And now I can add lecturer to the list, as well! I spoke to a class of remarkable young ladies at Newnham College in Cambridge. I discussed the importance of Sidney Lanier's poetry. I loved it, but at the same time, I was so nervous I feared I would faint right in front of the students! I can finally eat again, now that the task is done—but why bother with this bland English food? Next we are off to Paris, where I will surely find the time to write you a proper letter!*
Your affectionate sister partner—
Sis

Once in Paris, Grace and Nan found housing at the Institut, a boarding house for women run by the Vicomtesse du Peloux. They lived there with numerous other women, mostly teachers and governesses from Russia, Germany, and Australia, and, of course, France. Madame du Peloux referred to all of her guests as *les hirondelles*—little birds.

They celebrated Christmas Eve there, with their new eclectic family, where they exchanged small gifts, drank rum punch, and laughed and talked until well after midnight. The next morning, Christmas Day, Grace and Nan suffered terrible headaches as they forced themselves to go to church.

One Saturday afternoon in April, Grace sat at the breakfast table with the other *hirondelles* and listened as they commiserated about their charges.

"And worst of all is how the little beast treats me," said one, a young German girl of around eighteen years of age. "He screams as though I beat him and makes all who see think I am terrible. Last week, he refused to leave the park, and when I picked him up, he bit me! Of course, I dropped him, but he cried foul and said I'd done it on purpose!" She held up her forearm and pointed to the bite marks, still healing.

The others clicked their tongues and shook their heads, while several offered ideas for how to deal with the impish young boy.

One of the young women, a tall Russian girl, looked to Grace. "You are lucky you have no such challenges to meet! What will you do with today? More lectures?"

After breakfast, Grace and Nan usually made their way to the Sorbonne, where they would sit in on various lectures for the morning. Grace usually chose, and so they learned about history, philosophy, and literature.

"Not this morning," Grace said with a smile. "Today, Nan is off on her own adventure with a friend, while I am meeting my dear friend, Madame Blanc."

Grace had been invited to attend a salon with Madame Marie Blanc, a literary editor and writer in her small, bright apartment on the Rue de Grenelle, near Les Invalides, and the women had become immediate friends. Every Monday afternoon that Grace had been in Paris, Madame Blanc had expected her to attend her salon, and so she did. Grace enjoyed visiting Marie's beautiful apartment with its white and gold furniture almost as much as she admired her rise to financial independence. Though Marie had married in her youth and had a son, she raised him as a single parent while she worked as editor for the literary magazine, *Les Revues des Deux Mondes*. Grace wasn't sure if Marie's husband had passed away or abandoned the family, and she felt it inappropriate to ask.

During their weekly chats, Marie had taken on the role of Grace's intellectual mentor, and she enjoyed sharing her American friend with other intellectual circles. Grace's life had quickly become a whirlwind of social circles, but not the kind she was used to in New Orleans. Here, in Paris, she felt at home in shabby chic salons surrounded by intellectuals debating philosophy, politics, history, and literature. They challenged each other's ideas and welcomed Grace's own.

Marie had wanted Grace to meet Madame Lily de Bury, the widow of a French nobleman, and it had finally been arranged.

Grace bid her breakfast companions adieu and set out to meet Marie en route to Madame de Bury's salon. As she approached the small park that was their meeting place, she spotted Marie seated on a bench, reading a small booklet.

"*Bonjour,*" Marie said, standing to embrace Grace.

"Marie, how are you?" Grace said, in her now-fluent French. Since their arrival in France months before, Grace and Nan had hardly spoken in English, and though it at times had proved a challenge, Grace loved how easily the language rolled off of her tongue now.

"Quite well, my friend. How goes your research into Bienville this week?" Marie said, as the women linked arms and walked slowly together.

During these months, Grace continued to review the pages for *Tales,* but she had also been working on a biography of Sieur de Bienville, the early French colonialist. "Well enough," Grace said, pleased that Marie had not only remembered the project, but that she seemed to value it as Grace did. It was odd to Grace that her male mentors were not as welcoming to genres that were outside of their own wheelhouse. Judge Gayarré, Grace's history mentor, did not much encourage her literary pursuits, and Mr. Warner, her literary mentor, did not see much value in her historic interests. Neither openly discouraged her, but she had noticed their immediate lack of attention the moment she referred to another project.

Marie, on the other hand, seemed to see value in any of Grace's projects.

"I've been trying to locate some old maps," Grace admitted with a laugh. "I'm not even sure why. I just have a hunch I need them and might find them in Paris."

Marie furrowed her brow. "Write down some description of these maps, and I will send it to a colleague. He may be able to help us."

"Oh, thank you, Marie, you are too kind, to guide me and share so many of your own friendships and colleagues with me," Grace said.

"So it should be, with women," Marie said. "We need to protect each other, support each other, in all things."

Grace smiled and lowered her voice a bit, as though sharing a secret. "I've started another little project, as well."

"Ah, you must tell me," said Marie.

"I am putting together many small stories, such as the women in New Orleans would tell each other. Stories about women, the way women tell them," Grace explained. "Like this, between us. Sitting together the way we do, sharing little pieces of ourselves."

"This sounds lovely, my dear friend," said Marie. "Women confidantes. And what will you call this project?"

"For now, I simply call them my balcony stories," Grace said. "Because that's where they are often told in New Orleans. On balconies. Just outside of the children's ears but not quite in the intense public view."

"This sounds more intriguing the more you tell me," Marie said. "You must tell me more as you progress. Now, my dear Grace, it is time for you to meet the wonderful Madame de Bury."

Marie had stopped walking, and Grace looked at the exterior of Madame de Bury's little apartments at 20 Rue d'Oudinot, near Les Invalides. The building was the traditional Parisian stone, with small wrought-iron fixtures under the windows. Grace and Marie passed through the double door entrance, where Grace admired the deep shade of blue on the door.

De Bury's apartment was filled with furniture and clutter—piles of books and papers sat in various mounds throughout the flat. Compared to Madame Blanc's bright apartment, Madame de Bury's flat was dark and a bit dank.

Expecting to find another petite French woman, Grace was surprised to see a large Scottish woman in her sixties. She was even more shocked to realize that de Bury didn't wear a corset. Up close, she noted the smallpox scars that marred Madame's face. And yet, the woman exuded confidence. She greeted Grace loudly from across the room, "Welcome, Miss King! Madame Blanc tells me wonderful things about you! I'll be happy to have you join our little circle of friends here!"

"Thank you," Grace said, noticing how soft her own voice sounded in comparison. "It's a pleasure to meet you and to be included in such a collection of intellectuals."

Grace sat on a dusty brown couch and spent most of her first afternoon observing the group. De Bury wore a black skirt, gray jacket, and a red silk belt. The style was simple and understated; De Bury did not need her clothing to speak for her. She opened the informal salon by jumping right into her discussion of French politics with her loud voice.

"We need a moral revolution here in France," Madame declared, looking for support from those in the room. Several men nodded their heads, but Grace had no idea who they were. There had been no formal introductions. De Bury continued, "Desjardin's assertion is right! Drug addiction and drunkenness too heavily affect the lower classes, and the higher class is too caught up in science and sensuality. Everything is about sensation, but what about the spirit? The soul? These must not be forgotten! *L'union pour l'action morale!*"

A tall, ruggedly handsome man answered her forcefully, "Absolutely! And a reunification with nature is necessary! Religion and spirit are found in all things in nature, and many in France today have forgotten this." Grace found herself intrigued by the man, whose voice took easy command of the room. He quoted Emerson and Thoreau, prompting many nods from both men and women. Grace felt overwhelmed and too shy to participate in the vigorous discussion, but as the others began to trickle out or mill about the room, Marie joined Grace on the sofa.

"And so, what did you think?" she asked, gazing at her friend curiously.

Grace nodded for a moment, trying to feign nonchalance. "It was...absolutely wonderful! Thank you, dear Marie, for sharing this and inviting me here! I was deeply moved by what...the man who sat in the armchair was saying."

"Ah! That was Charles Wagner, a well known Presbyterian pastor. His sermons are quite popular," Marie explained. "We should go soon to hear him on a Sunday morning! He will be most appreciative."

"That would be wonderful," said Grace. "Nan will love that, too."

"Though I must caution you a tiny bit, my dear friend," said Marie, lowering her voice and smiling gently. "He is married!"

Grace's face flushed pink as Marie laughed.

"Not to worry, though! You are simply joining his many admirers!" she said conspiratorially.

"Miss King," said Madame de Bury from across the room. "Tell me what you thought of our little discussion today."

Grace sat up, as though scolded by a schoolteacher for talking in class. "I am most impressed, Madame, and humbled to have been in attendance at such a discussion. Please excuse my timidity in such large crowds. It isn't in my nature to speak out of turn or to be forceful in speech."

"Of course, my dear, of course," she said. "A good southern, American lady you are: bottled and kept on a shelf. But you must sit by me and share your thoughts afterwards from now on, as your ideas and thoughts are most welcome here! Come! Someone, bring us tea!" she called, making room for Grace to join her on the small sofa across the room.

Madame de Bury smiled at Grace and said, "I only surround myself with intellectuals, and I consider you to be one of them. Now, let us hear your voice. Tell me first of your adventures in England."

"Well, I must confess," Grace began slowly. "I did not much care for it."

Madame de Bury burst out laughing. “Who does? It’s cold, and the food is terrible. Did you have a terrible time?”

“I spent much of my time there feverish and had to remain in bed,” Grace explained. “I tried to pass the time writing letters and resting, but it has tainted my experience a bit.”

“Oh no! Were you able to get out at all? The social scene in London can be nice, and Hyde Park is often a favorite.”

“I was able to a bit, yes, but...” Grace hesitated.

“Go on,” urged Madame.

Grace hesitated. “Hyde Park was a bit of a disappointment.”

Madame laughed loudly. “I hate it, too. Why are the carriages so big? And the dresses the girls wear so ugly!”

Grace laughed. “They seem to exist merely to be seen—to be show ponies. They were paraded up and down the pathways. Frankly, the poor creatures were so badly dressed and plain, it made me quite melancholy,” she blurted before stopping herself abruptly.

Madame guffawed again and reached out a reassuring hand to squeeze Grace’s own. “And there it is, *mesdames et messieurs*, the little American bird has some color!”

* * *

In May, 1892, Grace and Nan spent a few days at a boarding house in Barbizon at Marie’s recommendation. The country home was near the Forest of Fontainebleau, and there, they met other creative residents, mostly painters.

Grace felt relaxed, surrounded by beauty, art, and intellect. She sat writing under the trees in the garden, enjoying the late morning breeze. The green leaves blew softly, rustling around her, and she found a moment of stillness in an otherwise very busy world and life she had created for herself in Europe. She looked around her and sighed happily, leisurely jotting notes in her notebook about Bienville and the research she had been collecting while in France.

She felt...*different.* Energized and at peace, simultaneously. She could write and work now, without feeling the need to obtain validation or approval from others. She could write for herself alone. She could fend for herself, make her own money, and shape her own life. The realization dawned on her slowly: she was simply Grace here. She could study and write in any direction, with nothing to prove. She was not Miss Grace King, of the New Orleans' Kings, daughter to Mrs. William King. She didn't feel the overwhelming need to run her ideas and projects by someone else in order to validate their importance. They just were. She could exist here without apology or purpose—and it was freeing.

Nagell, a Swedish painter, walked across the garden toward her. He gestured to the other chair without speaking, to be sure company was welcome. Grace smiled and nodded. He grinned and eased into the black wrought-iron seat.

"You look at peace, out here," he said in thickly accented English.

"I feel at peace here," Grace said, sighing again contentedly. "I've never been able to write so easily and freely as I do here."

Nagell grinned again. "It is easier to create when surrounded by beauty and not having to do with the ordinary, yes?"

"Yes, it is," she agreed. Just then, Nan waved from the doorway of the stone and stucco country house.

"And your sister? Is she as happy in France as you?"

"I'm not sure," Grace said thoughtfully. "I think if she weren't, she would say so, but she may, in fact, be getting a bit homesick lately." She looked at Nan and smiled across the large garden. Nan had been a bit quieter recently, but Grace had thought that was simply because they had been surrounded by so many creative, talkative people.

Nan walked to join them, holding several envelopes in her hand.

"Grace, you have a few letters in the post," she said, handing them to Grace and smiling shyly at Nagell, who kindly returned her smile.

Grace took the letters and scanned the envelopes. She glanced at Nagell. "Do you mind if I open these? I am expecting an important note."

"Of course not," he said, helping himself to the bread on the table. He lathered the dry bread with butter.

Grace skimmed the letter from Livy and said to Nan, "The Clemenses have invited us to spend some time with them in Italy, near Florence. What do you think, Nan? I'd love for you to meet them!"

Nan nodded, helping herself to the bread and butter, as well, while casting the occasional glance at Nagell. "Of course. We can change our return route to leave from Italy, instead of England."

"Good, then," Grace said, watching Nan curiously. Nan glanced at Nagell and blushed. Grace frowned. "Nan, here's one from Mimi." She handed the letter to Nan and waited while Nan skimmed through.

"Mimi says she misses us, hopes we are well, and that Fred's wife, Nellie, is driving her crazy, but that she's thankful for Will's wife, Jennie. Looks like Jennie and Will are getting on well, and he's doing quite a bit better," Nan said, looking back up at Grace. "Well, that's good news, isn't it?"

"Mm," said Grace, only half-listening.

Nan waited patiently but finally spoke up when Grace said nothing. "What is it? Is it something wrong?"

"No, quite the opposite," Grace said, scanning and re-scanning the letter. "Marie says an acquaintance of hers, a Madame Toulon de Vault, is backing a project of translating letters believed to be written by George Sand to one of her lovers. They are offering me the opportunity to translate the letters from French to English and publish them in an American journal. And to top it off, Marie's acquaintance may have found the maps I've been searching for these last few months!"

"What wonderful news!" said Nagell, jumping up to embrace Grace. "We shall celebrate! I will make for you my favorite Swedish dish—beefsteak pudding!"

Grace laughed. “Why on earth would anyone put beefsteak in a pudding!”

“No, no! You have never had the beefsteak pudding? You must! You must! It is traditional and wonderful! I will go now for the ingredients!” Nagell strode happily across the garden.

“You know, maybe we should make Mimi’s bouillabaisse for everyone tomorrow evening?” Nan suggested, watching Nagell walk away.

“Ah, now there’s an idea. Are you getting a bit homesick?”

“Maybe. But, we’ll see part of Italy this fall. I am homesick a bit, yes, but when will we ever get this chance again?”

Grace nodded thoughtfully and turned back to the letters. “I’m not so sure about this translation project,” she admitted to Nan, looking back over the letter. “How proper would it be for a lady to translate love letters? What if they are scandalous?”

Nan shrugged. “I guess that will be up to you to decide.”

* * *

September 25, 1892
Dear Mimi,

You would not believe the experiences I have had recently! Madame Toulon de Vaulx has invited me to work on a special project connected to George Sand! We had dinner to discuss the project at the most beautiful salon I have ever seen. There were gilt chairs, a grand piano, and paintings all over the walls—floor to ceiling.

I cannot begin to tell you of the importance of this trip for my writing—and my spirit. I have found such an incredible spirit and intellectualism in France that I lament returning to New Orleans. How is it that the daughter of Paris—New Orleans!—did not inherit her mother’s intellect and creativity? It makes me wonder what could have been if we had come to France during the War—would we have retained our status and wealth? Would I, and all of us, have had very different lives?

Even with my feeling with this way—Nan and I are a bit homesick as of late. We made your famous bouillabaisse for some friends recently, and they simply raved about how wonderful it was!
Lovingly,
Sis

* * *

That fall, Grace and Nan travelled to Villa Viviani, the Clemenses' rented home near Florence. Mossy stone urns stood vigil at the gate posts of the small, cottage-like villa with yellow stucco and green shutters. The interior was impressive with its two story salon, filled with green plants. Tall pine trees surrounded it, casting a lovely shade over the gardens, which were filled with pink and yellow roses.

As they sat under olive trees for breakfast, surrounded by blue mountains dotted with white villas, Grace tried to relate their many adventures in France to the Clemenses, but Mr. Clemens continually cut her off and changed the subject.

"Youth, dear," said Livy, gently steering the conversation back to Grace. "Grace was telling us about some of her work with Marie Blanc."

Grace smiled patiently. In the time she and Nan had spent in Europe, she suddenly realized that very little of it had been spent speaking with American men. She had forgotten the deference they expected. She opened her mouth to speak but closed it almost immediately when she was cut off yet again.

"Bah," said Mr. Clemens. "That Blanc woman has no sense of humor! She tried to translate my 'Celebrated Jumping Frog of Calaveras County,' but she failed to capture any of the wit or humor. But that's just like the French! They have no sense of humor! Now, the Germans! There's a respectable people!"

Grace sighed and settled back into her chair. Clearly she was merely an audience for this show. Across the table, she made eye contact with Susy who smiled sadly. She, too, was just an audience member.

After breakfast, they decided to take a day trip to put flowers on Elizabeth Barrett Browning's grave. As they prepared to leave, the post arrived, and Grace received the first copies of her Bienville manuscript.

"Wait," said Nan, looking over her shoulder. "They didn't send you proofs first? They just printed it?"

"It appears so," Grace murmured, raising her eyebrows.

Mr. and Mrs. Clemens came behind them, and each picked up a copy of the text.

"Well, it's lovely," said Livy, flipping through the pages.

"Uh oh," muttered Mr. Clemens.

"What is it?" asked Grace, panic filling her voice.

"Page four. Misprints," he said.

"And page seven," said Nan.

"And page twelve," said Grace, sighing in despair. "What am I going to do? It looks like I put together a shoddy text! They've botched it!"

Mr. Clemens set the text down. "You just need to speak with the editor. Convince them to reprint it. For now, my dear, let's pay a visit to the departed. Proof the copies while you are here, and meet with them in New York on your way back to New Orleans."

Grace nodded. "Thank you, Mr. Clemens."

That afternoon, Grace approached Browning's tombstone. The others had not reached the plot just yet, so Grace had a few quiet moments between Browning and herself. The white marble structure rested on six short columns and another marble foundation platform and was decorated with elegant scrollwork and trimming.

She placed a small bouquet of flowers on the bottom platform alongside other well-wishers' gifts and reflected over Browning's writing and life. She wondered whether anyone would one day do the same for her—place flowers or ribbons in remembrance of her life as a writer. This European trip had deeply changed her, and she knew it. She felt it. She was becoming her own person, with her own interests outside those of her previous mentors. Returning to New Orleans meant that she would need to reconcile this new Grace with the old one.

Chapter 19

Dear Ms. Mandin,

On behalf of the American Women Writers Society (AWWS), we welcome your presentation, "Liminality and Grace King" at our triennial conference this November in Philadelphia, PA.

Sincerely,

Selection Committee

* * *

As the newly hired Program Assistant for her fourth year in the doctoral program, Meredith was supposed to manage the office and assist the other grad students with their pedagogy and teaching skills, since this was their main means of finding a job post-graduation. She'd started by bringing in bulletin board paper and trying to pretty the office space up. It was like putting lipstick on a pig: the overwhelming beige was simply broken up into mostly beige sections with little posters here and there.

She spent many hours in the fall semester in grad students' classrooms. For the most part, Meredith loved this part of the job. She liked watching her colleagues teach. She learned great ideas from them: that she should add her lesson plans to the online class shells for students to access them. That she could create hyperlinked lesson plans as little walk-though exercises for students to self-pace their way through, after the initial lessons, like Leigh did with her lesson plans. That she could relax in her own classes and establish a nice rapport with her students without losing control of the classroom, like Gavin with his students.

These observations were enjoyable.

She was, also, presented with various challenges with this responsibility.

As she entered the office one early afternoon, Carol, a grad student in her fifties, sat with one of her students. Carol had disliked Meredith since they once had a deep disagreement over whether women's welfare funding should be stopped if they didn't tell the government who the fathers of their children were. Meredith had pointed out that this is a private issue and a form of slut shaming. Carol had pointed out that she used to be a social worker and therefore knew the truth about "those women." Meredith had stared, open mouthed, in complete shock and let the issue go right there. *Don't play chess with pigeons. They'll just shit on the board and strut away like they won.*

"So, yes," Carol said to her student. "Black people can say a lot of things, but the moment a white person says it, it's racist." The young woman stared at Carol, confused, somewhat shocked, and clearly offended.

Oh, fuck. What the hell is she doing?

"Hi, Carol," Meredith said, setting her bag on the table with an overly sunny smile. "Are we all set for our meeting?" Meredith asked, purposely interrupting the conversation.

"Uh, sure, I guess," Carol said, her eyes wide at the interruption.

"Great!" Meredith said, looking to the student. As the girl packed her things, she tried to give her a look that she hoped said, "I'm so sorry!" The student slung her heavy backpack over her shoulder and left the office, saying nothing to anyone.

Turning to Carol, Meredith said, "So, the class was good. I think you mentioned at some point that it's your first time teaching intro to composition. In the class I attended, you presented a PowerPoint lecture on the evolution of horror films. Is that tied to an assignment?"

"Oh, not really, but I want to appeal to student interest."

"So...you gave a one hour presentation on horror to appeal to students?"

"Oh, no. That day was day three of the lecture."

"Okay," Meredith said slowly, trying to make sense of the information. "And do you see the lecture as connected to one of the course learning objectives?"

"I don't really know. I mean, I can teach whatever I want," she said, her tone growing harsh. "I want *my students* to have this knowledge."

"About horror films?"

"Yes! They're important."

"But the class is English 101, Intro to College Writing. Are they going to write about the horror films?"

"Well, no, but I'm not clueless," she said, growing more frustrated. "I know you think you know everything, but I was a teacher in Florida *and* a social worker, so I know what I'm doing."

Clearly. Then, with a sigh and a softened tone, Meredith said, "I'm simply worried about their next professor in their next class. What if they're asked to write something different? Will they be prepared? What if they have one of our own grad professors, like Professor Dougal?"

Carol paused. "Well, I hadn't thought of it like that."

After settling Carol and gently explaining that students really needed to write in their college composition class, Meredith saw Katie, a new grad student, in the corner.

"Hi, there," she called to her, smiling. She sat down in the chair opposite her at the table. "How's it going? Are you settling in okay?"

Katie gave a look that said clearly Eat-Shit-and-Die. "I'm fine."

"You doing okay with the teaching load? It can be a bit stressful, with all the coursework," Meredith said.

"You people are ridiculous. This is so easy. Try being in a real program, like Virginia Tech," Katie said, rolling her eyes.

Meredith noticed, however, that Katie's words did not reflect the nervousness Meredith could see in her eyes, but she sighed and walked away anyway. Katie picked up her things and left the office, and Meredith braced herself for the next meeting with David. As she settled in at the large shared table to wait, Laurie, a TA one year behind her, walked in. Laurie was always smiling, always friendly, and always a bit scattered.

"Oh! Meredith! I know we weren't going to go over my observation until next week, but I'm so nervous! Could we do it now?"

Meredith smiled. "Sure, Laurie. Do you want to settle in first?"

"Nope! I've been so nervous! Let's just talk about it," she said, as she settled herself in at the table with Meredith. Her bright red, embroidered blouse contrasted deeply with her dark blue trousers but brought out her rosy cheeks.

"Sure," Meredith said. "So, from your perspective, how do you feel about your classroom and the lesson I sat in on?"

"I'm not sure," Laurie said. "On the one hand, I know I'm doing the right lessons. But something's off. I'm terrified of my students, and nothing seems to get the class going in the right direction."

Meredith nodded thoughtfully. "I can see that," she said kindly.

"Oh no! You could see that, too? Does that mean I failed teaching?" Laurie asked, genuinely panicked.

"No, no, no," Meredith said, reassuring her. "Laurie, my first year teaching, I taught junior high kids. Those little shits stole every pen and marker on the very first day—before first period was even over! It was tough. It takes awhile to get the hang of this, and the fact that you *want* to be better is a good thing. Hell, I want to be better, too! We all do. So, let's talk about some classroom management strategies to help you with your nerves, so you can feel more comfortable and help your students feel more comfortable, too. Would that be okay?"

"Oh, God, yes," Laurie said with a deep sigh of relief.

They chatted for awhile about Laurie's class of students and how she could shift the pacing of her class to put her students in a better frame of mind. By the time they were done, Laurie felt better, and so did Meredith. At least she felt needed and useful after chatting with Laurie. David had come in during their chat, and as Laurie headed out, he walked over to Meredith at the table.

Last week, Meredith had sat in David's class for ninety minutes while he'd talked at his students about Yeats.

"How's it going?" David asked as he plopped into a chair and tipped it away from the table. He propped his sneakers up on the table. "So, we're still looking for people to send articles to the campus journal. Are you submitting anything?"

"I'm afraid not," Meredith said. "I'm just writing on the diss right now."

"Psh," David responded. "You just think you're better than our little journal," he said in a half-playful, half-serious tone.

Meredith smiled. "Yup, that's what it is," she said in a flat tone, trying to play along. Since overhearing the other students speaking about her, she had made it a point not to submit her name or work for anything on campus anymore. Even sending materials and conference proposals was becoming more and more difficult, since she felt she had to attempt everything alone. In a perfect world, she'd have a team of colleagues giving her feedback on her writing and work before she sent anything. As part of that team, she would be doing the same work for others. Under this competitive environment, however, Meredith felt like she was suffocating. She couldn't grow or stretch, because at every angle, there was someone there saying nasty things; there was always something just there, out of sight, ready to pounce on her. At this point, she tried not to even talk about her projects to anyone.

"So, what'd you think of my class?" David asked, bringing her back to their conversation.

"It was good. You have a good bunch of students," Meredith said. "Are you happy with the way the class is going? Can I offer any specific feedback to help address any of your own concerns?"

"Nope, I'm happy with it," David said, looking at Meredith. He put his hands behind his head. "But what did *you* think?"

"Well," Meredith said. "I noticed that some students seem to be struggling with paying attention," Meredith hesitated.

"Horse shit, Meredith. You're just nit-picking," he said in a harsh tone. He slammed his chair back to the floor.

Meredith took a deep breath to try to rebalance herself after feeling like she was under attack. In the softest voice she could muster, she said, "David, on the day I sat in the classroom, you did almost all of the talking for ninety minutes straight."

"Whatever," he said, crossing his arms and glaring at the wall.

"Look, I'm not saying don't teach the things you love about literature. I'm saying, from what I saw, most of the students weren't following the lecture. You were teaching a class to, maybe, two students, while everyone else just sat there," Meredith said gently. "I'm happy to help with student engagement, to help you share your interest in the lit with the students in the room."

He clenched his jaw and refused to make eye contact. "I think we're done here," he said, pushing his chair away from the table and storming out of the office.

Meredith sighed and rubbed her eyes. She hated arguments, and she hadn't wanted to argue with David. But she also couldn't avoid what she'd seen in the classroom. Glancing at the clock on the wall, she stood to stretch and gather her bags.

She turned to a large box of materials she needed to carry upstairs for a workshop. She hoisted it up, her bags dangling from her shoulder and bouncing into chairs as she made her way to the door. Reagan glanced over from the computer where she worked as Meredith struggled to open the door.

"Reagan, could you..." Meredith watched as Reagan, keeping eye contact, slowly placed in her ear buds and turned back to her computer.

Meredith sighed, set the box down, opened the door herself, and dragged the box outside.

Over the next few weeks, the plants and watering can in her cubicle were repeatedly tipped over, spilling dirt and water. Her papers were rifled through, and her personal notes and files scattered around the desk and floor.

* * *

A week after the semester ended, Meredith and Liam took the girls for a short trip to New Orleans. They booked a small tent site at a campground just outside of the city to keep the costs down, and that night, the girls loved sitting by the tiny fire and sleeping in their sleeping bags.

The next morning, Liam and Meredith packed everyone up and drove to the nearest streetcar stop. They parked their truck on the street and led the girls to the stop.

"What are we waiting on?" Lila asked.

"The streetcar, remember?" Meredith replied, smiling and holding Emmy's hand.

"What's a streetcar? I don't remember," Lila responded, spinning in place.

From down the street, Meredith heard the bell.

"*That's* a streetcar," she said, pointing.

Lila froze in place and looked up, her mouth opening. "We're going to ride in *that?*"

"What? Don't you want to?" Liam asked, handing her a dollar and a quarter.

"YES!" She squealed, jumping up and down in place.

"Emmy, too?" Emmy asked, looking up.

"Yes," Meredith said, laughing. "Emmy, too!"

"Yay!" Emmy said, half dancing.

The streetcar screeched as it pulled up to the curb, and Meredith lifted Emmy up the steep steps. She slid their fare into the feeder and led them down the aisle. Lila slid into the seat against the window, and Meredith sat beside her, while Liam did the same thing with Emmy so both girls could have a clear view of the passing Garden District.

Lila's hair blew back from her face as the streetcar moved down the lane, and she squinted in the sun at the mansions sliding by.

"Mommy, what are all these fancy buildings?" she asked.

"Most of them are houses."

Lila's mouth dropped open. "People just *live* in them?"

"Yes, they do. Very rich people, anyway," Meredith said, laughing.

"Look at that one! Oh—and look at that one!" Lila kept pointing at the homes along St. Charles Avenue. "That's my favorite! No, wait. *That's* my favorite!"

Meredith leaned forward to Liam and Emmy in the seat in front of them. “How is Emmy?”

“She’s fine,” Liam said, as Emmy turned around, wearing Liam’s oversized sunglasses on her tiny face.

“Emmy no see, so Emmy wear Daddy’s gasses,” Emmy shouted, pointing to Liam’s sunglasses.

Meredith laughed. “I see that! Are you having fun?” Emmy nodded stoically and turned back to her window, her hair blowing back from her face.

“So, where to?” Liam asked, putting his hand up for Meredith to hold over the seat back.

“Lunch, I guess,” she responded. “I was thinking of picking up some sandwiches and having a picnic in Jackson Square. What do you think?”

“Emmy loves ’nics!” Emmy shouted, turning to them. “Emmy want ’nic!”

Lila smiled, too. “Let’s do that, but what’s in Jackson Square?”

“I’ll show you,” Meredith said. She settled back against the wooden seat and reveled in the feeling that she was home and that she was showing the girls something so very dear to her: New Orleans.

In a short time, they had picked up muffulettas and had arrived at Jackson Square. They spread out the thin tablecloth Meredith often kept in her bag to use as an impromptu picnic blanket and settled the girls down to eat where they could watch the various street performers.

“Look at that one!” Lila said, pointing to a small car that buzzed along the sidewalk, stopped, and unfolded into a person, waving at the crowds of people.

Emmy’s jaw dropped and eyes grew wide as saucers as though she just could not reconcile the magic she had just witnessed. “Wow,” she whispered, as she leaned a little closer to Liam.

“Mommy, horsies!” Emmy cried a few minutes later, as the familiar clip-clop of the carriage horses came down Decatur Street.

"Yes, lots of big horsies and carriages. Would you like to go see them?" Meredith asked.

Lila and Emmy nodded, as they cleared away their tablecloth and trash. Liam picked Emmy up as they approached the draft mules.

"They're *big!*" Lila said, tilting her face back to look up into the big brown eyes of a large, dark gray draft mule.

"They sure are," said the carriage handler nearby. The middle-age woman wore simple jeans, a button up blouse, and straw hat. "That's Morticia, and she's sweet as a lamb, so you can go right ahead and pet her."

Lila grinned as she reached out a tentative hand to Morticia's shoulder. The draft mule leaned her head around so Lila could pet her muzzle. "She's so soft," Lila whispered. Morticia blew out a sweet breath into Lila's hands. "Mom, can we go for a ride?"

Meredith glanced at the posted rates and began calculating the cost in her head. Twenty dollars per person times four.

"Um..." she said, hesitating. Eighty dollars for maybe twenty minutes.

"Now, there's a special today," the handler said, setting her water bottle back inside the edge of the carriage. "Two for one for families with extra cute kids," she said with a smile and a wink.

Lila's eyes lit up, and Meredith looked to Liam with a silent *Can we afford this?* Liam smiled and nodded.

"Woohoo!" Lila said, petting Morticia's shoulder again.

"Thank you," Meredith said quietly to the handler as they handed the girls up into the carriage.

"It's my pleasure," she said quietly in response as she climbed into the driver's seat.

The girls pointed at every street performer they passed, from magician to musician to acrobat. Meredith watched as Lila grew quiet and stared at a string quartet in the middle of Royal Street, her head tilting to the side as she listened.

They passed Bourbon Street, where the girls laughed at the party-goers singing karaoke inside different clubs before turning back towards the square. On a quieter block, Emmy pointed up at the balconies dripping in flowers and plants. "Pretty," she said.

After the carriage ride, Meredith led them over to Cafe du Monde for an afternoon pick-me-up. As the big plate of beignets were set on the table, the girls stared, wide-eyed again for just a moment before digging into the piles of sugar and dough. Lila settled back into her chair to watch another musician nearby. The middle-aged man played blues on his guitar, tapping his foot to the beat. Meredith and Liam sipped their cafe au lait and breathed a collective sigh at sitting still for a few minutes. Meredith kept watching the girls' faces for signs of boredom or exhaustion. She had two identical, small coloring books and baggies of crayons in her bag, as well. She also continued to glance at Liam's face. Cafe du Monde was notoriously crowded, which tended to strain his nerves. For now, he looked slightly pale but okay.

Still watching the musician, Lila leaned her arms on the railing beside the table, resting her chin on her folded arms. "This is awesome," she said quietly. "Will we get to ride the streetcar again?"

"Yes," Meredith answered, handing Liam a wet wipe for Emmy's sticky fingers. "I thought we could head that way here in a few minutes, so we don't get too tired. There's a park I want to stop at on the way back."

"Okay," Lila said, never taking her eyes off of the musician. As they packed up again, Liam swinging Emmy up into his arms to cross Decatur Street, Meredith handed Lila a few dollar bills.

"What's this for?" Lila asked.

"We're going to pass the musician you've been listening to. See how his guitar case is open at his feet?"

Lila looked and nodded stoically.

"That's so people can give him money for playing for them. And we enjoyed his music very much, right?"

Lila nodded again. "So, I just put the money in the case?"

"Yup."

Lila pursed her lips in concentration and as they walked by the man, she leaned down and put the bills into the case, holding tightly onto Meredith's arm the whole time.

"Thank you, young lady!" the man called out.

"Mommy," she hissed as they walked across the road on the crosswalk. "I did it!"

"Yes, you did. Now, let's go find the streetcar again, okay?"

Lila grinned and skipped the rest of the way up Royal Street to reach the St. Charles streetcar.

Twenty minutes later, Meredith led them down a narrow street.

"Mommy, where's the park?" Lila asked, looking at the narrow houses suspiciously.

"Up here. And just to be clear: it's a park, not a playground, remember? I thought we could play..." Meredith reached into her bag again and rummaged around inside. "Frisbee!"

Lila smiled and jumped up and down, while Emmy clapped her hands. "Emmy like fisbee!"

They turned the corner, and the Coliseum Square opened up in front of them.

After entering the grassy area, Liam set Emmy down, and she and Lila began running in circles and spinning around.
As they walked about halfway down with the children playing in a kind of orbit around them, Meredith pointed over to a large, Greek revival mansion: 1749 Coliseum Street.

"See that one right there?" she asked, pointing it out to Liam.

"The big apricot colored one?"

"Yeah. That's Grace King's last home."

"Really? It's massive! I thought she struggled with poverty," he said, still gazing at the large home.

"She did. For most of her life. Eventually, her brother, Branch, bought it for her and her sisters, and they lived there until the ends of their lives. Together," Meredith explained. "Sometimes, they thought they'd have to sell it, and sometimes they rented it out for awhile while they traveled and such, but it gave them security. Roots."

"Mommy, are there more toys in your bag?" Lila asked, running up.

"Yup. I brought a Barbie for each of you. Go ahead and poke around in there," Meredith said, handing the bag to Lila, who immediately pulled out the table cloth and dumped the contents of the entire bag onto it.

"No, please don't..." Meredith sighed. "Too late."

Lila and Emmy dug into the pile, Lila wrinkling her nose at Meredith's wallet and phone and throwing them back into the bag.

"So, where do you think we'll be living in a year?" Liam asked, leaning back against a tree and pulling Meredith in front of him. He stretched his arms protectively around her waist as they watched the kids play.

"Hopefully, here. But I don't know how likely it is. It's hard to find a university job anywhere, let alone in a specific city with no personal connections to help me out."

Liam nodded. "Wherever we go, it'll be okay," he said softly. "We'll be okay." He squeezed gently.

Meredith shook her head. "I'm not so sure. I don't want the girls to have the struggles I did—that we did—growing up in a poor county."

Liam sighed. "I know. You're right. But we're already in a much better position."

"If I fail, though, we'll be right back at the beginning. Working shit-jobs to pay rent and put food on the table," Meredith said, feeling angry all of a sudden. "Everything will be for naught. The stress, the moving, the hardships...I want stability. I want roots. I want *them* to have roots. I want them to think of a certain place as *home*." She sighed. "I don't think of Kentucky as home anymore. After everything with my parents, I don't ever want to go back there. There's nothing there but pain."

Meredith grew quiet. Her own challenges weighed heavily on her shoulders, and she watched the girls playing, dancing their Barbies close together and giggling. Her eyes drifted over the park and rested on the Grace King House. She imagined an elderly Grace sitting on the porch, her short white curls framing her face. For Meredith, the past, present, and future all threatened to crush her.

Meredith had known that she had chosen a hard path. Earning a doctorate is one thing, but finding a job to support a family of four was another entirely. Liam was doing better now, since leaving the Army, but Meredith knew the strain that interacting in regular civilian life put on him.

She felt afraid.

"I'm so tired, Liam," Meredith finally whispered. "But I'm terrified of resting, because resting might lead to failing. I could lose the momentum, and then where would we be?"

Liam sighed. "I'm sorry, Meredith. I'm trying. I really am. I don't know why doing regular things is so damned hard right now. I should be able to attend classes and be in crowds and do regular jobs...but I just can't seem to function. It's like I just freeze up."

"No, Liam," Meredith said quickly. "I know you're trying. This isn't me complaining, I promise. I'm just..."

Liam nodded, smiled tightly, and pulled her closer. He gave a small nod. "If I could just...be normal...this would take the pressure off of you, though..."

Meredith snorted. "Since when have either of us ever been *normal...*" She waited for Liam to snort in response before continuing. "How are the therapy sessions going, by the way?"

Liam paused before answering. "Pretty well, I think. It was a good thing, to start on that path. I just wish I could get down it a little faster, so you would be able to—"

"Nope," Meredith said, stopping him. "You'll go at whatever speed you go. Besides, it's my turn. My turn to support us, and when you're able and ready, we both will. Okay? I'm just scared I'll fail. And it wouldn't just be failing myself. It'd been failing you...and them." She nodded towards the girls still playing on the grass.

Liam took her hand and kissed her fingers. "But what if you don't fail? What if neither of us fails? We have the chance to pull our kids out of the poverty we grew up in. No trailers for them. No traumatizing childhoods. No violence. Just—normal. Ever notice how we build off of each other?"

Meredith furrowed her eyebrows in a silent question.

"When we first met," Liam explained. "I had an okay job that allowed us to save a tiny bit of money. That money got us out to your first teaching job. Your teaching job supported us and allowed me to go back to school for a bit and figure some things out before joining the military. My time in the military supported us while starting our family and getting you into grad school. Now, you going to grad school will support us for the next leg. We just have to keep going a little while longer, sweetheart."

Meredith nodded and gave him a tight, tiny smile, trying to ignore the tears behind her eyes. Liam kissed her cheek and held her in his arms as they stood together, watching the girls play happily.

Chapter 20

1893
Dear Mr. Warner,

I have made some progress on a project I undertook at Madame Blanc's encouragement: the translation of letters believed to be composed by George Sand. Though I am a bit shocked by the risqué content, they are nonetheless beautifully articulated. Such sentiment this woman possessed! I have enclosed the beginning of the project for your advice on possible publication opportunities.
Yours
G.E.K.

* * *

1893
Dear Miss King,

I am shocked by the sample you've sent. This is no work of a true lady—your own reputation as a lady writer would be deeply damaged by publishing such inappropriateness! I am ashamed you would even think to submit such a project to an editor! Thankfully, you have sought my direction—My advice to you is to end this project before it ends your career. No respectable editor would work with material such as this, and it makes this editor hesitate concerning other projects, as well.
C.D.W.

* * *

1893
Dear Mr. Warner,

Thank you for your honesty. I have obediently set aside the project and will no longer pursue it. I am grateful for your feedback and guidance.
Your Southern Friend,
G.E.K.

* * *

New Orleans

In 1894, Madame Blanc came to New Orleans to visit Grace and to study the state of American women in the South for her own research. Grace relished showing her favorite city to her favorite friend. Luckily, Marie was in time for Mardi Gras, so Grace made a point of taking her to the Mystic Krewe's Ball, where Marie delighted in the festivities. During the rest of the visit, Grace arranged performances by the best pianists she could find and afford. They rode the newly electrified St. Charles streetcar through uptown. Grace was relieved to find her own family—for the most part—in complete accord for Marie's visit, with Branch even playing a bit of the flirt. Will and Jennie had missed most of the festivities, sending a note with apologies because Will had taken ill. The family learned on the last day of Marie's visit that it was actually because Will had been missing, and Jennie had been too embarrassed to say so. Grace had entered the kitchen on the last morning of Marie's visit to make coffee only to find Jennie and Mimi already sipping a cup at the table, Mimi patting Jennie's hand reassuringly.

"He usually comes back after a few days," she'd said kindly. She'd met Grace's eyes, and they shared a guilty gaze. They could have spared Jennie the pain and heartache, but they had kept Will's secret from her in the hopes that she would help him. Grace had sighed and steered Marie clear of Jennie for the morning, which was easy to do in a big household.

After leaving New Orleans, Grace and Marie took a luxurious steamboat trip to Arkansas for Marie to meet with Alice French, another American writer and acquaintance of hers. En route, the women enjoyed spending the day solely in each other's company, watching the countryside slide by from their comfortable deck chairs. Glasses of lemonade sat on a small table between them.

"You know," said Marie one afternoon. "I have a friend, Louise Sullivan. She would be good for your brother, Branch."

Grace laughed and held her hand to her chest in mock outrage. “You mean you will not marry him yourself? And reject being my sister?”

Marie tossed her head back in laughter. “*Mais non!* No more marriage for me, my friend! One short one was more than enough!”

“And there, we agree. No marriage,” said Grace softly, her eyes crinkling in amusement. She watched the landscape of her beloved Louisiana and the occasional plantation viewable from the river. “Besides, after publishing my history book last year, I’m earning my own strong income now. What need have I for marriage?”

“Well, I can think of one need, but marriage is not required,” Marie said, her eyes twinkling with mischievous humor.

Grace felt her face turning crimson, and Marie laughed.

“So squeamish!” she said. “Then I suppose I cannot convince you to stay at Alice’s plantation for a bit with me?”

Grace shook her head. “No, my friend. I’m afraid I am not ready to...to...”

Marie chuckled. “To see two women who love each other? Alice and Jane have been together for many years now.”

“Yes, I’ve heard,” said Grace in a flat tone.

“Ah, what is wrong with that?” asked Marie. “No marriage binds them, so if they are unhappy, they can simply separate. No fears of babies, and always a dear friend nearby,” she added softly.

Grace’s face continued to burn, and she cleared her throat uncomfortably. “So, I will see you to Arkansas, but then I must return to New Orleans,” she said kindly.

Marie let the issue go with a shrug and shifted the topic for her friend’s comfort. “Will you work on another history volume, then?”

“Well, I am an historian first,” Grace said. “I always was. Even my stories, I tell them because they are part of history. Luckily, I had the best training from Judge Gayarré, and my work for the local historical society has led me to meet other historians, like Mr. Ficklen, who co-wrote the history book with me. I may continue in this field for now."

"Ah, but the literary one will miss you too much," Marie said sadly.

Grace thought about that for a moment. The literary field had been lovely, even if a bit uncomfortable at times. Other people, however, seemed to want to control her voice; editors, publishers, and even acquaintances felt the need to constantly weigh in and tell her what she should write—and what she most certainly should not. For her history projects, they simply *were*. She enjoyed the research process and, even better, she enjoyed feeling productive without feeling criticized. "I will dapple in literature from time to time, but for now, my histories are sustaining my soul peacefully." No tricky waters to navigate, no gossip mongering, no catering to male editors.

Marie nodded slowly. She sighed happily and gestured to the banks of the river. "It is too bad our dear friend de Bury could not be here for such a beautiful journey."

Grace felt her eyes prickle. "I'm still in shock that such a vibrant woman could be gone from this world."

"It is shocking, indeed. But other voices will come forward and take her place."

"And what of us? Will the same happen to us?"

"But, of course. What else *could* happen?"

By the time Grace returned home to New Orleans, Will had returned, and Mimi had agreed to pay the debts he had accrued in her desperate act to save his marriage.

* * *

The following winter, Grace received word that Judge Gayarré was rapidly declining. He was 91 years old. Grace began visiting him every Sunday to write his anecdotes and stories for him, so they could live on after he passed.

One afternoon, she arrived to find him in his dressing gown with his wife's shawl over his shoulders and a derby hat on his head. His memories were fading, and he was grumpy most of the time. The Judge sat hunched over in his arm chair by the fireplace. A cup of hot chocolate sat on a nearby table, and Grace could see the other chair had been prepared for her; pens, extra ink, and fine paper all rested on the table near the arm of the chair.

Grace took her place and settled in.

"Oh, Grace, is that you?" Madame Gayarré called from a back room.

"Yes, Madame, it's just me."

"Oh, good, dear! I do think he's improving! You let me know if you need anything at all!"

"Thank you, Madame," Grace called, as she turned to the Judge and raised her eyebrow. "Is that true? Are you improving?" she asked skeptically.

"Bah," he said, with a dismissive wave of his hand. "Let her think what she wants," he said gruffly. "It's cold in here."

Grace leaned over to place another log onto the fireplace, while subtly wiping a small bead of sweat from her forehead.

He grunted and nodded curtly. "Have you spoken to Charles?"

Grace furrowed her brow. "Mr. Warner?"

"No," he said, annoyed. "*My* Charles."

Grace thought carefully. She had known the Judge since she was sixteen years old and never had she met a Charles she associated with the Judge. "Who is Charles?" she asked softly.

"Charles," he said irritably. "I want to know how Charles is faring before I go."

"Judge," said Grace, feeling a sense of worry creeping into her throat. "You've never mentioned a Charles."

The Judge glared into Grace's sharp brown eyes and sudden recognition came into his eyes. He inhaled sharply, held it for a moment, and then released it. "I might as well," he said to himself. "This is never to reach Madame Gayarré. Understood?" he said in a voice that sounded more like himself than Grace had heard in ages. She nodded and leaned forward. "Delphine was a...servant. Of mine. Ages ago. Octoroon. Barely even colored. Before I met Anne, of course. And we...she...has a son. Charles."

Grace swallowed the lump in her throat and waited.

"She had a temper, so she had to leave after that. I heard she burnt down a plantation and was eventually married off to a free Black. They thought Charles could *passe blanc,* but I disagreed. He still had a look that was recognizable. He would never have passed. So, I sent him to Paris. I haven't heard from him in decades."

Grace nodded slowly, processing this new image of her old mentor. "I don't know that I can ever find him on so little information, Judge, but I'll do what I can." Inside, she felt her temper rising. The man she had viewed as a father-figure and had held in high esteem had fathered a son. Illegitimately. With a slave. And then he had sold her. Her image of the intellectual Creole gentleman with ancient, regal ancestry shifted abruptly.

He nodded and leaned back in his chair. Before Grace could pick up the pen and paper, she heard a soft snoring beside her. Sighing, she quietly let herself out, thankful for the cool air outside.

A few weeks later, Grace paid her final visit to the Judge, though to hear Madame Gayarré speak, he would recover his full strength any day now. As Grace sat by his bedside, he glanced over at her. He never mentioned Delphine or Charles again, and neither did Grace. She decided to let his shame die with him, to protect Madame Gayarré.

The Judge turned to Grace on that final visit. "What do you think of all this women's suffrage business? Isn't it the greatest nonsense you ever heard? I tell you it's impossible for women to be free—the men have subordinated them and will always keep them in submission—always. They cannot be mistresses of themselves!"

Grace offered a tense half-smile and almost—*almost*—reminded him that he had just spent several decades training a woman historian. Ever since her talks with Isabella Beecher Hooker in Hartford, Grace had thought there wasn't a thing wrong with women voting. In fact, she'd rather like to vote herself. And yet—expressing that idea to the men around her would lead to constant criticism, and possible financial issues, if the men decided to no longer support her career and publication efforts. And how would Branch or Fred react, the King family's strongest financial supporters? Would they stop funding the household?

"Of course not, Judge," she said through gritted teeth. Inwardly, she cringed, and her anger began to boil.

Judge Charles Gayarré died shortly after, and on February 15, 1895, the unthinkable happened: Nine inches of snow fell in New Orleans.

* * *

In 1898, Grace had taken ill with malaria and had retreated to a light teaching position in Ruston, Louisiana, at the recommendation of an historian friend, Dr. Dillard. He had arranged it all: her teaching small classes in the late morning and even setting up historical visits in the afternoons, when she wasn't resting in her room. She had enjoyed the routine—almost as much as she had enjoyed the time away from her family.

The summer of 1899, she'd been persuaded to join Nina on a trip north to visit May. This trip was the first she'd made in awhile, and she found herself deeply fatigued at the smallest activity.

She, Nina, and May had spent several weeks at Blowing Rock, North Carolina, a mountain retreat that Grace found beautiful. There, the sisters had passed afternoons chatting over iced tea and watching the playful antics of a young boy, Warrington. They'd met his family over luncheon, and when they learned that the family was soon to move overseas, Grace shared her experiences in England and France. The Dawsons had been lovely, and Grace had exchanged contact information to keep in touch.

On the train ride further north, however, Grace and Nina sat on blue velvet seats, side-by-side, hardly speaking to one another.

Finally, Nina turned to Grace. "It's not my fault people thought you were my mother," she said harshly.

Grace sighed in frustration but said nothing. She closed her eyes for a moment, feeling a wave of fatigue wash over her.

"I mean, you're nine years older than me, but look at you. You're old."

"I'm forty-six. I'm not 'old,'" Grace said, pouting a bit as she closed her book and reached into her carrying case to retrieve another.

"Forty-six is old," insisted Nina. "You're old fashioned, prefer old things over new, and use old words. You...are...old." Grace sat in continued silence.

"The other day, you said 'rag' instead of 'cloth.' What kind of country bumpkin says 'rag'? But I guess it's fine, since you're terrible at most domestic duties now, anyway. Useless, really," Nina muttered, more to herself than to Grace.

Grace clenched her jaw in anger and opened her book. Some days, she was used to Nina's nagging and could ignore it; other days...it was best she force herself to read. She pretended to read the rest of the way to Hartford, where she'd planned a short visit with Mr. Warner. They parted ways in New York, with Nina insisting she was tired of Grace's company and her old friends. In Hartford, Grace checked her bags at the station, since her visit was to be a short one.

She walked slowly from the station to the Warners' home and purchased two small bouquets from the florist on her way. As she neared the Warners', she looked with deep sadness toward the path that led to the Clemens' home. It had been months since Livy's last letter. She had been bedridden with grief over the sudden passing of Susy from a short illness.

The path was somewhat overgrown with lack of use. Grace glanced toward the steamboat house, but untrimmed trees blocked her view. She set down the little bouquet of flowers against the trunk of a tree. She strained her ears and listened, but she could no longer hear the happy laughter and excited conversation of her first visit.

She sighed and turned to the Warners', noticing that the once pristine landscaping had been neglected. The Warner home, too, had begun to show age. The porch needed a sweeping, and the yard had a few broken tree limbs scattered around it. Grace noticed peeling paint on some windowsills.

Grace was invited inside for luncheon, and she waited in the library for Mr. and Mrs. Warner to join her.

Grace looked around the dark room, but the excitement and grandeur it had held on her first trip seemed to have gone, as well. Had it aged, or had she? This room looked stale. Dust rested on the edge of the shelves, and the rugs looked faded and somewhat worn on the corners. Grace heard Charles making his way down the hallway, and she stood to greet him. Instead, however, an old man slowly hobbled in, assisted by a sturdy cane upon which he leaned heavily.

"Grace," Mr. Warner said, smiling, though breathing heavy from the exertion.

"Mr. Warner," she said. "How are you feeling?"

"Ah, well, my heart has given me some trouble of late, but I'll get better soon. It happens from time to time," he said, sinking into a nearby armchair. "Would you mind terribly if we have luncheon here in the library?" he said as he sighed and sank into the deep chair.

"Of course not," said Grace, sitting on the sofa nearest him. They chatted about every day pleasantries, and Grace told him recent news about the happenings in New Orleans.

She noticed a marked change in his demeanor. Something was off.

"I trust you have been writing with your historian friends," he said stiffly.

"I have, yes," Grace said carefully. "And your own writing has continued?"

"Mm," he grunted, as Mrs. Warner walked into the room.

Grace stood to embrace Susan, but she stopped abruptly when their eyes met. Susan glared through narrowed eyes at Grace. "Miss King," she said curtly. "Charles, you *must* be sure to show Miss King our newest acquisitions. We've been quite fortunate in business and have so added to our collection. It's such a shame you haven't been around to partake."

Charles grunted in response but did not stir from his chair.

"Oh, I almost forgot," Susan added. "Isa will be arriving shortly, so you'll have to excuse me. I need to prepare for her," she said with a pointed look at Grace as she turned and left the room.

"Antoine's has created a new menu," Grace said, trying to lighten the tension. "Oysters Rockefeller. You'll love it on your next visit."

"My next visit," Charles said slowly. He smiled sadly and closed his eyes. "That will be lovely." Within moments, he was asleep.

Deciding to skip luncheon, Grace said her goodbyes to the butler, Mrs. Warner having disappeared, and returned to the train, confused and offended. She spent the ride trying to understand the odd scene at the Warners' home.

As she waited at the train station in Boston for her publisher's agent who was to meet her, she heard a great commotion around the corner. Curious, she walked over and saw an automobile pulling up to the curb. She had seen a few of them but never from so close a vantage. It looked like a pony carriage with a bench seat for two people. The rear wheels were slightly larger than the front, allowing for easier entrance. Instead of reins, the driver controlled the auto with a handle that sat off to the right side of the carriage, and this shaft turned the wheels to guide the automobile's direction. A motor in the rear made a great racket.

The driver climbed down and removed his hat. "Miss King!" he said loudly, waving to her. "I'm Walter Hines Page, with the publishing company. I've been sent to see you to your hotel!"

"In that?" Grace asked, shocked and pointing to the auto.

"Yes, ma'am," he said, grinning. "In that. Here, let me get your valise." After loading her things, Walter turned to hand her into the automobile. People gathered on the sidewalk to watch as she settled her skirts and sat properly. She watched in amazement as Walter turned a crank, swung into the seat beside her, and steered them away from the curb. The first motion was jarring, and Grace reached up to steady her hat, while Walter laughed at her shocked expression. She found herself laughing as they tumbled over bumps and ruts in the streets, thoroughly enjoying herself.

Chapter 21

In November, Meredith flew to Philadelphia for the largest literary conference she had ever attended: American Women Writers Society, usually called AWWS for short. Once again, she felt more than a little out of her league. She entered an immense two-story hotel lobby filled with dark blue sofas and arm chairs. A bar and coffee stand stood in the back, and trays of champagne flutes were being offered to guests as they entered.

She checked into her room and was shown the conference check-in table, as well. She stole little glances at the other conference-goers, who were dressed in everything from comfy track suits with beautiful jewelry to elegant pant suits. All around her, people were greeting each other warmly, embracing, and talking quickly.

As she checked in at the table, she recognized the name on the conference worker's name tag.

"Oh," she said, without thinking.

The blonde woman looked to be maybe a decade or so older and was dressed in a simple green polo and khakis. She stared at Meredith and raised her eyebrows. "Yes?"

"Oh, uh, I'm sorry," Meredith stumbled. "I was just surprised. You wrote an article on Grace King awhile back."

"Yes," the woman said, surprised.

"I really enjoyed it," Meredith said. "It's helping me in writing my dissertation on her."

"Well, that's nice to hear," she said with a kind smile, handing Meredith a thick packet. "Have a wonderful time, and if you need anything, stop back by and see me!"

"Thank you!"

She tucked the thick conference packet under her arm and headed to the elevator, almost skipping.

The next morning, Meredith had been too nervous to go to the breakfast being hosted by the conference in the hotel. She sat in an overly air-conditioned ballroom, listening as some of the top scholars in the field discussed their research on

American women writers. One scholar presented her research on literary salons, referencing Grace King's Le Salon des Amis.

Afterward, Meredith shyly joined the line of audience members patiently waiting their turn to speak to the panelists individually. When finally the scholar looked up at her, Meredith stumbled over her words.

"Hello, I, uh, am a Grace King scholar, and I spoke about King at the Salon just last fall," she said, hearing her own words and realizing that she sounded like a kindergartner proud of a finger painting. "Um, anyway, I really enjoyed the recent piece you did on King and the literary marketplace."

She started to turn away when the scholar said, "Why, thank you. You must be Meredith Mandin. Call me Marian..."

What...the...actual...

"Um, yes," Meredith said, her face heating up as she shook Marian's hand. The room was so crowded she could barely think straight.

"Well, it's very nice to finally meet another King scholar," Marian said. "There are so few of us!"

The tall woman beside her leaned over and touched the other speaker's hand.

"Marian, did I overhear that she's a Grace King scholar?" the woman asked. Marian nodded. The tall woman turned to her. "I'm Katherine. I have an acquaintance who is working on a King project. Here, let me write down her email address for you."

As she walked out of the conference room, Meredith remembered that her phone had buzzed with an unfamiliar number during the panel. Meredith looked at her phone and saw the unknown caller had left a message. Listening to the voicemail, she heard her mother's voice:

"Meredith, I know I made some mistakes, but I'd really like to talk to you. Hear about the girls. Please call me if you get this."

* * *

That night, Meredith lay awake in the overly fluffed, down-filled hotel bed. The room was too quiet, which let her memories make all the noise they wanted. Repeatedly, she turned on the television to something mindless until she felt herself sliding into sleep, but when the sleep timer kicked off, the room went silent, and the memories and anxiety resurfaced.

When she was about five, her parents bought the house her dad still owned. Her bedroom was in the basement of the split level house. She had created a little nook behind the catty-corner headboard of her bed and filled that little corner with stuffed animals, pillows, and blankets. She didn't share it with anyone. It was her place, and she could only access it by sliding under the bed and crawling up to the corner. She hid there at night when her parents fought upstairs—the sounds of shouting and furniture slamming too much to sleep through. One night, she fell asleep there and woke up the next morning to her mother leaning over the headboard. She said Meredith had scared her and not to hide like that anymore. She made her take all the animals and blankets out, and shortly after, she rearranged Meredith's bedroom so the headboard was flush against the wall. No more hiding allowed.

After her parents divorced, her mother moved to Indiana with Meredith. They lived in Meredith's aunt's basement. Meredith, however, spent more time at home complaining of stomachaches than at school. She couldn't shake the feeling that something terrible was about to happen; the feeling gnawed at her stomach, making it ache and hurt all the time.

She couldn't sleep at night and so fell asleep in the classroom. She was scolded by teachers for this and avoided by the other students. She had eaten lunch alone every day and hardly spoken to anyone, and hardly anyone had ever spoken to her. There were only two things she liked about the school: the courtyard they passed each day on the way to the library where they would apparently garden come springtime and a beautiful painting of a unicorn on one wall in the hallway. The unicorn stood on its hind legs, ready to launch into the blue sky. She loved passing the mural on the way to specials.

But it turned out, the feeling was right.

A few weeks after their move, Meredith had sat in a school assembly, criss-cross applesauce like all the other elementary school students. They were giving out school awards, and Meredith only half-listened, since she still didn't know anyone there. She had watched the teachers moving around the front of the gymnasium, near the stage. A teacher had come through the side door, walking quickly. Meredith had known immediately: that teacher was coming for her. The teacher made her way across the floor below the stage, and Meredith felt her heart speeding up, her air coming a little tighter. The teacher walked down the aisle to where Meredith sat.

"Your dad's here to pick you up," the teacher had said quietly, half kneeling down.

Meredith went with her so as not to draw attention from the other students. Once they were in the hallway, she told her, "My dad's not supposed to take me. My mom said so."

"He's your dad, so you have to go," the teacher said, leading her to the office where her backpack and things waited.

All of her things—even from inside her desk. Meredith realized then that she would not be coming back to the school. Her father had stood there waiting, large and imposing. She felt brave for one single moment: "You're not supposed to take me. I'm not supposed to leave school," she said, looking up.

"Well, I'm your father, and I'm taking you. You'll see your mom later," he said, glowering at the receptionist.

He took her back to Kentucky and hid her at her grandparents' house out in the country. They lived at the tail end of a long, dead-end road. She wasn't allowed to talk to her mom on the phone. She wasn't allowed to go back to school yet either. She wasn't allowed to do anything except play video games, and Meredith hated video games.

She sat in the field beside the old white house, watching the sun and clouds day after day. The wind seemed sad then. Meredith had begged for it to bring her mother. She imagined it reaching over the hills and roads and guiding her mother's little red car up the gravel road to pick her up. She imagined the wind pushing the car, faster and faster to reach her. The wind reassured her: *Help will come.*

When it finally did, Meredith was hiding behind the couch in the living room. The sheriff stood in the doorway with her mother behind him. Meredith's grandfather argued and tapped his shotgun on the floor by his feet. The sheriff turned around...and left. Meredith had started to cry, and her grandmother heard her. She grabbed Meredith's shoulder and sent her back down the hallway to the bedroom with the video games.

Again, she was scolded for hiding. *No hiding allowed.*

She was able to go with her mother the next day, though, after additional paperwork had been filed, but her mother was not allowed to move out-of-state anymore. Meredith was re-enrolled in her old school and had to spend every-other-weekend at her father's home. He worked night shift, so he mostly slept all day. Meredith watched television or drew all day—alone.

At that time, all she had wanted in the world was her mother, so what changed?

In junior high, Meredith had suffered a minor injury, hurting her knee. Gayle had taken her to see a doctor, but within minutes of meeting him and deeming him *handsome*, Gayle was the one on the exam table, laughing with the doctor over an old knee injury of her own.

Within months, Gayle's first knee surgery was scheduled. Then came her wrists and carpel-tunnel. By high school, Meredith had learned how to remove stitches from her mother's legs and clean the wounds. What she had not learned to do was monitor the multiple prescription bottles on her mother's night stand.

* * *

The next morning in Philadelphia, a sleep-deprived Meredith entered a reception room for breakfast and a morning talk about the job market and how best to navigate it. She smiled at other conference goers as she poured herself a cup of coffee and selected a croissant and yogurt cup and made her way to a vacant seat at the too-large round tables. As she settled in, a woman with a stylish dark bob and wearing a blue skirt suit clapped her hands to get the crowd's attention.

"Welcome to our breakfast chat session, everyone. We here at AWWS take mentoring scholars very seriously. For this session, we have asked our more seasoned scholars to share their experiences and guide small discussions about the job market and search that so many of you are navigating or are about to navigate. So, relax, get a cup of coffee—or two—and have a wonderful chat!"

The crowd applauded gently, and each table turned inward, smiling awkwardly at their new companions. Meredith looked around her table: two young women on both sides of her with long hair curled to perfection and a woman in roughly her sixties directly across from her with her graying hair in a long bob.

The older woman spoke first, her eyes crinkling with her smile. "So, how about we introduce ourselves first? I'm Susan. I specialize in nineteenth-century American literature, and I've been teaching at a state university for nearly thirty years now."

Next to Susan, the first young woman spoke up. "I'm Melissa, and I, too, specialize in nineteenth-century American literature. I finished my Ph.D. two years ago, and I'm currently teaching where I studied. I've just published my first book, and I'm hoping to find full-time employment this year."

Susan responded, "That's wonderful! Was the book your dissertation?"

"Yes, it was," Melissa responded. "I've been on the market for the last two years, but nothing took, so I just powered out the book. I'm hoping that will give me an advantage and let me move out of my parents' house."

Susan smiled politely, nodded, and turned to the other young woman on Meredith's left. "Wonderful—welcome, Melissa. And you?"

"I'm Stacey, and I focus on modern American literature. I am in a full-time position right now, but it's not ideal. I have an annual contract renewal, and it's very competitive. The new administration at the university has openly said that no one is safe at renewal time each year, which I think is more common now. I'd like to find a better fit. My boyfriend is a surgeon on the west coast, so I'd like to move out west. I turned my diss into a book, as well, and have a few other articles out, too."

"That happens quite a bit, finding a full time gig for awhile before finding your true place," Susan said. "Welcome, Stacey." She turned to Meredith and raised her eyebrows to nudge her response.

"I'm Meredith, and I study nineteenth-to-early twentieth century American lit, so right in between Melissa and Stacey. Um, I'm writing my diss currently and will be on the market for the first time this year."

"Ah, and your publications?"

"I have one article coming out in a text shortly, but that's it, I'm afraid."

The three women cringed.

"Well, welcome," Susan said, gesturing to all three of them. "Tell me about your experiences on the market so far."

"It's tough," Melissa said. "I landed five interviews last year, out of the fifty packets I sent out, but none of them worked out. I spent so much money traveling to different campuses, since their reimbursements didn't fully cover the actual travel expenses. After two of those campus visits, I found out that the divisions hired their inside applicant. There was absolutely no reason for me to take that time or spend the money. Thankfully, my parents helped pay most of my expenses."

Stacey nodded. "Same here. I had four interviews last year—after sending out over eighty application packets all over the country. I had to interview for one of them in a man's hotel room, with no one else there. He kept staring at my legs and asking about how my husband would feel about me having such a job. I didn't land that job, either."

Susan sighed and shook her head. "I wish I could say that that is a rare occurrence, but it isn't. I experienced the very same thing when I entered the market two decades ago. And once you find a position, salary negotiation is another mountain. And I'm afraid many institutions now pay starting professors less than public high schools do their teachers. How about you, Meredith? What have your experiences been?"

"Um, well, this will actually be my first year," Meredith said. "I'm preparing one packet for a school in Northern Georgia, and I'm watching the job sites like a hawk."

"So, you've really not done this before?" Stacey blurted, seemingly shocked at Meredith's naiveté. "Sorry. I just can't remember a time when I *wasn't* working to find a job. To be at the start of that—wow. I don't envy you that."

Meredith spent the rest of the session smiling and nodding politely. The more the women shared their horror stories—wasted time and money, disappointment, sexual harassment—the more Meredith's anxiety rose. How was she going to enter this market and compete to find a stable income to support a small family of four, when these accomplished scholars hadn't been able to even support themselves?

* * *

By lunch time, Meredith's nerves were shaken up. The conference was hosting a formal luncheon in the ballroom, but Meredith decided to head out for a walk and a light bite to eat, if she could stomach it.

She decided to walk toward Christ Church and visit the small cemetery to see Ben Franklin's grave. She hoped the short outing would help clear her mind before her presentation later that afternoon.

After visiting the Church, Meredith found a seat in one of the small gardens nearby, enjoying the shade of a small tree and the peaceful shrubs. She thought about a scrapbook she had recently found in their garage. Years before, she had placed some pictures in it that Kay had sent her of her father's baptism in the small pond near her grandparents' home in Kentucky—the same place she had been hidden from her mother.

She had liked the woods that surrounded her grandparents' place, but she had despised spending time near the home, especially after being held there waiting for her mother. It was a simple enough house: white vinyl siding, black trim. A front porch and side deck. The front porch had an old porch swing and giant aloe plant in a wooden stand. There's where they went for bee sting remedies. The house was small inside: three bedrooms, all on the main floor with an unfinished, stone basement. There were always spiders in the basement. An old, beat-up pool table was also there, but the kids were forbidden to touch it. In the living room, on the bottom of the end table by the sofa, slept the great family bible. This bible was the largest bound book Meredith had ever seen as a child. It was bound in white leather with gold letters on the cover. It was only ever used for the annual family reunion—nothing else.

Alongside the house was a small creek where they would catch crawdads and tadpoles every summer. Meredith preferred catching the tadpoles and left the crawdads alone.

She remembered her grandmother, her dad's mother, taking her for a hike in the fall when she was maybe eight or nine. They walked for a long time—the leaves crunching under their feet—and came upon several wooden structures deep in the woods. One was some kind of round house, but only the frame remained. In a semi-circle near it were platform structures, raised up over Meredith's head. Like beds on stilts. Her grandmother told her this was where the Indians had burned their dead.

Up the hill behind their garage was the pond from the picture. The pond had terrified Meredith as a kid. Even as an adult, dark water still terrified her. The pond was small and muddy, and Meredith could never see the bottom, and the trees always gathered around it, hiding it in deep shadows. As a child, she had imagined that it was bottomless, and she feared falling into the muddy depths and being taken down into the dark muck.

Her cousins had skipped rocks across the water, trying to reach the other side. Every now and then, they fished, caught a tiny bluegill and threw it back. Nothing of value came from the pond. The stagnant water smelled of silt and mud, and mosquitoes and bugs were drawn to it, so they never stayed near it for very long.

As she grew up, her visits to her grandparents' house grew less and less frequent, until they only went for the family reunions.

Meredith remembered the family reunions. They were always held in July, the hottest damn month of the year—until August. Her grandmother would start cleaning the house two weeks in advance. She started cooking one week in advance. Her grandfather would arrange seats and benches and chairs in a giant circle around the front yard. Even old church pews were placed into the circle that stretched from the front porch down the sidewalk—that had been mostly reclaimed by grass—all the way to the road, down the side of the road and back to the driveway and up to the porch again. In front of the porch steps was a podium. The great family bible would be set out on the podium, and her grandfather would stand at it and preach sermon after sermon to the gathered adults in the front yard for hours. They sang hymns and shouted, "Hallelujah!" and "Amen!" Some brought guitars or banjos to accompany the hymns.

Eventually, everyone would file into the house for dinner—chicken and dumplings, fried chicken, mashed potatoes, giant bowls of green beans, made-from-scratch biscuits, and corn grown in her grandmother's garden.

It almost sounded like it would be a pleasant memory, but Meredith had hated these events.

After her father married Kay, she had stepsisters with whom to attend these weird social gatherings. One year, they sat on the hot, concrete bridge that went over the little creek—they were too old to gather tadpoles anymore, but too young to drive away from the gathering with some excuse. Her cousin, Lucy, sat nearby, telling them how she'd like to screw the neighbor kid. She was ten. Lucy lived with Meredith's grandparents. Everyone knew her mother, Clerise, had dropped her off there and never picked her up again. Every few years, Clerise turned up for a few days, then left again.

That was the summer Meredith had realized that Lucy was being abused by her grandfather. When Ginny asked her, point-blank, if someone was touching her when they shouldn't be, Lucy had yelled: "So what if boys like touching me? I like it, so you shut up! If you say anything else about it, I'll tell Papaw you were being mean to me!"

Meredith was eleven—maybe twelve, and she was terrified of her grandfather. She always had been. She didn't say anything to anyone, but she never went near him again.

Meredith remembered this scene while sitting in the church yard in Philadelphia. Soon after that, she had tried to tell Kay what Lucy had told them. Kay had shrugged it off, saying something about Lucy telling tales. Meredith hadn't known what else to do. Kay was a grownup; if she didn't think it worth taking action, why would anyone else? And so, Meredith dropped it.

In the picture in the scrapbook, Meredith's dad is standing in the middle of the pond. The water only comes to his waist, and the sun blasts over the water. The preacher is tilting Steven backward, and they're wearing khaki shorts and polo shirts. The pond looks like a tiny mud hole in the picture—no longer imposing and frightening.

* * *

That afternoon, Meredith prepared for her panel. As they started to walk into a smaller ballroom, she overheard someone say, "I can't believe Elaine Showalter came out of retirement to present this year!"

"Yes, but the room is already beyond capacity. Too bad. I guess this panel will do," said another, as she and her friend walked into Meredith's room. *Awesome. Not only do I not get to hear Showalter speak, but I get to catch all the people who'd rather be in the other conference room.*

Then, Meredith recognized Marian in the front row, and she relaxed a small bit.

Her panel members gave their presentations first and second as Meredith listened patiently. They were polished and smooth—and clearly in complete control. They both read their papers seamlessly, clicking through their PowerPoints with ease. Meredith felt frumpy and childish next to them, but there was nothing that could be done about it now.

"And now," said their moderator. "Meredith Mandin..."

The audience clapped politely as Meredith took her place at the podium. The room had filled, with most rows having one or two empty seats left. Meredith's heart raced, so she took a long, slow breath to steady her nerves. As she read from her prepared manuscript, she heard her own voice: deceptively steady and smooth.

After her reading was over, the panel answered questions from the audience.

Marian raised her hand to ask a question after the other panelists had finished speaking. "Meredith, do you view King as continuing on in the traditional nineteenth century southern pastorals?"

Meredith smiled. She knew the answer to this one. "Actually, I view King as bridging two larger literary movements: the southern pastorals and the coming modernist movement. For example, her use of what is called literary trans-lingualism shows that she was thinking about her language use in a different way from other writers in her time period. She could write in English but the reader knew that the characters were speaking in French. She also embraced the notion of what would come to be referred to as the grotesque, and asserted, in numerous tales, that the only way to survive was to adapt. And I think that's what she did ultimately: she adapted. Or at least, she tried to, in some aspects."

Meredith let out the breath she'd been holding and was pleased to hear murmurs of agreement and to see nodding heads throughout the audience.

* * *

That evening, Meredith paced the hotel room for fifteen minutes before finally picking up her cell phone and calling her mother.

"Meredith? Are you there?" Gayle said immediately.

"Yes."

"I'm so glad you called. I...I've missed the girls so much."

Meredith remained silent. By now, Emmy had no idea who her grandmother was, and Meredith wasn't sure of Lila's feelings.

"And you. I've missed you, too," Gayle added quickly. "Um, so my doctor thinks I had a mini-stroke last week."

"Oh. How are you feeling now?"

"I'm doing okay now, but I'm in a lot of pain. Had to increase my pain meds a bit."

Meredith said nothing.

"Do you think you could let me talk to Lila sometime?"

"Nope. Let's just see how this goes first."

"I-I understand." Long pause. "I met someone."

Of course she did.

"That's nice."

"His name's Roger, and he takes good care of me. Claudia introduced us, up in Dayton."

"That's nice." Meredith could hear her mother trying to be normal, as though they hadn't not spoken in two-and-a-half years, but even knowing how hard she was trying, Meredith couldn't find a way to care. She felt numb. And cautious. Any second now, she knew Gayle would ask for money.

"He sold his business in Dayton to come and live with me. He takes real good care of me," she repeated. "Don'tcha, honey?" Gayle called out to someone in the background. "He's got a nice truck—brand new, even—and we're really happy."

"That's nice."

"So, I also overextended my achilles tendon the other day."

"Oh, how did you do that?" Meredith's voice was flat and emotionless. She could hear it, but she didn't care to change it. She was trying to care about her mother's health, but after everything, she just couldn't. She remembered suddenly back to a conversation they'd had when she was finishing her bachelor's degree. Meredith had offered to get an extra job and pay for her mother to go see a nutritionist to balance her medical needs with her nutrition; Gayle had recently been diagnosed as diabetic. Her mother had declined, saying it wouldn't help her anyway. That was when Meredith began thinking that, on some level, her mother liked having the medical issues. They defined her, in some way, and created part of her identity. Without them, what would she be? *Who* would she be?

"So, I was driving the truck—you know, that old thing was always a pain in the ass to drive, and my foot slipped on the brake. Doctor said I was lucky I didn't rip the tendon right in half!"

Meredith paused. "Why are you driving Gene's old truck, if your new guy is so well off and has a new one?" Her stepfather, Gene, had used the old truck for his many small farm and lawn-mowing jobs.

"Oh, oh...it's in the shop. Getting some minor work done."

Sure, it is.

"Oh." Long pause. "Well, I better get going."

"Oh, okay. Call soon, you hear? Love ya!"

"Yup. Bye!" Meredith pushed the little red button and ended the call.

Shortly thereafter, she unblocked her mother on her social media accounts, just so she could know what was going on. She still had baby pictures of the girls on her cover, from two years earlier. She posted things like, "God Bless Granddaughters" and "I believe in Jesus." People would comment: *What lovely grand babies, Gayle!* And she responded: *Yes, I don't get to see them as much, but I love and miss them!* If her friends ever realized the pictures were never updated and the kids never aged, they politely never said so, so Gayle continued to live in her own world of picture-perfect Grandmotherly devotion.

Chapter 22

1899
My dear Grace,

It has been so long since last we saw you. Clara sends her love, and Youth says to tell Branch thank you for the latest gift of pipe tobacco. As you know, we have all been shattered by the loss of our Susy, and Youth struggles to write of late. I feel we need to reassert our roots in Hartford, but I'm not sure if we can bear the always-present memories. We have avoided it because of the pain it could bring on, and yet...I wonder if Susy's presence there might ultimately be a comfort. What do you think we ought to do? I value your opinion and will be interested to hear it...
Your Affectionate Friend
Livy Clemens

* * *

My dear Livy,

Go home, dear friend.

I have suffered true poverty and hardship in my life, and I tell you now that you will go on. There is no point in running from home or running from the memories; they will come with you, always. I am sorry—deeply and sincerely—for Susy's loss—and yet, if this is the first real hardship you have faced, then you are still luckier than most.

Without the Clemens' family, Hartford is sorely changed. My recent visit somehow brought the chill of winter into the month of July. It was as opposite as it could possibly be from the once intellectual epicenter it was. Boring, dull, and materialistic.

But a home like the one you and Mr. Clemens created? That was remarkable. Yes, the memories will be there, but eventually, they will cease to ache and hurt and will instead soothe your soul.

Clara, Jean, or even their children and grandchildren will one day be grateful for the home so filled with laughter, love, and stories—and yes, memories. They will have a home to return to again and again—do not sell the home, Livy. A home like yours sets the roots deeper and gives a healthier tree.
Yours Affectionately
Grace King

* * *

New Orleans

By 1900, the King family was living at 2911 Prytania Street in a lovely cottage near the St. Charles streetcar line.

Grace sat in the kitchen, looking over the paper. She had spent the morning writing at her desk in her room, and her fingers now ached from gripping the pen. Nan came into the room and set down a basket filled with tomatoes and green onions.

"There you are," she said. "I'm thinking shrimp creole for dinner. Warm things up a bit."

"Sounds good," Grace murmured, as Will shuffled into the kitchen. He had rejoined their household after a painful separation from Jennie and children. He had visited them recently but had been in a dark mood ever since.

He poured himself a cup of coffee, but when he joined her at the table, Grace noticed the redness of his eyes. His cheeks were pale, and his neck was flushed. His shirt smelled of spilled bourbon.

"Again, Will?" she asked quietly.

"Again, what?" he shot back. Grace noticed that Nan stayed away from the table, organizing for dinner.

"So, your wife and children have to go live with her family because you and your drinking can't provide for them. We allow you to come home, and you *still* can't figure out that perhaps you should stop drinking and get yourself together?" She said angrily. She glanced at the doorway and kept her voice down. Mimi despaired when she and Will argued.

"You don't know," he snarled. "You don't know my struggles."

Grace rolled her eyes. "Well, it's not your job causing it, that's for sure," she muttered.

Will swung his hand at the table, knocking the coffee cup across the room. It slammed into the wall and shattered to the floor.

"You spoiled child," she said. "Grow up. Your mother is growing old and needs her children to start caring for her. She shouldn't be having to bail you out constantly. If it were me, I'd never have let you move back home!"

"You arrogant bitch," he hissed. "What makes me different from Nan? Or Nina? You, Fred, and Branch support them, but not me. You don't support me. You don't help me. You never have. You insult me and purposely make things harder!"

"You are a man," said Grace. "Start acting like one."

Will threw back his chair, letting it tip and slam to the floor as he stormed out.

Grace simply returned to her paper, pretending not to care.

Nan shakily began collecting the broken pieces of the cup as Nina walked into the room.

"What was all that about?" asked Nina, helping herself to the coffee.

"Will thinks we mistreat him," Grace mumbled, feigning only half-interest. "He thinks he should be fully supported financially and cared for like an invalid."

"Maybe he should be," said Nina, sipping her coffee. "You're too hard on him. And me. The two of us. We're not your favorites, and you've decided you're better than us. The whole family has neglected Will and me, and so we have more health problems than the rest of you because of it."

Grace sighed and set the paper down on the table to face her, but Nina had already turned and walked away.

* * *

By October, the family fights were near constant. Grace kept up with the family's social events with Nan's help, while Nina and Will came and went as they felt they needed. Branch sat in the parlor late one night, smoking a cigarette and sipping on a brandy when Grace walked into the room. She sank into the armchair next to Branch. "What are you doing here? I thought you'd be at the club."

He shrugged and puffed on the cigarette, staring at the fireplace. He had a small fire in it, even though it wasn't quite cold enough for one just yet.

"So, you're avoiding someone? I assume another man's wife? Or daughter?" she said, half-playfully.

Branch sighed and looked at her. He reached over to the brandy bottle and poured more into his tumbler. He turned another tumbler right side up and poured some brandy into it, too. He handed her the glass. "Drink this and criticize less," he said.

Grace sighed and looked at the amber liquid.

"Go ahead," he said. She frowned and set it on the table beside her.

"Here, you got a letter today," he said, handing her an envelope. She glanced at the return address: her editor in New York. Grace slid the letter out of the envelope and skimmed it.

"Oh my," she murmured in shock. Branch grunted an inquiry. "Charles Dudley Warner has died of a heart attack."

Branch raised his eyebrows. "He hasn't been well for a while, has he?"

"No, he looked dreadful when I last saw him in Hartford," said Grace, still reading the letter. "Hamilton says Mr. Warner was out for a walk and collapsed while walking in the negro part of town. He took refuge at a colored woman's cottage. How odd," she said. "Why would he be walking down there?"

Branch looked at her pointedly and raised an eyebrow. "Really, Sis? You can't read between the lines here?"

"What do you mean?"

"She was his mistress, Sis. He didn't 'take refuge at a stranger's house.' He was visiting his mistress. He almost had a heart attack doing the same thing on his last trip here."

"What?" Grace said. "But...he's married. And a gentleman," she said stubbornly. On one level, she had known. She had always known. She just hated to admit that a man she had once loved and respected could do something so base as to take mistresses. She was reminded of her final visits with the Judge all over again. Were all men like this?

"Sis," said Branch softly. "By now, surely you understand: there are no gentlemen."

Grace sat back into the arm chair as a deep exhaustion overtook her. She glanced at the brandy on the table. She reached over and picked up her glass, as Branch held his out in a silent toast.

They sat in silence, sipping their brandies and staring at the fire in the hearth.

* * *

The following July, Grace fanned herself on the back gallery, trying to escape some of the heavy heat of the early evening. Inside the back door, she heard Will and Mimi chatting in the kitchen. In the distance, the sky looked ominous and heavy.

"Will, you look terrible," Mimi said, her voice heavy with concern.

Grace rolled her eyes. *I'm sure he does,* she thought.

"Grace," Mimi called.

Grace sighed deeply as she climbed to her feet, which were a bit sore after a busy day of cleaning the house. She walked inside to see Will sitting at the kitchen table, his face and neck crimson and irritated. Sweat trickled down his forehead. Mimi carried a large bowl filled with cool water and a damp cloth. She set the bowl on the table and began blotting the cloth over Will's head, reminding Grace of the many times Mimi did the same thing for her childhood fevers. Mimi's hands trembled now with age as she attempted to care for her grown son, her frown and concern set deeply in her face. For a moment, she watched the scene: elderly mother tending to her son. It was touching, Grace thought, until she focused on the grown man sitting in the chair, smelling heavily of bourbon. Suddenly, Grace felt her temper rising.

"Enough, Mimi," Grace said. "He's clearly just drunk...again."

"Grace," Mimi said, her voice conveying decades of exhaustion and fatigue in a single word.

Will looked up at Grace, tears in his eyes. Though his forehead was still bright red, his lips were almost white.

"She's right, Mimi," he mumbled, still looking into Grace's eyes. Grace could see tears forming in the storm in his eyes. "I'm not worth it." He tried to stand but stumbled and fell onto Mimi's shoulder. "I'll go rest, *Maman*." He rebalanced himself, kissed Mimi's forehead, and walked slowly from the room.

Mimi watched him go without protesting, and Grace listened to the stairs creak as he climbed them before she could meet her mother's eyes. When she did, Mimi was livid.

"How dare you," she hissed. "Can't you see he's had a sunstroke? He isn't drunk! Not this time!"

"Mimi, he smells like bourbon," Grace insisted, trying to defend herself.

"And even if he was drunk—which he is *not!*—can't you get it through your stubborn head that he has a problem?" Mimi dumped the water from the bowl into the sink.

Grace looked up at the stairs where Will had gone. *He was acting even more oddly than normal,* she thought. Finally, she sighed. "Okay, Mimi. I'm sorry. What can I do? Should I go for the doctor?"

"No, no," she said, sniffling. "He needs something to calm his nerves. Just go to Mr. Ammons next door."

Grace nodded and left the kitchen through the back door. It was luck that they now lived next door to the druggist, Mr. Ammons. Within minutes, she returned with a sedative for Will, which Mimi immediately took to him while the rest of the family had a quiet dinner downstairs. The pressure of a coming storm weighed heavily on them all.

In the middle of the night, Grace woke at the sound of the thunder shaking the walls of the house. She and Mimi ran around, closing windows against the pouring rain. They entered Will's room and closed his window, while he slept through the storm, not even stirring while they were in his room.

The next morning, Grace rose at 5 a.m. to make coffee, her usual routine. Mimi joined her, though the silence was still heavy between them.

"I'm going to check on him," Mimi said, barely audible.

"Of course, *Maman*," Grace said, trying to be the dutiful child. Mimi returned almost immediately.

"His water closet door is shut. He must be up, then."

They sat at the table, sipping the hot, sweet coffee.

"*Maman*," Grace said, finally. "I'm sorry. I just see how tired you are from caring for him—"

"I will never tire of caring for my children," she said, holding her head high. Grace could still see her mother as a southern belle—straight back, graceful tilt of her head and neck, like a dancer's—but she had aged with so much stress, strife, and worry in her life. Dark circles were now permanently fixed on her mother's face, as were the heavy lines around her mouth and her always-saddened eyes.

Mimi stood, leaning heavily on the table in her fatigue. "It's been too long. He should be coming down for work," she said, leaving the room. Grace walked out onto the back gallery, enjoying the tiny breeze and damp air that lifted the hair from the nape of her neck.

"Grace!" Nan called from the stairs. "Come help! Will's locked the water closet door and won't answer!"

Grace sighed and pressed her lips shut. Would this drama ever end? The constant fights, yelling, and tears had added a weight to all of their shoulders. She tried to keep her temper in check as she walked up the stairs, but hearing Mimi's voice in the distance calling and begging Will to open the door only upset her more. A lump of frustration tightened in her throat.

"That is *enough!*" Grace half-sobbed as she reached the top of the stairs. She joined Nan and Mimi and pounded on the door with them. Nina and Branch were out of town, so the three women beat their hands on the door, not knowing what else to do. No answer came.

"William King! We've had enough of your nonsense!" Grace screamed, kicking the wooden door. "It's too much! You're too much for us to keep putting up with this! I'll have this door broken down, William! Open it! You've scared Mimi for the last time, I tell you!" Grace curled her hands into fists and began waylaying on the door, turning her knuckles red. Mimi and Nan stepped back.

"When Branch gets home, we will send you away! We don't deserve this! It isn't fair! Open this door and face your responsibilities! *Grow up!*" Grace beat her fists until several of the knuckles turned bloody. Angry tears stung her eyes until she couldn't see the door anymore, and she leaned her face against the door, sobbing. Then, an odd smell reached her nose: gas.

She flinched when Mimi touched her elbow gently. "Nan's coming with Mr. Ammons, and I've yelled for the watchman from the front gallery. They're coming up the stairs now." Grace hadn't even realized that Nan and Mimi had stepped away. Mimi's hands clutched at her heart, and she looked close to fainting. Her face was drained and paler than Grace had ever seen it.

The two men rushed into the room, with Nan right behind them.

"On three," said Mr. Ammons to the watchman. "One, two, three!"

As the door gave in, Grace caught a glimpse of Will lying on the floor of the water closet, his body curled around the toilet with his face just inches from the gas pipe.

"Oh my God," said Mr. Ammons. He turned to Grace and gestured for the ladies to leave the room, so Grace swept her arm around Mimi's back and guided her into Branch's room next to Will's.

"What...what's happened?" Mimi murmured, her lower lip trembling uncontrollably. "Will? Will? Oh, my poor wayward Will!" She began rocking herself back and forth on the edge of Branch's bed, as Grace held her.

"*You,*" hissed Mimi at Grace as she gasped for air. "*You* pushed him! *You* threatened him!" Mimi pushed Grace away violently.

"But, Mimi, I didn't mean for..." Grace said, the lump in her throat choking back any other words. She felt a hand on her shoulder and looked up tearfully into Nan's soft eyes.

"It's okay, Sissy, I'll take care of her for now," said Nan gently.

Grace nodded and let Nan take her place beside Mimi. She walked back into Will's room, where the men had moved Will's body onto the bedroom floor. He lay there, twisted at a grotesque angle, leering up with his lip fixed in a snarl. Grace took a deep breath and tried to control her tears as she arranged his arms and legs in a more restful pose before Mimi saw him. She then placed her white handkerchief gently over his face.

* * *

The family mourned Will's death deeply, and Grace was no exception. She was plagued by guilt for years of anger and unkindness toward her brother. By the end of 1903, the family prepared for another death; Mimi's health had been failing steadily, and losing Will triggered a deep fatigue in her. In early December, Grace began bracing herself for the loss that she knew would devastate her. She devoted herself to caring for Mimi around the clock, staying awake for days at a time.

One evening, she drifted off to sleep sitting straight up in a chair near Mimi's bed, only to find someone had placed a light blanket over her. When she awoke, the rest of the house slept peacefully. She remained still, appreciating a moment of quiet in what had been a bustling—and burdened—household.

She thought about her writing, left upstairs on her desk. After Will's death, she had received word about George Preot's death, as well as one of her editors in New York. Her mentors and guides were disappearing, leaving Grace to find her own way. Her historical work had been her focus for some time, but she'd felt that old calling, stirring up that tingling in her fingers once again. She had decided to write a novel about the King family's struggles during the War and Reconstruction eras, but the writing of it had been so painful that she'd barely progressed at all.

She leaned forward to check on Mimi, who slept fitfully at best. The only sound in the room was the ticking of a nearby clock and the swish of Grace's skirts as she tidied up Mimi's night table.

"Sissy?" murmured Mimi.

"Mimi, I'm sorry," Grace whispered. "I didn't mean to wake you."

"I wasn't really asleep," she said wearily. "I want to talk to you. Help me sit up, Sis. Light a lamp, too, so I can see you."

Grace struck a match and lit the small bedside lamp, casting a gentle glow over the room. She carefully rearranged the large pillows behind Mimi and helped her lean back against them.

"Would you like water? Or broth? It's late, but I'll fix whatever you want, *Maman*," said Grace.

Mimi patted the side of the bed for Grace to sit beside her, as though she were a child again.

"Sis, I don't have much time left," she started. "I want you to know that I am proud of you," said Mimi, leaning back against the pillows. Her eyes half closed.

Grace opened her mouth to speak.

"No, don't interrupt. I am proud of you, Grace Elizabeth King. I thought I would see my daughters all wed and having children. I never thought that I would have a daughter who would be a writer," she said. "You are beautiful. I want you to know that, my dear girl," she said, barely loud enough for Grace to hear.

Grace felt the sting of tears building behind her eyes, and the lump gathering in her throat almost choked her words. "*Maman*," she said, her voice deep and trembling. "I'm so sorry," she said, laying her head in her hands and letting the tears fall freely. "I'm so sorry about Will. You were right. I was too hard on him, and I'll never forgive myself for it..."

Mimi placed her hand on Grace's head and weakly tugged her to come closer. Grace curled up next to Mimi in the bed and placed her head against Mimi's shoulder. The tears continued to slide down Grace's cheeks and onto Mimi's nightdress.

"Sh, sh, sh," Mimi cooed, running her weathered hands over Grace's head—soothing her child. "You didn't know. You never understood men, and you understand women almost too well—so you see the faults of men more than those of women. Well, except maybe Nina. You seem to find her faults easily enough," Mimi said with a chuckle that was barely more than a breath. "I carry regret about Will, too, you know."

"You do?" Grace asked.

"Yes. I regret not having my children christened. Maybe that could have helped poor Will. And you and Nan, too. You might find some peace there. And Nan," she said. "Well, Nan will follow you always, won't she? Let her. She needs you. Take care of your sisters, Grace."

Grace sniffled and started to sit up. "You should sleep, *Maman*," she said. "Fred and the children are coming tomorrow."

"Stay right here with me tonight," Mimi said, snuggling down into the pillows and blanket. "You need sleep, too." Mimi wrapped an arm around Grace's shoulder, and the two drifted off into light sleep.

The next morning, Grace crept out of the bed and prepared the house for Fred's visit. When he arrived, he arrived alone.

"Where are the children?" asked Grace, as he came in and hung his coat.

"I thought...I thought I'd better make this trip alone," he said quietly.

Grace nodded, the reality finally setting in that they would be saying goodbye to Mimi.

"Besides," Fred added. "Mimi really hates Eleanor."

"She's not the only one who hates your wife, Fred," Grace said flatly. "But who knows? Maybe Eleanor's a sweet woman, underneath that pesky laudanum addiction."

Fred grunted in amusement. “Maybe. To tell you the truth, I don’t really remember.”

Branch walked in and clasped hands with Fred. “Eleanor’s not with you?” he asked quietly. Fred shook his head. “Good. Mimi truly hates that woman.”

Fred sighed, shrugged, and followed Grace and Branch to the kitchen where Nan filled trays with finger sandwiches and set out champagne glasses. Nina came in to join them, setting out the nice silverware.

“Grace?” asked May, coming in from Mimi’s room. She had arrived a few days before. “*Maman* would like her old music box. Do you know where it is?” May rarely visited the family in New Orleans, as busy as she had been as the mayor’s wife in Charlotte. Though childless, she had adopted numerous charities and worthwhile endeavors.

Grace nodded and opened a nearby cabinet. She set the box down on the table and ran a quick cloth over it to remove dust. She looked at her siblings, and they each exchanged a look of sadness before nodding gently. They filed quietly into Mimi’s room, with Nan coming in last carrying a tray of champagne glasses. Grace and May sat on the bed on both sides of Mimi, while Nina and Nan sat at the foot, leaning against the footboard. Branch and Fred sat in the armchairs to the side, with a small table in between them. They each held a glass filled with champagne. Mimi leaned against the pillows, scanning her tired and sad eyes from one face to the next, smiling gently.

Grace began. “Mimi, you always liked to have champagne with breakfast, like the Creole ladies.”

May chuckled quietly. “It only confused our American friends even more, thinking for sure we were Creole!”

“Oh, May, you should have seen Mimi last Mardi Gras!” Nan said. “Fred’s children came over, all disguised in their costumes, and Mimi pretended to be frightened of them and to not know who they were! They were in stitches, but of course, eventually removed their masks. They thought they’d truly frightened her!”

Mimi smiled from her nest of pillows. “They are good children, Fred,” she said softly.

“Remember the swamp?” asked Branch.

“How could we ever forget!” said Grace.

“Well, I don’t remember it,” said Nina, who was only an infant at the time.

Branch continued. “It was Mimi who led us away from danger. And then into it. And then out of it again!”

They all laughed, but Grace felt tears surfacing through the happy memories. “And the alligator shoes! And the sickness, and the hunger, and all of it—Mimi, you took care of us. You did your best...for *all of us*,” she added slowly, reaching out to gently squeeze Mimi’s hand.

Mimi smiled, happy tears sliding down her cheeks. “My children. So proud of you,” she said, her voice thin. She swallowed and closed her eyes. May reached over and opened the music box. It alternated between “Don’t You Remember Sweet Alice, Ben Holt?” and “The Last Lily of Summer,” Mimi’s favorite songs. The King siblings sat in silence, listening to the music box as Mimi’s breath evened, deepened, and finally stopped several hours later.

Sarah Ann Miller King died in the Prytania Street house on December 5, 1903. She was eighty-two years old. On January 23, 1904, Grace and Nan were baptized and confirmed. They visited their mother’s grave in Metairie Cemetery every single Saturday, rain or shine.

* * *

The following autumn, Branch led Nan, Nina, and Grace through the lower Garden District.

“Branch, what are we doing here? What is this thing you want to show us?” asked Nan, huffing and puffing to keep up with Branch.

They reached a pleasant park dotted with oak trees, but Branch hardly slowed his stride. As they approached a white Greek revival home, he finally stopped.

"Here. We're here," he said simply. He opened the black wrought iron gate and led them up the short walkway.

Grace, Nan, and Nina exchanged confused looks but followed him to the front gallery.

"What do you think?" he asked, gesturing to the house.

"It's a lovely home," Grace said, looking at Nan. "Branch, are you finally getting married?" she asked slowly.

Branch stared at her. "No. Why would I do that?" he asked, his brow furrowed in confusion. "I bought the house, Grace."

"What?" Grace asked, incredulous. "You *bought* this house?"

"Yes, for us to live in together," he said. "A new start. A better start."

Grace reached over to hug her brother.

"There's more," Branch said. "After Mimi passed, I realized I should have been doing more for the family, too. This house is my way of making up for it."

"Branch, you do what you can. We know that—" Grace started.

Branch shook his head. "Mimi asked me to make sure you three would be okay. No matter what. To help give you the financial support you might need. And she was right. That is my duty now, and one that I'm happy to do. I should have done it long ago. Grace, Nan, Nina. The house isn't mine. It's yours. I'm signing it over to the three of you. You need stability and independence."

The sisters looked from one to the other in shock. Grace pursed her lips to keep them steady while her eyes filled with tears. She stepped forward to embrace Branch. "Thank you," she whispered into his shoulder.

On November 17, 1904, they had a small ceremony at the lawyer's office who oversaw the transaction. Grace teared up throughout the process because Mimi was not alive to know or see the house.

The following October, Branch died unexpectedly from a severe bout of pneumonia.

Chapter 23

Notes from a Grandfather's Journal to His Grandchild
For My Granddaughter Lila and her future little (sister?)
from Grandpa Gene

If I could have anything in the world, it would be...enough money to never have to worry about having enough to get by.

Memories about my mother...I'm sorry. My mother died when I was four years old. I don't have any memories of her.

My father wanted me to be...more than a farmer.

The kind of car we drove when I was a kid was...We did not have a car. We had neighbors who would give us a ride to town.

My goals today...have a decent home, an okay car, and enough food to last the month.

A popular fad when I was in high school was...bell-bottom blue jeans.

Lessons or classes I took were...I never took any.

I always wanted to...hike the Appalachian Trail.

You remind me most of...your mother. I became her father when I married Grandma Gayle, making us a family. Your mother is brave and smart. She is never afraid to try new things.

My greatest fear is...that the young people of today will not want to remember their older relatives or the struggles they had to go through.

One thing I learned from my children is...it's hard to be a kid and it's hard to be a grownup.

* * *

An unusually warm Saturday arrived in middle Tennessee in March, and Meredith finished dressing Emmy. Lila popped her head into Emmy's room.

"Is she finally ready to go?"

Meredith shot Lila The Look. "Yes, she is, but patience, please."

"Yay! She's ready, Dad!"

Meredith and Emmy walked into the living room to find Lila jumping up and down.

"Let's go! Let's go!"

Liam smiled and stood. He gestured toward the cream and taupe journal on the end table. "Is that Gene's old journal?"

Meredith nodded. "I came across it recently. I forgot it even existed, but I'm so glad he made it. It gives the girls some way to connect to him."

"Who's that?" asked Emmy, as Meredith held her hand as they walked down the stairs and outside into the warm sunshine.

"Gene was Grandpa," Meredith explained.

"He died before you were born," Lila said, skipping along beside Liam.

"Do you remember Grandpa?" asked Meredith.

"Some. We played games and laughed a lot."

Meredith smiled sadly. She had fond memories of Gene pulling an infant Lila through the house in a wagon full of pillows until she fell asleep so Meredith could sleep a few minutes on the sofa. Liam was deployed for the very first time, and Meredith had been completely overwhelmed and was staying with Gene and Gayle for a bit for help.

"Look! Look!" Emmy shouted, pointing excitedly.

The apartment complex had rented a giant inflatable castle for the kids as part of their spring cookout event. Normally, Meredith avoided social events like these, but how does a parent hide a two story inflatable castle visible from their front porch? She kept an eye on Liam, however, just in case the crowd size became too much.

She and Liam walked the girls to the castle entrance and helped them take off their shoes. Lila and Emmy didn't hesitate or look back as they plunged inside, squealing with laughter. Meredith found seats at a nearby table where they could watch the castle and keep an eye on the kids, while Liam picked up a few drinks and snacks and joined her.

After a few minutes, Emmy came over. "Too many big kids," she said, her eyes falling on the snacks and lighting up. "Chippies!"

Liam opened the bag and helped Emmy, while Meredith looked for Lila inside the castle.

"Do you see Lila anywhere?" she asked, her eyes scanning the castle from end to end.

Liam looked up. "No, but I'm sure she's there somewhere. Or maybe getting her own snack with her friends?"

Meredith stood up and walked toward the castle. As she did, another table came into view, and Lila stood beside it looking annoyed. A woman with a serious expression was talking to her.

"Excuse me?" Meredith called. "Is there a problem? I'm Lila's mom."

"Oh, we just took care of it, didn't we, sweetie?"

Meredith fought her immediate impulse to punch a complete stranger in the face. "Lila, are you okay?" Meredith asked.

"Yes," Lila said, looking glum. "Can I go get a snack with Dad and Emmy?"

Meredith nodded and turned back to the woman.

The woman smiled at Meredith. "It seems your daughter made my son move from the top of the slide."

"Okay..."

"And it seems they fought a bit, but I told her that everyone must take turns. I had them hug it out, and everything is fine now."

"Hold on," Meredith said. "So you're saying that one—you disciplined another parent's child without even bothering to tell that child's parent? And two—you forced my daughter to hug your son? Did she give consent for some boy to touch her?"

The woman sat back, her eyes growing wider. "They're just children. Children fight, and making them hug is a simple way to teach them to love one another. I'm a teacher, so I—"

"Then you must be a pretty shitty teacher, then," Meredith blurted. "Because child psychologists, pediatricians, and educators have known for quite some time that forcing children to allow people to touch them against their wishes trains them to see their bodies as not being their own. This is why so many children don't fight back against sexual assault or tell an adult when it happens. Dumb bitches like you making them 'hug it out' makes them think they did something wrong, and physical touch is the punishment. Don't you ever even think about talking to my daughter again. Is that clear?"

Meredith spun on her heel and walked away. Her hands shook, and she fought hard to keep walking and not buckle at the knees.

"What's going on?" Liam asked as she returned to their table.

"Lila," Meredith said. "Did you get in a fight with that boy?"

"Yes," Lila said, her face burning red. "He's a bully. He was sitting at the top of the slide, telling all the kids that it was his slide now, and no one could slide down it without his permission."

"And what did you do?"

"I moved him."

"By hitting him?"

"No, by picking him up and moving him," Lila said slowly, staring at Meredith. "Look at him. He's, like, Emmy's size. I wouldn't hit a kid that small, and it was easier to just move him."

Liam snorted, but Meredith wasn't ready to laugh it off.

"His mom made them 'hug it out.'"

"Oh, shit," he muttered.

"Lila, did you want to hug that boy?"

"No."

"So why did you let some strange woman make you hug him?"

Lila shrugged, and Meredith's frustration only grew. How could she have let her own daughter get this far without providing her the tools to stand up for herself against adults? Adults were the worst perpetrators of crimes against children.

Meredith, of all people, knew that. *How could I have failed as a parent on such a level?*

"Can we go home now?" Lila asked, looking sullen.

Meredith nodded tightly. After they cleared their table and began the short walk back to their apartment, Liam reached over and squeezed her hand. Meredith concentrated on just trying to breathe.

* * *

Dear Meredith,

I submitted the essay you sent me in a recent book proposal, and I'm afraid I've heard back from the publisher: Your chapter has been declined. The editor cites a lack of argument in your writing. You might consider taking greater pains with your writing in the future, especially when submitting it for possible publication. You had plenty of time for this submission and still failed to produce a quality text.

Best wishes in your future endeavors,

Amanda

* * *

"I don't understand," Meredith said to Liam over cold beers the Saturday after receiving the message from Amanda. "Amanda had that essay for almost two years. Why didn't she read it or provide direction if it wasn't what she wanted? Why just dismiss me like that? The other editors sent feedback for the essays I sent them. They were direct about what changes they wanted to see, and I followed their guidance—no questions or challenges. I did exactly what I thought I was supposed to do. I'm so confused."

Since their meeting several years ago, Meredith and Amanda had emailed regularly, even chatted on the phone about getting together again for mutual projects.

"I don't know. The whole thing seems odd," Liam said. "You okay?"

"Not really," Meredith admitted. "In all honesty, I'm less upset about a possible publication and more upset with her complete and sudden dismissal. What did I do that was so terrible? Submit a weak essay? So, if I slip, even a little—just once—colleagues or mentors, like I thought she was, will just write me off completely? I sent that essay *two years* ago, and no one ever sent any feedback. Jesus. I'm so fucking tired of trying of so hard to guess what it is I'm supposed to do."

Meredith felt tears prickling behind her eyes, so she looked down and away to keep them hidden—even from Liam.

"It's not right, the way it was done," Liam agreed, reaching over and holding her hand. "I'm sorry this happened."

Meredith took a deep breath and squeezed his fingers.

"I just thought..." she started. "I just thought I was beginning to find my people, you know? Starting to build that network? And now...holy shit, I'm exhausted. And I don't know how much longer I can keep this up..." Tears slid down Meredith's cheeks, dropping onto her shirt.

Liam reached over and pulled her to her feet before settling her onto his lap.

"Fuck 'em," he said. "We've come so far from where we grew up. We're going to be okay."

"How? Even *if* I finish my diss on time and do everything exactly how I was taught, it won't guarantee a damn thing. I could still end up working some shitty retail or coffeehouse job, with a Ph.D. And how are we going to give the kids a better life if I can't find a decent job, even after all this?"

"My own stuff is getting better," said Liam. "I did okay with that crowd the other day, and I didn't pass out in class when I was put on the spot and asked to explain a concept. I mean, I stumbled over the words and don't think they made any sense, and I don't remember most of what I said, but I wasn't as bad as I was a year ago. Maybe..."

Meredith snorted. "No. Not yet. You just do you, and keep getting a little better each semester. It's been easier here, right? Closer to the VA hospital and services?"

Liam nodded and pulled her against his shoulder. "We'll figure it out, sweetheart. Together. We always do."

* * *

That night, Meredith awoke to hearing Lila crying down the hall in her bed. She immediately hopped up and walked quickly to Lila's room.

"Lila?" Meredith said softly, tapping on the door and coming into her bedroom. "What's wrong?"

"My legs hurt," she whimpered, still half asleep.

"Okay, give Mommy a minute," Meredith said. She retrieved the children's Tylenol from the bathroom and returned, handing Lila one of the chewable tablets. "Now, remember, it takes a few minutes for the Tylenol to get from your tummy to your legs, so let's keep your legs warm, and Mommy will stay here and rub them until they feel better, okay?"

Lila nodded and sniffled sleepily, while Meredith rearranged the stuffed animals on the bed to make room for herself.

"It hurts..." Lila said, drawing her legs up and stretching them back down.

"I'm sorry your legs hurt, sweetie," Meredith said quietly, running her hands slowly and reassuringly over Lila's aching knees. "You're growing, and sometimes, it hurts to grow. But it'll get better, okay?"

Meredith settled in for what she knew would be quite a while. She often spent nights in Lila's room, rubbing her legs to ease the pain away until they both usually fell asleep. Tonight was no different. When Meredith awoke at 5 a.m., she was stiff from being curled up on Lila's bed for hours. She tiptoed out and headed to the kitchen to put on the coffee. It was time to get to work on her writing.

* * *

A few days later, after spending her whole day writing and reviewing articles, Meredith decided to head out for a walk before picking up the girls from school and daycare. She pulled on a light jacket in case of rain and walked by the mailbox. Usually, Liam checked the mail, but today, he had class until later in the evening, so Meredith stopped and opened their tiny box. She shuffled the stack of mail over to the tall, always-overflowing recycling can the apartment complex had placed there. She tossed the various ads and sales papers into the bin but stopped when she held the last envelope in her hand.

She knew the stick-like handwriting, though no return address was listed. She put it in her oversized jacket pocket and turned left out of the apartment complex towards the park, where she walked most weekends. Within minutes, she walked through the narrow sidewalk entry on the paved walking trail. Giant rocks sat under the trees throughout the field, where Lila and Emmy often played, pretending they were in a fairy forest. Meredith followed the path around the ballfields and back to the paved trail that led through the woods and to the nearby river. She passed the occasional afternoon walker, like herself, but for the most part, the park was quiet and still. She reached the river, which was up after the recent rains, and climbed down the steep path to its bank. She found a flat, stone outcropping and sat, crossing her legs, watching the water glide by for a bit as she caught her breath from the quick walk.

She took the envelope out and stared at the handwriting on the front. There was an odd shape to the "r" that was distinct. A capital "r" but the loop didn't touch the line; there was a gap there that had always been there. In every "r" she'd ever seen him write.

The envelope was pitifully thin. *What kind of answers could I possibly get from such a thin envelope?* She sighed, pursed her lips, and finally slid her finger under the flap to tear open the top.

A single, half-sized notepad page was tucked inside, with writing on just one side.

Dear Meredith,

I asked your Aunt Clerise to send this letter to you. You can send a letter back to me by sending it to her first, then she

can bring it to me. I miss you. I have found myself through the church, and you can, too. I want you to know that I pray for you. For your family and your daughters. You have led them away from God, and children should not be raised without God. I will continue to pray for them and you.
Love you.
Dad

Meredith stared at the letter, her brow furrowed and lip half curled in disgust. *That's it?* She flipped the page over repeatedly and looked inside the now empty envelope. Nothing. No answers. No explanation. No begging to be forgiven. In fact, it was the opposite—his concern about her leading her children away from God.

Meredith glared with shaking hands at the letter.

How could he? After all that had happened, how could he have sent such a stupid note? She couldn't even call this a letter. This was a note. And after destroying several women's lives, *this* was all he could bother to do? Meredith's anger seethed from deep in her heart. All of the events of a what she now saw as a ruined childhood—and Ginny's—and here he had a chance to answer for those things, to show some kind of penance or regret—and he had chosen not to.

The realization dawned slowly. It crept so quietly into her heart that she almost didn't hear it: Meredith had deserved more.

She had deserved parents that were supportive and encouraging. She had deserved to be loved for who she was—and not to be told repeatedly by one parent that the other did not love her. That they were only being nice to her to get at the other parent.

Gayle and Steven had been very young when they had her, barely old enough to vote. They were children. And they'd parented like children: selfishly—never seeing it as anything beyond themselves.

She would be different. Meredith swallowed the lump in her throat. The letter had not given her any answers, but

Meredith found that suddenly, she wasn't asking any questions.

The note didn't matter. Her father didn't matter. Her mother's actions didn't matter. She would release the weight of the past so it didn't crush her future—or Lila and Emmy's. Her past felt like a weight, threatening to drag them into the dark water. Best to let it go.

She slowly ripped the note into tiny pieces and expected tears to sting her eyes, but none came. She closed her fist around the pieces of paper, her knuckles turning white with the pressure. When she opened her hand, a breeze swept gentle fingers down and lifted the scraps from her hand and across the water. Meredith watched as they were swept away, carried by the water over the rocks and around the bend in the creek.

She glared at each piece until every single one went under the current or out of sight. Finally, she turned back home, her shoulders a tad lighter, deciding to stop by the grocery store on the way to pick up the girls to purchase the most ungodly-sized cupcakes she could find.

Chapter 24

October, 1912
Fred—

Grace has taken a turn. I think the stress of the finances have taken their toll. She no longer writes. She says she can't find the strength to sit at the desk. Nina and I are at a loss.
Nan

* * *

To my Sisters,

Pack your bags, my dear Sisters! This retiring widower is ready to set sail and finally see Europe. And what better guides than you world travelers! We leave in two weeks, and you needn't stress over the cost. Everything is taken care of.
Fred

Grace took the still-unpublished novel with her on the trip out of desperation. She stood in the large cabin on the steamer and stared at the worn manuscript. This book had taken more out of her than all the others combined. The others had been stories waiting and wanting to be told, ready to flow out of her and onto the page. This one, however, had to be pried out with blood, sweat, and tears. Many, many tears. Five drafts, and still the publisher wanted a different story than the one she wanted to tell. She was beginning to feel resentful of the "Yankee publishers," as she now called them, and she hoped she might find a European solution to the problem. *One last go-round,* she decided. *If this book doesn't find hope on this trip, I'll set it aside as a lost venture.*

While sitting on the deck a short while later, Grace watched wealthy women walking by on the arms of their well-dressed gentlemen. She sipped her lemonade as the wind snapped the flags flying above her. She needed time to think. She was the head of their small family now, ever since Branch's passing, but their income had dwindled. They had only the royalties from her writing and the income their property earned from renters—and both of these were drying up.

She considered whether to sell the Coliseum Street house or L'Embarrass Plantation lands for money—and yet, the properties' potential for future income made her reluctant. The plantation had once been their respite; would they ever return there, though? Grace jotted figures and notes for other possible options, scratched them out, only to write them again. The strain exhausted her, and she braced herself for the return to poverty she felt was coming.

She crumpled her small paper in frustration and shoved it into her pocket just as she spotted Nan and Nina approaching. They joined her at the small table and watched the sun set while sipping glasses of champagne.

Nan smiled. "It's going to be different having Fred with us in Europe."

Grace nodded thoughtfully, trying to shift away from her financial worries. "It already is. This liner is much nicer than what we're used to—and champagne? I'm glad he was able to take the time, and gladder still that he wanted to share the trip with us."

Nina set her glass down, having only taken a few sips. "I'm worried, though. I think I saw a very suspicious jug in Fred's things."

"Well, we'll have to wait and see," Grace said, sighing and setting down her own glass. "Why do men have to ruin drinking for everyone?" she asked. "Already, I feel guilty for drinking, like somehow my sipping a glass of champagne has such an influence over him that he cannot control himself. Why am I able to control myself, but he, a man, cannot?"

Nina scoffed. "Don't you understand? Women are pushed by society to be perfect—to be educated, poised, graceful, beautiful, and accomplished. And so, we are, but men are not. Because we are also taught to be forgiving and kind, so we hold them to a lower standard than they hold us. The result is that we are ultimately stronger than they are. And they are jealous of our strength, so they continue to keep us in a lower social order."

Grace and Nan looked at one another in surprise. "Nina," said Grace. "That might be the most profound reading of men and women I've ever heard."

"I'm full of such wisdom. Maybe you should stop being so bossy and listen to other people sometimes," said Nina, refusing to make eye contact.

"And it's over," said Grace, sitting back in her chair. *A good Southern woman is not supposed to let her spine touch the seat back,* she thought, remembering Mimi's directions from her childhood. But old age and an aching back were making that more difficult as of late. She looked down the walkway to see Fred strolling toward them. He wore a nice, linen suit, but Grace noticed with a sigh that his cheeks were already flushed and his hat was tilted at an overly jaunty angle.

"Are you ready to dine in style?" he asked cheerfully, offering Grace his arm. She eyeballed him suspiciously before accepting.

She leaned in a bit closer and asked under her breath, "How drunk are you right now?"

"Enough to listen to three old ladies all through dinner but not enough to throw any of them overboard," he joked quietly, while smiling and nodding happy greetings to passers-by.

Grace sighed as they entered the dining room and took their seats. As dinner progressed, Fred's stories became steadily louder and cruder as he regaled the guests at their table.

By the time they left the dining room, Fred was stumbling, and the sisters were mortified. They'd exchanged grimaces, worried frowns, and cringes all through dinner. Nina and Nan walked beside Grace for a moment on the deck.

"Grace, distract him. Give us time, and we'll get rid of the whiskey," said Nina quietly. "This is the first night. We *cannot* do this for the whole trip!"

Grace nodded as Fred caught up. "Whoa now, ladies! I'm an old man! Slow down!" he said, puffing and leaning over with his hands on his knees to catch his breath. The sisters weren't at all winded.

"Nan, Nina, why don't you go along? Fred and I are going to have a rest right here," Grace said, gesturing to two wooden deck chairs. As Nan and Nina went ahead, intent on their mission, Grace turned to Fred and eased him into the chair.

"Good lord, Fred, haven't you learned a damn thing?" she said, sinking into the other chair.

"Well, now, that's not very nice," he said good-naturedly. "Grace, my wife is dead," he said, suddenly serious.

Grace sighed deeply. "I know, Fred. I'm sorry—"

"No, no," he said, waving a hand. "I mean, yes, she's dead. But she also wasn't very nice. Not after the first few years. And now...I'm seeing the world. I worked, I supported her and the children, sent money to Mimi. And now...I'm reaping some of the reward for that."

Grace suddenly felt guilty for their mission of relieving Fred of his jug of whiskey.

"'Course, you know my boys hid a big ole jug of good whiskey in my luggage," he whispered very loudly.

"Yes, Fred, I know."

"They thought traveling with three old ladies required an entire jug of whiskey!" He joked. "They're not wrong, you know," he added.

Grace pursed her lips. *Maybe less guilty now.*

"You ladies," said Fred, laughing. "You've traveled everywhere, haven't you? Who would have thought, my prim little sisters, traveling the world?"

Grace laughed gently. "Certainly not me, Fred."

They sat in silence for a bit until finally, Fred climbed to his feet, groaning as he did. "Well, time to turn in."

Grace walked with Fred to their rooms, watched him enter his own, and turned to the one she shared with Nan and Nina. The door creaked open a tiny bit, and Nan whispered, "Is he inside?"

"Yes," said Grace.

"Good," said Nan, opening the door more. Nina stood inside with a small barrel. "It's heavy," said Nan. "It took both of us to lift it!"

"Well, there's three of us now, but let's hurry!" said Grace. The three women juggled and jostled the small barrel up to the deck, avoiding the more populated sections in order to dodge any questions. Finally, they stood beside the rail, sweating and panting.

"Here we go," said Grace. They lifted it up, balanced precariously on the rail. "May our dear brother's drinking habits—"

"Someone's coming! Just chuck it in!" Nina grunted, as she tipped the barrel up and over the rail. A middle-aged couple turned the corner, arm-in-arm. Nan went into a loud coughing fit just then, as Grace heard a distant splash from down below.

"Are you quite all right, ma'am?" asked the gentlemen, leaning toward her in concern.

"Oh, yes," said Nan, her fit over just as quickly as it had started. "Quite fine. Thank you!"

The sisters returned to their room then, giggling like little girls.

* * *

Grace arrived at the small restaurant a few minutes late and looked anxiously around just as a man stood up from a table by the window. He smiled as he crossed the room to her.

"Miss King, I am but your humble servant," he said. "And I am honored to meet you again."

"Again?" she asked, confused.

"Why, Miss King," he said, offering his hand. "I am Warrington Dawson."

She eyed the young man: twenty-eight years old, tall, handsome, and polished. No longer the ornery little boy running around the resort in Blowing Rock, North Carolina. She smiled warmly. "You're taller now, and clearly are quite the gentleman. How wonderful!" She had kept up writing to the Dawsons well after their move to Paris and had extended that correspondence to young Warrington.

He gallantly offered his arm as they crossed back to the table. She patted his hand as he held her chair and saw her comfortably seated at the table before sitting himself.

"It's so wonderful to see you again," she said. "And somehow, you're more handsome now ever! I'm not sure why, but I think part of me still expected a ten-year-old version of you to appear!"

"You flatter me, Miss King," he said, smiling. "I've ordered tea and finger sandwiches. I hope that is to your liking."

"I'm sure it will be lovely," said Grace.

"Now, I could continue with the usual pleasantries: how was your trip, is your family faring well, and such. But what I really want to know...is how your book is coming along," he said.

Grace sighed deeply. "It isn't. I'm afraid that I just don't have it in me, anymore," she added. The words surprised her and yet...they were honest. "Mr. Brett, my publisher, wants a different story, and I just can't do it. He's asked me to write a Reconstruction novel, but he doesn't like what I have to say. He says it needs more romance, a lovely southern belle who will find a handsome Yank. But Reconstruction wasn't romantic. It was terrible! I just can't be untruthful like that, and I don't know if he will publish it if I don't do exactly what he says."

"So, he's telling you the story you should write? Won't that make it his story and not yours?"

"Yes," said Grace, pausing to carefully consider Warrington's words. "Exactly. I want my story—*our* story—told, not his."

Warrington nodded. "Would you happen to have a copy with you?"

"In my trunk, yes," she answered.

"I might know someone who could be of help," he said. "A friend of a friend, really. I've recently been spending time with the writer Joseph Conrad, and his agent, Edward Garnett, is quite talented. I'd like to take the manuscript to him and get his ideas for possibilities for it, with your permission, of course," he added quickly.

Grace stared at him for a moment. *Publishing outside of Macmillan,* she thought. For a moment, she felt disloyal. Wasn't loyalty in business important? *But the royalties are so badly needed...*

"I only mean," he said, rushing his words. "You've worked so hard on this. You deserve to see some result for it, and I only wish to help..."

She smiled gently as she felt the tears behind her eyes. "My dear Warrington...your kindness..." She swallowed the lump in her throat. "Yes. Please. I would deeply appreciate any suggestions for placement you or Mr. Garnett might advise."

Warrington reached across the table to hold her still gloved hand, giving her a gentle squeeze. "Send me the manuscript, dear Grace, and we will fight for it together."

She nodded and blinked back the tears of exhaustion just as a server arrived with a plate of delicate cucumber sandwiches. She fluttered her hands near her eyes and laughed a youthful laugh.

They spoke animatedly about a plethora of intellectual topics for almost an hour over tea when Grace suddenly paused. Warrington looked at her curiously. "Why, Miss King, is something the matter?"

Grace returned to their conversation and shook her head. "No, not at all. I just suddenly realized why, all those years ago when I first came to Paris as a young woman, why a dear friend of mine surrounded herself with young intellectuals, like you. Madame De Bury was in her sixties while I was in my thirties, but she relished engaging in intellectual conversation. It struck me—just now—that I may have inherited part of her role. Or at least, I certainly hope to have."

Warrington smiled. "And you're doing a fine job of it, Miss King. You've always told me that we need to change in order to grow, to adapt. To be always flexible and ready to accept new paths."

Grace said with a sad smile, "And so we should."

"Will you be visiting her? Your friend?"

"I'm afraid Madame De Bury passed quite some time ago. But I will be visiting another friend, Madame Blanc," Grace said.

"Perhaps this visit will bring you peace and help you on this next part of your path," Warrington said.

"Perhaps," Grace said softly. "Perhaps."

* * *

She made her solo visit to Madame Blanc at her country home, while Fred and her sisters visited a few other sites. Marie, however, was gravely ill from a relapse of pneumonia. She was weak and pale, and her persistent cough concerned Grace deeply. Only days after Grace's arrival, Marie's doctor took her aside.

"Madame has not much strength left," he explained. Grace choked back tears. She would be saying yet another goodbye for which she was not in the least prepared.

Grace stayed with Marie, keeping her company, reading to her, and accepting her visitors. While Marie slept or visited, Grace often walked to Bellevue, a nearby ruined chateau.

One afternoon, Grace answered a knock on the door to find Charles Wagner had arrived to visit.

"Mr. Wagner," Grace said in surprise.

"Miss King," he said, as he entered the small entryway. "I had heard you were attending Marie's bedside. I've come..." He paused painfully. "I've come...to pay my respects."

"Of course," Grace said, the lump rising in her own throat. "Let me tell her you are here."

After escorting Charles in to visit with Marie, Grace retreated to the kitchen. She liked to give Marie privacy to say the things she wanted without an audience. After awhile, Charles came in to thank her. Grace sat at the table staring at an untouched cup of tea.

"Marie tells me you read to her constantly and handle all of her visitors. That you wouldn't even leave her to visit Rodin's studio because it would take you away from her side for longer than you wished."

Near Marie's small villa, across the hill, was Auguste Rodin's studio, but Marie had little strength or interest in visiting the famous sculptor, and Grace did not wish to leave her for more than an hour or so at a time. Grace said nothing but smiled sadly and gave a small nod.

"You know," he said, after a pause. "What you're doing for her, for Marie, is the kindest thing anyone could ever do."

"What I am doing for Marie is the very thing she would do for me, if the roles were reversed. It's the very thing I've done for too many others in recent years. My mother, my brother. Marie, to me, is a sister—deserving of the very same care." Grace felt her tears sting her eyes and slide gently down her cheeks.

Charles stepped forward and knelt beside her. He placed his hand over hers and an arm around her shoulder. Even kneeling, Charles was larger than her, and she felt herself leaning against him. "I am here, Miss King. Don't hesitate to send for me if...if..."

Grace nodded, drew a shaky breath, and leaned back from him. She quickly recomposed herself and stood, gesturing to the hallway to see Charles out.

As they parted, Grace kissed his cheeks. Soon after, Marie passed away with Grace by her side. For Grace, it felt as though the European part of herself—that youthful intellectual and fiery young woman—went with Marie. With so many parts of her past coming to a close, how much of Grace would be left to face her present or future?

* * *

A few days later, Grace stood on the beach, looking at Mont St. Michel. The sun warmed the sand on the beach, even if the wind still held a chill to it. The famous gothic spires stood tall, even from this distance. They were preparing to be escorted across the walkway, and even a usually cynical Nina smiled in excitement. Nan reached out every so often to squeeze Grace's hand. Even May and Brevard had traveled from North Carolina for their own European travel and had met them for this part of the visit.

Their guide, a man in his fifties, gestured to them as he approached. "*Bonjour mesdames et messieurs! Et vous êtes prêts?*" *Hello, ladies and gentlemen. Are you ready?*

Grace and the family exchanged smiles and nods and gathered around the guide. "Now, you must remember, no matter what, you cannot walk across the sand outside of our path," he said. "There is sand that moves under the feet and is not always safe for walking. We, also, must walk all the way across at once, without lengthy pauses en route. I'm afraid the tide does not give much time to cross, so we cannot dally."

The group nodded. As they made their way across the sand, Grace felt goosebumps erupt on her arms. Somehow, the walk felt other-worldly, as though they had left the earth and had stumbled into...into...

"It's almost like walking into heaven, isn't it?" Nan whispered to Grace with a shy smile.

Grace looked at her younger sister. Shy, timid Nan, who made every trip to Europe with her. Never questioned Grace's leadership. Grace reached out a hand to Nan, who grinned and took it. "I could not have said it better myself, Nan," Grace said softly. They linked arms and walked side-by-side across the sand.

Chapter 25

Dear Ms. Mandin,

On behalf of River State University, we would like to thank you for your interest in the open position of Full Time Instructor. We would like to schedule a first round phone interview with you next Monday at 3:30 p.m. Please respond to this email to confirm this appointment.

Sincerely,

Dr. R. Frank

* * *

Dear Ms Mandin,

On behalf of Tulane University, we would like to thank you for your interest in the open position of Postdoctoral Fellowship. Another candidate has been selected for this position. Please consider re-applying in the future.

Sincerely,

—

* * *

Dear Ms. Mandin,

On behalf of New Orleans Community College, we would like to thank you for your interest in the open, tenure-track position of Writing Center Director and Assistant Professor of English. We would like to schedule a first round virtual interview with you next Friday at 8:00 a.m. Please respond to this email to confirm this appointment.

Sincerely,

Human Resources

* * *

Dear [Applicant],

This position has been filled.

Sincerely,

[Fill in Blank with Appropriate Department]

* * *

Meredith stood in their garage and stared at the towers of foot lockers and trunks. Liam came up behind her and put a cold glass of beer in her hand. She sipped it and sighed.

Emmy slowly rode a small bike with training wheels in circles in the driveway. Meredith had parked the car sideways to block the end of the driveway for Emmy, while Lila rode her own bike around the neighborhood with her friends, swinging by every so often to check in.

“How are we going to do this?” Meredith asked, as Emmy rode her bike by the garage door, ringing the little bell on her handlebars. “Yay, Emmy!” called Meredith, clapping dutifully.

“What do you mean? We have to pack, even if we don’t know where we’re going. It’s kind of exciting, isn’t it?”

“Maybe,” Meredith said hesitantly. “I’d rather know.”

“Let’s just sort what’s here first, then start packing the apartment slowly,” he said, setting his own beer on a nearby trunk. Meredith nodded and followed his lead.

She plopped down on the garage floor and opened the nearest foot locker as the bell sounded again.

“Yay! Good job!” Turning to Liam, she said, “You realize she’s training us with that damn bell, right? It’s pavlovian at this point."

“She’s going to be a great leader one day,” Liam said without looking up from the container in front of him.

The containers were left over from his deployments and time in the military. They stacked nicely and interlocked, so they held onto them for their frequent moves.

Liam queued up a playlist of music on his phone, set it aside, and they got to work.

Meredith’s first trunk held remnants from his last deployment. Faded pictures of her and Lila were stacked against an unused journal. He wasn’t ready to write his story yet. A wrinkled American flag rested in the bottom, under his worn combat boots and old equipment.

“Obviously, we should keep some of this, but all of it?”

He glanced into her trunk and furrowed his brow. “Hm.”

"Or we can keep all of it until you're ready."

"That might be best," he said, turning away and back to his own trunk.

Meredith smiled and rearranged the items to make room for more, as Emmy's bell sounded again. "Yay!" Meredith called.

Lila rode up to the garage on her bike and hopped off.

"Hey, Gabbie's having a sleepover for her birthday in August. Can I go?"

"Lila, it's only May now," Liam said.

"I know, but she's excited," Lila said. "Can I?"

"We'll see," Meredith said. "There's a chance we'll be moving by then, sweetie, remember?"

Lila frowned and her eyes darkened. "I don't want to move. We already moved here! My friends are here! Why can't you just get a job *here*?" Lila stomped back to her bike, hopped on, and rode off.

Meredith took a breath to stop her, but Liam shook his head.

"She'll understand eventually," he said quietly. He reached over and squeezed her hand and glanced into another open trunk beside her. He reached in and picked up Lila's tiny baby shoes. He held them up and smiled. "Was she ever this small?"

Meredith smiled, too. "We've been working so hard, we're missing them growing up," she said sadly. He put the shoes carefully back into the trunk.

"And what about River State? I know you don't want to take a non-tenure track job, but we could live near my mom, and the girls would love it," he said, lifting occasional items out of the box to show Meredith and then replace. Memories stored in boxes. A red and white striped, baby dress that both girls had worn as infants. A tiny sunhat.

"I'm not sure. I feel like that one went really well, but they haven't called. The job sounds okay, even if it doesn't come with any healthcare or retirement benefits. And even though I'm not thrilled about it not being tenure-track, it would be nice to be close to your mom. But how many CNN specials do we have to watch about rural Kentucky, corruption, and opiate addiction? I don't want that for our girls."

"Well, no one *wants that* for their kids," he said, laughing.

Meredith threw an old green and tan Army shirt at him. "No, I mean, I don't want them to see that kind of poverty and drug abuse all around them."

"I know, I know," he said, crumpling the shirt up and tucking it into a trunk to serve as padding.

"I want to be near your mom, but I can't return to that area. All it is to me is ramshackle trailers, trash everywhere, and grunge. We can't take them there," Meredith said, her voice shaking. "There's no *home* there, or it seems...anywhere else. I just want to find a place to put down roots for them."

"Okay," he said. "We'll figure something out. How did the NOCC interview go?"

Meredith smiled. "That one actually went really well, I think. Everyone seemed nice and like they actually liked each other. There were a ton of people on the search committee, though. Like, normally, there's three people, but this time, there were, like, six, I think?"

"So, why aren't you more excited about going to New Orleans? That's been the goal, right?"

"I'm scared it won't happen. Like, really afraid to even get my hopes up. I want stability. And weekends with our kids. If that takes us to New Orleans, so very much the better. But I'm afraid of being crushed if it doesn't work out." The bell rang again, and they both clapped their hands for Emmy as she giggled and turned her bike for another lap. Meredith held up a tiny, outgrown sandal. "We're missing their childhood."

As she turned to start on another trunk, her cell phone rang in her shirt pocket. She glanced at the area number: 504. New Orleans. She waved to Liam to turn down the music before she answered.

"Hello?"

"May I speak with Meredith Mandin, please?"

"Speaking."

"This is Carol from New Orleans Community College HR," said a chirpy voice. "I'm calling to invite you to come to New Orleans for an on-campus interview on June 9th."

"Oh, that's great! Yes, yes, I'll be there," she stammered.

"Wonderful. I'll be in touch via email with the items you should prepare. Make your own travel plans, keep the receipts, and the college will reimburse you after you file the paperwork. Have a good day," she said, as the line went dead.

Meredith looked at Liam, shocked.

Liam grinned back. "Now, can we get excited?"

* * *

A few weeks later, Meredith sat on a bench along the Riverwalk near Jackson Square after her interview with New Orleans Community College. She took deep breath after deep breath to steady her nerves after interviewing with the hiring committee and meeting what felt like dozens of administrators for over six hours. She'd toured the small campus, looked around the newly renovated writing center, and even had a sit down with the small college's president.

Her mouth felt dry, and she felt oddly empty. She had poured everything she had into preparing for the interview. She'd reviewed every English faculty member at the college, their CVs, their backgrounds, even their blogs. She'd read up on the history of the college, its place in the local community, and even the history of the writing center—who had directed it, when, various archived websites.

And she'd tapped into every ounce of energy she had for the interview. She'd taught sample lessons, presented her teaching portfolio, and discussed her administrative and teaching philosophies.

The committee warned her: teaching at a community college was tough. Faculty carried teaching loads of five courses per semester. There was little funding for research, and the students would be from a wide range of educational backgrounds with extremely diverse needs.

"We're no Tulane," Dr. Tamara Smith, the search committee chair, had said, smiling. The others had nodded in collegial agreement. Meredith had felt more relaxed the more the committee members bantered and chatted.

Now that it was over, Meredith went over and over the day in her head, examining each part to see if she had answered accordingly or if there was anything she could have done differently.

A warm breeze plucked at her hair as she watched the boats moving steadily across the river. It was June now, and she knew that her time was running out to find a job for this upcoming fall. Most colleges and universities had sent out their hiring notices months ago. If this didn't work out, Meredith couldn't think of a single option beyond hoping for an adjuncting gig, which would pay peanuts. They'd have to move back to Kentucky for less expensive living, but where there were few to no jobs in her field. And between their last move and this next one, she couldn't imagine uprooting the kids yet again, so once they moved this next time, they would need to stay put awhile. It was New Orleans now or not at all.

Her phone buzzed in her bag, and she pulled it out to see Liam was calling.

"Hey," she said.

"Hey, there," he said. "Sorry I couldn't call before now. How did it go?"

"I think it went really well," she said. "Like, really really well. But I'm so afraid to get my hopes up."

"That's understandable," he said. "But it's done, whatever the outcome may be. It's done. You did everything you could."

Meredith sighed. "I think so. I keep running back through everything and can't think of anything I could have added or done differently."

"Then, it's time for you to rest. Go get something delicious to eat, do something fun for yourself, and sleep. You get a whole hotel room to yourself—with no kids!"

Meredith laughed. "Yeah, you're right. Okay, that's what I'll do."

"Good. Call me later tonight. Love you!"

"Love you! Bye!"

Meredith walked back toward Jackson Square, standing on the landing overlooking the park with the river behind her. She leaned her arms on the hot railing and sighed. The city buzzed and hummed lazily below her, unfurling its languid energy in the hot summer afternoon. The breeze carried the smell of flowers and silt as the gusts of wind from the river rolled over her in waves. She took a deep breath and suddenly realized that the *push push push* she felt constantly was finally silent. Here in this moment, she could merely exist.

Near the Cathedral, a brass band began playing a version of "Wade in the Water", while crowds of people gathered around to listen. Meredith smiled as she listened and gazed over the Square with its Pontalba buildings reaching out from the Cathedral towards her.

Was the city welcoming her home...or bidding her farewell?

* * *

The following Tuesday, Meredith sat in the writing center back in Tennessee, jotting notes, when Preema walked in, waving to her from the entrance.

Meredith smiled and hopped up to greet her.

"Oh, Meredith!" Preema said, opening her arms for an embrace. "I wanted to stop by and thank you for your help these last few years!"

"Preema, of course!" Meredith said, returning the warm hug. "You've been my favorite client!"

"Oh, I thought I was never going to make it! But," Preema said, squaring her shoulders. "My senior paper was approved, and now I am taking an internship in a social work office!"

"That's so wonderful!"

Preema grinned. "Well, I'm off to pick up my cap and gown. Thank you, again, Meredith, and good luck to you!" Preema reached out for a last hug and waved as she set off down the hall.

Meredith turned back to her table just as her cell phone buzzed again: New Orleans. Her heart leapt into her throat, and she almost dropped the phone as she picked it up.

"Hello?" she said softly, walking quickly out into the hallway so not to interrupt those working.

"Hello. Is this Meredith?"

She immediately recognized the voice of the search committee chair.

"Yes, it is. How are you, Dr. Smith?" she said, pacing the long hallway that overlooked the marble entryway three floors below.

"Super, just super!" Dr. Smith said. "Well, my dear, we loved you. And we would be honored if you came to join us here," she said. Meredith could hear the smile in her voice.

"Yes, I'd love to! Thank you so very much, Dr. Smith," she said in a rush.

"Wonderful! And you can call me Tami, my dear! I'm so glad you'll be joining us! Normally, we wait to go through HR for these offers, but we didn't want anyone to snatch you up!"

After saying their goodbyes and see-you-soons, Meredith sat on the bench in the hallway, feeling so relieved tears misted her eyes. A job. An income to keep their heads above water. *And tenure-track to boot!* And now...she was finally going home.

Chapter 26

New Orleans

On the evening of April 27, 1923, the Louisiana Historical Society arranged a reception for Grace. She had dedicated herself to the group for decades, and she had decided it was time to slow down a bit. She was now seventy years old.

The King sisters had reined in their travel and had been living simply: visits with friends on salon days, tea in the afternoons, giving French lessons to children in the neighborhood. Grace had published a few works on the city of New Orleans, which pulled in a small, steady income for them. Their usually sedate life, however, had Grace reeling from all of the activity of this evening.

She sat in a lovely armchair that had been brought to the small dais for her on the second floor of the Cabildo in Jackson Square. The Society had invited all of its members, past and present, to the reception, and Grace nervously adjusted the folds of her skirt and tucked escaped tendrils of her now-white hair into her hat. The long gallery let in the beautiful evening light from the massive, arched windows along the left side as the crowd continued to grow. A small band played on the opposite side of the hall, and Grace looked nervously for Nan and Nina in the front row. Nan gave her a light smile and tiny wave as people continued to fill in the seats in the back. Grace had lost count of how many were in the large hall.

Finally, the Society called the reception to order, and the first speaker, Henry Dart, stood to the podium to her right.

"I would like to invite you all here tonight in celebration of one of our most esteemed members, Miss Grace King," he began. The crowd applauded politely, as Grace fought the urge to shift in her seat and instead smiled graciously. Henry continued by giving the long history of the Society and how important Grace had been in her roles as Vice President and Secretary. He listed every book of history she had written, and as Grace listened, she thought for a moment that surely this list belonged to someone else. “Just look around you, ladies and gentlemen, as you sit here in this glorious historic building. Look around you at the beginnings of the revitalization of the Quarter. Miss King ushered in change and evolution—why, she and her loyal sisters were even at the front of the line to vote in 1920.”

Grace smiled gently at the memory. She had spent months writing letters assuring Fred and Brevard that she had not “turned militant”, but she’d been frustrated, too. She hadn’t been able to understand why men did not support women or trust them to make good voting decisions. Hadn’t the women done just as much to carry the burden of life after the War? She had finally taken a hair and published a letter in the local newspaper, publicly calling for the men to support the women as the women had so often supported their men. They hadn’t. The men of Louisiana declined to give voting rights to women, and so the federal government had done it, instead.

Back in the reception hall, the audience clapped obediently for something Henry had said, but that Grace had missed. She smiled and tilted her head, trying to focus her attention.

“Miss King has also led the initiative to save the beautiful history and identity of our city—in her literature, her research and histories, and even our buildings and parks, and for that we can never thank her enough. Miss King is truly the greatest living author of Louisiana! And to expand more on her literary achievements, let me introduce Professor Reginald Somers-Cocks of Tulane University.”

As Henry left the podium, he walked to Grace and reached out a hand to warmly and gently squeeze her own. She smiled and returned his gesture as he took his seat in the front row and turned his attention to Professor Somers-Cocks. Grace smiled kindly; she and the professor had become friends through the Society and had shared many afternoon luncheons in recent years.

“Miss King is the foremost authority on the history of New Orleans. She knows its stories and understands its people,” he began. “She has lived here her entire life and watched the city and its people change and grow during one of history's most challenging eras, Reconstruction. Her literature has helped to capture those struggles forever, so the past is not forgotten. And yet, Miss King has not lived without her own struggle. Being a fine Southern Lady, she had to fight to get her stories into the world. Why, even after so many well-received and esteemed volumes, Miss King struggled to find publication for her grandest work, *The Pleasant Ways of St. Médard*, which was published with the help of a dear friend, Mr. Warrington Dawson," the professor nodded to a gentleman near the middle of the crowd.

Grace scanned it to see Warrington grinning back at her. Her face lit up in surprise, and for a moment she forgot she was being watched by such a crowd. "Oh," she said, waving her gloved hand in a tiny, shy greeting. Warrington waved back, still grinning. The crowd laughed gently, as the professor continued.

"After Mr. Dawson had the kind heart and good sense to send it to Mr. Edward Garnett, who called it, and I quote, 'a story rare in its historical significance' in the same review where he claimed it would certainly become an American classic," the professor said. He then read a long list of Grace's fictional works, where again she listened, surprised at how long the list was. Had she really written all that much? "I'd like to introduce our next speaker this evening, Mrs. Dorothy Dix."

Mrs. Elizabeth Gilmer, as Grace knew her, stood calmly and walked to the podium as the professor followed Mr. Dart's route of coming to Grace to squeeze her hand as she thanked him quietly. The audience clapped loudest for perhaps the most famous of the night as Mrs. Gilmer took her place.

"I first met Miss King," she began. "As an acquaintance of the late Eliza Nicholson, who was the first woman to own a newspaper. Mrs. Nicholson believed in me and gave me a job, mentoring me as she often did young writers. 'Keep an eye out,' she told me long ago, 'For Miss King. She's doing big things for our little city!' And she was right. Miss King not only captured images of the city of New Orleans—the *whole* city of New Orleans, I might add, but she did so in a way that helped the people remember their strengths and regain their dignity. She gave the people a past, and then she put a rose in its teeth and a pomegranate behind its ear," she said with a grin.

Grace laughed and wiped a tear from the corner of her eye. "And now, I give you our last speaker of the evening, Miss Grace King," Mrs. Gilmer said, gesturing for Grace to take the podium herself. As she stood, the audience erupted into applause. Mrs. Gilmer waited patiently as Grace walked slowly to the podium and lightly embraced her.

Grace turned to the audience and smiled. "My word," she said. "I started my career with a public speech, and now here I am again to start winding it down with one," she said to gentle laughter. She spoke for a bit about the history of the Society and how it had changed over the years, but a sudden lull made her pause. She looked over the audience, locking eyes with Nan and Nina.

"When I began my career, I wanted to show the stories of the women in my life. I wanted to showcase their strength, their dedication, and their love. For their families, yes, and for each other. As many of you know, our family has lost two more members in the last few years. Our dear sister, May McDowell, who we lost to illness, and most recently, our dear brother, Fred, who we lost in an automobile crash last fall. I wish more than anything they could be here today," Grace paused for a moment as tears tightened her throat and choked her words. *Louder, Sis, so they can hear you in the back of the room.* Grace swallowed the lump and took a deep breath. "It took me many years to realize that I had a voice. And even now, I'm still learning how to use it," she said with a small chuckle. The room again filled with kind smiles and light laughter. "I am a realist *a la mode de Nouvelle Orleans*. This city is my home, my heart," she said. "And I hope—I dream—of seeing our lovely city continue to grow and evolve into the artistic and intellectual center that I see in her heart and soul. Thank you." The audience applauded politely as Mrs. Gilmer walked to a small table and returned with a beautiful, slender silver cup. On one side, Grace's name had been engraved, and on the other...

"Scholar, Historian, Essayist, Writer of Fiction," she read aloud. Tears spilled down from her eyes as many audience members began a procession to Grace, where most left flowers or small gifts. The King sisters had to find help to deliver all of the bouquets home, as there were simply too many for them to carry.

* * *

The next day, Grace and Nan sat quietly on the front gallery, exhausted from the previous day's flurry of activity. They sat in silence for some time, staring at the park across the street. Grace smiled as she watched a young family—husband and wife and two little girls—walking and playing in the park.

"Yesterday was beautiful, Sissy," said Nan.

"Yes. I do think yesterday was probably the highlight of my career...maybe of my life," said Grace softly.

"I wish the others would have seen it," said Nan, tears in her eyes. "Nina and I are very proud of you. And the others...they would be, too. Grace?"

"Mm?"

"Will you continue to write? Now that you've earned such rewards and acknowledgment?"

"I guess so," Grace replied with a deep sigh. "I'm not sure what else I would do, to be honest. It's exhausting at times, but I don't think I would know who I was if I wasn't working on something."

"You could let me help some more, you know," said Nan, so quietly Grace almost didn't hear her.

She looked at her sister curiously. "You know, Nan, I think I must be an abject fool for not thinking of that myself. And sooner," she added, rubbing her sore hands.

Nan smiled. "We can use the typewriter more, too. That should help your hands."

"Well, then it's settled. I could use the help with the historical novel I'm working on."

"*La Dame de Saint Hermine*," Nan said thoughtfully. "And what about the Friday salons we've been holding? Should we continue with them?"

"I suppose we should, don't you? Though I have been thinking about establishing something a bit more permanent. Some of the ladies have approached me about such a salon. More formal. Something that can continue, even if we do not," mused Grace, before adding, "What do you think?"

"Something more established might be nice. A little salon. Maybe The Little Salon?"

"That has a nice sound to it," Grace said. She thought back to the French salons that had so cultivated her own sense of intellectualism, even as a pang of sadness accompanied it. Somewhere in her memories, she thought she heard Marie's laughter. "What about *Le Salon des Amis?*"

"Even better," agreed Nan. "Let's make it a women's club, Grace, where we can learn from one another. Who could we invite to speak first?"

"How about a writer I've been reading recently: Sherwood Anderson. He has a modern way of writing that I think will be quite important, in the long run."

Nan smiled and nodded. "You know, we could rent a property or small meeting room in the Quarter for a small sum, if we get enough members and everyone pitches in a little. Do you think we could have a real club? With its own parlors and such?"

Grace smiled at the thought. She remembered the clubs that Fred and Branch had frequented. Men's spaces. Would it be possible for such a thing to exist for women? "Let's bring it up with a few others. I can think of a number of ladies in the historical circles who might be interested. Maybe eventually, we could even gather the funds to purchase something."

In 1924, Le Salon des Amis was officially formed by a group of intellectual women. In 1925, it purchased the Victor David House, a property on St. Peter Street, just next to the cathedral, that was built for Victor David's daughters. A property designed for women, purchased by women, and used by women. The spiral wrought iron stairs in front still stand, and an historic plaque has been added to the building.

* * *

In 1932, Grace, Nan, and Nina continued to live at the Coliseum Street house. They filled their time with salons, receptions, and social events.

Grace, now seventy-nine years old, sat in the drawing room, looking over the page proofs for her latest project: *Memories of a Southern Woman of Letters*. Her memoirs. She had taken two years to write them, and they were finally complete. She sighed and closed the manuscript. *Finis. The journey is done!*

She set the work and her pens on the side table and climbed to her feet, stretching her back from the long hours seated. She glanced at the framed plaque hanging on the wall:

"Be it known that in recognition of her exalted character, her eminent attainments in Arts & Letters, her constant devotion to the advancement of Truth & the Welfare of Society, the Administration of the Tulane University of Louisiana have this day conferred upon Grace King the degree of Doctor of Letters."

The corners of her mouth turned up in a tiny smile. Contented, she let out a deep breath and decided to head to bed.

She climbed the stairs, but after reaching the hallway, she suddenly felt such a fatigue that she stopped to catch her breath for a moment. A quick, sharp dizziness shook her head, then was gone, but when she tried to step forward, her legs wouldn't move and she tumbled down onto the hallway floor. Grace sat on the floor for a moment, breathless. She blew a shot of air up to push her hair away from her forehead. She leaned against the wall and tried to push herself to her feet, but she couldn't feel them. Her legs felt numb.

"Nan!" she called.

Nan opened her bedroom door. "Grace! What happened?"

"I don't know. I just took a tumble, and now I can't get my balance."

Nan stooped down and wrapped an arm around Grace's shoulders. She groaned as she tried to lift her but had to lower her back onto the floor.

"I can't! Hold on. Nina!"

Within a minute, Nina, too, stood on Grace's other side. They lifted Grace halfway up before all three fell back to the floor.

Nan and Nina exchanged concerned looks, but Grace burst out laughing.

"What are you laughing at?" Nina said crossly.

"We're all so old," gasped Grace, breathless from her laughter as much as the effort to stand. "When did we get old?"

Nan and Nina sat on the floor on both sides of Grace and joined her in laughing. Eventually, they caught their breath.

"Nan," said Grace. "Do you think you could bring something for me to lean on? A light chair, maybe?"

Within a few minutes, Nan returned with a small wooden chair. With Nan and Nina's help, Grace climbed to her feet by holding onto the chair for balance. They helped her stumble into her bed, where she fell asleep within minutes from the exhaustion.

The next morning, the doctor arrived and said Grace had suffered a stroke, though she wasn't paralyzed. He put her on bed rest. At first, she felt fine, but a few days later, she began to feel very tired. Nan stayed with her, rubbing her arms and legs for circulation.

On Thursday morning, January 14, 1932, Grace's breath grew softer, and she died peacefully at 9:30 a.m. Nan said afterward that she watched a small light hover above Grace's bed for a moment before it disappeared.

Crowds filled Trinity Church for the funeral, and tributes of flowers were taken to Metairie Cemetery.

* * *

In 1933, just one year after Grace's death, Nan, too, passed away. Nina followed them in 1942. All of the sisters are buried in the King family plot in Metairie Cemetery, just a few rows from the entrance closest to the streetcar stop. Meredith recommends wearing comfortable shoes and asks that visitors please pull the weeds.

Chapter 27

Attention All:

Ms. Meredith Mandin will defend her doctoral dissertation entitled, "Between Grace and Grit: Liminality in Grace King's Fiction." Dr. Pat Bradford served as director. The defense is open to the public and will be held on May 15 at 2:00 p.m. in Bush Hall 301.

* * *

Meredith sat curled up in an armchair in the living room, her laptop propped on the arm and a massive binder across her lap, trying to work before the kids arrived home from school. She frowned at a scribbled note in the margin of a chapter of her dissertation and looked up at the screen to make the adjustment. On the nearby end table, her cell phone buzzed and flashed her mother's number.

"Hey," Meredith said, picking up the phone and still squinting at her laptop.

"Hi, there. Just saw you called," Gayle said.

"Um, yeah, so it's official: I'm defending my diss next week."

"Oh, that's great," Gayle replied. She hesitated. "What does that mean, exactly?"

"That means I'm done with my doctorate."

"Oh, cool. And the diss is, like, a really big paper, right?"

"Um...more like a book." Meredith explained.

"Oh, and it gets published?"

"Sort of. In a database for academics, not like, on Amazon or at a bookstore."

"Oh, well, that's okay," Gayle said, as though she were consoling Meredith. "But, you know, my poem was published in a real book. You know, you could probably pay to get your paper published, too..."

Meredith sighed. Her mother had written a poem once two decades prior and had paid to have it published in an anthology she'd seen advertised on late-night television. This meant she, unlike Meredith, was a published writer.

"Um, well, I think that was a bit different from this..."

"Well, yeah, I mean, people can buy the book with my poem..."

Meredith held her breath for a moment, then let it out quietly and slowly.

"So what happens after that? You're just going to move to New Orleans?"

"Um, yeah. We'll be stopping in up there for a few days. We're staying with Maggie."

"Can I...can I stop by for a visit?" Gayle asked haltingly. "I'd love to see the girls."

Meredith and Liam had already talked about this very idea: whether or not to see her mother.

"I think we can arrange something," Meredith said carefully.

"Oh, I'm so glad," Gayle rushed. "Thank you, Meredith."

"You're welcome. I better go, though, I have a lot of revisions to make on the diss."

"Oh, you're still working on it? I thought it was done. Taking you long enough, isn't it? I mean, a whole year on one paper?"

"I'll talk to you later," Meredith said in a flat tone.

"Okay, bye!"

"Bye!"

Meredith touched the off button on the phone just as Lila came through the front door. She walked straight over to Meredith but stopped and hovered a few feet away. Her backpack was hanging off of her arms, and she let it drop to the floor. Her eyes were large and tear-filled.

"Lila, what's wrong? What's happened?" Meredith said, shoving her binder and computer out of the way and sitting forward.

"I did something bad, I think..." Lila's lower lip wobbled, and the tears slid down her cheeks.

"What did you do?" Meredith patted the ottoman for Lila to sit.

"I hit someone."

Meredith took a deep breath. "Okay. Why did you hit someone? Tell me the story."

"That stupid Dwayne kid."

"The boy that keeps throwing dirt on your books? The one I already spoke with the school about his harassing you?"

"Yes. I was on the bus, and stupid Dwayne kept trying to touch me. He was trying to take my book, then he was kicking my legs. And then he tried to touch my stomach."

Meredith fought the urge to show her anger at someone picking on Lila. She didn't want Lila to mistake it for anger at her, so Meredith forced her voice to be soft and kind when she asked, "And did you tell him to stop?"

"Yes. I did. You told me no one is allowed to touch me without my permission. I told him no, and I did it loud and clear so I know he heard me. Other kids even heard me say it."

"And then what happened?"

"He tried to touch me again."

"And then?"

"I punched him square in the jaw."

Meredith fought back a snort of laughter. "Okay. What did he do?"

"Cried like a baby."

"And the other kids? The bus driver?"

"The driver didn't see me, and now the other kids know I'm serious when I say stop touching me."

"Good girl," Meredith said, holding out her arms to hug Lila.

"You mean I'm not in trouble?" Lila said as she hugged Meredith.

"Of course not. And I dare any elementary school principal to try to punish you for this," Meredith assured her.

"So I won't be in trouble at school?"

Meredith sat back so she could look directly into Lila's eyes.

"Sweetie, a boy tried to touch you without your consent, so you defended yourself. I'm so proud of you, and I hope the other kids learned something from it. You are *never* wrong to say you don't want to be touched, and anyone who says otherwise is lying. If that person refuses to stop, then, yes, you can defend yourself to make them stop. Understand?"

Lila nodded and half-smiled through teary eyes. "Mom?" she asked in a small voice. "I punched that kid from a whole seat away, clean on his fat chin. For once, I'm glad I'm so much taller than the other kids. I was careful, though, and made sure to miss his eye and his mouth. I didn't want to hurt-hurt him—just make him stop."

"I know, honey. Don't worry about this. If there are any phone calls from school tomorrow, I'm on your side. Now, don't go and brag about it tomorrow, or turn into some crazy bully. You've made your stance, now let it stand. We stand up for ourselves and others who aren't as strong yet, but we don't become bullies. Got it?"

"Got it. Can we go swimming after Daddy gets home?" Swimming in the apartment complex pool had become an almost-nightly event.

"Sure. Get yourself ready. Want to invite your friend, Gabby?"

"No, she's mean now."

"What do you mean?" Lila and Gabby had been pals for almost a year.

"She says I can't play with her and her other friends because I have a skateboard and not a scooter like theirs. I want to play with them, but they ride off in a different direction every time I try to join them now."

"That's stupid. And mean. Don't be like them. Daddy and Emmy will be home soon, and we'll head down to the pool after that."

"Okay. I'll go get ready."

An hour later, they plodded down to the pool, dragging towels, drinks, and pool noodles with them. Liam and Emmy swam together, Emmy squealing as he lifted and dropped her into the water, while Meredith and Lila dog-paddled side-by-side.

Lila looked up as Gabby and her friends came through the gate and jumped into the pool with them. Meredith watched as

Lila's struggle flashed across her face: to try to play with her old friends or not.

Gabby and the other girls splashed and squealed, and Meredith noticed that Gabby kept watching Lila, who stayed with Meredith, practicing her dog-paddle skills.

After awhile, Meredith glanced up at the clock on the side of the building. "Okay, kiddos, we need to head out. We have a lot to do tonight. And Emmy, remember that if you get out of the pool without a fight, there's a popsicle for you at home."

The girls toweled off quickly and gathered their things. Just as Meredith and Lila reached the gate, Gabby piped up.

"Hey, Lila," she called. "I'm having a sleepover Friday night. Don't you want me to invite you?"

"No thanks," Lila answered. "I'm moving before then."

Gabby rolled her eyes. "Yeah? Where to?"

"New Orleans."

Gabby looked at Meredith who said nothing, just nodded in agreement.

"*You're* moving to *New Orleans*?"

"Yeah. Bye!" Lila said, as she walked through the gate.

Meredith heard Gabby and the girls chirping behind them. "*She* gets to move to *New Orleans*?"

"Two bullies shot down in one day. Big day for you."

"Yup. There's a popsicle for me, too, right?"

"Yes. Yes, there is."

* * *

"Hold my hand, please," Meredith said the next day to Emmy as they waited to cross the parking lot. Meredith carried an armful of bags filled with everything they might need. Lila and Emmy trudged along, a little excited to be doing a "grownup" thing, but Meredith knew the excitement would wear off quickly, and then she'd be defending her diss with two small, bored children in the room.

Liam carried a few bags as well, and they climbed the wide stairs to the third floor of Bush Hall. They approached room 301—the graduate lecture room, and the very same room where Meredith had sat for her first class with Dr. Bradford four years before.

"Okay, let's settle in," she said to the girls. She placed their bags on side of the table closest to the door, in case of bathroom trips. She placed her own bags by the podium and logged into the computer to cue up her presentation slides. Liam settled the girls in and carefully stacked new coloring books, fun magazines, new gel pens, and little bags of pretzels in front of each girl.

"Oh my God, do we all get coloring books? I want to color, too!" said Laurie, as she entered and sat beside Liam. Lila looked up, wide-eyed. "Yeah, adults like coloring!" Laurie said and asked, Will you share?" Lila smiled shyly and nodded.

The graduate director popped his head into the room. "Everything okay in here? Do you need anything?"

"No, I think we're all set," Meredith answered from the podium. The committee filed in, filling the seats at the back of the conference table, and other grad students followed suit. Before long, the room was filled, and it was time to start.

"Hello, all, and welcome to the dissertation defense of Meredith Mandin," Dr. Bradford started. "Meredith will present an overview of her dissertation, and we will open the floor for questions and discussion. Then everyone will leave the room while the committee discusses the results of the defense. Meredith, please begin when you are ready."

"Thank you, Dr. Bradford. And do forgive me for being a bit unprofessional. I wanted Liam to be here, but with packing and moving, we couldn't find a sitter," she said. The girls both colored in their books, oblivious to the world around them.

Meredith spoke for about twenty minutes, presenting slides and parts of her dissertation. As they opened up the floor for questions, Emmy looked up and climbed down from her seat. Liam started to reach out to stop her, clearly bracing himself for her to throw a tantrum, but Meredith smiled and shook her head. Emmy ran across the front of the room to hug Meredith's legs, who reached her hand down and returned her hug, while beginning to answer the first question. As Emmy let go and went to the window, Meredith kept talking, but she turned and checked to be sure the window was latched properly and that Emmy couldn't wiggle it open. *Safe.* She turned back to her audience, still talking about Grace King's place in the literary canon.

Dr. Bradford smiled gently at Emmy, who went back to clinging to Meredith's legs. "Now, Meredith, you've been struggling for some time with Grace's stance on race. Could you elaborate on your resolutions there?"

"I have struggled with this issue," Meredith said, with a deep sigh. "She really did privilege lighter skinned people of color over darker skin people of color, according to her letters to Charles Dudley Warner. Now, she *did* do positive things for minorities, like representing women and new American realities, but she was ultimately a creature of her own time period. And though she writes occasionally progressive ideas, she never befriends women writers of color," Meredith paused. "Now, maybe she never saw herself as having that kind of power. That's entirely possible; we can't act with authority, power, or strength if we think we have none," she said. "It's not an easy acceptance, but there's nothing I can do to change the attitude of a dead woman."

Dr. Bradford nodded. "Can you tell us, then, why you were pulled to and driven to study King? Ultimately, she is a minor figure in American literature."

"She is," Meredith agreed. She took a breath slowly, letting her thoughts unfurl in her own mind first. "She's a survivor. In a time of deep historic uncertainty, she found herself through writing. She helped formulate the entire world's understanding of New Orleans as a place and culture, all because she dared to pick up a pen. Her work and descriptions of the city brought it literary and artistic attention. And her work as an historian? Well, that led to the establishment of the French Quarter as an artistic and cultural district. She wasn't perfect. She's not a role model. I think people realize this about male writers, but they still tend to think women writers need to be perfect role models for the next generation. Women like King started clearing the path for others to find the way to their artistic selves, for other voices to be heard, and without those women, who knows where we'd be now."

Dr. Bradford nodded and smiled kindly. She gestured to the door and said, "At this time, the committee respectfully requests to meet alone."

Everyone filed out of the room. Meredith sat on a bench in the hall as Emmy climbed into her lap, and Lila hovered by her shoulder.

The door to room 301 opened, and Dr. Bradford motioned for everyone to return.

Dr. Bradford stood by the white board and smiled. "This is always my favorite part: Congratulations, Dr. Mandin."

Hugs and handshakes encircled her, and Dr. Bradford was the first among them. Meredith handed out the gift bags she'd brought for her committee members, a small gesture of her gratitude for their work and support: Cafe du Monde beignet mix and cafe au lait.

Within minutes, everyone was gone, and she and Liam packed up the girls' things. They stood in the hallway of Bush Hall, just the four of them. Everything was still and quiet, with the exception of the girls tugging on Meredith and Liam's legs to go to an early dinner.

"Come *on!*" Lila said, rolling her eyes. She and Emmy were already heading towards the stairs.

Liam and Meredith followed them hand in hand, leaving Bush Hall and graduate school behind them.

* * *

Dear Mr. Liam Mandin,

Thank you for your recent application packet for the position of Armed Forces Support Program Assistant at the New Orleans Veterans Affairs Office. We would like to schedule a phone interview by the end of next week. Please respond with your preferred times.

Sincerely,

——

* * *

They packed their household items into three moving pods and sent them ahead. Every dresser drawer held socks, spices, kitchen utensils—whatever they could fit inside them. Every bookshelf had linens and boxes tucked inside the shelves. Meredith even tore open the bottom of a box spring to stuff clothing and blankets inside. Liam had already scouted ahead and arranged a rental house. The morning after Meredith's defense, the pods were picked up, and they drove the six hours to northern Kentucky to visit family and friends before heading back down south.

The next day, Meredith heard, rather than saw, her stepdad's old pickup truck pull up to the curb outside of Maggie's house, where they were staying. *Yup. Same old truck. What happened to "he's well-off financially and not a mooch like the last guy"?*

She answered the door awkwardly and watched as Gayle walked up the short sidewalk to the porch. "Hi," Meredith said. "Come on in."

Gayle wrapped an arm around Meredith's shoulder. "I missed you," she said, holding on tight. "Roger drove me, since I'm not supposed to drive right now because of my health. I guess he's just going to go run some errands for a bit, unless you decide it's okay for him to be here. He really wanted to meet the girls."

Meredith felt her warm welcome shrivel up. Even now, after not seeing them for years, she felt Gayle was putting the feelings of some man ahead of Meredith's. Lila and Emmy were overly timid around strangers, and at this point, Gayle was barely more than that. Meredith knew the only way to start to mend the relationship was a simple afternoon of chatting and maybe playing with the girls. "Do you want to actually visit with the girls? Because there's no way they'll have anything to do with you with some strange man sitting beside you," Meredith said quietly.

"Oh, okay," Gayle said, sitting in a faded recliner. "Liam, good to see ya."

Liam nodded politely.

"Lila," Meredith called into the dining room where Lila was playing, pretending not to listen. "Would you like to come say hi to Grandma?"

"Sure," she said, coming in and standing beside Meredith.

"Hi, doll baby!" Gayle said in her old baby talk. It had been almost three years since she last saw Lila. Lila was no longer a baby.

"Um, hi," Lila said, suddenly shy.

Gayle held out her arms to give Lila a hug, but Lila hesitated and tensed her shoulders, stepping closer to Meredith's side. Meredith said softly, "When and if you're ready, okay?"

Gayle put her arms down, disappointed. "So, how's the move going?"

Lila quietly moved back to the other room to rejoin Emmy and their village of Barbies. Meredith noticed that Emmy did not come in, nor did Gayle ask to see her.

"Okay. We've got most things ready to go—"

"So, I may have had a stroke last week. That, or a heart attack, that's why Roger drove me. The doctors don't even know which it was," she said, laughing. "I'm a medical anomaly!"

Meredith faked a small laugh. "Yup, I guess you are."

"Would you believe it? I'm now allergic to the hydrocodone I've been taking almost every day for twenty years! My body just won't accept it now, so the doctors gave me Percocet to use, instead."

"You mean, you're still taking those pain meds?"

"Well, yeah. I'm deathly allergic to all other kinds of pain medicine. I tried to stop taking the hydrocodone, and I almost *died!* I had migraines so bad I threw up. After that hell, I'm on Percocet now. It's working really well, though—better than the lor-tabs and even better than those old pain patches."

"I see," Meredith said, suddenly realizing what she should have known all along: *Gayle was an addict.* How on earth had she not seen this?

"But I'll still get out and mow that hill, probably this weekend," Gayle said, laughing about the steep grassy hill in front of her house.

"I thought you said you'd just had a stroke or a heart attack and couldn't drive because of it," Meredith reminded her.

"Yeah, well, it's not a big deal," Gayle said, looking away.

"Why can't your guy mow the grass?"

"Well, his back is bothering him," Gayle said, as though this explanation justified her mowing the grass one week after a stroke...or a heart attack...

Twenty minutes later, Meredith heard the truck pull up outside again. She glanced at Liam, who seemed surprised, too. She had thought Gayle would have wanted to play with the girls, talk to them...anything.

"Well, I guess I better go," Gayle said in a chirpy tone, standing up and picking up her Pepsi bottle from beside her. "Bye, doll baby!" she called.

"Bye," said Lila from the other room. Meredith mentally noted that Gayle still said nothing to Emmy, who had been playing quietly with Lila the whole time.

Meredith was surprised at the sudden and quick exit, but she walked Gayle to the door. They hugged lightly. "Good luck with the move. Call me sometime!"

And she was gone. Like a distant aunt or cousin. Not a mother or a grandmother who hadn't seen her daughter or granddaughters in almost three years. Twenty minutes. That was enough for her.

"That was really weird," Liam said gently, after Meredith had shut door and returned to the sofa where he still sat. "Are you okay?"

He reached a hand to hold Meredith's lightly. She squeezed gently and released a deep breath she didn't realize she'd been holding.

"Yeah. I get it now. She isn't my mother," she said slowly. "I'm not sure what did it: losing my stepfather, or being on pain meds for the last twenty years. Either way, that's not really my mom, anymore," Meredith said quietly. "That mother is gone and replaced with this different version." Somehow, the realization brought a sense of peace, along with deep sadness.

"So what comes next?" Liam asked softly, drawing her down onto the couch beside him and nestling her in against his hip. "We both know you'll need to set your sights on something after this."

"You mean starting an entire new life isn't enough?" Meredith said, laughing.

"Not for you," Liam said, kissing her forehead. He paused. "You should write."

"Write what?"

"Whatever you want. But you should write."

Emmy came running into the living room and threw herself into Liam's lap. "Daddy! Bug in there!" She squealed as Liam tipped her upside down.

"Were they..." he paused, making a face at Emmy, "*tickle* bugs?"

Emmy squealed in laughter as Lila came in to join the fun.

* * *

A few days later, the family arrived in New Orleans, driving slowly through narrow streets and neighborhoods. Lila and Emmy watched each street come and go, asking if each one was their new street.

"That house right there," Liam finally said, nodding his head at a small, neatly kept shotgun house. The simple home had been painted a sage green, and red trim highlighted the windows, doors, and eaves. The red brick porch was wide and inviting, and the realtor stood in the open doorway, waving a welcome.

"Wow," said Lila.

"Wow," said Emmy, mimicking her sister.

"Well, hello, Mandins!" the chirpy realtor called. "I was just here spiffing up a few things! I knew y'all were coming in after a long drive, so there's a few goodies in the kitchen."

Meredith and Liam helped the girls out, and everyone stood stretching their legs and looking around at their new neighborhood. The realtor walked over and stretched out her hand. "Mrs. Mandin—excuse me, *Dr.* Mandin—it's so nice to finally meet you! I'm Shannon," She shook Meredith's hand. "And Mr. Mandin, it's good to see you again!" She turned to Meredith and lowered her voice as though sharing a deep secret. "You know, he is proud as a peacock of you!"

Meredith laughed and nodded, smiling over at Liam, who was picking up Emmy and pointing out the small trees in the backyard.

"Now, this is Bayou St. John, a great neighborhood for families! You'll find the park right on up that way," she said with a gesture. "And there's a lovely local cafe just around the corner. And these," she said, holding out the keys. "Belong to you." She handed them to Meredith and turned back to her small sedan parked on the curb in front of the house. "Enjoy," she called. "Oh, and welcome home!"

That evening, Meredith stood in a small office off the kitchen of their new home. She took a frame out of her bag and carefully stood on a stool to hang it on the wall:

This certificate certifies that
Meredith Mandin
Has been granted the degree of Doctorate of Philosophy in English
From Tennessee Valley State University

That fall, Meredith sat on the back steps of their home, sipping coffee and reflecting over their new lives. The early morning had a slight chill to it, but Meredith enjoyed it. She pulled her loose-knit sweater a bit closer and stared at the small trees that shaded the yard. Birds flitted in and out in the quiet of the morning. An empty notebook rested on the step beside her with her favorite black gel pen sitting on top. Waiting.

They'd settled in quickly, and Meredith had been relieved when the *push push push* she'd heard and felt for so many years had finally quieted.

The girls were happy; they loved their new school and were making new friends. Emmy had started kindergarten, and Lila had entered the fourth grade. It turned out, the aide in their classrooms lived just down the street and had offered to babysit anytime. Liam had landed a job working for the Veterans' Affairs office, running various support programs for veterans and active duty members. Meredith's classes had started, and her students and new colleagues had been wonderfully welcoming.

They had made it. All four of them, and in one piece.

One important thing Meredith noticed: The wind blew differently here. As she sipped her coffee, the breeze pushed in and lifted a few pieces of her hair. The sun felt hot, but this breeze felt cool and almost sharp. She could feel the wind pushing the seasons and changing the weather here, whereas in Kentucky and Tennessee, it had felt stagnant. Heavy and suffocating, like a muddy blanket. But here, the wind smelled fresh, and the air *moved.* Even on a sunny or hot day, the breeze that blew here felt restorative to Meredith—reassuring, almost moving life along, so no one else had to do it.

She glanced again at the empty notebook.

Her new job did not depend on her ability to navigate the complicated academic publication system. Her promotion schedule and performance, instead, rested entirely on her ability to teach her classes and run the writing center. She could write whatever she wanted.

After all the work as an academic and scholar, Meredith decided to walk a slightly new path. She felt ready to write and to begin a new story.

This one.

Grace's and her own.

Author's Note

In fictionalizing the life of Grace Elizabeth King, I have attempted to be as accurate as possible to the actual facts of her life. In some instances, I have had to recreate scenes or take creative license in arrangement of the scenes for better flow and effect of the narrative.

Though inspired by actual events, the story of Meredith Mandin is fiction and should be treated as such. Any likeness or similarity to actual persons is purely coincidental.

Works Consulted

Bush, Robert B. *Grace King: A Southern Destiny.* Louisiana State University Press, 1983.

—. *Grace King: A Selection of Her Works.* Louisiana State University Press, 1973.

Nystom, Justin. *New Orleans after the Civil War.* Johns Hopkins University Press, 2010.

King, Grace. *Balcony Stories.* 1893. Reprint. General Books, 2010.

—. *Memories of a Southern Woman of Letters.* Macmillan Co., 1932.

—. *Monsieur Motte.* A.C. Armstrong and Son, 1888. Reprint. BiblioLife, LLC, 2012.

—. *The Pleasant Ways of St. Médard.* Holt & Co., 1916. Reprint. Kessinger Publishing Rare Reprints. 2012.

—. *To Find My Own Peace: Grace King in Her Journals 1886-1910,* edited by Melissa Walker Hiedari, University of Georgia Press, 2004.

Pfeffer, Miki. *Southern Ladies and Suffragists: Julia Ward Howe and Women's Rights at the 1884 New Orleans World's Fair,* University Press of Mississippi, 2014.

—. *A New Orleans Author in Mark Twain's Court: Letters from Grace King's New England Sojourns.* LSU Press, 2019.

☾

Acknowledgments

Writing and publishing a book is not done in the romantic-poet bubble that many envision. Rather, a large team with many players participate along the way.

I wouldn't have been able to create this work without the academic guidance and support of my professors during my own time in graduate school. Dr. Pat Bradley provided gentle and kind guidance through my doctoral work on Grace King, and kindness in graduate school is worth more than the givers of it often know. Drs. Mischa Renfroe and Ellen Donovan served as readers on that same project, offering their ideas and encouragement through the process. Additionally, grad school was made better for me by Dr. Bene Cox, who taught me a great deal about leading a writing center with grace and skill.

Further afield, I want to thank the ladies of Le Petit Salon, who offered their kindness and appreciation for my work on King and the many scholars associated with the Society for the Study of American Women Writers (SSAWW) and the Intercontinental Cross-Currents Network for mentoring new scholars and welcoming them into the ranks. I would also like to thank scholars Miki Pfeffer, Sandra Petrulionis, and Julia Nitz, all of whom let a wide-eyed graduate student into their clubs and taught her the ropes.

Without the guidance and inspiration of my editor, Shana Thornton, this would not have been possible. Not only does Shana inspire me with her desire to accomplish the impossible—whether that be in her business goals, community projects, or personal aspirations—but she does so while retaining the heart of an artist.

I am also grateful for my earliest readers: my mother-in-law, Sharon Lute; and my dear friends, Patricia Baines and Wendy Story. Without these sounding boards, the novel would have plateaued ages ago.

And above all else, I am grateful for my husband, Sam, and our two wonderful children.

ଔ

About the Author

Khristeena Lute is a writer and English professor currently residing in upstate New York, where she spends as much of her time outdoors as possible—running, hiking, and camping—or following whatever projects or topics interest her that week.

She earned a Bachelor of Arts degree in English from Ohio University before she became a junior high literature teacher in Yuma, Arizona. During her time as a teacher, she completed a Master of Arts degree in Elementary Education from Northern Arizona University just as the Army shipped her family across the country to Fort Campbell, Kentucky. While there, she finished both a Master of Arts in English from Austin Peay State University and a Doctorate in English from Middle Tennessee State University, specializing in American women writers from the Civil War to present.

Khristeena has written several academic chapters on Grace King, which have been published in various anthologies of literary criticism. *Finding Grace and Grit* is her first novel.

Find Khristeena on Instagram, @khristeenalute, or at her personal webpage, khristeenalute.net.

For information about authors, books, upcoming reading events, new titles, and more, visit thorncraftpublishing.com